Promissory Notes

A NOVEL

by

PAUL MAZZARELLA

This is a work of fiction. Names, characters, places, and incidents either are the product of the author's imagination or are used fictitiously. Any resemblance to actual persons, living or dead, events, or locales is entirely coincidental.

ISBN-10: 0615686567

EAN-13: 9780615686561

Library of Congress Control Number: 2012947603

Muzzy Publishing , Lynnfield, MA

Many thanks to all I've ever shared a hug and a smile with.

Chapter 1

It was a serene Tuesday morning in March as the shiny black limo turned off Ford Road behind the flower-packed hearse. Carol Schrudel sat staring straight ahead, entranced by the memory of having taken the same route many times before in other funeral processions of passed relatives and family friends. There had been Uncle Mo's funeral in a driving blizzard. Carol remembered the delay as mourners had poured out of their vehicles to push a stuck car embedded in at least a foot of snow. She recalled how she and her cousin, Edna, had laughed as their cousins Albert and Francis kept slipping and falling, trying in vain to move the disabled car, their black dress shoes providing zero traction. Carol wondered what had made their faces redder, the whipping wind or sheer embarrassment. At least today the weather wasn't a factor.

She was wearing a black hat-and-veil ensemble to match her plain black mid-length dress. Her dark hair was up and folded beneath her hat. While getting ready, she had stressed over whether to pin the hat down but decided to wear it freestyle. Her head was hurting enough without any bobby pins biting at her scalp. It was just about the only thing on this day so far that she felt relieved about. She was about to bury her dear mother, Mary, and little else mattered.

Next to Carol in the limo sat her seven-year-old nephew, Keith, and his nine-year-old sister, Kate. Keith had just dug out a Budweiser cap from underneath the seat cushion and was showing it off as some kind of treasure find. Kate sat there seemingly annoyed and fidgeted with one of the zippers of her designer handbag. Carol thought how strange it was that some mourners needed to drown their sorrows during the actual funeral. She hoped the limo driver hadn't left the bottle cap there earlier that morning after chugging a quick beer.

Across from Carol, facing her, sat her older brother of two years, Kevin, and his dutiful humdrum wife of ten years, Kristin. Both were appropriately dressed for the occasion. Kevin had on a dark-gray suit with a patterned black tie, while Kristin wore a smart black pantsuit. Next to them sat her younger brother of two years, Chris, dressed in designer black jeans and dark-gray cowboy boots, with a white dress shirt and wool navy sport coat. He was applauding Keith's dented beer cap discovery and held his hand out for closer inspection. Keith, however, wasn't giving up the relic. No doubt, Chris was contemplating how a frosty beer now might take the edge off. Carol envisioned drinking something similar but much stronger when they got back home. She always seemed to know what Chris was thinking and vice versa.

The procession finally stopped, and the driver opened the door for everyone to get out. Carol always marveled how down pat these funeral folks were with their timing of the rituals and their polite take-charge grasp of the situation at hand. From the prayer endings to the proper placement of the orange funeral cones, these guys were in lock-step mission control. What made the job easier for them was that mourners during such a trying time wanted to be led. Their minds were filled with grief, memories, and thoughts of how much more tightly their nice clothes fit since the last funeral. They were drained from fatigue and sedatives. Carol placed a mental checkmark for herself personally next to all of the above.

* * *

The burial service took all of five minutes. Carol always had thought how strange that was. So much time had been spent on arranging the choosing of the casket, the funeral songs, and the get-together at the house afterward, but the cemetery seemed to be a blur. Her cousin, Edna, had been a rock for her during the entire ordeal. Carol had been a puddle, incapable of making any decisions. She knew her mother always had worn brightly colored dresses, but she couldn't decide between the rose- or violet-patterned dress. She had stood by the clothes rack at Macy's with a dress in each hand, looking back and forth. On the left was the rose dress; on the right was the violet one. She stood in a catatonic state, and Edna had had enough. She grabbed the violet dress, declared it the one, and whisked them off to the shoe department.

The dress was the easy part. Carol remembered how shoe shopping with her mom had turned into such a nightmare in recent years. It had become all about comfort. Her mother's feet had succumbed to the ravages of time: fallen arches, corns, and circulation issues. Years ago, her mother had worn the latest high-heel styles, even to the supermarket. At the end, every shoe she owned resembled a sneaker, but she was too proud to just buy a pair of sneakers.

When Carol and Edna had entered the women's shoe department, Carol headed for the walking-shoe display. Edna quickly had steered her to the dress shoe aisle and picked up a light-purple, size-six, sensible, heeled pump and declared they were done shopping. Carol muttered something about her mom needing comfortable shoes, and Edna, ever conscious about overstepping her boundaries, reminded her that Mary would want to be seen as if she were in her prime, which didn't seem to be so long ago. Carol had agreed; her mom was what they would call a "dish" in her day, keeping herself slim and in shape, not needing to color her light-brunette hair until she was well into her mid-sixties.

It was only during the last three years or so that she seemed to age twenty years almost overnight. She even had kept it together after Carol's father had died of a heart attack at age fifty-nine. They had been married thirty-three years, and Mary adored him. She always had said the fond memories of their life together kept her going, and even though she missed him terribly, he wouldn't want her going down the path of despair so common after such a sudden tragedy. Still, they'd had their spats, mostly about finances and who to invite for Thanksgiving or Christmas. Carol always had been in awe about how things never erupted into full-blown pan-and-pot throwing sessions and how a cup of coffee and a slice of pie together seemed to be some sort of peace offering, followed by content smiles and a sweet rubbing of hands. Carol picked up the same shoes in a size seven just in case the other pair was too tight. It was still all about comfort as far as she was concerned. She couldn't stand the thought of her mother's feet being forever pinched. Edna had given her a reassuring pat on the back as they both walked away misty-eyed.

* * *

As Carol walked back to the limo, she counted more than twenty cars parked by the gravesite. Two people in each car would add up to forty. Would there be enough food back at the house? She hadn't expected so many people. She realized she had underestimated how many friends her mom had made from her volunteer work at Divine Child Church over the years. She walked one car back to where Edna was and tapped on the window. Edna had watched her looking at the people getting into their cars. She knew instantly what was the matter and rolled down the car window to assure Carol there was more than enough food and drink for all to enjoy. They shared a smile, and Carol blew her a kiss and returned to the limo. The driver got out to rush her along, offering his arm for support. Once again, she thought about how good these funeral guys were. *Just like wind-up dolls*, she thought with a slight chuckle.

Carol stepped out of the limo and entered the house first. She had read about how burglars scanned the obituaries to rob houses vacated due to funerals, and as she quickly inspected the china and TV, she was glad that being a crime victim wouldn't add to the day's misery. Edna quickly followed and headed straight for the kitchen to reheat the food and prepare the salad. When Carol put on her mom's apron, a dash of sadness overcame her. Her mother had worn this apron on so many holidays. It was nothing much to look at; it was more of a smock than a tie-around apron, colored white, with an outline of a big turkey. It had a brown stain on it that would never come out no matter how much her mother had obsessed about how the latest cleaning product would do the trick. Carol reached inside the side pocket and found a wrinkled slip of paper with a recipe for sausage stuffing her mother had tried for last year's Thanksgiving with mixed results. Mary had vowed to go back to her old stuffing fixings for the next turkey, but now she would never get that chance.

Kristin came in and offered to help. Kevin followed, and upon surveying the situation, decided that Edna and Carol had things under control and mentioned to Kristin that the kids may need some kind of entertainment; off she scurried to tend to her children. Carol deeply wanted her sister in-law to stay—not for the help but for the conversation. She always had wanted to have a more sisterly relationship with Kristin, but every time they were about to share anything more personal than what their favorite color was, Kevin seemed to appear out of nowhere. He'd either change the conversation or tell Kristin he needed her to do some mundane task that he easily could perform. One of these days Carol would call him out over this, but now wasn't the right time.

Carol exited the kitchen with a tray of chicken, ziti, and broccoli and placed it on the dining room table. It always seemed to her that this was the meal of choice for all office, graduation, and anniversary parties and was a no-brainer for this occasion. Edna followed with a tray of antipasto and a bag of rolls; then the guests formed a line to fetch the paper plates and plastic silverware. While Edna and Carol walked back to the kitchen to retrieve more food, both smiled as Carol whispered, "I didn't recall telling everyone to dig in yet. Funerals have a way of making people think their next meal could be their last, I guess."

It was five hours or so before the last person had left. Kevin and his flock had said their goodbyes long ago and probably had been back home in their Grosse Pointe mansion for a while now. Chris and Edna were cleaning up while Carol sat on the living room couch reminiscing about the day. So little of the day's chatter actually had been absorbed into her throbbing brain that she was fearful she'd made a bad impression by seeming so uninterested in hearing the many accolades others had offered regarding her mother, especially the ones that came from her mom's church group.

She was so glad Chris was staying over for a few more days. Unfortunately, his business and life partner, Arthur, had to stay back in Ogunquit, Maine, as their deli and catering business was just starting to take hold. Carol was disappointed, as she had been eager to meet Arthur. All she had seen was a few pictures of him on Chris's cell phone. He was supposed to visit last Thanksgiving, but as life would have it, his grandfather had passed away the day before. Chris made it out to Dearborn for the holiday but flew out the morning after with a doggie bag of goodies her mother had made for Arthur. They only had been together two years—nine months presently in Ogunquit, the rest in New York City. Carol never had seen her little brother happier.

It was Carol who Chris had come out to first, and they both improvised a plan to tell their parents and her older brother, Kevin. They decided to tell people in stages. First in line was their mom. She had just finished organizing the cupboards and sat down with a cup of coffee. Chris walked in first with his head down, and Carol followed, being there for support only. Chris was only seventeen and a junior at Divine Child High. Catholic school wasn't exactly the best place for a gay teen, and Carol was fearful the road ahead for her little brother would be laden with thorns and thrown Bibles.

For many years, their mother had suspected that Chris was gay. She had noticed that Chris had shown little interest in sports while growing up and surmised that his limited participation in soccer and track had more to do with his wanting to stay in shape than his love of competition. He despised the brutality of football and seldom sat down and watched the Lions' or Wolverines' games with Kevin and their father, preferring to gossip with Carol and Edna during family occasions. Still, their mother couldn't render an opinion based on circumstantial evidence or stereotypes. What solidified her suspicions was the collection of gay porn books she had stumbled upon underneath his bed one day while looking for a missing sock.

Carol, Chris, and their mom all hugged one another. "My dear Chris," Mary exhorted, "you are filled with humility and God's grace. I always will love you for the person you are from the bottom of my heart. I'm so proud that you're my son. There are many ways to show courage. You'll need it more than ever, and I have no doubt you'll persevere and make others as happy as you've always made me and the rest of this family."

Carol had blurted out, "Wow! Go, Ma! How inspiring! Can you please shine your infinite wisdom on me now to help get me through my daily hell working with Angela, our acid-tongued nosy neighbor and my obnoxious coworker at CVS?"

Both Carol and her mother knew this powwow would be the easy part for Chris. Kevin and their dad would be a much tougher audience. *Good luck with that one*, Carol thought. It was decided that they didn't need to know right away . Kicking the can down the road for a little while longer wouldn't change a thing for the time being.

A few months later that notion would be proven wrong. Both Chris and Carol worked part time at the local CVS drugstore—Chris as a stock boy and Carol as a cashier. Carol was vying to be transferred to the film counter, as she couldn't take working alongside Angela Sheridan and her incessant boorish banter. Their mother urged Carol to be extra patient with Angela, citing that her parents were in the midst of a divorce and Angela was seeking attention any way she could, but Carol was already past the breaking point. In her mind, working the film counter was similar to receiving a promotion, but in reality it was more of an escape, as there was no pay raise. Angela was a very immature sixteen-year-old, and Carol, being three years older and preparing for her sophomore year in college, never felt the need for her friendship. They had attended different schools throughout their lives and had no friends in common either.

One summer evening just before closing time, Angela ran out of the back room hysterically ranting about having seen Chris making out with another guy behind a stack of paper towels. It was with another teenage boy who worked at the store. He was Chris's first love and the reason he had outed himself to his mother and Carol. Right away, Carol knew this was bad news for Chris. Angela's older brother, Jack, and Carol and Chris's brother, Kevin, hung out together and were inseparable. There was no way Angela would let go of this one. This news would rock the family framework and be the talk of the neighborhood. Thank God, Chris had only one year left in high school.

Their father was waiting outside the store to drive them home. He didn't do this as a regular course of action, but severe thunderstorms had pounded the Dearborn area all evening, and he insisted on giving them a lift home. Chris came out from the stock room staring straight ahead at the front door. His face was ashen and his gait robotic in nature. He hadn't even bothered to clock out. He calmly opened the passenger-side door and slowly slid into the vinyl seat of the family's Ford sedan. Carol followed, hoping she could turn invisible. She screamed as a lightning bolt eerily crackled, and she dove headfirst into the backseat.

The ride home was just a mile or so, but it seemed as though they hit every red light. Their dad was trying to listen to the Tigers game on the radio, but the reception was terrible from the rainstorm. They were playing in Baltimore, he explained. Otherwise there would be a rain delay if they were playing at home. Carol nervously nodded, as if she couldn't figure that out on her own. Neither sibling spoke.

When they turned the corner into the Fairlane neighborhood and veered onto their street, Carol spotted Jack Sheridan sitting on the front steps of the Sheridans' house, soaking wet from the downpour and his legs shaking in anticipation. He had a front row-seat, and a little lightning and thunder wasn't going to deter him. His family lived across the street, and Angela obviously had called him with the news about Chris.

"Tell me it's not true!" Kevin shrieked as the car pulled up.

The swirling wind and distant thunder helped drown out his screams but not enough, as their mother rushed to the front door. Chris dashed out of the car but stopped in his tracks long enough to look Kevin in the eye. Instead of denying it, or saying it had been a misunderstanding, he said nothing. When Kevin saw Chris's blank expression, he instantly knew it was true.

Chris walked past their mother into the kitchen. He opened the freezer and took out a slice of frozen pizza and placed it into the toaster oven. He and Carol often stopped for a slice on the walk home from work but not with tonight's weather and unfolding drama. He tuned the small kitchen radio to a top-forty station and fetched himself a glass of milk as he danced back to the table, where he sat down calmly, awaiting the onslaught.

Their dad was clueless to the commotion going on, as he was backing the car into the driveway. Kevin eventually informed him, and their mother grabbed them both and reminded them that Chris was still their flesh and blood. Carol had gone into the kitchen to check on Chris. He looked so sure of himself. His body language made him appear as if he didn't have a care in the world. He was going about things so nonchalantly, and she was very impressed by his nerves of steel. Carol realized that if Chris could accept himself for who he was, everyone else should too.

The door swung open slowly, and the rest of the family entered carefully, as if they were going to find a ghost. Kevin paced from the sink to the table, saliva dripping down the left side of his chin. Chris offered a napkin to Kevin, who hastily took it and wiped his face. Then he rolled the napkin into a ball and pretended that he was about to throw it at Chris's head. It appeared Chris's demeanor had calmed Kevin down immensely. In all probability, what he ultimately cared about most was his precious jock image, which had taken him years to cultivate. He left the room shaking his head while staring at the ceiling, traumatized by the thought of having a gay brother. It was all about Kevin.

Their dad had been more distraught by the fact that his wife had kept a secret from him. Mary just fluffed him off and fetched him a cup of coffee. She was most concerned about Chris. The toaster oven beeped, and Chris took out the slice of pizza and meticulously sprinkled salt and pepper on it, careful as always not to overdo it. This was part of his nightly pizza ritual. Mother began to beam, and her smile lit up the room. She went over to Chris and hugged him. Carol remembered that so vividly. It was as if her mom had siphoned Chris's inner strength into her body. Their mother had repeated the same hug with Chris this past Thanksgiving, holding it a few seconds longer despite the pain in her chest and the weakness in her arms. That hug may have kept her alive a few months longer, Carol liked to think.

* * *

"Hello! Hello! Come in, Carol," Chris barked. "Edna just said goodbye to you three times. I'll take out the garbage."

Carol got up immediately and walked Edna to the door. She thanked her for all the help and told Edna to get some rest and not to worry. Chris would be here, and everything would be fine. Tomorrow would be another day. Edna hugged her and promised to call. "Stay away from the vino tonight and get some rest yourself," she said while walking out the door.

Carol surveyed the house and was surprised it was already so neat. *Fringe benefits of Chris being here*, she thought. Chris returned from his garbage run and appeared content with the results of the cleanup. "I should open up a bottle of that cheap Merlot you insist on poisoning yourself with," he said.

Carol winked, and he got the glasses. She laughed right away at the sight of him holding the dirty glasses up to the light. "Just pour it, fool. The alcohol will kill any germs," she said.

Chris obeyed. Besides, he had cleaned up enough today. It was time to relax with his big sister—the only immediate family member he had left who really understood him.

The front door creaked open and in sauntered Edna. "I knew it. I'll have a quick glass," she smugly proclaimed.

The three of them laughed as Edna flipped off her shoes. Carol and Chris did the same. When the three of them had their shoes off in the past, it meant a long night ahead. Edna assured them her limit was two glasses, and she stuck to it. She had to be at work the next day by nine o'clock and had to show up, as she already had taken two days off to help Carol prepare for the funeral.

Edna worked as an administrative assistant for an up-and-coming law firm that specialized in criminal and divorce law. It was her dream job. She had worked in the legal department at Ford Motor Company for nine years but had been let go during the last major downsizing effort. It took almost three years for her to find a job, and if it hadn't been for a stellar recommendation from her old boss at Ford, she still might have been searching. He was the proud father of her current firm's senior partner and chief executive, and he felt no one was better suited than Edna to watch over his son while he started out on his own. She had the right organizational aptitude necessary to help build a startup, along with a certain spunk that added levity to any situation. Edna could keep her boss grounded so that he could better devote his energy toward growing the practice. There were only eleven employees in the firm, and Edna's duties included everything from ordering office supplies to scheduling appointments and managing payroll. Sprinkle in some HR duties, and she was truly invaluable.

Before taking the job, Edna had consulted with Kevin for advice. He was a junior partner at a big downtown corporate law firm. Predictably, he told her not to take the job. "It's too risky," he'd said. "Most criminals don't pay the fees. Why do you think they say crime doesn't pay?" She was glad she hadn't listened to him. The firm had grown quickly by the end of its first year, and she was dating a lawyer, Nick, whom she had met at a deposition at her office during the first month the practice had opened.

It wasn't for fear of dismissal that she had to be at work the next day. If she missed any more days, her work backlog would just be too much. She worked ten-hour days as it was. Any more time spent at the office meant less time at the gym. She would turn forty in a few months, and even though she had a slim figure and a young complexion, she prided herself on having "less jiggle in her wiggle," as she called it. Both Edna and Carol had similar body shapes and features, along with the same spellbinding blue eyes, and were often mistaken for sisters. Their mothers were sisters and also had looked very much alike; Edna's mom, Helen, was the older sister by four years. Just to see their reaction, Edna often told strangers that she and Carol were twins, that their mother had been in labor for the longest time, and that Carol had been born two years later.

Helen had died much sooner at age fifty-eight, a victim of a hit-and-run accident while walking across the street on her way to the corner store to get milk. That had happened eighteen long years ago, and she would be seventy-six if she were still alive. The police never identified the driver of the car. Edna often wondered how a person could go through life living with someone else's blood on their hands. There wasn't even a skid mark on the pavement; the driver had just kept going. Every time there was a news story about an unsolved murder case from decades ago being solved, Edna felt a kinship with the victim's family. At least those families now had some kind of closure. She had given up hope of that ever happening with her mother's death. The only witness had been an eight-year-old boy who wasn't sure whether a bright-green truck or a blue car had been going by as he sat preoccupied counting change behind his lemonade stand when the accident had happened.

* * *

Carol awoke to the fury of the city street sweeper passing below her bedroom window. She glanced at her alarm clock. It wasn't even nine a.m. Half-asleep, she took baby steps to the bathroom, pausing to snoop and see whether Chris was still sleeping. His bedroom door was open, and his bed already was made. She plopped on top of the toilet seat and settled in just right. The seat had a broken hinge, and either a person adjusted their weight just so or they ended up bare-ass on the cold linoleum floor. Carol had meant to replace it before the funeral, but it had slipped her mind. She wondered whether anyone at the house the day before had fallen victim to the sliding seat. A seat belt or a bungee cord might have helped. She didn't recall hearing any thuds, but in truth she didn't remember much of anything from yesterday. Looking in the mirror, she noticed her mascara had run a bit. She had stumbled into bed the night before, right after Edna had left, neglecting to wash her face or brush her teeth for that matter. It had been a trying day, and hygiene hadn't been her top priority.

Carol never wore much makeup and often was told that she looked five years younger than her thirty-seven years; she rarely used any of those nighttime skin products sold relentlessly on infomercials. Every now and then she'd have a weak moment and take out her credit card and buy something, but it had been years since she had. She scoffed at all those celebrity hawkers promising everlasting youth. Most were well beyond their prime and could no longer command leading roles. Obviously the products weren't working very well if the only work these women could find was doing those silly commercials, Carol thought, chuckling at how every one of them seemed to have a doctor appearing near the infomercial's end, presenting scientific evidence trying to tip over anyone who was on the fence with their credit card in one hand and the phone in the other. It didn't matter what the product was for. Weight loss, wrinkles, baldness—an "expert" doctor appeared on all of these infomercials.

Also, why did an alleged world-renowned dermatologist need to have a stethoscope around her neck? Why did they all have to be wearing their ghastly green scrub garments as if they got called out of surgery to film a commercial? Was the patient still lying on the table? If so, hopefully things got done on the first cut so they could rush back into the operating room! Dial now while supplies last. Ha! All Carol used was good old-fashioned petroleum jelly. It did the trick for pennies per application.

The smell of coffee downstairs lured her to the second-floor landing. "Chris, are you down there?" she asked. There was no response. All she heard was some kitchen contraption's motor wheezing. Chris was conjuring up some goodies, for sure. What a way to start the day. She rushed down the tiny staircase.

Chapter 2

Carol walked into the kitchen. Her floppy SmartWool extra-thick plaid socks and her bright-orange sweat outfit caught Chris's puzzled eyes. She explained that the socks were a comfortable purchase she had made once while shoe shopping with their mother. "DEARBORN" was emblazoned across the front of her sweatshirt in solid black.

Chris chuckled. "How old are those hand-me-downs? They've got to be at least twenty years old." He was right on. They had been Edna's.

Edna was an only child. It wasn't planned that way. Her mother had suffered three miscarriages. One had occurred before Edna was born, and two after; the last one was so bad that the doctors told Helen she could never conceive again. Edna was eight when the last one occurred, and Carol was six. That was the only one Carol was old enough to remember. Edna had been so excited by the thought of having a baby brother or sister. She'd play with her Annie doll and pretend she was helping her mother change a diaper, and then she'd feed the doll and burp it ever so gently. Edna had stayed over at Carol's house when Helen had gone to the hospital. A couple of days later, she anxiously waited on the stoop with her doll carriage so her little sister or brother could sleep inside it. When her parents arrived home without a baby, she ran to the car and looked in the window as she jumped up and down in tears screaming, "Where's the baby?"

They informed her that God had taken the child. Edna was visibly shaken as she yelled, "God is selfish! I hate him!"

Her father, Sam, a happy-go-lucky, third-generation Irishman, was a laborer who did odd jobs. He was more of a handyman than a craftsman. He couldn't afford private-school tuition for Edna, but she never wished for it or complained about it. The family lived in a modest home in East Dearborn that was kept up the nicest on the block by far. For years, Sam had fixed just about everything that had gone wrong at the Schrudels' house and always refused to take any money—a beer or two or three, but never cash. He could even fix washing machines and ovens. Sam was still alive and lived upstate in good health with Patty, a widow who had one son and two grandkids; he had met her at an AA meeting. Edna really liked Patty and tried to visit as much as possible, given that it was almost an eight-hour drive.

Carol was happy that Uncle Sam and Patty had driven down for the funeral, but they had insisted on driving back right after, passing on even coming back to the house for a bit. Uncle Sam made the dubious claim that he didn't want to drive back in the dark, but they had made more than half of their early-morning drive to the funeral before dawn. Edna even offered to have them stay at the same family house in East Dearborn where she had grown up and where she still resided. They passed on the invite. Edna and Carol suspected that had been Patty's doing and that "driving in the dark" was just an excuse. They could completely understand if she didn't want to be around the dozens of pictures of Helen around the house, not to mention sleeping in the same bed where Helen and Sam had slept.

Carol's dad had been an accountant and never had been handy. He tried at times, but he always seemed to make things worse. That's when Sam usually came to the rescue. After a while, Carol's dad was relegated to mowing the lawn, raking leaves, shoveling snow, and taking out the garbage. He'd had his deadly heart attack while mowing the front lawn. No one had seen it happen. His wife had gone out to check on him because she thought it peculiar that he hadn't come in yet. The front lawn was only twenty feet long and about the same in width. She found him facedown with his right hand still clutching the mower handle. It was one of those old-fashioned, quiet, manual push mowers. He hadn't even let out a scream. The doctor said he probably was gone before he even hit the ground. Carol was at the mall when it happened. Her dad was wiping off the mower blades before she had left. That's the last image she had of him.

She remembered reading his obituary and shaking. "Eric Schrudel, survived by his loving wife Mary, etc., etc., etc." She had been too young to fully understand the finality of death when her grandfather had passed away. Her paternal grandma, Sylvia, was still living—that is, if you want to call it that. She was ninety-one and suffering from dementia and diabetes. She'd had her left foot amputated and had lived in a state-sponsored nursing home for years.

Carol's father's sudden death was the first one that really hit home. He was a stoic man of German ancestry. Sometimes Carol didn't even realize he was in the den while she watched TV. He always had the newspaper held up high so that she couldn't see his face. Carol likened it to closing a door for privacy. The only time he'd put it down was when he wanted to see what everyone was laughing about. People were often impressed by how he could recall any Tigers' statistics, past and present. Family life suited him fine. He really was a homebody with the exception of his weekly Tuesday night bowling league. He had been a curious but never intrusive father.

For thirty-three years, Carol's dad had worked as an accountant for a local Ford dealership, six days a week. There always had been plenty of food in the fridge, but the family was far from affluent. He was very serious about academics, helping the kids with their homework and scrutinizing every report-card detail. He wasn't Catholic; he was raised Lutheran as a child. The youngest of five, he didn't see much use in religion over the years, and when his wife, being Irish Catholic but not overly devout, had asked if the kids could be raised Catholic, he didn't object. In his mind, all religions were basically rooted with the same feel-good messages.

Financially, it was difficult for Carol's parents to put three kids—especially ones so close in age—through Catholic school. They even insisted Carol take piano lessons, which she excelled at and enjoyed. Most family vacations were only day trips to one lake or another. Her mother initially had volunteered at the church to get a slight discount on schoolbooks. After a while, she became uplifted by the spirituality that volunteering provided her, and it was her passion to her dying day. Carol always had understood and admired the sacrifices her parents had made for all three of the children to receive a good education.

Carol's fantasy of a decadent breakfast came to a screeching halt. Chris had mixed wheat germ with granola in the blender. She watched in awe as he poured skim milk into a bowl and sliced a banana, placing each piece perfectly around the rim. "You're going to actually enjoy that?" she asked in bewilderment. He slid an empty bowl toward her and pounded his chest like he was Tarzan. Carol pushed it away and poured herself a cup of coffee.

Chris was a lot taller than Carol and very trim. He ran five miles about four times a week and had a full head of dark-brown neck-length hair that he slicked back. She did a double take. "You don't have a gray hair on your entire head, do you?" she asked.

Chris shook his head and smiled, showing off his milk mustache. Carol thought how much he looked the same as that night when his gay secret was revealed. He was even sitting in the same chair. Except for the fact that Carol had to use hair coloring every three weeks to achieve the same natural result as Chris's mane, she would have thought that time had stood still for both of them. When he had arrived, Chris had remarked that Carol was a different shade of brunette every time he saw her.

She didn't even want to tell him she briefly had gone blonde last year and didn't like it. She had needed a change to brighten up her life but quickly realized it had more to do with her drab lifestyle than her hair color.

"Let's go shopping today and do lunch," Chris said. "I only have three days left here, and we can't sit around moping."

Carol nodded. She felt the same way. Besides, she'd have plenty of time to figure out what to do with her mothers' belongings. Things would sink in later, and she needed Chris to help her forget right now. She could remember well enough on her own.

They both rushed to take showers. Chris ran down to the basement. Edna's father had built a makeshift bathroom down there when Kevin had wanted his own room. For years he and Chris had shared the same bedroom, and at fourteen Kevin had wanted his own space. There weren't many four-bedroom homes in Dearborn, so Kevin moved his bed down to the basement right by the furnace to keep warm. He used an old stained bureau with a half-broken leg to place his clothes in. There was just one light bulb on the ceiling without any shade attached to it. He thought he was the coolest kid on the block. As Carol scooted upstairs to hit the shower, she remembered how Kevin's clothes always had a musty scent.

Chris was already on the couch watching a *CSI: Miami* rerun intently when Carol got back downstairs. She glanced at the clock. "There's still forty-five minutes left. It's never the first suspect, silly. Horatio hasn't even taken off his sunglasses yet. We're not getting sucked into this," she ordered.

Chris aimed the clicker at the TV to shut it off. No, that one didn't work. He picked up another one. Nothing doing! He let out a groan, as what he thought would be an easy click of a button had turned into an arduous task. The beach scene was still on, and the body was still lying on the sand, cordoned off by yellow tape.

"What bikini-clad beauty would want to get up close and personal with a smelly, bloody corpse basting in ninety-degree heat?" Carol asked, as she picked up the first clicker and pressed a button, and off the TV went.

Chris didn't even question it. "Thanks, we could have been here for hours. I don't even want to know how you did that. By the way, the towels in the basement smell a little musty," he said.

It was decided they would go to the mall, and Carol would drive her old black Camry. She had to make a return there, a pair of light-purple size-six shoes. Chris always teased her about buying a foreign car in Greater Detroit, but it was cheap and dependable, and most important, it got great gas mileage. On the short drive to the mall, they passed the infamous CVS store. Chris noticed the pizza place they frequented next to the CVS they'd worked at as kids was now a nail salon, the fourth such salon they had driven by in less than a mile. "Please tell me Angela doesn't still work at CVS?" he jokingly asked, expecting Carol to say she had gotten married and moved out to the burbs.

Carol didn't say a word at first then turned to Chris. "She's still there. I went in there to get some meds and because I had a coupon for the new nail salon next door. I hadn't been to that store in some time, not since they built another CVS a mile closer down the road. I looked up when I got to the register, and there she was. At first I didn't recognize her, even when she called out my name. Then I saw her name on a tag pinned on her ample chest with 'Assistant Manager' stenciled on it. I just answered her questions with monotone 'yes'es and 'no's and walked out of there with my heart racing. It was awkward, and Angela seemed more nervous than I did for some reason. She's gained at least fifty pounds since high school. Maybe she was ashamed of that. She certainly can't dress in those skimpy outfits she used to strut around the neighborhood in. I noticed the Halloween candy display as I walked out and thought that she must have tried every candy bar in the store a thousand times over. Twenty years working there, and she moved all the way up to assistant manager. The world is her oyster."

Chris laughed so hard tears were streaming down his face. "Life's a bitch!" he said and slapped Carol's knee so hard she let out a yelp.

"Hey, those cold Maine winters are turning you into some macho animal. Ouch!" she screamed.

They circled the mall three times to find a parking spot that seemed to be a mile away. "You'd never know it was almost lunchtime on a Wednesday during a nasty recession. Where do all these people come from?" Chris asked in a perplexed tone.

Carol didn't want to talk about money. She wasn't planning on spending much at the mall. She made barely more than twenty-five grand a year giving piano lessons at the house. Her mother never would take any rent from her, ignoring Carol's objections.

For eight years Carol had worked in the music department for the Dearborn school system. She bounced around from school to school, depending on the need, and had taught on every level, and then the “Great Recession” hit. In reality, the Greater Detroit area already had been in a depression for years. Municipal budgets had shrunk every year, and the school systems suffered the deepest cuts. The arts departments were slashed the most, and Carol’s job was eliminated.

She became very busy scheduling piano lessons right away, as parents had few alternatives to ensure their children had some sort of musical background. As the economy improved, however, more parents canceled their kids’ lessons as more schools increased their music and arts budgets, and students could learn an instrument for free or for a minimal fee again. Carol could have attempted to get her old job back, but her mother had just been diagnosed with lung cancer, and she wanted to take care of her. Giving lessons on their old piano kept her close by so she could check on things. Her mother had bought the piano from Divine Child on the cheap when its elementary school had refurbished the old auditorium and bought a brand-new piano.

Chris struggled a bit with opening the car door and let out a groan. Carol giggled. “It sticks a little. Put your shoulder into it, tough guy.”

They carefully walked to the mall entrance. All they could see were heads behind steering wheels bobbing left to right looking for parking spots. Pedestrians were of secondary importance.

Chapter 3

Dodging stroller after stroller, Carol and Christ entered the cavernous, labyrinthine mall. Chris remarked that he had never seen so many kiosks and pointed out the many traffic bottlenecks they caused. They darted into Macy's like they had just broken out of jail.

"This store is my safety net. I always find something here," Carol said, out of breath, as she made a run for the women's department.

Chris followed, knowing all too well that he soon would be playing the role of Carol's personal shopping critic. Carol grabbed a pair of straight-leg, dark-blue Lee jeans and walked over to the full-length mirror near the dressing room. She put the jeans next to her waist in front of the mirror and held the legs against her own legs, picking the pant legs up and down one at a time. Chris noticed how blue her eyes were in the mirror and commented that the store lighting made her look years younger. Carol rolled her eyes and headed into the dressing room.

Chris was actually being sincere. Carol was a good-looking woman. She wasn't a classic beauty with high cheekbones but had more of a Midwestern look. Her face was angular and proportionate, and her deep-blue eyes were set as if they were smiling on their own. Her skin was silky smooth. She had those "angry eleven" frown wrinkles situated above the bridge of her nose between her thin brown eyebrows. No crow's feet—just three tiny freckles in a row underneath her left ear cascading down to her jaw line.

Growing up, Carol had had few bouts of acne but never any weight issues. She was a bit of a tomboy and had an athletic figure and long, lean legs. She kept her hair shoulder length and periodically changed from bangs to parting it on the side. The only time Chris had seen her hair up was for senior prom and a girlfriend's wedding, but that seemed like a lifetime ago. He couldn't wait for them to sit down at lunch so he could interrogate her about her love life and, of course, Edna's too.

Carol came out of the dressing room all smiles. "This never happens. I picked up a size four, expecting them to be way too tight, and I think they fit. What do you think?" she asked, as she slapped her right butt cheek.

Chris could see that his sister had lost some weight, about five pounds or so, since the last time he had seen her at Thanksgiving, and concluded it may have been stress induced. He nodded in approval but suggested she try on another pair one size up as a comparison, just in case. Right away, he knew that idea wouldn't be well received, and he went into retraction mode. Carol was forming the beginning of a pout. "I mean, they fit perfectly fine. I was more concerned about the length," he hastily added, hoping that would pacify her.

Looking at Chris in disbelief, Carol opened her purse and headed for the cash register line a few feet away. "Nice try," she said, wagging her finger at him. She was able to buy the jeans and return the shoes at the same time and didn't have to walk across the store to the return window like she had in the past, which always had broken her purchasing momentum. In her case, it was probably better the old way.

Carol and Chris braved it back into the mall. Carol was proud she had only bought one item and in record time. She swung her shopping bag up and down and skipped a few steps as she hummed to the music blaring above. Her gait slowed to a crawl as she realized the future expense of a new wardrobe. Maybe it was best for her to put on a few pounds in the long run, but for now the euphoria of fitting into her new skinny jeans trumped everything else.

Chris was beginning to seem disinterested in any continued perusing of the gigantic mall. He turned to Carol with an exasperated look.

"Your turn, my lost-looking brother. Don't you want to buy anything? Do you even own a suit?" Carol asked.

Chris crankily responded, "I have access to huge outlets down in Kittery, a few miles down the road back in Maine, when I feel the shopping need. When does food and drink factor into the equation? My gizzards are gurgling from drinking that lousy wine out of your detergent-stained glasses. I think soapsuds are forming in my esophagus. Any bubbles foaming out of my mouth?"

Carol laughed and led him by the hand to the food court. They twice changed direction, walking as if they were in a maze then finally found it. What a mistake! They encountered long lines with screaming and coughing children.

"There's a P.F. Chang's in this mall somewhere," Chris said. "It was calling out to me when we pulled in. I have limited Chinese food options back home. I think the car is parked close to the exit by Victoria's Secret. The restaurant is probably easier to drive to. Do you need help picking out a little something at Vicky's?" he asked, hoping to set the tone for Carol to open up about anyone new in her life. The only response he got was a soft punch in the arm, but he knew a few drinks might help move things along.

Carol led them out of the mall for the treacherous walk back to the car. She felt a little annoyed that her brother was about to get his way, but after being around those bratty kids, she reasoned that a nice sit-down meal and a few drinks would do her some good after all.

They walked into the restaurant and headed straight for the bar, where they found two seats situated near the kitchen entrance. Carol ordered an Appletini, and Chris told the bartender to make it two. They clanged glasses carefully so nothing would spill. At twelve bucks apiece, every drop mattered. Carol expressed how guilty she felt being out the day after the funeral. Chris admitted he felt the same way, but sitting in the house with all the family memories stirring in their heads wasn't exactly the best therapy either. She half-agreed, believing there wasn't anything wrong with feeling sad, as long as it was for the right reasons, and their mom's passing fit that criteria for certain.

Neither of them talked for a few minutes as they took in the festive atmosphere and deeply inhaled the delicious aroma every time the kitchen doors swung open. The dark Asian decor made for a soft tranquil feeling.

Chris finally broke the silence. "I'm worried about you more than ever, Carol, living alone now in the house, both from a safety and an expense issue. I noticed half the block has foreclosure signs in front of the houses. Across the street and two doors down are recently purchased foreclosed properties, and everyone appears to be strangers. It's not the same neighborhood we grew up in, and it's still one of the nicest parts of the Dearborn, which points out the sorry state of the city even more."

Carol leaned back and responded, "Whoa. It's not that bad. Except for a little exterior TLC, the house is in pretty good condition. New hot water heater, furnace, front door, and the appliances aren't that old. Dad had a very good life insurance policy, and Mom only dipped into it a few times to keep up the house. We even got Wi-Fi, and Mom learned to be quite adept at retrieving recipes off the Internet. She was planning on painting the house in the spring and getting a new front fence. The floors may creak a little, but I can live with that. Better to hear a burglar that way."

Chris struggled with choosing his words carefully and finally said, "I'm more concerned about you. Is there anyone in your life right now? Someone you can lean on? A person you can hug and actually share your life with? You took care of Mom like a saint. Now you need someone to take care of you."

Carol's eyes were moist. She was so touched by her little brother worrying about her. She knew he was right, but good men don't grow on trees, and she wasn't about to venture out to singles bars or seek out companionship online.

Her last serious relationship had been three years ago. His name was Carl, and she had thought they would have a future together. He was a musician in a wedding band and played both the trumpet and the clarinet. A few times, the only way she could spend time with him was by attending the weddings of people she didn't know. She'd sneak into the hall about an hour before the reception was over when no one would notice and have a few drinks, hoping it was an open bar. In retrospect, it was a little sad, considering she had no one to dance with because her boyfriend was playing in the band.

One time, Carol had decided to come in earlier than usual. The band was between sets and standing at the bar. When she didn't see Carl, she asked where he was, but all she got was four frozen penguins in tuxedos staring at her with their mouths wide open. She found Carl through a fogged-up window of a BMW getting his trumpet blown by a bridesmaid, and that was the end of him.

Chris had met Carl when he had come home for Christmas and right away had told their mother there was something about him he didn't like. Carol didn't find this out until she told Chris they had broken up. Kevin was a big fan of Carl's because he had been a standout high school hockey player and Carl's older brother once played for the Wings for half a dozen games before getting busted for steroid and cocaine possession while trying to gain entrance into Canada on a road trip. Naturally, Kevin chose to discount that part of the story. After all, Kevin was a lawyer and those were only "allegations."

Carol always trusted Kevin's instincts. He had insisted she go to college out of state, as it would make her a well-rounded, worldly person. When she told him she was leaning toward attending Michigan University, where Kevin was a sophomore, he drove to Dearborn and pleaded with her to change her mind. She laughed and called him a social misfit. Kevin had always had a sense of humor growing up, but once he moved up to Ann Arbor he became so serious. Carol believed it was the pressures of college life, along with his heavy course load. Chris found it rather peculiar that Kevin would drive that far just to keep Carol from cramping his style. Carol wanted to attend a Catholic liberal arts college, and Chris suggested Marygrove, which was about ten miles from home. They visited the campus together, and both came away very impressed. Carol was thrilled when she got accepted. Her time there was primarily full of fond memories, and it seemed to have flown by. She eventually graduated from Marygrove with a masters in education; she had commuted from home the whole time. Without the urging of Chris, she never would have gone there.

Carol ordered two more drinks and some egg rolls. Chris added chicken fried rice and spare ribs. The conversation reverted back to Carol's love life, initiated by Carol this time. Chris took note that his plan was working. She told him that she, Edna, and at times, other friends frequented a few local hangouts, but it wasn't stimulating meeting sweaty guys dressed in softball uniforms, splitting pitchers of beer, and screaming at one another. The last time she'd had sex was almost a year ago. It had been with a vendor who owned a copier service that Edna's firm used. She and Edna double-dated a half-dozen times with him and Edna's current boyfriend, Nick. He was a good person and could hold a conversation without cussing every other word, but it wasn't going anywhere as he had an ex and three kids monopolizing his time and money. Carol didn't offer his name, and Chris didn't ask since it seemed to be long over.

The food arrived, and Chris switched to Coors Light, claiming that any more martini rounds would make this day way over budget and they might have to wash dishes.

Chris talked about his life with Arthur and how beautiful Ogunquit was. Some days, he said, neither of them would even drive. They could walk to do all their errands, and the beautiful beach was right there. Arthur was overweight, and Chris had tried to coax him into exercising and dieting. They walked regularly up and down Ogunquit's long and wide sandy beach, talking the entire way, content with their lives. Arthur had gained twenty pounds since the "Dilly Dally Deli" had opened. It was too easy for him to nibble, especially while slicing cheese. Plus, he always had to give things a taste test for his seal of approval. The deli had a lot of other temptations, and to make matters worse there was a bakery next to it that made the best lemon cake, as well an ice cream parlor across the street that made everything right on the premises.

Arthur was the life of the party. He sang along at the local bar, was a wine expert and a fantastic cook, had the quickest wit, and could recite hundreds of famous quotes. Carol wondered why she couldn't find a man like that. Maybe all the good men were gay. She pledged someday to come out and visit Chris and Arthur.

There was no need for a doggie bag, and they paid the tab. Chris put it on his AmEx, saying he wanted to get his air miles up. He and Arthur were planning a trip to Tuscany in the fall. Arthur's family was from a small village outside Florence with a name that Chris couldn't pronounce.

"Hey, it's St. Paddy's Day in a few days. Is that Irish pub—Kiley's, I think—on Telegraph still open?" Chris asked.

Carol really wanted to head home, but Chris had asked so innocently and his big dark-brown eyes were open wide and so earnest looking that she agreed with a smile.

As they drifted toward the door, Carol thought about how Chris was the only one in the family with brown eyes. When he said something goofy while growing up—which, since he was the youngest, happened frequently—their father would jokingly ask if he was adopted. She wondered whether her father really felt that way once he had learned that Chris was gay.

Chapter 9

They pulled into Kiley's jammed parking lot and walked into the long, dark bar. The contrast from the brightness outside blinded them momentarily. As their eyes adjusted, they found an opening, and Chris knifed in between two patrons sitting at the bar. Carol feared bumping into someone she knew, as she was in no mood to hear empty excuses regarding why they weren't able to attend the previous day's service. She and Carl used to go to Kiley's about once a week and had gotten to know a few of the regular patrons, St. Patrick excluded. She had been there as recently as two weeks ago with Edna after an early movie and stumbled across an old classmate from high school who was married to the bartender. At the time, she was in a nostalgic mood. Going down memory lane provided her with a snapshot of her once carefree life—a time when being late for history class or forgetting to bring lunch money had been her biggest daily issues.

The void in her life now—the sorrow and the reality of the impending solemn days ahead in a quiet, empty house—was all she could think about. Going through life drinking one's troubles away wasn't the best answer. She took one step toward Chris and leaned in to tell him she had to get out of there, as the Irish music was loud. An old purple-nosed chap next to them was singing along gratingly off key, waving his hands up and down and exhorting others to do the same.

"I just ordered you a beer. We have a tab going. The prices here are so reasonable," Chris barked into her ear.

Great, she thought. Not only did she not want to stay, but now a tab ensured that multiple drinks were forthcoming. She knew Chris all too well; in his mind "cheaper" meant "more." Well, she didn't get a lot of face time with Chris, might as well turn her personality radio dial up a few decibels to a fun station. Forcing a smile, she clinked bottles with Chris and took a hearty swig, feigning her enjoyment of a modernized rendition of "Danny Boy."

When it came to music, Carol was old-fashioned. She liked the original versions—the ones that had made a song famous in the first place. It was bad enough to listen to a 1970s R&B oldie being absorbed into some twisted hip-hop medley. Messing with a song like "Danny Boy," a centuries-old classic steeped in tradition, by increasing the tempo with an acoustic guitar backdrop was akin to a mortal sin.

Chris led Carol deeper into the jubilant, crowded bar, excusing himself as they bounced past people. Carol followed and graciously nodded, all the while dreading that they were now out of sight of the front door—or was it the back door they had entered through? She felt lost as it was. Her only escape now truly was alcohol, and it was still light outside.

After a few more beers, Carol felt a finger tap her shoulder, and she turned around.

"Hi. I saw you from across the room, and I wanted to say hello. You look the same. I had no doubt it was you."

She knew who it was right away, Jack Sheridan, Angela's older brother and Kevin's best buddy growing up. "Oh, my, how are you, Jack? We haven't seen each other in almost twenty years," she said. "Do you remember my little brother, Chris?"

Jack nodded and gave Chris a bear hug. He mentioned how grown up Chris looked and said he wouldn't want to wrestle with him now like they had when they were kids because he had grown so big and tall. Carol looked at them embracing and was surprised. Jack always had been a big dude, and Chris was now taller than him by a few inches and had much wider shoulders. Chris was definitely not effeminate looking and carried himself more like a John Wayne man's man. They shared a few more pleasantries, and Carol thought it odd that Jack hadn't yet expressed his sympathies. Then he explained he had come in to get a burger for carryout, as he drove a semi for an auto parts manufacturer and had just returned from a haul out to Arizona, and he had to do it all over again the following morning. It was clear he hadn't heard about Carol's mother's death.

Chris offered to buy Jack a drink, and he accepted. Carol felt a sense of comfort. Jack seemed to be a regular guy living with a wife and three kids in nearby Allen Park. He pulled some wrinkled photos of his family from his wallet, apologizing about the quality because he sat on his wallet for hours at a time. Carol and Chris gave out the obligatory oohs and ahs, nodding in approval. Jack asked Carol whether she had a family of her own.

"Nope. I haven't gone down that path yet, but you never know," she replied with a pleasant enough tone. It was a commonly asked question, and she made a sport of answering it differently each time to deflect her discomfort.

Jack quickly turned his attention to Chris and asked the same question. Chris was completely taken off guard. He turned to Carol with his mouth agape, his bulging eyes begging for help. "We've thought about adoption. We're a little leery about going the surrogate route right now," Chris calmly replied.

Jack placed his hand on Chris's shoulder, and Carol shuddered as the words spilled out of Jack's lips. "There are plenty of things today that doctors can do. My wife and I tried everything. We went through a lot of time and expense, but it was worth it. We finally got not one but three little miracles. Be patient and supportive. It doesn't matter who the issue lies with, you or your wife."

Carol wondered whether she had misheard with the music being so loud and all. Jack and Chris clinked beer bottles. Carol almost swallowed hers.

Chris raised an eyebrow. He was trying to figure out whether or not Jack was being a clever ass; suffering from the onset of some brain-function disease or something else degenerative, like possibly his sense of humor. To Carol he seemed quite sincere. Chris decided to get it over with once and for all. He blurted out, "Surely you must remember that I'm gay."

Now it was Jack's turn have a puzzled look on his face. He scratched his head a few times. "No, I'm pretty sure I'd remember something like that, my man."

Carol interjected with her voice slightly elevated so she wouldn't have to repeat herself. "You were there! On that rainy night! Soaking wet on your front steps! We all got out of the car, and Kevin was screaming at the top of his lungs. I remember it so vividly. I was surprised I didn't see you peeking into our kitchen window later."

Jack was understandably agitated. Someone he hadn't seen in years was questioning his sanity, not to mention his character. "I swear I didn't know. Even if I did, it wouldn't bother me at all, you guys. I was out there that horrible night because my parents were having another screaming match, and I couldn't take it anymore. That was one of the nights my father would pack his suitcase and leave. That night was the first he didn't come back. We all remember that night for different reasons, I guess. Kevin never told me anything. I was watching you guys because it made me feel optimistic. In a way it gave me affirmation that other families argue and have their problems and that they can be solvable."

Carol believed him. No one would open up like that unless it was true. Jack always had been a caring and sensitive kid. Once, when he was about ten years old, he had carried a neighborhood dog that had been hit by a car right in front of their house and ran with it down the street to its devastated owners. He had gotten in trouble, she remembered, because he had jumped into the owners' car to go with them to the vet and his parents had been furious when they found out.

Carol commented in jest, "If anything, Jack, I wondered at times about Kevin and you being an item, sharing those disgusting peanut butter, jelly, and marshmallow sandwiches. Climbing trees and staying up there for hours. Last, but not least, all those camping excursions in the backyard in that leaky pup tent."

Jack smiled. He loved those sandwiches.

Chris believed him too. Now that Chris thought about it, after that rainy night, Jack always waved to him and acted like he always had around him. All these years, Chris had figured Kevin had told people not to mess with his little brother. Maybe he had been wrong about that. Kevin was four years older than Chris. During Chris's teen years, the age difference seemed almost generational. Kevin hadn't shared much with him and took little interest in forming a deep friendship with him, but he knew Kevin loved him in his own way. Chris had convinced himself it was the age gap and an adjustment to adulthood, not the "gay issue." Kevin acted like he usually did toward him until after he came back for summer vacation after his junior year at U of M. Then he turned dour and distant—not with just Chris but with everyone, including his family. Most people who knew Kevin shrugged it off. His grades were outstanding, and he worked hard to save money doing odd jobs with his Uncle Sam a few times a week every summer. He even bought his own car during his sophomore year with a little assistance from his father and the dealership. No one questioned his work ethic and resolve to become an attorney.

Jack picked up from their body language that they believed him. He switched the subject to Kevin and said that since his college days he had only seen him once or twice by chance—at a wake of an old hockey coach and at Home Depot a few years back where they had swapped phone numbers and e-mail addresses. Jack had mailed Kevin an invite to their twenty-year hockey league reunion and followed up with a voicemail but got no response from either. He wondered aloud what he had done to deserve that kind of treatment, since he and Kevin had been friends for years and never had said a cross word to each other. Ultimately, Jack just chalked it up to life. Carol sensed that he was being all too kind.

Chris asked about Angela, and Jack responded as if he thought Chris would never ask. "Our parents' breakup hit her hard, " he said. "She went down a dark path for a bit, smoking, doing drugs, being flirtatious, and the like. It was as if she was trying to get them back together by abusing herself. Thankfully that only lasted less than a year. When I got back from an upstate hockey camp, she seemed fine. Mellow but serious, and understanding of others. No more chip on her shoulder. A complete turnaround, if you ask me. She claimed she had an epiphany and wanted to devote the rest of her life to making our parents proud and making a difference in people's lives. She even put herself through nursing school. It was like she was doing penance for some sin she committed. She still works part time at CVS on weekends when she isn't volunteering at the hospice. During the week, she's a visiting nurse for Whitehurst. She just did a job in the old neighborhood recently. I don't know how she can give people needles—I would faint. To this day she has a great relationship with both of our parents. I feel a little guilty on that front. She's had a few boyfriends along the way, but she's never been married. I tease her all the time that she's turned into the second coming of Mother Teresa," he proudly joked.

Carol never felt more inadequate in her life. She even thought she heard church bells and angels singing. Chris placed his hand over his heart, overcome by the tribute Jack had just bestowed upon his sister. Jack bought another round and asked about their mother, again making Carol feel guilty, as she hadn't asked him how his parents were doing.

"Our mom passed away last Saturday. We buried her yesterday. Chris flew here for the funeral. Friday night he's flying back to Boston, and then he'll drive up to Ogunquit, Maine, where he lives. Please don't judge us for being here. We're not staying much longer," Carol said with her head lowered.

"I didn't know," Jack said with an understanding smile. "My sincerest sympathy to both of you. I'm not much of an avid obits reader. I always considered it bad luck. My father jokingly called them the 'Irish comics.' Your mother was a nice lady, always made me feel so welcome. I'm so sad. The childhood memories I had of your household were so great. You'll miss her terribly, I know, but it'll get better as time passes."

"It would have been tough for you to know with your traveling schedule," Carol added, thinking how strange it was that Kevin hadn't called his best friend from childhood; it was almost as if he were sheltering the news from him. Carol always had assumed they had stayed in touch. Jack pointed to the plastic bag with his burger and fries in it that had been sitting on the bar for almost an hour. "That's why the good Lord gave us the microwave," he bellowed as he hugged them goodbye and fought his way through the crowd, holding the bag like a quarterback trying not to fumble.

Carol was annoyed by all the religious references. What a waste of money her lifelong Catholic schooling had been, she thought. She pulled rank on Chris and ordered them to pay the tab and leave. Visions of leftover goodies from the day before danced in her head.

"Praise the Lord, Angela, and the almighty microwave!" she mockingly yelled into the quiet night, turning a few heads from the circle of people who stood smoking in the parking lot. Chris was mortified and walked behind her looking the other way, taking a different path to Carol's car and hoping the people hanging around wouldn't think he was with his peeved sister.

Chapter 5

Carol wanted to get an early start on the day as the morning sunlight slowly crept into her bedroom. She strained to look at the tiny radio digital alarm clock situated on her nightstand next to a jar of Vaseline and an *In Touch* magazine that was almost three months old. "Have to throw that sucker out. The Kardashians already had a divorce and another baby in the family since that edition," she said out loud, hoping her voice would stir up Chris, who she could hear flipping around in bed across the hall.

The clock's blue digits read 7:09 a.m. She had driven to three stores with Edna riding shotgun before settling on this bare-bones device. She had to get one with blue digits. She had read somewhere that red digits could somehow burn themselves through people' closed eyes after they looked at them. Edna highly doubted that and demanded to see the scientific evidence to back up that assertion, since she knew Carol immersed herself in the tabloids with her mother daily, and that's basically all she read, besides the *Detroit Free Press* comics.

"All that garbage you read, Carol. The most troubling part is that you believe it. Get an alarm clock with some bells and whistles. This one has the capacity for just one person—as in *solo*! Someday you may need one with settings for two, if you know what I mean, and you'll thank me," Edna had pleaded to no avail.

A single ray of sunlight shot through the space between the blinds and windowsill like a laser beam. It bothered Carol enough that she sprung out of bed.

"Chris, I have to return those fold-up chairs we borrowed from the funeral home," Carol called out. "We were supposed to do that yesterday. You can help. Then I want to get in a good workout at the gym. You can come as my guest. How about it?"

"Okay. I'll be right down," he grunted.

Carol put on some black spandex pants and a nondescript light-gray T-shirt. She wasn't into fashion these days. Chris came downstairs and told her he had brought white athletic socks and sneakers but had neglected to pack any gym wear. He sat down and grabbed the TV clicker.

Carol would have none of that. She ran into the mudroom and opened the hamper. On top sat Edna's old orange sweat outfit that Chris had ridiculed Carol for wearing the morning before. She picked it out, gave it a couple of sniffs, sprayed a couple of squirts of Febreze on it as an extra precaution, brought it to the den, and gently placed it on Chris's lap. He looked at her completely immersed in wardrobe horror.

"Try it on. No bellyaching. It's way big for me. I never wear it out of the house. Might be a tad short, but that's it," she demanded in a hurried tone.

To her surprise, Chris got up and tried it on. She was sure it was because he wanted to prove to her that it wouldn't fit. Much to his chagrin, it did fit for the most part. It was a tad short as Carol had predicted, but there was more than enough room for him to move around in.

"The reason you don't wear this monstrosity out of the house is because it's plain ugly. We're half-Irish Catholic, and we aren't supposed to wear any orange St. Paddy's Day week," he pleaded.

Carol folded up the chairs and went out to stack them in her car. Chris begrudgingly followed. There were only ten chairs, and with a little rearranging they all fit in the car. They were determined to make one trip, even though the funeral home was only a mile away. Chris appeared to be over his wardrobe tantrum, and before they knew it, the car was in the funeral home parking lot.

The funeral home used to be named Murphy & Sons, but Chris noticed the name on the sign had a corporate ring to it—Heavenly Rest Associates. He hadn't noticed that before.

"This place is some kind of national chain now, like a Wendy's or a Starbucks. Why don't they just name it Dead Depot or Burial King?" he said. "I'm surprised they haven't put in a drive-thru window. Mourners could just drive in, see the body in the casket through the window, state their name, wave to the grieving family, say a prayer, order a coffee specially brewed in holy water, and drive off. They could even have a machine that sprays an assortment of floral scents into the car . Or maybe they could give away a floral-scented car deodorizer with every jumbo cup of coffee purchased!"

Carol laughed. "I know it's morbid. Capitalism to the extreme. I get it. Enough, please. At least I'll have tears running down my cheeks when we get in there. They won't realize they're from laughter!"

Carol and Chris walked into the funeral home, a chair under each arm, and placed them against the hallway wall. After the last trip, they attempted to surreptitiously tiptoe toward the front door.

"I thought I heard someone in here. Thank you for returning the chairs." The funeral director's voice echoed through the empty room. As he came closer, he noticed the tears running down Carol's face. "My poor dear. It will get better," he said as he reached for a Kleenex in a box atop the credenza and handed it to Carol. It was a required move right out of the corporate manual.

Chris reached in, brought Carol's face against his chest, and hugged her. He prayed to himself that she wouldn't burst out laughing. It was all he could do to maintain a straight face. "Thank you so much, sir. I think coming back in here so soon got to her. Thanks for the chairs," Chris responded while simultaneously walking Carol out the door, unaware that his warm embrace had turned into a full-fledged headlock until she began to squirm so she could catch her breath.

Upon entering the car, they both broke into wild laughter. Now tears were rolling down Chris's cheeks. He punched the glove compartment so hard it opened, and a bunch of tampons out spilled onto his lap. They heard a slight tap on the driver's side window. Carol slowly rolled down the window halfway, and in popped the funeral director's head.

"Please read these brochures. They may help ease your pain, and please check out our website if you're interested in getting the CD collection," he offered in monotone corporate speak, as his baffled face became red and distorted upon seeing both of them laughing, with Chris chomping on a tampon. Carol nodded and quickly rolled up the window, almost catching his nose. She sped off as they laughed harder and harder until they reached the gym.

The two regained their composure and went into the gym. Chris joked that Carol already looked like she had put in a good workout as her sweatshirt was soaked. She got on the elliptical, and Chris went to the weight room at the other side of the gym.

Both agreed on a time limit of one hour. After twenty minutes, Chris appeared next to the elliptical machine and complained that he couldn't get into a groove because of his outfit.

"That is so lame. Go away, and put it out of your head," Carol said, out of breath. "No one cares, and there are only five people in here."

After another forty minutes, she got off the machine and wiped it clean with a towel. She found Chris on the imitation leather couch near the locker rooms looking content and reading *Muscle and Fitness* magazine. There wasn't an ounce of sweat on him.

"Sit and relax. I'm almost done with a good article on male menopause. I want to take the test afterward," Chris said.

Carol responded in a disappointed tone, "First, my thighs always stick to that couch, and it hurts getting off it. Second, how can such a drama queen be worried about such things? You just had a tampon in your mouth." She gently pulled the magazine out of his hand, patted his completely dry mane, and motioned for the door.

Chris once again slowly followed her. "This is becoming a trend. I feel like a lemming walking toward a cliff every time we leave a place," he lamented in a sheepish tone.

Chapter 6

Chris gave Carol a hip check and galloped upstairs to run the shower. He was anxious to rid himself of the twenty-year-old orange outfit he'd been forced to wear. He didn't care to shower down in the dungeon. There was little natural light, and he liked Carol's bath products much better—Clinique! All that was in the basement shower stall was a crusted plastic bottle of Head & Shoulders and a milky bar of soap with a fossilized pubic hair planted deeply in it. He almost needed a blowtorch to remove the bottle cap; no shampoo would squirt out of the clogged hole no matter how hard he squeezed it.

The shower was so warm and inviting that his mind drifted in the mist. He thought about Arthur and how much he missed him and wondered which one of them missed the other the most. He worried about their business and how important this summer season was for it. Last year it was just getting started, and word of mouth was the only way to get more people in the door. The website hadn't been up and running until almost Labor Day, and they missed the deadline for an ad in the travel brochures. The "Dilly Dally's" great location on Route 1 by the beach access path was a coveted spot, a huge help, but the rent was higher on average than most of the shops for that very reason. The last tourist season had been blessed with great weather, which is a crucial factor in New England as there's a finite window of time to make the most of the yearly take. Every rainy day hurts the pocket, and two in a row can wipe out a whole week of profits.

A gourmet deli has thin margins. The ingredients and higher qualities of meats and imported cheeses have variable costs that are tough to pass along to cash-strapped vacationers. Clothes and trinket shops have it much better. They always can discount their goods to move old merchandise and offer sales to push new products. Chris and Arthur didn't have that stopgap insurance. The plain and simple fact is that food spoils and must be thrown out. When that happened, they couldn't recoup anything; an outbreak of E. coli traced back to their shop could severely impact business. Add in the dynamic of the power of Internet reviews, justified or not.

That was the main issue with Arthur's rapid weight gain. It pained him to waste good food so much that he'd eat it. Chris imagined how bad it would be if the weather hadn't cooperated so well last summer. Maybe he was being overly harsh. It was only twenty pounds or so, but Arthur already had a thick frame. Arthur, however, was far from obese. His waist size was forty, but Chris worried about stress and weight-related conditions, such as high blood pressure and diabetes. Arthur didn't seem to have impotence issues yet. *God forbid*, Chris thought with a shudder.

He turned the shower off and rubbed the plush bath towel against his face, taking in its fresh smell. He heard his cell phone ring and reached across the sink, grabbed it, saw Arthur's name illuminated on the screen, and answered it. "I was just thinking about you. I'm standing naked in the shower. Me so horny. Is everything good with you, my playful paisan?" he asked in a sexually alluring tone.

Arthur was calling to check on him. He asked how Carol was then whispered a few sweet nothings into Chris's ear. He sounded surprised to hear that both were doing so well. "Are you sure you're not trying to be strong for me, baby?" he asked Chris, sounding a bit skeptical. Chris assured him things were going as well as could be expected and that he would be home late the next night as scheduled. Arthur told him he was glad to hear that, but if more time was needed, Chris should stay longer.

Carol pounded on the semi-open door and raised her voice for Arthur to hear. "Thanks, Arthur, or should I say, 'my playful paisan'? Chris will be home as scheduled. I'm fine." Chris gave her a sneer, as it was obvious she had heard most of his conversation. He gave Arthur a phone kiss, and they exchanged goodbyes. He put the towel around him, indignantly walked past Carol into the bedroom, and closed the door. "Tell me...is 'Schrudel the Noodle' your pet name?" she joked through the door.

A short while later, Carol came downstairs refreshed and hungry. She found Chris in the kitchen scouring the cupboards. It was lunchtime, and she suggested they go out for pizza and maybe take in a movie matinee. Chris instantly warmed up to the idea with a devious smirk. It was obvious he would do anything to get out of the house. He told her Edna had called on the house phone and said she was planning to stop by this evening after work and mentioned she could bring food over.

Carol called her back right away. "Hi. You know what? I want to cook. I'll make something fun. It'll be therapeutic for me." She turned away from Chris, cupped her hand over the receiver, and whispered to Edna, "It'll keep me out of trouble. I can't wait to tell you about our bizarre day yesterday. I can't let this madman of a brother coerce me into going to a bar today. He's not on vacation. This isn't homecoming. He's here to mourn." She hung up and saw Chris had a phony innocent look written all over his unshaven face. "Didn't care to use my razor? What's the matter? Don't you like pink?" Carol clowned, rubbing his two-day old stubble, then added, "I'm on to you, little brother."

Chris insisted her remarks weren't fair. He predominantly ate deli food back home, so he welcomed eating anything out of his current daily realm. Most weeks he worked twelve-hour days. He spent his mornings preparing delicacies such as grilled calamari, stuffed peppers, and assorted homemade sausages. The deli also served made-to-order breakfast sandwiches, bagels, and hot and cold deli sandwiches first thing in the morning for the beachgoers who wanted to eat on the run or have their coolers fully stocked for the whole day.

Okay, Carol got it. Chris ate the same stuff every day and worked hard nonstop. His whining paid off. She would cut him some slack. Her thoughts turned to the evening's menu, and she wanted to appease Chris more than ever now. She would have to use her imagination. "We're going to the supermarket later, and I'm warning you that it'll take some time because apparently you're a fussy customer. I don't want you to start throwing your food on the floor and banging your spoon on the table, you big baby," she said sternly.

They went to a local pizza-and-sandwich shop near the cinema complex. It was in a strip mall that was half vacant, and Chris once again noticed yet another thriving nail salon. "Detroit is in a depression, yet it's nail salon galore around here. Who can afford such a luxury every week? When did this place turn into Beverly Hills? Why would anyone frequent such an environment, where all the workers are wearing surgical masks, while they, the customers, sit unmasked, breathing in toenail dust? You watch. You heard it here first. Studies will find that stuff is worse than asbestos. I'm talking about you, sister," he amusingly carried on as only he could do.

This was part of the reason Carol coveted spending time with him. Chris had a rare talent for churning his acute powers of observation into a symphonic comedic episode within seconds.

"Those are the sacrifices one has to make to look good," Carol said. "Actually, I'm overdue for a manicure. Maybe they can take us both in right away after we eat."

Chris picked up her left hand, examined her un-chipped mahogany nails, and declared, "They're fine. You, my dear, are most certainly not. You need therapy and Nails Anonymous. There's a vile epidemic going on around here. *60 Minutes* will be here soon doing an exposé on all this madness. You'll see!"

They walked up to the counter and ordered a half-cheese and half-pepperoni pie. Carol grabbed a large Diet Coke out of the cooler to the left of them. She tried to distract Chris so he wouldn't notice the beer and wine cooler to the right, which was partially shielded by the trash barrel and the large chip-display tree. Too late—he took out two beers. They both sat in a tiny booth. Carol looked at the beer bottles on the table and waved her hand and shook her head.

Chris laughed. "They're both for me. I'll be done with one by the time the pizza gets here."

The thin-crust pie came out quickly. They waited for it to cool, and Chris carefully picked up a slice of pepperoni so everything would stay intact. Then he took a temperature-test nibble and gave Carol the okay.

She couldn't contain herself. "Hey, isn't pepperoni a big deli staple? Aren't you sick of eating that too? You just like to whine!"

Chris smiled and chewed and took a final sudsy swig of his first beer and twisted the top off the second one. Both ate in silence for about ten minutes until there was only one slice of cheese pizza left. Carol pushed it toward him, and he pushed it back and burped. She threw the slice in the garbage and placed the tray on the counter, and they slowly trudged out the door holding their full bellies.

Carol was actually in the right frame of mind for a movie. Entertaining a person for days at a time can be a grind—even someone she loved. Knowing that she was going to miss Chris soon didn't alter her current state of mind. She felt like she always had to be "on," and winding down in a plush seat for two hours of escapism sounded fine. Chris sat in the car thinking the same thing in reverse. They ruled out any animated, action-adventure, sci-fi, or teenybopper movies. That basically left romance or comedy. Chris fumbled with his phone and chirped out the movie playlist. They decided on *The Vow* with Channing Tatum and Rachel McAdams, as it fit their criteria.

They rushed into the cinema with barely five minutes to spare and got the tickets. As they walked into the dark theater, Chris pointed to the rows near the top, and they schlepped up the dimly lit stairwell and sat down panting. Within seconds of getting situated, Chris started to get fidgety and whispered that he had to pee.

Carol softly murmured, "Didn't we just pass not one but two men's rooms no more than a minute ago? You didn't have to go then? You waited until we climbed Mount Everest? Great move downing those two beers, by the way."

She let him pass through as she watched the last of the trailers. As the theater darkened further, Chris returned. He whispered, "I'll bet you Channing punches out at least one person. He does that in every movie he's in. Macho son of a gun, that boy is." Carol bet him a buck just to shut him up.

The movie was entertaining enough. At the end, Carol took out a dollar and gave it to Chris. Satisfied, he gladly took it then threw it back into her purse. "That was a layup. I was getting a little nervous, though. It was almost at the end when he whacked the ex," he said while pretending to rub sweat off his forehead. "Okay. I'm only going to say it once. She could remember everyone else in her life, her wrinkly manipulative mother and her Svengali of a father and also her conniving ex, but she couldn't remember doing Channing Tatum, with that ripped body? A little farfetched if you ask me. With that temple of a body, she couldn't remember one nook or cranny her tongue had worshiped."

Carol laughed in agreement. "It's supposedly based on a true story. Maybe if the real guy had a body like that she wouldn't have forgotten who he was."

The next stop would be the supermarket. Carol offered to drop Chris back at home and was relieved when he accepted. "Kick back and watch a little TV. I'll be gone an hour or so. Do you want me to come in and show you how to use the clicker?" she jokingly asked as she handed him the house key.

Carol had planned a feast worthy of a blue ribbon for the two most entertaining people in her life. Edna wasn't as fussy to cook for as Chris. She watched her calories but didn't count them, as she had a metabolism people envied. Her weakness, as well as Carol's, was cheese. Any kind, soft or hard, sharp or mild, cow or goat—it didn't matter. A cheese-laden snack often allowed them time to decide which direction the evening was going. Often, crackers and cheese shamefully was the meal. Tonight would be different. Carol was overly determined to give Chris an epic gastronomic send-off, as she rarely had the opportunity to pamper him. Edna had better stay focused and play along. Wine tended to distract her.

Carol fancied herself a pretty good cook. All these years she had learned under the tutelage of her mother. Every big holiday they toiled in the kitchen together for days. They studied the lip-smacking reactions of the people sitting around the crowded table, and her mother would give her a secretive wink. Carol would put her hand over her eye and give her a hidden wink back. It was easy to remember how a dish came out from one year to the next, as they followed the same boring recipes. They could cook blindfolded and achieve the same results. Mary was content with that for the most part, until she mastered the use of the Internet, and then things changed quickly. Her cooking went to the nouveau-chef level, as she mixed and matched ingredients from around the world. She reached a plateau unrivaled for a seventy-something, flirting with the limits of people's taste buds and teasing all the olfactory senses. Carol tried to keep up with her but didn't have the same passion. It was as if her mother knew she was on borrowed time and on a worldly pilgrimage based in her own kitchen.

Together they enhanced tired recipes and unleashed new ones. Unfortunately their test market was typically limited to each other and occasionally Edna. Tonight, Carol wanted to cook a meal her mother would be proud of, both as a tribute to the good times they'd had together and a testament to her unruffled refusal to embrace death and her quest to savior the remaining days she'd had left.

Since Carol was on a limited budget, achieving this would be a challenge. On a mission, she pulled into the supermarket with coupons in tow. The store wasn't crowded, and she grabbed a cart with two wobbly back wheels and instantly replaced it with one that had a two-for-one soup coupon tangled in the steel mesh. *Ahead of the game already*, she thought. She still had no idea what to pick up. It would come to her, she knew. She made a game of it, pretending she was a chef on a Food Channel show forced to make a mouthwatering dish with a handful of ingredients.

She buzzed through the produce aisle and tossed one item after another into the cart: shallots, red potatoes, Vidalia onions, fresh basil, spinach, eggplant, and vine tomatoes.

Then she hit the dreaded cheese section. She could spend an hour here. She mustered the willpower to avoid drifting into her usual hypnotic cheese-induced trance and went straight for the ricotta, making sure it wasn't past the expiration date, and placed it in the cart. Off she scurried to the meat section, where she whipped a baguette into the cart without breaking stride. She found a 30-percent-off coupon clutched in her hand for pork tenderloin, wheeled over to where the pork products were, found a nice long piece draped in plastic that passed her freshness eye test, and added it to her collection. Next she picked up Panko bread crumbs, spicy barbecue sauce, low-calorie syrup, black Greek olives, pine nuts, cream, and golden raisins. She reversed direction with the cart's tires screeching, headed to the soup aisle, and picked up two cans of chicken noodle, happy she had remembered her found coupon.

There wasn't a line at the checkout counter, and no one was behind her as she unloaded her items and sorted her coupons. Only three matched, but she still figured she was saving about twelve dollars, a minor victory. Her attention drifted to the tabloids. Sadness overcame her as she suddenly remembered the fun times she'd had with her mother. Carol would put the groceries away at home, and then they'd head for the kitchen table or the den and spend time reading the tabloids. They'd wager a penny on whether or not a story was true. Carol always had been suspicious of how a "family friend" always appeared to be the main source for an embarrassing or stinging story. Who were these people and why did these celebrities have these kinds of "friends" hanging around?

At the end, Carol's mother owed her fifty cents, as she was overly credulous. Still pending was whether or not Jennifer

Aniston was pregnant. In the future, they would have to go double or nothing up in heaven. Carol's eyes filled with tears as she stared at a *Star* magazine. Her hand reached for it, and she held it for a few seconds, waiting to hear her mother's approval. She stood frozen until a grandmotherly voice interrupted her thoughts. Her eyes shifted to the kind-looking, elderly cashier who had been waiting patiently to ring her up. "I'd get it if I were you. I just read it in the lunchroom. There's a lot of juicy stuff in there. It's a shame that she had to die like that." The woman startled Carol for a moment until she realized she was talking about Whitney Houston. Carol smiled and gently handed the tabloid to the woman as she wiped the tears from her eyes. It was one of those odd moments she'd later share with Edna but not for a while. She wasn't quite ready to laugh at the expense of her deceased mother.

Chapter 7

Chris was watching *Law & Order* when Carol got home—no big surprise, as some version or spinoff of the show seemed to be on every other channel. She told him to stay put as she carried in the groceries. There were only four plastic bags, and one just had a carton of brown eggs in it. She put everything away and walked back into the den, noticing Chris was flicking channels during the commercials.

"I see you finally mastered the clicker," she said.

Chris admitted he wasn't really watching anything. He had fallen asleep on the recliner, and she had awoken him. He glanced at the wall clock and complimented Carol on how fast she had gotten back. Carol informed him that Edna was due to arrive at six-thirty and was picking up some wine. She also reminded him that Kevin was stopping by in the mid-afternoon the next day to go over their parents' estate and the will. It was best they went over things as soon as possible while Chris was in town. Kevin was the executor, and his firm had advised on the will. He had cleared his schedule but had to attend a fundraiser in the early evening up in Grosse Pointe, so he couldn't stay for dinner. Carol was going to drive Chris to the airport. Edna had picked him up before, as Carol had been inundated with funeral arrangements and taking nonstop phone calls from friends and relatives.

Chris wasn't looking forward to any of this business. He just wanted his mother back. He always had felt guilty that he had left home right before his father had died, and now he hadn't been around for either of their deaths. He had moved to Greenwich Village in Manhattan and lived there for more than ten years. His mother actually had persuaded him to go. He had seemed stifled in Dearborn, and she wanted him to spread his wings. He loved New York at first sight and was in awe of all that it offered him as a young gay man. During his time there, he bounced around from apartment to apartment and a number of roommates. The rents were overly expensive, and at first he had three or four roommates so the cost would be spread out more. He tended bar and over the years developed a good reputation as a dependable employee. The gay community was close knit, and word of mouth traveled fast. He was eventually asked to manage a new bar and restaurant venture and jumped at the chance. He loved working nights and required little sleep. He spent his afternoons running errands and going to the gym. He made enough money to get a tiny flat in the West Village on the third floor and loved the independence of living solo. He designed it all by himself and felt proud when his designer friends came over and applauded his creativity in making the flat appear much bigger than what it was through blending color and scheme with the natural light the only four windows provided.

Chris really missed that place. It was where he had blossomed as a person and become more confident in social situations. He had toyed with the idea of going to design school but decided against that as a career. There were more interior designers in New York than tea in China. Arthur loved that place. Chris never would forget the first time Arthur visited—how his eyes had darted from one wall to the next looking at the furniture, artwork, and accessories. It felt like a sanctuary when they were together in there. There was no dishwasher, and Arthur would crank up the stereo and sing loudly as he washed and Chris wiped. It never felt like a chore, just shared time together.

They had wanted to keep the apartment as a *pied*-à-*terre*, but the cost was too high. They sobbed as they walked down the stairs for the last time and embraced in the hallway as the movers waited for them outside. Chris sent as much stuff as possible with them to Ogunquit, where Arthur already had a house, but it seemed foreign and awkward combined with the layout and the furniture already in place. They tried the best they could to mix and match things but decided to sell most of Chris's furniture through a consignment store down the road. All that was left of Chris's was a set of funky red-velvet shaded lamps for the master bedroom and an exotic pair of candelabras.

Arthur and Chris had first met at a birthday party that the neighborhood dry cleaner owners, John and his wife Joyce, had hosted for themselves in SoHo. The couple's birthdays were a day apart. Chris was a loyal customer and stopped by often just to chat. He even brought them coffee once in a while. Joyce joked that she refused to believe Chris was gay and that he would love her single girlfriends attending the party. When he arrived, she was introducing him to her girlfriends when Arthur tapped him on the shoulder and asked if he wanted any of the egg rolls he had on a silver tray he was carrying. Their "gaydar" eyes met, and they both smiled invitingly at each other. Arthur was catering the occasion and took John aside and asked if Chris was seeing anyone, while Chris was asking the same question of Joyce. What made it more fateful was that it was mostly a "straight" party and their meeting was so by chance. Chris remembered he had goose bumps when he first saw Arthur. Arthur had been too busy working the crowd and organizing servings in the kitchen for them to have any further conversation that evening.

It was Chris who took the initiative and asked Joyce for Arthur's phone number. When he called the next day, Arthur instantly asked him what had taken him so long to call, even before Chris could identify himself. They met later in the day for coffee before Chris started his manager shift at the lounge. They were inseparable ever since; in fact this was the longest time they had spent apart.

Chris kicked off his shoes and realized another episode of *Law & Order* had started. *Once you miss the beginning*, he thought, *it's an exercise in futility to catch up.* He turned the channel to the local news. "Five murders in Detroit so far, and the day isn't over yet," he said to Carol, noticing she was in a reflective funk of her own and hadn't heard a word he'd said.

Carol stared at her worn piano in the parlor while she was strewn on the couch dangling her SmartWool-protected feet off the side. She used to see the piano as being good for the soul. Lately it had become her livelihood, and she felt somewhat uneasy about that. It was an upright dark-brown Steinway, devoid of decorative molding or detail. It was very drab and quite dissimilar from those fancy grand pianos played in concert halls or storied hotel bars. One of the foot pedals stuck a bit, and the piano was full of scratches that she once thought gave it character, but now all she saw was ugliness. She was pragmatic about her playing talent from the start, and Juilliard would have been a pipe dream. She could play all the show tunes and popular music really well but never had developed an ear for the classics. Not too long ago, she would sit down and play a few songs for her own pleasure and enjoyment. Now she only played to keep sharp. Her relationship with the piano had gone from amorous to acrimonious. She looked at the piano as merely as the breadwinner. At fifty bucks per hour-and-fifteen-minute lesson, however, it was a relationship she couldn't walk away from. She wanted a divorce, but the piano was her sugar daddy.

Understandably, Carol had canceled her lessons this week. She currently had twelve students per week and eked out a decent living, had no commute headaches or cost, and paid no rental fees. She missed the camaraderie, however, of working in the public school music department and the work agenda it provided—not to mention the comprehensive medical plan, as she currently had a bare-bones plan she paid for herself. It had been a good vocation that she'd always thought had strong job security, but the challenging economic landscape had changed that perception. She still stayed in contact with a few of her old work friends, but mostly via email. Now there was no one to say hello to in the hallway or to go out with for an after-work drink. Maybe she was just being melancholy and next week she'd get back in the groove. Carol closed her eyes and thought how nice it was that she and Chris were in the same room for all this time, just sitting quietly. In a strange way, it seemed like they were sharing the same feelings without actually conversing. Edna would be coming over in two hours. It was time to prepare dinner.

Carol got up off the cozy couch and ordered Chris to continue whatever he was doing on the recliner. He wasn't sleeping or reading, and most certainly he wasn't paying attention to the Disney Channel, she concluded. She was wrong about that. He was partially focused on some teen family sit-com. The main stars didn't appear to be old enough for high school and seemed to be close to the age of the characters they were portraying. He remembered the old sitcoms like *Happy Days* when a thirty-something Henry Winkler played Fonzie and the rest of the cast played teenagers still in high school while in their mid-twenties in real life. He always thought that was a little weird and also insulting to both the viewers and other legitimate teenage actors at the time.

What attracted Chris to the TV was the innocence of the kids and the carefree life they had. It was the life he'd once had too, being in the same room he was in now, sitting with his family, and he missed it. Mom fetching a TV tray and snapping it together in an instant in front of the chair and coming back with a sandwich, chocolate milk, and a cookie while he watched TV. He missed her doting on him, and he still pined for her attention. Those trays weren't very dependable. They tended to collapse at times if plates were imbalanced on top, or if they were accidentally kicked, but they were a challenge and made eating fun. Maybe it would help if they had dinner tonight on the TV trays, he thought. He got up and clumsily put together four of them and situated them in front of the couch and chairs. He applied slight pressure on top to test their sturdiness. He figured one would be needed to put bread, condiments, and the wine on.

Carol placed the food on the counter then looked to see what she had in the fridge and cupboards. She had an outline in her mind of the menu but wasn't sure she had the proper inventory. Finally, she was satisfied she had enough stuff and put on her apron. The stove clock showed an hour-and-a-half until Edna's scheduled arrival. They would start off with sliced provolone with stuffed jalapeno olives, along with crackers and bread. That would be wine-sipping and nibbling food for an hour or so. The first course would be an eggplant tower, with three round slices fried with seasoned bread crumbs in olive oil, with a dollop of room-temperature ricotta placed between each layer. On top of each dollop she would gently sprinkle powdered sugar for a bit of sweetness to hit the palate. Around the base of the fried eggplant, she would place black Greek olives and drip a little balsamic glaze over the top of the tower. On the same plate, surrounding the tower, she'd arrange sliced tomatoes with leaves of basil on top and drizzle extra-virgin olive oil over them. She'd finish with a dusting of finely grated Parmesan cheese over the entire dish.

For the entrée, she planned to baste the pork tenderloin in spicy barbecue sauce. Next she'd roll the pork in Panko bread crumbs and pan sear it all in vegetable oil, rather than olive oil, so the crumbs would fry lighter and fluffier. Then a small amount of syrup diluted with orange juice would be applied on top. She'd slice Vidalia onions and place them on top for added crunch. This would add a little acidity and sweetness to the spicy flavor already sealed in by the bread crumbs. She'd bake the pork so it would be slightly pink in the middle. After letting it stand for ten minutes, she'd slice the crusted pork into medallions. For sides, she'd serve shallot mashed potatoes, as well as spinach steamed with pine nuts and golden raisins. For dessert she had chocolate ice cream in the freezer in case things got that far. Usually more wine was dessert when the three of them got together.

Chapter 8

Carol was upstairs in the bathroom freshening up when it dawned on her that her mother always had wanted Edna to have her emerald broach. Edna's mother, Helen, had given it to Carol's mom as a twenty-first birthday present. Mary had worn it religiously on every special occasion. It wasn't ostentatious or expensive, but it had high sentimental value. It featured tiny emerald chips within a raised gold-plated teardrop-shaped ornament. When Edna was a little girl, she had admired how shiny it was and told her Aunt Mary that green was her favorite color. Everyone in the room chuckled when Edna blurted out that she wanted one for Christmas, as not many seven-year-olds had a green broach at the top of their wish list.

Carol went downstairs into her mother's room and picked the broach out of the jewelry box. The box had been a present from Kevin when he was a small boy. He had made it himself with assistance from Uncle Sam. It never closed completely and was a little warped, but her mother never minded. Carol sat on the bed polishing the broach with her sweater, careful not to stick herself with the pin. She thought of all the history stored in the room, from faded photographs to stacks of old letters. It felt like a museum. Actually the entire house did now. The doorbell rang, and she placed the broach on the bureau and went out to greet Edna.

Edna brought four bottles of red wine. She couldn't decide between Merlot and Chianti, she said, so she got two of each.

She had to work late and was still dressed in her work clothes, a figure-hugging, light-blue-and-black, horizontal-thin-striped sweater dress with black nylons and high heels.

"You didn't have to get dressed up on our account," Chris said, pointing at his jeans while looking at Carol's frumpy sweater and jeans. Edna handed him the bottles of wine, and he read the labels and gave her a thumbs-up. "If you weren't my cousin and if I weren't gay, I'd say you were hot," Chris noted.

Edna kiddingly gave him a smack and said, "These days I'll take any adulation I can get. That was your intention, I assume. Hey! Something smells real good!"

She started to walk toward the kitchen to peek in the oven, but Carol cut her off and herded her into the den. "What is this?" Carol uttered, looking at the TV trays. Chris explained to her that he wanted tonight to feel so homey like the old days when they were kids. The girls laughed. "Do you want me to go down to the basement and get your old highchair?" Carol snapped.

Edna said she thought the TV trays might be fun. Carol got them to agree that the tables would stay for the wine and cheese only, and then they'd move to the dining room table and eat like adults. She admonished Edna for going along with Chris and wondered aloud what else was in store for the night.

Chris opened the Merlot first, as he thought it was a better wine for appetizers. Carol walked in with a large cheese-and-cracker platter in one hand and tiny paper plates in the other. No sense in using the fine dishware on the flimsy tables. She gently placed the platter on one of the TV trays and stared at it for a second, as if to ready herself to catch the platter. Temporarily appeased, she grabbed the wineglasses, and Chris poured the wine and then found a '90s cable music station on the TV. Edna sat down and grabbed a slice of cheese and placed it between two crackers. Chris handed her a glass of wine, and she placed it on the tray.

"Try not to breathe hard," Carol said in a sardonic tone, intently staring at Edna's wineglass.

They all laughed, and Chris noticed how straight and still everyone was sitting. Edna was saying she'd been so busy that she had skipped lunch, and as she reached for another piece of cheese, her right breast bumped against the tray and her wineglass almost spilled over. It was only a matter of when, not if, the tray was going to collapse.

Carol couldn't wait to mention that she and Chris had run into Jack Sheridan at Kiley's the night before. They took turns chiming in and telling Edna the whole story. Edna was struck by how Angela had turned her life around, but living across town and being older, Edna never really knew much about her, except for what Carol had told her, and not much of it had been positive. She knew Angela was pretty with long dark hair, and from seeing her across the street while visiting Carol's family, she knew she always dressed in skimpy outfits and couldn't envision her being heavy.

Carol was getting frustrated that no one asked the obvious question. If Angela didn't call her brother Jack from the store, then who did she call and how did Kevin find out so quickly? There was silence in the room as all three pondered that with perfect posture.

Edna broke the silence. "She must have called Kevin."

That answer seemed too obvious, and that's what flustered Carol the most. Back then, Angela barely talked to Kevin, and they were far from friends. Carol recalled only a few times when Angela had even set foot in their house. Kevin was almost five years older than Angela and intimidated her. Both he and her brother Jack teased her. Most of the time, he completely ignored her. She had to have called someone else.

Chris didn't seem concerned with the question. Some of Kevin's other hockey teammates had worked in the store, he said. They may have been on shift that evening. Any one of them could have made the call to Kevin. He had been too busy in the storage room to take attendance. Besides, that was a lifetime ago. Did it really matter now how Kevin found out? Carol reluctantly considered that a plausible explanation, as she couldn't recollect who had worked that night, and she dropped the subject as her level of suspicion ebbed. Chris sounded so convincing, and if he didn't care about it much, why should she?

Edna brought up her relationship with Nick. It was one of those on-and-off-again deals. He'd been on the rebound from a three-year relationship when they'd met and was still hurting. Like Edna, he had never been married and wasn't looking to. He was content with having a more peripheral relationship. Edna knew she wanted something more but wasn't sure if she wanted it with Nick anyway. He was a very guarded person and too quiet for her at times. He had mood swings, but she was drawn to his intelligence. He was very polite, and they never fought. That was the problem. There was little passion or spontaneity. Everything he did was calculated. Still, they were good company for each other.

Chris laughed and said, "There's not a man on the planet who can keep up with your yapping. I wouldn't say that's a shortfall for him. You ever think he might tell people you talk too much?"

Edna shot him a dirty look and changed the subject to the weather.

Chris was curious how Carol could afford Clinique products and told Edna it was a welcome surprise when he had stepped in the shower. "The petroleum jelly and baby shampoo queen moves up to Clinque," he joked. Carol and Edna looked at each other, and Edna put her hand over her mouth. Sensing there was a story behind this, Chris urged them to tell him the details. "Do tell. They just didn't jump on the shower caddy by themselves."

Carol sighed. "It was at an Elks Club fundraiser last year. There was an auction toward the end. I had eaten very little and had a few vodka tonics. A Clinique basket was next in line to be auctioned off. Edna had just redone her bathroom. I had been procrastinating about getting her a present, and I felt really guilty. I came up with the inane idea of getting her that basket. A large audience stood in front, and I was way in the back. The bidding started at sixty dollars, and I bid seventy-five. Someone in the front of the crowd was adamant about getting that basket and kept outbidding me. The price got up to a hundred and fifty bucks! I was determined to get that basket. I bid a hundred and fifty-five and won it! I walked up to the stage to collect the basket and heard Edna scream. She was the person bidding against me! I could only see an arm being raised and didn't know it was her. She apparently wanted to give it to *me* as a birthday present. She had been trying unsuccessfully to get me to step up my beauty regimen for reasons I still don't know. She figured I'd use the products since they were a gift from her."

Chris tried to contain himself. There he was, sitting straight and upright, afraid to move for fear of knocking over his TV tray. His laughter erupted from his belly, and as it traveled up his diaphragm to his larynx, his right leg spasmed and nudged the tray over. He was holding his wineglass, but his plate of cheese and crackers tumbled to the carpet. The disaster of red wine spilling on to the beige carpet was successfully avoided.

This was why Carol had felt much trepidation about allowing the trays to be used in the first place. She breathed a sigh of relief, discounting the slight mess of a few cheese and crackers on the floor, and went on with the story. "I really didn't want the gift basket for myself. I knew Edna would use it, so we struck a deal. She wrote me a check for seventy-five dollars, and she kept all the anti-wrinkle creams, body lotions, and nail stuff, and I got all the shampoos and conditioners. We were both culpable for what had transpired, and if I'd had the nerve to maneuver down front to where Edna was, it never would have happened. I'd never participated in an auction before and was very comfy standing in the back. I don't know how I got the gumption to keep outbidding her."

"Shame on you guys. Your hearts were in the right place, but your heads were up your asses. Correct me if I'm wrong, my sisters, but you paid around seventy-five bucks each for fifty bucks worth of products. The power of alcohol! I'll open up another bottle," Chris sputtered while still in full belly-laugh mode.

Carol and Edna weren't as amused and defended themselves in tandem, "Hey, it was for charity!"

Carol motioned toward the dining room and playfully snarled, "Playtime is over. Time to move to the grownup table. Please take a comfortable seat with plenty of legroom, and I'll get us some adult food."

They all laughed as Carol got up and dragged her left leg across the rug, complaining that it had fallen asleep from being still for so long.

A few moments later, the kitchen door swung open to the sight of Carol holding three plates of fried eggplant towers and a baguette in its paper sleeve under her arm, her leg still noticeably limping. Edna applauded her dexterity, and Chris added that he would have clapped also if she were balancing a ball on her nose at the same. Carol broke off a piece of bread and passed it to

Edna, who was busy developing a strategy regarding how she was going to devour the tower. She decided on cutting it in half down the middle. Chris already had taken off the entire top layer and then ate it whole. Carol decided to start on the perimeter with the tomatoes and work her way in, as she had a medieval fantasy going on. She visualized her prince had to cross the moat first to rescue her from the burning tower. Carol knew the eggplant towers were a hit from the silence that ensued and the smiles on her guests' face. Chris commented on how the different flavors snuck up on him, and Edna was impressed by the crispiness and lightness of the eggplant, as it didn't seem to be fried. Carol watched as their plates emptied and her anxiety subsided. The first course had been a winner. She was one for one so far.

Edna helped her clear the table, and Carol bent down and pulled out the crusted pork tenderloin, which was warming in the oven, and sliced it into medallions. Edna attentively watched over her shoulder, trying to learn something. She liked to cook nice meals also, but because she lived alone, it was more prudent to do carry out and simple dishes like mac and cheese and grilled chicken with a garden salad. Edna helped bring out the steamed spinach and the scallion mashed potatoes. Chris already had topped off all their glasses of wine by the time they returned.

Once again, Carol watched as they took their first bites. "This is absolutely delicious. Arthur needs to take cooking lessons from you, but never tell him I mentioned that," Chris said.

Carol cut into a medallion. It was perfectly pink in the center and fully moist. She noticed right away how well the tanginess and sweetness meshed. Her main concern had been that one might overpower the other. The side dishes were also right on. Chris commented on how the golden raisins gave added flavor to the spinach, saying he would have always eaten his spinach as a kid if it had been made this way. Edna reached over and piled two more medallions on her plate, justifying to herself that she'd walk an extra mile on the treadmill the next day to work it off.

Carol thought about how her mother had inspired her to become a better cook and privately thanked her. It was more than just that, though. Her mother had taught her how to deal with adversity and to appreciate all the good that life has to offer. Now she would have to go forward without her. Her mother had been her compass, and hopefully she would be in heaven, still steering her in the right direction.

Chris broke Carol's daze, and asked her whether she planned to redecorate the house. "I can give you some great ideas, " he said. "The maudlin wallpaper across the first floor has to go. The window treatments and drapes are absolutely hideous. You need to paint the rooms some vibrant colors. Things are way too beige and brown around here. I would sponge-paint in the kitchen and bathroom to give them a modern, fun feel. The couches in the den and parlor are over twenty years old. You need to pull up the carpet and do hardwood floors with brightly patterned area rugs. The lighting is horrid. The lampshades in the den have burn marks on them, for crying out loud. I read in the newspaper that Home Furnisher's is offering zero-percent financing and no payments for up to a year. We can go there tomorrow morning before Kevin stops by. I'm only here one more day."

Carol knew he was right, but a flash of panic overcame her. It was much too soon. It would seem like she was trying to forget her mother, who had been so proud of what she had done with the house over the years. Her mother's tastes had been rather conservative, but she had been far from a plain person. Out of respect, Carol couldn't do it. She still needed to grieve and reflect. Chris, forever the optimist, was always full speed ahead in his outlook on life. In fact he was a bit of a Pollyanna. It was what Carol loved about her little brother the most—only not this time.

Edna patiently waited for Chris to finish. She knew Carol so well and correctly sensed her discomfort and smartly interjected, "I can go with Carol anytime. Maybe it's not wise to rush into such a project. Perhaps you all should see what Kevin has to say tomorrow in terms of what your mother's wishes were."

Carol's eyes darted straight into Edna's as if to say, *Thanks so much for bailing me out.*

Edna got up, grabbed her plate, and headed toward the kitchen, relieved that the subject had been dropped. Chris followed suit. Carol picked up her plate, and her eyes scanned the table. The only leftover was a couple of scoops of mashed potatoes. *Crisis averted*, she thought as she looked up to the ceiling.

She went to the bedroom and retrieved the broach from her mother's bureau. Her timing couldn't have been better, as Edna had just brought up Carol's mother's wishes. Chris was opening a bottle of Chianti and bitched as a piece of cork fell into the wine. He poured the wine into his empty glass and let out a muted roar of victory as the piece of cork floated to the top. He picked it out with his fingers, grabbed a pair of fresh glasses for the women, and poured the Chianti into them.

Carol turned toward Edna and held her hand. "I have something to give you," she said, while clutching the broach in her other hand. "Mom always wanted you to have this broach. We don't have to wait for any reading of the will. She mentioned it numerous times. She would have been wearing it this Saturday for St. Paddy's Day. Now it belongs to you. Wear it in good health. I love you very much, and so did she."

Edna looked down at the broach and into Carol's watery eyes. The spigot opened up, and they both sobbed profusely. Edna slowly took the broach from Carol, and with her hands shaking she pinned it on her dress. They both got up and lovingly hugged each other. Chris was crying too. He walked over to the two of them, and they all hugged for at least a minute, carefully wiping the tears from one another's eyes. It was a moment all three would never forget.

Chris broke up the scrum, went into the den, put on a disco station, and raised the volume. "We need to liven it up," his scratchy voice said.

Edna kept touching the broach against her heart and promised to wear it on Saturday. Forever a gracious hostess, Carol asked whether anyone wanted ice cream, already knowing the wine was to be the dessert. All three picked up their glasses and clinked them. Chris got up and danced to "Bad Girls" by Donna Summer, invitingly reached for the girls' hands, and pulled them off their seats. They danced together for the entire song, as well as an obscure thumping disco house tune none of them knew. All three sat down wiping the sweat off their foreheads and let out a collective giggle.

Edna turned down Chris's offer of more wine, as it was getting late. She retrieved her pocketbook, took out her car keys, and jingled them back and forth in a moment of indecision. "It's been a great night, from the company to the meal. It can only go downhill from here on out. Let me leave while I still have my wits about me," she said, as if she were trying to convince herself. She quickly walked to the door, not wanting to look her cousins directly in the eyes, as she didn't want to get emotional again. She wished Chris a safe trip and told Carol to call her if she felt up to going out Saturday night.

Chapter 9

Carol got up the next morning and tidied up the kitchen. She glanced around and reflected on Chris's redecorating suggestions. She had visited him a few times in New York and admired what he had done to his last apartment. Her kitchen walls were drab. The stove and oven were one and the same. It did bother her mother's back when she bent over to get food in and out of the oven, but not hers so much. The stovetop had four basic burners without an intermittent simmer option. There wasn't enough room for a wall oven unit, unless she knocked down a partition leading to the pantry, but that would reduce the pantry space. The linoleum floor was ancient and lifting up a little at the seam that went through the middle. The kitchen set was more than thirty years old but in great condition, especially considering the daily use it had gotten over the years. The steel tabletop had touches of silver, gray, and baby blue running through it, with chrome sides and legs. The seats were made of soft teal vinyl and also had chrome sides and legs. One chair had a slight rip in the vinyl, which could easily be attended to. Carol chuckled; the set was so old it was new, as its retro style was making a comeback.

For years her parents had primarily used the downstairs bathroom, as their bedroom didn't have an attached bathroom. To this day, no one had ever used the tub-shower except for her parents. Far from a master suite, the bedroom wasn't even the biggest in the house and could only fit a full-size bed and little else. The upstairs bedroom, which Chris and Kevin had shared for years, was much larger.

Carol peeked into the bathroom and noticed all her mother's stuff sitting there. Kevin had had a railing installed along the wall to make it easier for their mother to maneuver in and out of the shower. She had broken her left ankle within the last year. The cancer treatments had left her so weak. Despite the relatively high doses of calcium injections and a strict regimen of vitamins, her ankle snapped on her one morning as she walked from the den to the kitchen. She hadn't tripped, stumbled, or fallen. It just gave way. The tumor in her left lung had been long removed, and the chemotherapy treatments were keeping the cancer in check.

The cancer had been discovered during a routine physical. Her mother had shown no symptoms except for a slight cough. She wasn't in much physical pain and had surprisingly few side effects from the chemo. Her hair was basically intact, although it had gotten a little frizzier. She joked that at seventy years of age she had split ends; she predicted acne would come next. Carol had called her "Mary Button," a spoof on the Brad Pitt movie. Her mother had suffered temporary bouts of severe weakness, which made it difficult for her to keep her balance. Periodic testing after her chemo treatments showed no signs of damaged cells in the surrounding area, which had been the biggest initial concern. She didn't entirely get a clean bill of health from her doctors, as she was still on oral cancer medication, but in her mind, the scourge as she called it, was beaten. Her strength slowly returned, though Carol sensed it never completely returned to her pre-diagnosis level. Just when her balance and mobility issues were clearing up, she wrecked her ankle.

Breaking that ankle was a huge setback. Her mother embraced it with full ebullience, however, and accepted it as yet another test God was giving her. She was determined not to let it interfere with her quality of life. Her physical limitations had given her more impetus to expand the reaches of her mind. That's when she experienced her renaissance with cooking. Once her cast was off, a home nurse came in twice a week to give her physical therapy, and she enthusiastically worked hard to regain her strength and balance. The kitchen turned into her gym, and she got her exercise from walking around it, frenetically cooking up a storm in the process. Carol encouraged her to scour the Internet for recipes. Together they'd go into culinary overdrive with the blender blasting, the pans sizzling, and the pots steaming.

Once Carol's mother got approval from the doctor to drive again, she'd venture out with aluminum containers filled with their creations to the nursing home down the street, as she knew a lot of people there from her church group. Carol wasn't so sure that was the best idea. Many seniors were on bland diets, and their delicate systems might not be able to handle all the flavors and spices. She was proven to be right. After a few weeks, the chief dietician paid their home a visit and respectfully asked they no longer feed the troops.

Carol's mom gracefully accepted the woman's wishes and renewed her focus on feeding the local police precinct two days a week. There was a kiosk that was really more like a trailer a few blocks away, part of a new "fighting crime" program, which infused police presence deeper into neighborhoods so that they got to know the residents. The cops even rode bicycles and walked the beat. A few policemen even paid their respects at Mary's wake dressed in full uniform, causing Chris to wonder aloud in jest whether their mother would receive a twenty-gun salute at the burial.

Chris came downstairs looking very morose. He missed Arthur and wasn't looking forward to the lonely dark drive from Boston to Ogunquit. It would take him about an hour and fifteen minutes. Ordinarily he would have flown in and out of Portland, Maine, which was only thirty-five miles away, about half the distance, but due to the suddenness of their mother's death, he had to scramble to find the soonest flight out to Detroit. She had been doing well, and he was taken off guard when Carol had called him. Mary had been out having lunch with some of the ladies from her church group and had excused herself to go to the restroom. She must have gotten disoriented or needed fresh air. One of her friends noticed she was gone a long time and assumed she had stopped along the way to chat with someone she knew. The woman finally decided to check on her whereabouts and went to the ladies' room, but Mary wasn't in there. The valet eventually found her lying between two parked cars. Mary's friends estimated she had been away from the lunch table for more than twenty minutes. She had collapsed from a massive stroke in the parking lot. Despite their exhaustive efforts, the EMTs couldn't revive her. It just wasn't fair, Chris thought. After all she had gone through, fighting cancer and a debilitating broken ankle, seemingly turning the corner on both, she had died due to a stroke and never had a chance to fight for another day.

Chris thought it peculiar that both his mother and her sister were found on the hard pavement when they passed. Both of his parents and his Aunt Helen had died alone, without comforting family members at their sides holding their hand. It was creepy. His thoughts turned to Carol, who was now living alone. He called out her name, but she didn't answer. He eventually found her outside in the backyard filling the birdfeeder.

She looked up at Chris, who was standing on the porch. "Last week a hungry cardinal stopped by for a bite," she told him. "Its feathers were painted such a vivid red. Mom was infatuated with it. She loved sitting out here reading and watching her feathery visitors as they chirped in satisfaction. One time an irascible raven invaded the feeder and loudly cawed, intimidating all the other birds. It was almost as if it were pounding its chest, daring them to try to get past it. Mom had enough of the winged bully. She'd give squirrels a pass, though. They were stealthy and never overstayed their welcome, but not this noisy critter. She grabbed the plastic cover off a trash barrel and flung it at the troublemaker like a Frisbee, and as it flew off, she warned it to never come back. I'm going make it a point to refill this as much as possible. There's a pile of rocks over there in case that raven comes back."

Chris was enamored by the story. His mother had despised bullies. She always claimed their day would come. Kevin had gone through a bullying phase when he was around ten, but Mary saw to it that it didn't last long. When the nuns at Divine Child informed her of his behavior, she marched right up there and boldly asked them to round up his usual victims. There were four known. She asked the kids to stay after school and made Kevin apologize for his actions to each and every one. On the drive home she gave him a simple math lesson; there were four of them and only one of him. Now all his victims knew one another and had a common bond. Four against one did not equate to favorable odds. Chris had been in the backseat paying close attention. Kevin was contrite and very astute in math. It was the last time any of the Schrudel children ever bullied anyone.

Carol and Chris decided to take a walk around the neighborhood. It was a partly sunny morning and in the high fifties. The forecast said the area might break the old temperature record of seventy-seven degrees. Lately it seemed every day was flirting with or breaking some record. Carol dressed in her workout clothes. Chris opted for jeans and a T-shirt. He was going to wash all his clothes today so when he got home he could just unpack his suitcase and put his clothes away. Carol wondered how many guys she'd dated over the years would do that.

They walked at a fast pace and tried to remember the names of the kids who used to live in the houses they walked by. They were surprised how many they could recall. Chris wondered aloud whether the streets were quiet because it was a Friday and the kids were in school. Carol sadly informed him it wasn't much different on the weekends. It wasn't a family-oriented neighborhood as it had been in the past. More young professionals and fixer-uppers were coming in. Most bought distressed properties with cash at rock-bottom prices. She thought it was good for the long term. Vacant houses invite trouble. She was trying to subdue Chris's fears regarding her living situation.

Sensing her attempt, Chris remarked, "Don't try to paint a picture that isn't there. It still doesn't change the fact that you're a thirty-something woman living alone. Don't let the recent weather fool you. This isn't paradise."

Chris offered to make them an early lunch. Neither one of them had eaten breakfast. The hour-long walk had made them hungry. After showering, they took inventory of what was available to eat. The best option without going out was tuna. Carol took out celery and mayo from the fridge and whole wheat bread from the freezer. There were pretzels and chips in the cupboard. Chris commented it wasn't the gourmet meal from the evening before, but it was food for the soul. Carol decided to air-dry her hair out on the front stoop while checking her email on her laptop.

Chris found the can opener and went to work in the kitchen. At the deli, he was primarily the counter person and sandwich maker out front. Arthur concentrated on cooking meals, appetizers, and the daily specials in the back kitchen. Arthur was also in charge of inventory, the vendors, the menu, and the catering business. He dealt with almost all of the vendors, some as far away as Italy and France. Chris dealt with the bread guy, balanced the books, and did the marketing. Doing the paperwork was time consuming. Chris usually did it in the evenings at home with a glass of wine. Often, Arthur would pay a vendor with cash during the day and forget to tell Chris. That was Chris's biggest pet peeve, but he understood why Arthur did that. Cash was still king with meat and produce suppliers, and they could get close to wholesale prices by paying cash. The discount was well worth it. It would just make things easier if Arthur told him. He could forgive him for that, though. It was a caring partnership, full of love and respect—and lust.

Chris called Carol in and passed her a sandwich plate with pretzels and chips. He had toasted the bread, as she always preferred, and lightly buttered it. Carol was impressed that he had remembered how their mother had made it for her. She watched as he opened up his sandwich and schematically placed the potato chips on the tuna, softly placing the bread back on top so the chips wouldn't get crushed. He always was so meticulous, as if he were an architect designing the perfect structure. That's how he had developed his interior design talent, she thought. They decided to enjoy their food sitting outside on the stoop, just like when they were kids. Carol gave Chris a hug and a peck on the cheek as they sat in silence. She would drive him to the airport in less than four hours. Then she would be alone for the first time since her mother's passing.

Chapter 10

Carol glanced at her watch. Kevin was due to arrive in less than two hours. Chris was taking his clothes out of the washing machine and placing them in the dryer. She decided to make some brownies to kill some time. Her thoughts turned to Kevin. He had been so instrumental in finding the right doctor to care for their mom. He had the right temperament to deal with Henry Ford Hospital and tackle the mountain of Medicare red tape. He had learned how to use the system to their mother's advantage and patiently explained every option she had at her disposal. She always had a private hospital room and was assured of little wait time for much needed tests and procedures. Carol was proud that Kevin was her brother. He had stopped by the house every Wednesday after work to check on things, always ensuring not to disturb Carol's piano class as he tiptoed through the back door. He got up early on Sundays and routinely drove to Dearborn with a box of freshly baked muffins. He'd have a cup of coffee and chat for an hour with her and their mother and then head back home. There was always a soccer practice, a birthday party, or recital he had to rush back for, but he never seemed excited to do so. Carol marveled at Kevin's energy and always told him he needed to chill out and relax more.

It was Kevin who had taken Uncle Sam to AA for the first time. His drinking had gotten much worse after Aunt Helen died, and Edna feared for his health. She mentioned her concern to her Aunt Mary during a Fourth of July celebration at Ford

Field. Uncle Sam was never violent or belligerent when drinking. In fact he was a happy drunk and always had a funny story to tell. He could captivate a crowd for minutes at a time while telling an animated joke.

Kevin, on summer break from law school, was sitting on the lawn behind Edna and Mary when he overheard them discussing their concern about Sam's drinking. He was fond of his uncle, and they had grown very close. Kevin had worked with him every summer since he was sixteen through his senior year at Michigan. He had been interning at a downtown law firm while on break from law school and hadn't seen his uncle since the summer break had started. His mother and Edna saw Kevin walk toward his uncle. He put his arm around him as they slowly strolled away from the crowd and talked for a while under the shade of an oak tree. At times the conversation appeared to get heated. The next day Sam was in treatment at a free state-sponsored detox shelter. Edna never could show her gratitude enough. Her father had a few setbacks over the years, but was now, at almost eighty years old, clean and serene.

As time passed, Kevin never appeared to be having a good time in life. He was certainly living, but he never seemed truly alive. He had a vapid existence for sure, Carol thought. His demeanor was often silent and introspective, his eyes blank and staring off into space. Something was always on his mind, but no one could pinpoint what it was. Chris postulated that he was so intelligent that everyone bored him. Kevin had graduated magna cum laude with an economics degree, followed by a law degree at Michigan for an encore. In jest, Edna said she suspected he may have been recruited by the CIA on campus and knew mind-control techniques. How else could he have so easily persuaded her father to get the help he needed? She had sought his advice countless times, almost as if she had him on retainer, mostly regarding financial and real estate matters concerning the house. Edna had no complaints with respect to her cousin. She lauded how he helped her and often followed up with her to see how things went. Kevin always had a soft spot in his heart for Edna and her father.

For all of Kevin's inordinate good deeds through the years, a lot of his actions unsettled Carol. She loved her brother, but there were gaps in their relationship. Once he and Kristin had gotten serious, he spent every major holiday in Minnesota with her family. It was Carol's understanding that marriage was full of compromise. So why didn't they alternate holiday visits? Her brother had a strong personality. Why didn't he put his foot down at least once? What troubled her more was the possibility that she was wrong about Kristin. She always appeared so polite, caring, and genuinely nice. Carol never had heard her say an unkind word about anyone. Kristin always seemed so interested in Carol's life, particularly work, as she was interested in teaching someday. When she asked Carol any romance-related questions, she was careful about not prying too much. Carol liked her and regretted they didn't spend more time together, other than at funerals and occasionally on Easter Sunday.

Even when Kevin and Kristin did visit, it seemed hurried. Kristin would help herself to another cup of coffee and appear to be relaxed and enjoying herself. Kristin and Carol would be talking about a movie or something in the news, and Kevin would come out of nowhere holding Kristin's and the kids' coats. Carol could see the startled look on Kristin's face. To Carol, these were all signs that Kristin was far from being a domineering wife. Kevin clearly was calling the shots.

When Kevin phoned Carol, it was always for a reason—never to just say hi or catch up like Chris would. Carol would ask about Kristin and the kids, and Kevin would reply with an answer more suited for a work colleague or even a stranger. She was his sister and felt she needed more than "Good" or "Getting big." How about a cute story to go along with that response? Before their mother had gotten sick, Kevin never had stopped by. Every workday, on his commute route, he'd only be a few highway exits away. One would think he'd drop by for a spur-of-the-moment visit. He didn't need an appointment to see his family. Their mother constantly made excuses for him. He had a career and a family of his own, after all.

Kevin was always courteous to Chris. He'd greet him with the requisite hug and ask him how he was doing. He never had visited him in New York, however. A few years ago, at their mom's seventieth birthday brunch held at a local Italian restaurant, Kristin had mentioned that Kevin had been in New York City the entire previous week on business. An eerie silence settled over the table. Kevin glared at Kristin for a second then turned to Chris, who had flown out for the weekend, and said, "My schedule was hectic and preplanned for me. I had a client dinner and retired to bed early every night."

Chris gave him an understanding nod and defused the moment by clapping his hands to the music with Kate. A little while later, Chris and Carol went to the bar to get a Bloody Mary. He whispered into her ear in a fake British accent, "I thought just old Yankee bluebloods and we British used the term 'retired to bed.' I say, our brother is becoming a bit of a bore." Carol had whispered back, "Becoming? You mean you're just noticing that? You've been away far too long."

Carol knew Chris was hurt. He would have loved to show off his big brother and spend time with him. At the same time, she understood that it may have been awkward for Kevin, since he and Chris never had had constant contact over the years. To Carol, that was mostly Kevin's fault. She was sure he had Chris's number on his cell contact list, but to Kevin that was more for family emergencies. Chris did initiate calls with Kevin, and he would cordially answer, but the patented conversations were respectfully short, and Kevin offered little substance. Chris would tell Carol they had talked. When Carol would ask what was new with Kevin, Chris would chuckle and say, "You know him, not much." She would cringe at that. She felt that Kevin considered family to be like something you put in a drawer—an old coin collection for example. Every now and then, you'd look at it, shine a few coins, then put the collection back in the drawer. To Carol, a real family relationship was sharing everyday life one another, knowing what they did last weekend, or whether they had a recent fender bender, or whether they were still seeing the same guy. That's the relationship she so badly wanted with her older brother. Lately she felt as if they were just connected through their genes only. It wasn't just about when duty calls. You just can't arrive on the scene, save the day, then ride off into the sunset on your white horse.

The doorbell rang, and Carol knew it was Kevin. Even that irked her. Why couldn't he quickly tap on the door, come in, and call out that he had arrived? He had grown up in this house and didn't need to make a formal entrance. Chris and Carol greeted him with smiles at the door. Kevin was dressed in navy pinstriped suit with a red tie snuggly attached to his neck. In his right hand he held a suitcase and in his left a BlackBerry. He looked as if he were about to conduct a business meeting. Carol didn't expect him to come sauntering in with a bottle of wine, but he could have at least loosened his tie.

They all embraced. This was the first time they had seen one another since the day of the funeral, and they got a little emotional. They wiped tears off their cheeks and nodded to one another that they were okay.

"It's a beauty of a day out there once again. Nice flying weather for you, Chris," Kevin said, his voice wavering for a moment. "It's probably best we go over things at the dining room table. It shouldn't take long."

Carol brought in some cans of Diet Coke, a few bottled waters, and the brownies she had made. There was an empty spot on the plate, and she looked at Chris. He silently raised his hand in guilt and gave her a crooked smile.

Kevin opened his briefcase and handed them each a copy of the will, along with a few pages of financial statements. Carol told him it was okay for him to take off his suit coat and loosen his tie, but he shrugged her off while clearing his throat. He calmly said, "You guys can read the will in full when I leave. I highlighted the important parts so we don't have to go over all the legal mumbo jumbo. Basically it says the three of us split all the assets equally. The house gets split the same way. Mom stipulated that it not be sold as long as Carol wants to continue living here, and I, as executor of the estate, couldn't agree more and will abide by her wishes. The furniture, china, jewelry, her car, and the artwork are technically part of the estate. She trusted we could sort that stuff out on our own. Let's move on to the liquid assets. There's a credit union savings account with a little more than a hundred and five thousand dollars that hasn't seen one withdrawal in twenty-two years. How many people could do that in today's world? Mom called it her 'rainy day fund' and was afraid to invest it in stocks, so we left it in the credit union. It shows you the power of compounding interest. The rates weren't always this miniscule. We've been rolling it over in CDs, and the last one expired just four days ago. Dad had a three-hundred-thousand-dollar whole-life insurance policy that we invested in a blended portfolio of tax-free municipal bonds, corporate and government bonds, and a conservative mutual fund that invests in high-dividend-yielding equities. The investments have steadily averaged slightly above a four-point-five percent return for the last twelve-plus years. There's roughly three hundred and four thousand dollars remaining, as she withdrew from the trust to pay utility bills, house upkeep, property taxes, charitable contributions, et cetera. Mom used her Social Security checks for everyday living expenses and for traveling with her church group.

"She also had a whole-life insurance policy for a hundred and fifty thousand. Dad was responsible for initiating the two policies when Carol and I were barely teenagers. Chris, you were only nine at the time. The combined premiums were hefty, given their income, but Mom and Dad didn't go out much and were far from extravagant. Dad paid the premiums until he passed. Then the trust took over the payments for mom. Mom told me the policies were a covenant they sealed with a kiss to protect the family. My firm already has sent the insurance company a copy of the death certificate and started the paper trail to collect the money. These things can take time. I'd estimate a hundred and twenty days. Insurance companies don't like parting with money and tend to stall. Of course, that money deposited into the trust can be withdrawn equitably at any time."

"The value of the house is hard to exactly determine," Kevin continued. "In 2005, when the new roof was put on, the house was valued at two hundred and thirty-five thousand. In 2009 the estimated value fell to a hundred and sixty grand but has moved up to around a hundred and seventy. I myself don't trust any of the newly released real estate figures. The fluctuations are just too asinine, and there are too many variables in the comparisons. Not enough apples to apples for my liking. Are there any questions?"

Carol and Chris looked at each other as Kevin caught his breath, grabbed a brownie, and double-sipped his soda.

"Wow. We have to applaud Dad for all of this. Mom too, of course, but Dad was the shepherd. He always was so savvy with numbers, and his thinking was so prescient. They gave us their heart and soul and took care of us in life and now in death," Chris said in complete wonder.

Carol was feeling a bit uncomfortable about the house situation, and Kevin clearly was expecting her reaction. He held her hand and said in a comforting tone, "I know what you're feeling. Please don't feel that way. The money the trust uses toward the house is small compared to the big picture. Plus, in theory, the longer the family owns the house, the more value it'll have. I know things out there are upside down, but sooner or later, the real estate market will return to normal. Thanks to our parents, the house is paid for. We aren't under any pressure to sell it. There's not any short sale or any other dire situation in the mix here. This isn't something that needs to be addressed immediately. Mom was very vocal about it being your decision. I was in the conference room and heard her stern voice, while she repeated it twice, so there weren't any misconceptions. She even peeked at the secretary's notes to make sure, found a spelling error, and corrected it. We all laughed at that. She was in complete control of the room. You guys had to see it. My colleagues were spellbound and later told me how lucky we all were."

Carol started to cry. It wasn't from being sad. Rather it was from being overwhelmed and proud to be the daughter of such giving parents. She took a passing look at Chris, and he reached for her hand. There she was, looking back and forth at her two brothers, holding their hands, all three the benefactors of such undying love and devotion.

"All right. I understand," Carol said. "It's my decision to make. I guess Mom didn't want me to feel like an orphan. We're all kind of orphans now, really. I mean, in the physical sense. All we have is each other. As long as you guys are okay with this, I am too." Her brothers nodded and smiled.

Kevin turned to Chris and asked if the deli had a fax machine. There would be papers to sign with respect to withdrawals from the trust. The withdrawals could be done monthly, yearly, or in a lump sum. A certain amount had to be maintained within the trust for expenses, and the trust couldn't be dissolved until the house was sold. Chris was surprised Kevin remembered that he owned a deli with Arthur. He didn't think a lot of what he told Kevin in the past had resonated and wondered what else had.

"You should talk it over with Arthur to see what his thoughts are," Kevin said. "There are tax implications to consider also. I don't know the tax codes in Maine, and if same-sex marriage is finally a done deal like people thought before, that's something else in the future you may have to consider."

Chris again was taken aback that Kevin remembered Arthur's name and was so sensitive to the possibility of marriage for him at some point. Maine had passed a gay marriage rights bill in 2009, and the governor had signed it. The gay community had been so excited. Arthur had told Chris there had been countless engagement announcements right after, and Ogunquit had been in party mode for days. Chris was still living in New York at the time but was watching the story closely. Then, right before the law was supposed to take effect, there was a referendum, and the antigay marriage zealots won out.

Chris knew he may have been wrong about Kevin, and it was eating away at him. He previously had thought Kevin was behind his not having suffered any antigay bullying or slurs in the neighborhood years ago. Bumping into Jack Sheridan the other night had shaken that belief. Chris had to know and attempted to be clever. "We bumped into Jack Sheridan the other night at Kiley's. We talked to him briefly. He didn't know about Mom's passing and felt bad. He asked how you were doing too. That was about it. It brought back memories, though. Both of you guys did a fair share of teasing me. Telling me to run long-pass routes playing football in the street and never throwing me the ball after I had run over fifty yards. Throwing water balloons at me and taking the air out of my bike tires. Those were minor infractions in the scheme of things. I have to give you a long past-due, heartfelt thank-you, though. That night Angela called Jack about that incident at CVS and after Jack told you... Well, Jack never teased me again. Never a gay reference or slur whatsoever from him. I don't know what you told him, but he always had a big mouth and he kept his trap shut. You made my life a lot easier. His mouth always hurt a lot more than his pranks. Thanks so much!" Chris convincingly said but didn't let on to the long extent of time they actually had spent with Jack.

Kevin's face took on a confounded expression. Sweat shined on his forehead. His fingers rubbed his elbows, and his eyes looked down at the table. Chris knew he was nervous and waited anxiously for his response. Kevin smacked his lips a few times, then finally he carefully responded as if he were a trained witness on the stand. "That was a long time ago. There's no need to thank me." Chris knew immediately Kevin was hedging. His answer was so vague. At least he didn't plead the fifth. There were two smoking guns here. First, Jack claimed he never knew what had transpired that night, and he certainly never knew Chris was gay. So why didn't Kevin refute that part? Second, getting to what troubled Carol most of all, who had called Kevin that night? How did Kevin find out? Were these two points somehow connected? Kevin just had ample opportunity to divulge how he had found out and could set the story straight. He chose not to do so. He basically went along with Chris's version of what had gone down. Did he want Chris to continue to believe in the myth that he was his omnipotent protector? Maybe it would have helped if he had asked Kevin to swear on a Bible, he joked to himself.

Kevin abruptly shuffled the paperwork back into his briefcase and got up. Carol sat there perplexed, scratching her head in bewilderment. She didn't want Kevin to see her looking at Chris wide eyed. She partially hid her face with her hand, brushing back her bangs, and got up as well. She headed for the kitchen with the brownies and came back with the brownie plate wrapped in plastic.

"These are for Kristin and the kids. Don't eat them all on the way home. Don't worry about the plate. It's part of the estate, after all," she kidded while giving Kevin a hug.

Chris and Kevin hugged and shook hands, and Kevin wished him a safe trip. Kevin urged them to read the will in full and repeated that if they had any further questions to call him immediately, no matter how silly the questions might seem. He told Carol he'd call to check on her the next day, and just like that, he was gone.

"Riding off into the sunset again," Carol muttered.

Chris looked at the clock and mentioned he wouldn't mind getting to the airport early. Carol put on her flip-flops and grabbed her keys. Both of them kept looking at each other and shaking their heads.

"It's going to be a fun-filled ride to the airport. Take the long way. Kevin couldn't wait to haul ass out of here. It must have been something you said," Chris sardonically voiced as he picked up his suitcase in laughter.

Carol pulled the car out of the driveway. "I do feel somewhat guilty," she said. "There are two alleged versions of what transpired on that thunder-filled evening eighteen years ago. We assumed Angela had called her brother. Jack convincingly claimed he never knew. Kevin went along with your version. He may have done that just out of principle, or his memory of that evening may be cloudy. It may have never been as big a deal to him as it was to you. The onus was on you that evening, not him. We may have to consider that it wasn't a pivotal moment in his life, so his recollection might not be as sharp. I so badly want to give him the benefit of the doubt, but I can't. It pains me to believe Jack over my big brother. His expression and his body language were dead giveaways. His voice, while he went through the financial matters, was strong, confident, and clear. When he responded to you, it was weak and lacked conviction. It was a definite change from his earlier tone. I get the impression he's protecting someone, but it isn't you, as he'd like us to believe. It could be himself, but I'm not sure what his motive is. It's not like he's done anything sinister, but things don't add up."

Chris waited a moment to make sure his sister was finished then responded, "Last night, when Edna was here, I didn't want to make it seem as if anything was bothering me. All the while, I contemplated the many scenarios of what might have happened. Going back, I don't believe any of Jack's buddies were at the CVS that evening. We were shorthanded that night. That's why my boyfriend and I were boldly lip-locking in the stock room—we didn't think we'd get caught. The most logical conclusion may lie with Mr. Hufton, the store manager. He knew Mom and Dad for years from hockey practice. Do you remember? Eddie and Paul, his sons, played on all the same teams as Jack and Kevin. Sometimes he'd give Jack and Kevin a ride home after practice. Mr. Hufton bought all his cars at Dad's dealership. Dad asked him if he could find us work at the CVS. He's the one who got us our jobs. Unfortunately he passed away a few years ago. Anyway, he may have spoken to Mom or Dad that evening and told them what happened, or maybe Kevin, as he knew him well, too. Three out of four here are deceased, and the only one alive is skirting the truth for whatever reason. Kevin was so polished and at ease going over the finances. It was inspirational, and I was impressed with all the aspects of the investment choices and their performance. He was proud too, and he didn't take credit for any of it, when he had the right to flaunt. He was the most human I've seen in a long time, showing signs of charisma, love, and compassion that had been dormant for years. I waited until he was very secure in his element before I shifted gears. I wanted to surprise him first to better unleash the truth. However, in my eyes, I didn't see surprise. I saw chagrin and fear. Kevin's hurried exit gave credence to that. It was like he had been flung out of a catapult. His actions spoke much louder than his words. I had him up on a pedestal. All of his words today, with their upbeat nuances and conciliatory tone, had begun to tear apart at the emotional wall he had erected around us. In one swift second, my euphoria subsided, and the feeling of negativity I'd previously harbored took center stage again. He didn't just fall off a pedestal. He fell through a trap door."

Chris motioned for Carol to make a right turn on red as they approached the airport on-ramp. She had similar feelings. They just had learned the specifics of their inheritance. Both had never imagined the depth of the hard financial sacrifices their parents had made and the largesse of the fortune amassed as a direct by-product. Carol felt like they were a family in every respect. What should have been a moment of celebratory testimony to their parents, however, was stymied by a terse inconclusive response, which opened up new questions to an unresolved issue.

"We're not imagining things or overreacting," Chris said. "I should have confronted Kevin right away with the fact that Jack swore he never knew I was gay and let things go from there. I had my chance but was reticent to do so. I chickened out. Not to stir the pot more, but I'll leave you with something else to ponder. Why didn't Angela ever tell her Jack about the incident she witnessed? It seems so out of character for her before she allegedly turned into Miss Goody Two Shoes. Was Jack playing us all along? The plot thickens," he teasingly said.

Carol pulled into the terminal drop-off area for departing flights. She found a spot that wasn't blocking any vehicles and pulled in. "It could just be Kevin being Kevin, and we whipped ourselves into a lather over nothing. Did our eyes deceive us and our instincts abandon us? In a few days, all this will be a distant sight in the rearview mirror, getting smaller with each passing day until it's almost forgotten. Do you and I make a good or lousy detective team? Who the heck knows? We're a fun team. We should star in a comedy series. Brother-and-sister bumbling private investigators, cracking one-liners while catching crooks. The ratings would be through the roof," she joked.

Chris laughed at first, and then his expression grew serious. It was time to part ways. He never was good at this. Tears welled in his eyes, then they heard a tap on the driver's side window. It was a security officer waving Carol to move along. Chris jumped out of the car and pulled his suitcase out of the backseat. Carol ran to the curb, gave him a big squeeze, and watched him slowly walk away, dragging his suitcase behind him. It was the kind of quick goodbye both preferred. Otherwise they'd still be hugging and crying in the car. They both had done more than their fair share of crying over the past week.

Chapter 11

It was Saturday, and St. Paddy's Day, but it felt more like a gloomy Monday to Carol. The reality of living alone for the first time in her life was taking hold. Sure, she had spent a couple of weeks home alone while her mother was in the hospital, but that was temporary. Back then her time was filled with the hope of her mother getting well and returning home. Now things were permanent, and she hadn't yet come to grips with her solitary situation. Everything in the house reminded her of her mother—her winter coat and scarf on the coat rack, for one. Carol wanted to feel this way. It felt natural and also an essential part of the healing process.

Her thoughts turned to Edna. Years ago, when Aunt Helen had died so suddenly, Edna had confided to her that the house seemed to embody the spirit of her mother—not in a macabre sense but in more of an idyllic way. Edna accentuated the positive influences her mother had in the house and in her life. Her mother had designed the new layout in the kitchen, which made it much more user friendly. There was now an island and more counter space. The fridge and stove were right next to each other. The backyard porch now had a roof to provide shade so they could enjoy the outdoors better. The walls were painted in muted colors, giving the rooms a more tranquil feel. Before, they had been wallpapered in a hideous flower-patterned theme, which made the house resemble a funeral home.

Edna envisioned the house as a peaceful sanctuary as much as she possibly could. Her father had lived there with her for about a year after her mother's death, and his snoring was annoying, especially when he drank, which was almost constantly. He moved out when he got sober. It was the reason she still lived there alone to this day. She adored her mother and never wanted to forget her. By staying there, she was able to keep the memories intact.

The phone rang, and it was Edna. Carol thought that if she had a dollar for every time Edna called while she was thinking of her, she'd be rich. It was uncanny how many times it had happened. Carol answered in a downtrodden voice. Edna and a couple of girls from the office were going to do a pub-crawl starting at noon in Dearborn. She invited Carol to come along. "I realize you may have other things on your mind, but if you're lonely and in the mood for an attitude adjustment later in the day, stop by. Text me, and I'll hit you back with our current location," Edna said in an understanding tone. Carol thanked her for the invitation and said she would think about it.

Carol wanted to get to know the house all over again. She wanted to sit in silence and pay attention to any new creak or noise. Her sense of awareness was on high alert. The stairs seemed to groan when a large truck passed by. The fridge motor at times seemed to whine. The parlor clock appeared to tick more loudly. The front window shades were moving ever so slightly due to the heat rising from the floor register. Carol realized it was another warm morning, and the heat shouldn't be kicking in like that. She went over to the thermostat and lowered it, satisfied she just had saved some money. When she moved the kitchen chair out to sit down, the legs screeched on the linoleum, and the sound echoed through the house. While she sat down, the air whooshed out of the padded seat. She didn't really care for that sound. Was the chair trying to communicate to her that she was too fat?

Mad at the chair, she got up and decided to let out a scream where the front entranceway, parlor, and den merged. She peeked out a front window first, as she was afraid to startle any passersby. The coast was clear. She walked back to the designated spot and let out a loud, shrieking scream. The vibration bounced off all the walls. The wineglasses, which were placed closely next to one another in the old wooden dining room hutch, shook and performed a chiming symphony for a few rhythmic seconds. Carol was happy with the result. She hadn't let out a scream at the top of her lungs for years, and she was confident it would scare off any potential intruder.

It was getting past lunchtime, and Carol hadn't eaten all day. Her mind had been racing since she had gotten up, and she had been ignoring her hunger pangs. She got a box of Special K out of the cupboard and scooped a few handfuls into her mouth. Feeling better, she jumped into the shower. As the hot water beaded down her back, she considered meeting Edna and the girls. She felt her pulse quicken as her thoughts turned to music, drinks, and laughter. It was a little past two o'clock. The girls were way ahead of her and probably half drunk by now. She could be ready in a half-hour and have a drink in her hand by three. She excitedly toweled off in a hurry when the phone rang. *Edna again*, she thought, as she raced for the phone, leaving behind a tiny trail of water.

Nope—this time it was Father O'Malley from Divine Child on the line. He was calling to check on Carol and to inform her that in his Sunday Mass ceremony he would be mentioning her mother's name during a prayer if she wanted to attend. Her mother was well known in the church parish, and he wanted to give her a well-deserved tribute. Carol was so touched. She asked

Father O'Malley which service, the one at eight thirty or ten thirty, and he replied both, but he added that he would understand if she only attended one. They hung up, and she was elated. That feeling went away quickly, however, as she realized she had just talked to a priest while buck naked, and that kind of freaked her out. Her pub-crawl thoughts came to a screeching halt, and sanity once again took over. *There will be no reveling today*, she thought. *Today should be a somber day of reflection and homage.*

She looked down at her cell phone as it was charging on her bureau. The little red light was flashing. She had a text message from Edna. They were at the Green Olive drinking martinis, just in case. The rest of the message was almost unreadable as the spelling was atrocious. Carol got the gist of it. They were having a good time. She texted Edna back and told her about the services tomorrow at the church. She was content staying in. Besides, she didn't want to see her mother's friends while reeking of alcohol. Edna responded right back that she would love to tag along and that the service at eight thirty was fine with her. Carol laughed out loud at the thought of Edna drinking all day and then getting up early for church of all places. She probably was too drunk to think this out rationally. Carol sent her a text message back saying that the service at ten thirty was more practical. She wrote in capital letters, "I'M SAVING YOU FROM YOURSELF. LOL."

* * *

Groggy from an unintended nap, Carol opened her eyes. She had been flipping through an old family photo album and dozed off. She estimated that she had soundly slept for almost two hours. It was nearly seven, and she felt like having a snack. She decided to eat a light supper and popped a low-calorie frozen meal of chicken, vegetables, and rice into the microwave while still half asleep. She walked into the den with her meal and placed it on the coffee table. Her eyes darted to the TV tray stand. "Why not?" she said out loud. She opened up the tray and put it together next to the recliner. She grabbed her cell phone and took a picture of herself sitting with her meal on the tray and sent it to Chris and Edna. She ate without the TV on, making sure to chew her food well. She heard her mother's voice in her head, breaking the silence, *Don't talk while you're chewing either.*

Kevin called as Carol was putting the TV tray back in its stand. He was at a party at his country club, and it was pretty noisy. He asked how she was doing and seemed surprised he had gotten her on the home phone. She told him about the church services the next day, but he already had made plans to play golf. He apologized, but Carol understood. The priest had just called today, and if she hadn't been home, she wouldn't have known either. It wasn't like they were so tight that the priest could have reached her on her cell. Kevin told her he would be in Chicago the next week on business and would check in with her from the road. Convinced his sister was doing fine, he wished her a happy tomorrow and hung up. Carol never did get a chance to tell him how she was doing, which was why he had called. It was hard to hear each other anyway. She caught herself... *That's how Mom would think!* She went upstairs and surfed around on her laptop until she felt heavy-eyed. Despite napping, she felt weak and fatigued. It had been a trying week, and she was drained.

* * *

Carol awoke feeling refreshed and decided to take a three-mile run. She opened the front door and stepped out to the stoop to see if the weather was as forecast, another unseasonably warm sunny March morning with high temperatures in the upper seventies. She determined it was at least in the low sixties and decided her spandex shorts and a T-shirt would be sufficient. She would run her familiar route around the block, which she already had clocked with her car. Once around was a half-mile, so six times around would make three miles. Carol enjoyed gathering her thoughts while running and never found it monotonous. Music wasn't an option for her, as she found it more of a distraction. Her first thought when she set out was how pasty her skin was, particularly her legs. She hadn't applied any self-tanning lotion in more than a week and would do so when she got home. Everyone was in the same boat, she figured; summer weather in March was an anomaly, and the only people walking around with deep natural tans were those lucky souls who recently had returned from Florida or the Caribbean.

She thought about all the relatives who recently had passed away and how the holidays never seemed the same without them. She wasn't even thinking about her parents, more so of aunts, uncles, and grandparents. She would have needed to borrow a lot more chairs from the funeral home if they were all still alive. With the exception of Edna, Carol only regularly saw her cousins at weddings or funerals, mostly the latter, because you didn't need an invitation to attend. She actually preferred the funerals in a strange way. There was no gift needed, and she had plenty of black clothes in her closet.

Most of her cousins had grown up much closer in proximity to her house than Edna, but she could never bond with them as she did with Edna, who had a refreshing perspective on life that Carol adored. She was funny without trying to be and naturally quick to the punch. She had gotten that from her father. Kevin loved Edna's dad. It was so obvious, as he'd always sit next to him and laugh the most at his jokes. It was as if he didn't want to miss any of the show. By far, Uncle Sam was Kevin's favorite uncle. Aunt Helen and Uncle Sam were his godparents, and he shared a special bond with both. Uncle Mo, her father's oldest brother, was Carol's godfather, and her Aunt Edith, his wife, was her godmother. Uncle Sam was the only one still alive, and she and Edna barely saw him. It was almost faster to fly to Los Angeles and back than to drive one way to the Upper Peninsula of Michigan to Marquette, where he lived. It's beautiful country up there, but that's just it—you truly feel as if you're in a different country. Edna joked that at least they didn't need a passport to see him, as it was much quicker to drive to Canada.

Carol thought about the upcoming day. She was excited and wanted to treat Edna to brunch afterward. Easter Sunday would be in three weeks. It would be so soon after her mother had passed, and she wondered whether Kevin would invite her over. In the past, most holidays were celebrated at the house in Dearborn. Kevin would invite them up once in a while, mostly during summer for a poolside barbecue. It also would be school vacation week, so most, if not all of her lessons, would be postponed, which meant another week of little or no income. She recently had paid off most of her credit card bills, so she didn't mind using them for basic necessities. She felt comforted by that; she must have inherited her aversion to debt from her parents.

Carol lost track of which lap she had just finished around the block. This happened to her regularly when her thoughts wandered. It was either her fifth or sixth lap. Never one to shortchange herself, she always ran an extra lap, even if she may have already run six. This way her goal was achieved and her conscience cleared. Now she would possibly burn extra calories and worry less about her consumption at brunch, she rationalized.

* * *

Dressed conservatively in a black pantsuit with black heelless shoes, Carol waited for Edna on the stoop. She took out some lip-gloss from her pocketbook and was applying it when Edna wheeled up to the curb. Edna looked surprisingly good for someone who had done a pub crawl the day before. She wore a pale yellow dress and white heels.

"Lip-gloss has been the only solid I've tasted today so far today," Edna joked after Carol got in the car.

As she pulled away from the curb, she filled Carol in on the day before. Apparently, one of the girls had thrown up in Edna's car, but amazingly there was no lingering stench. Edna had spotted her friend holding her hand against her mouth, and she had pulled off the plastic green hat she was wearing and had her use it as splash-landing spot. This was only around seven, and they all called it a night. Carol took note that they never made it until dark and was glad she had decided to stay in.

They pulled up to the church, and Father O'Malley greeted them at the top step. He told them gruffly as they opened the door, "I reserved a seat for you in the front pew. I was getting worried when I didn't see you earlier."

That was his way of rubbing it in, as he knew Carol didn't regularly attend church. She informed Edna of her naked conversation with him the day before as they walked toward the front of the church, and Edna instantly remarked, "Thank the Lord you two weren't communicating via Skype. You don't know what he was wearing or not wearing either." They both giggled like schoolgirls as they genuflected and gingerly slid down the hard wooden pew so their delicate rumps would avoid sustaining any splinters.

The packed church was uncomfortable and sticky hot. Carol was getting frustrated as the roar of the turbine-like fans made it hard to hear anything. The smell of cheap perfume permeated the air, and she felt somewhat claustrophobic. Her mind drifted to the feel of a nice breeze as she held a soothing umbrella drink in her hand. The service, she estimated, was halfway through. She picked up a booklet to keep track of the proceedings and started to play a game inside her head. How many times was the word "thou" on the page she opened? She counted in her head, *One, two, three*...when a strange feeling overcame her. The cadence in Father O'Malley's voice had changed. Edna slightly kicked Carol's leg, and she looked up. Father O'Malley was looking at her, as was the entire gathering. She had heard a few muffled snickers behind her. Obviously he had mentioned her mother's name and had stopped to see her reaction. Carol smiled and gave a half wave, and everyone went about their business. Edna and Carol tried not to look at each other; Edna was trying hard not to laugh. She was sweating profusely through every pore and held the strap of her pocketbook so tightly it nearly broke. Carol was trying to think of something utterly disgusting to change her frame of mind in a heartbeat. They both stared straight ahead until they conquered the urge to burst into hysterics.

The Eucharist portion was just starting, and Carol knew they'd soon be home free. Father O'Malley walked over to her and gave her Holy Communion, as she was the guest of honor. When the service ended, Carol stood out front with Father O'Malley, and they hugged and shook hands. There were many well-wishers, and she was highly gratified that her mother had touched so many lives. The outpouring of support was beyond comparison, and Edna stood by her side in amazement. When it was time to leave, Edna hugged Father O'Malley and thanked him.

As they walked down the steps, Edna looked at Carol and thought out loud, "Oh, my God. Your mom was a star." She repeated it again and again until they got to the car.

Carol said she was treating for brunch and wouldn't take no for an answer. Edna wasn't about to pass on Bloody Marys anyway.

A brief feeling of cynicism overcame Carol, and she had to tell Edna so it wouldn't stay inside. "I don't know. You live a lifetime of volunteering at the church. You attend all the dinners, fundraisers, and donate to the best of your ability. You even work the bingo hall. You know, bingo, the stealth eighth sacrament that the church pretends doesn't exist, while it hosts Gamblers Anonymous meetings in the same hall once a week. Then all you get for a reward, in this life at least, is your name mentioned briefly in a prayer. It seems twisted. I'm not saying it specifically in regard to my mom. I'm talking in general. It could apply to anyone."

Edna rubbed her arm and empathized with her. "Sometimes I wonder too if that's all there is in this life. Then I remember there's always alcohol. Too bad you missed the one second of fame for your mom back there, you silly girl. I'm glad one of us was paying attention."

They both laughed as Edna pulled into the restaurant parking lot. They had decided to forgo the usual church brunch spots and headed for a sports bar, as the atmosphere was more to their liking.

The crowd was quite boisterous, with a good blend of age and gender. Carol and Edna were a little overdressed but didn't mind much; most people had on either Michigan or Michigan State athletic wear. The NCAA basketball tournament was playing on all the television sets. They went straight to the bar, found two empty seats, and ordered a Bloody Mary each, extra spicy, with olives, and no celery. "Here's to Aunt Mary," Edna said, as they raised their glasses.

"I can't thank you enough for coming and for being there for me all the time," Carol said.

Edna looked at the three large green olives on the toothpick in her drink, pulled off one with her mouth, and devoured it. "I'll save the other two as if it's a three-course meal," she cracked.

Carol told her a little about the reading of the will, without going into much detail regarding the financials. She did offer that there was a decent amount of money at her disposal if she needed it but not enough for her to seriously consider changing her lifestyle.

Edna understood that Carol wasn't talking about obscene, Madonna-like money. She was more concerned about her cousin's emotional well-being and suggested that after Memorial Day they go on vacation. They had gone to Playa del Carmen together three years ago, before Mary had received her cancer diagnosis, and had a wonderful time. That was the last time Carol had been on a plane. Edna had flown to Vegas with Nick for three nights a few months ago for New Year's but didn't have such a great a time. Nick had a bad head cold, never gambled, and wasn't much of a party animal. In addition, it had been too cold to hang around the pool at the hotel. Edna wondered why Nick had chosen Vegas in the first place. They surely hadn't gone there to get hitched. She joked to Carol, "What happens in Vegas stays in Vegas—definitely applied for the wrong reason. I'm trying to erase my memory of that awful trip."

Carol suggested they order some food, as she was hungry from her run. Edna pointed to her two remaining olives, insinuating she was content. Carol put up her hand. "Oh, no. I'm not falling into that trap again. Last time we came here for lunch, we never ate, and the next thing we knew it was nine o'clock and the band was starting. At least that was on a Saturday. I'm ordering us a burger each, and if you don't eat it, tough," she stringently declared.

Edna laughed and ordered another round of drinks. She knew Carol was right and respected the fact that she might not be ready to let loose yet. She responded without any resistance, "Make mine medium well with cheddar, and rice instead of fries."

They chatted some more about possible vacation destinations. Except for trips to Quebec City and Montreal, they never had been on a real cultural vacation together. It was decided Europe was the most logical choice, despite the Euro being so expensive. They would start looking seriously after Easter. The burgers arrived, and Edna's mistakenly came with fries. She raised an eyebrow in disgust, stuffed one into her pouty mouth, and gave out a satisfied moan. There was no way that plate was going back into the kitchen now, she proclaimed as she reached for the ketchup with a smile.

At the end, there wasn't a fry left on either plate. They were both so full. "A half-pound burger with fries, I guess, is too much food for me now," Edna said as she rubbed her tummy

Carol looked around the crowded bar and zoned in on the fans screaming at every basket, holding their heads and high-fiving, as if their lives depended on their team winning. She loved all sports, but baseball appealed to her the most. It was more relaxing and cerebral, as there was more strategy involved. She and Edna usually went to a few Tigers games a year and then would venture to nearby Greektown afterward for its festive Mediterranean ambiance. It was always a fun change of pace for them. The feta cheese was so fresh, and all the restaurants served it in huge quantities.

Carol also would go to Tigers games with Rita and Cheryl, two college buddies she still kept in touch with, but not as much lately, as they both were divorced with young kids. Finding a dependable sitter was always an issue with them. They all had played intramural softball together in college and were big baseball fans. Kevin had invited them to use his firm's luxury box once after he had made junior partner. It was a nice time, and they were treated like celebrities. Carol remembered how smitten the girls were with her big brother and how proud she was of him, but she found the luxury box a little too sterile for her taste and preferred to sit in the cheap seats. Kevin also would make sure that a different, local, underprivileged children's program used the box as much as possible, as he spearheaded many civic sponsorships for his firm. Rita and Cheryl couldn't say enough about that.

Carol and Edna witnessed two guys misconnect on a high-five and inadvertently slap each other in the face. It was getting late, and both knew this was their cue to leave. They certainly weren't going to match that intensity. Edna had noticed there were more lulls in the conversation than usual and figured Carol hadn't brought her "A" game to the table and understood that she might not for a while. They were basically matching yawns for the last ten minutes, and Edna's St. Paddy's pub-crawl was catching up to her. Carol paid the tab, and they headed out.

Chapter 12

Carol got back into her daily routine. Her first lesson usually didn't start until school got out in the afternoon, around two thirty. She averaged around three or four lessons a day. It would take her about fifteen minutes to prepare each lesson, making sure to design it to each student's playing acumen. A few of the students were grandchildren of her mother's friends. She would no longer have that built-in recruiting base. She did have a website, but she found word of mouth was still the most reliable way to promote her business. These days, parents were sensitive as to whom their children were spending time alone with and felt safer if it was someone known and trusted. Carol had one eight-year-old student whose mother insisted on sitting in the den until the lesson was over. She never thought the mother was being overly protective, as there were too many horror stories out there. It wasn't easy parenting these days, especially if both parents were working full time.

The biggest concern for Carol was the rising dropout rate. Every year, more students would lose interest after a handful of lessons, even the ones who showed promise. She liked to believe the reason wasn't rooted in her teaching techniques. She tried to create the lessons with eclectic flair to make them more interesting and fun. Her most steadfast rule was no cellphone use until after the lesson was over. The plain fact was that kids today had too many distractions, mostly due to technology. Carol reasoned with herself that if she were a kid today, with the myriad of apps on phones that one can use anywhere at anytime, why bother with old-fashioned piano lessons? You were more popular being adept at "Angry Birds" than being proficient on the piano.

Her personal sense of achievement was slowly dissipating. There wasn't a more satisfying moment than seeing a sixteen-year-old student, under her tutelage since age eight, on stage at a recital, school musical, or community function, playing the piano perfectly with poise, confidence, and grace. When the star-struck audience began their applause, she'd look at the proud parents, hugging each other with tears of joy in their eyes, blowing kisses at their loved one. Then those misty, appreciative eyes would drift toward her, and she'd be convinced it all had been worth it. Carol missed that exalted feeling and wasn't sure it would ever rise to the surface of her heart again.

The average age of her students was ten years old. Some genuinely looked forward to their weekly lessons and greeted her with a smile and sometimes a hug. A couple of sisters came twice a week. Carol actually tried to discourage that, as she thought it best they practiced a week between lessons. The parents, however, insisted on twice a week. Each sister would watch TV while the other took her lesson. Carol was troubled by their lack of progress but more bothered by why the parents hadn't noticed at home and why they hadn't inquired about it. She took it upon herself to call them. It turned out they had no piano at home on which to practice. The parents, who were well off and could certainly afford one, just wanted two precious hours of time alone together. The father had given Carol a disturbing wink when he told her that. They were new to the area and couldn't find anyone to look after the children, which made Carol more of a convenient, high-priced babysitter so the parents could fool around. She decided to lower her standards a little, as her initial inclination was to tell them off, but two hundred dollars a week told her not to do so. Who was she to deny them their whoopee time?

She had one student, Joe, who was forty-five years old. Their mothers had been friends. He was a divorced, chubby, balding sort who always had wanted to play the piano and figured it was never too late to learn. He worked nights as a computer programmer, and he'd drop by for his weekly lesson on Wednesdays at nine in the morning on his way home from work. He always brought coffee, and Carol looked forward to him coming, as he was the only student with whom she could have an adult conversation, and he also was very personable and understanding. Having him as a student forced her to start her day early, and she'd go to the gym and run errands after his lesson. In that way, Joe was good for her. He did have a lot of promising talent, and Carol told him that if he had started taking lessons at a young age, he might currently be very accomplished and even play in a band. Joe lamented that something always had seemed to get in the way. He had a nine-year-old son, Josh, who went to Divine Child and wanted to learn the drums. Josh lived with his mother, but she insisted the drum set stay at Joe's house. His weekends were noisy to say the least.

Joe was a complete gentleman, but there was no chemistry there. He had been taking lessons for about a year and certainly wasn't the shy type. If he wanted to ask Carol out on a date, he would have already done so. He had a girlfriend he met online and suggested to Carol that she should give it a try but didn't push it on her. All he proposed was that she should give it some consideration, as he had been leery of meeting someone online for years and regretted not doing it sooner, just as he had with taking piano lessons.

* * *

It was a windy, cold Wednesday night. The weather had turned more seasonable. Carol sat in her chilly bed, dressed in sweats, with the radiator clanging in the background. The week before, she had slept in just her undies and a T-shirt, eschewing the sheets and comforter. Things appeared to be getting back as closely as possible to normal, she passively thought.

Carol had found Joe to be somewhat convincing, as she thought about his comments from earlier in the day. He knew her mother had just passed. He supportively had stated, "From my experience, the everyday burden of caring for an elderly parent always seems to fall on the daughters, not the sons. I've seen it with my friends and firsthand within my own family. As you know, my mother lives with my older sister. It doesn't seem fair. You did the best you could."

Joe knew that Carol lived alone, without any chance of meeting someone on the job, and he sensed that her isolation was a detriment to her moving forward with her life. It wasn't as though she had a fulfilling career to keep her mind off things. She knew Joe meant well, but she never had thought of her mother as a burden. She had been a joy to be around and a cherished friend, as well as an adored mother. Joe was trying to steer her in the right direction. The pupil had become the teacher. Maybe she should be paying him fifty bucks a week. She could lie on the couch, and he could analyze her and offer advice between songs.

She couldn't do this online dating scene, could she? Did it reek of desperation or was it a twenty-first-century Internet avenue to meet the man of her dreams? She hesitated, and her frozen fingers started to Google "online dating services," when, oops, her incoming email alert pinged. It was from Macy's, and she instantly opened it up. They were having a big sale this weekend on linens and sheets—40 percent off. She took that as an omen and switched her screen to the safety of an unfinished crossword puzzle.

A few moments later, the phone rang. As she reached for it, she saw Kevin's home phone number flash on the screen. She knew he was in Chicago and figured it was Kristin calling to discuss Easter plans. She answered, and right away she knew something was wrong. When someone starts off a conversation with, "I don't know if I should be telling you this. I just don't know where else to turn," there's a high probability it's not a pleasant topic. Kristin was crying, and her voice cracked as if she were trying to persuade herself to go forward. "Can we meet tomorrow or whenever you can? I don't know your schedule, but can we meet before Kevin comes back on Friday afternoon?" she asked.

It was obvious Kristin wanted to speak to her in person. Carol slowly asked, "Kevin's okay, isn't he? What about you and the kids?"

Kristin assured her this wasn't an emergency situation and not health related. She insisted on driving to Carol's while the kids were in school. She would be there around nine the next morning.

Carol lay in bed with her mind racing. Why would Kristin confide in her after all this time? She had yearned for a more sisterly friendship with her sister-in-law but envisioned it lounging over cocktails on a hot summer day, by the pool, preferably while Kevin was at the office. Not like this! She wished Kristin were hightailing it over there right now. What could it be? Did her family know? Why her? There didn't appear to be any 911 call involved. At least she inferred that to be the case. She went back to the crossword puzzle to ease her mind. For the next ten minutes, all she filled in was one more word, and it only had three letters. She determined that trying to continue would be an exercise in futility. She closed her laptop and decided to feed her cheese addiction. She ran downstairs to the fridge, reached for a chunk of extra-sharp cheddar, and cut off a few slices. She gobbled up the cheese, went back upstairs to bed, and was asleep within twenty minutes. Eating a few pieces of cheese was better than taking a sedative.

* * *

Kristin arrived the next morning right on time and had brought a box of muffins from a local bakery. Kevin always brought muffins from the same place. Oddly enough, she didn't look weary or as troubled as she had sounded the previous night. She was wearing a yellow Michigan baseball cap and a tight-fitting, navy-blue, long-panted Michigan tennis outfit with sneakers that looked like they were right out of the box. Kristin said that she had her first tennis lesson ever later in the afternoon and that maybe hitting balls would be good therapy. She pointed to her sharp outfit, which she had obviously recently bought, and asked Carol with a mischievous smile if that gave it away. Carol took that as a good sign. It probably had been rather difficult for Kristin to reach out to her. Carol poured them a cup of coffee, and they both sat down at the kitchen table.

Kristin was more composed than what she herself thought she would be. She took some papers in a folder out of her pocketbook and apologized ahead of time if she said anything out of sequence, as her emotions might cause her to lose concentration. Carol told her to go slowly and to start whenever she felt ready.

Kristin got right into it. "It concerns Kevin. Last year he started coming home late on Thursdays. He said the firm began a weekly team-building strategy session, and attendance was mandatory. When he'd get home, he'd seem distant, and disinterested in everything, if you know what I mean. I gave him the benefit of the doubt. I know how important it is for him to make full partner, and I assumed he was under a lot of pressure. After a while, he seemed to really go into a shell. I started to get paranoid, smelling his clothes for perfume and even his underwear for any sex odors. I'm so sorry. I didn't mean to be so graphic. I'm just trying to show you my state of mind. His odd behavior drove me to such suspicious thoughts."

Carol rubbed Kristin's arm, saw how upset she was getting, and said that if it was too painful, she could stop, as even Carol wasn't so sure she wanted to hear the rest.

Kristin took a sip of coffee and continued. "I got a sitter and decided to follow Kevin one Thursday night. He drove to an office building in some area of Detroit I was unfamiliar with, and he went inside. I ran out of the car and saw him go alone into an elevator, making sure he wouldn't see me. It stopped on the third floor. I looked at the building directory, and the only tenants on that floor were two different psychiatry offices. Was he seeing a shrink for professional purposes or was it personal? In fact, the building housed nothing but healthcare-related offices. I ran back to the car and waited. He came out exactly one hour later by himself and drove to a Catholic church about a mile away. I'm not sure what neighborhood it was in. All I know is that it wasn't the church we belong to back home. Why would he go there? Was he meeting someone? Was he meeting his mistress in a church? I just didn't know what to think."

"I got scared and drove home," Kristin continued. "Kevin came home fifteen minutes after I did, in the same mood he was always in on Thursdays. I asked him how he was, and he said he was all right. I waited for him to fall asleep and grabbed his phone downstairs. There were no recent incoming or outgoing calls to any unknown females. I checked the list at least a month back, maybe more. All the calls had been to work colleagues, our home phone number, my cell, our landscaper, the local take-out pizza place, and your Uncle Sam. I felt relieved after that. However, later in bed that night, I realized he could be communicating with someone on his work email or via some other unknown email address. I never once confronted him. Maybe I'm the one who needs a shrink! I can't hold it in any longer. I'm not suggesting that you may know something about your brother's infidelities. I just figured you know your brother better than anyone and maybe you could shed some light on this or help me sort it out."

Kristin excused herself to go to the bathroom. Carol sat there pondering what she had said and wondered whether any of it was indirectly or directly related to Kevin's shift in character over the years. People have affairs all the time. She wouldn't approve, of course, if her brother were having one, but he certainly wouldn't be a criminal if he did—just a louse.

Kristin returned and apologized again for dragging Carol into her nightmarish problems so soon after her mother had died. She had struggled with whether to bring it up while Mary was still alive but didn't want to worry her, as she had hoped there would be a resolution well beforehand. She couldn't decide whether there was anything to really worry about in the first place. All she knew was that her husband was purposely keeping something from her that was very personal, and she, his wife, felt like an outsider. Whatever it was, it pained her dearly that her husband couldn't confide in her and seek comfort from her. She felt like a failure.

"What do you think so far? Am I overreacting?" Kristin softly asked as she crossed her legs and folded her arms, apprehensively awaiting a reassuring response.

Carol had to toe the line here. She and Kristin never had been close, despite Carol's elusive wish to the contrary. Anything she said could get back to Kevin and cause irreparable damage to their relationship, which already was distant enough. Carol carefully responded, "I'm not trying to defend my brother, and I don't want to insult your intelligence, especially after you sought my counsel. I covet our relationship and secretly have wished for years that it was much deeper."

Kristin cut her off and said, "Oh, my. So do I. Every time I expressed that feeling to Kevin, he'd dissuade me from calling you. He'd say you were too busy with your own life and helping your mother. It also prevented me from developing a bond with your mother. How could I seek out a closer relationship with her without including you? It was unsettling to me. Kevin hardly ever wants to step foot in this house, as if it were haunted. I'd joke with him that he was afraid you'd spill some dark secret about his past growing up, like that he wet the bed or something.

"I met Kevin at U of M and still have a few friends sprinkled around the area from there. My family is miles away in Minnesota, a plane ride away. Your family is a short drive from our house. The muffins were still steaming hot when I arrived today, for God's sake. It was lonely for me when I first got here, and it still is. I needed, and still do need, your love and friendship. I used to get lost all the time here until there was GPS. I've never felt fully assimilated here and I've never been a country club girl. I'm a family person. That's why I feel so emotionally trapped. I can't tell anyone in my family about any of this for now. They just don't know Kevin like you do."

Tears welled in Carol's eyes. She always had thought of Kristin as sort of a Stepford wife and could now ascertain the reasoning behind a lot of her submissive behavior. "I expressed similar thoughts to my mother," Carol said, "and she'd respond that you were too busy with the kids and that Kevin was too concerned about his job. I'd nod my head to pacify her. The longer you wait to confront Kevin, the more wound up you'll make yourself. Kids tend to have a sixth sense about when things aren't right. You don't want them to suffer. My advice would be to tell him what you saw, and if he doesn't come clean, ask him to see a marriage counselor with you."

Kristin expanded on that thought with regard to the kids and said, "That's another thing that bothers me, but shouldn't, and I feel bad that it does. Kevin is the most perfect, attentive, loving father he could possibly be. I don't know how he does it. He dotes on those kids and always assures they're well mannered and respectful of others. It's like he can't have enough love in his heart for them. I sit there and guiltily feel jealous of my own children at times. I so badly yearn for that kind of loving affection from him."

Kristin clearly didn't live in fear of her husband. He never possessed any violent or insidious tendencies. She feared the truth, even though she desperately wanted it revealed. "There's something else, if I may go on," she said. "I know I've taken a lot of your time already."

The papers in the blue folder had piqued Carol's interest. She wondered whether they had anything to do with her mother's estate, or even if they were divorce papers, but she wasn't betting on either. Maybe they were love letters that Kristin had found? She had to know! "Hon, I'm all ears," Carol said, trying not to sound overly eager.

Kristin continued, "We were at the country club on St. Patrick's night for a formal dinner dance. Who wants to be in a cocktail dress at a sit-down dinner on that night? I felt uncomfortable, like a fish out of water, rubbing elbows with those windbag overly made-up women. There's another twist to the story. One of the members there, Don Faust, is a senior partner at Kevin's firm. Kevin told me he was stepping out to the lobby to call you, as a matter of fact. Did he call you?" Carol nodded, and Kristin continued her story, content that he hadn't lied about that. "Well, Don came over to where I was standing. He was pretty drunk, slurring his words, and his eyes were bloodshot. He told me that he and the other partners were concerned about Kevin's recent actions.

"The firm always has done pro bono work for the poor and unfortunate. It's mostly for public relation purposes. They could give a crap about the poor. That's what that moron Don actually said! The majority of that work is generally assigned to the firm's newcomers so they can gain experience. Kevin was an experienced junior partner there and a large fee generator. He had greatly increased his pro bono caseload, and they were concerned it was reducing his focus and taking away from his revenue contribution. Don said that he had a meeting with Kevin about it, but it was all for naught, as he basically kept working for free. The other partners weren't happy, as they couldn't understand why he did any pro bono work at all anymore. Don wanted me to talk some sense into Kevin. He further explained that he had vouched for him, and now Kevin was making him look bad. He basically said that not only were Kevin's actions reducing his chances of being made senior partner, but his continued defiance could lead to his ultimate dismissal."

Kristin began to cry, and Carol was shaking her head in disbelief. Sure, it was very noble and civic minded to help the underprivileged. However, Kevin was gainfully employed at a high-power law firm that had a lot of influence in social, political, and institutional circles. He had worked so hard to get to this lofty level. Why would he risk his livelihood and go out on limb to assist the forsaken masses?

"It doesn't sound as if he's thinking rationally," Carol said. "He may be burned out already. Like it or not, you folks are part of the evil one percent everyone out there hates. It could be that he's having some kind of spiritual or moral internal conflict, and that's why he's seeing the shrink, as well as going to that church. Maybe it's something that simple. Look how helpful he's always been with his family, and now he's taken it to a frenetic extreme. It could be that whatever he's going through is spiraling out of his control, and he's trying to create some kind of balance."

Carol offered a little levity. "It could be that he has some compulsive disorder like those pat-rack people on that TV series. Just be thankful you don't have a house full of homeless people stacked on top of one another." She busted laughing, expecting the same out of Kristin. Instead she started crying louder than ever. "I'm sorry if I inadvertently said anything wrong. It was only in jest. Sorry if it was a bad analogy!" Carol ruefully said.

Now Kristin switched gears and laughed hard. Carol was confused. Could it be that everything was actually okay with Kevin and that Kristin was the one who was having a nervous breakdown? Kristin opened up the folder and spread the papers across the table. Carol could see some of them were bank statements. Kristin cackled, "I swear you're psychic! You hit the nail right on the head. After Don's comments, I took it upon myself to do some digging. Please look at these papers. Don't feel funny—I'm the one responsible for getting these. Thank goodness I guessed the password. It only took me a few attempts. I mean, really, 'Wolverines'? Not much of an imagination. I want to share these with you. As they say, the proof is in the pudding, and there's tons of it here. Look at these checks from Kevin's personal account. Go ahead. I insist." Kristin put one sheet down right in front of Carol. It was a check for ten thousand dollars made out to The Home for Little Wanderers. Another ten-thousand-dollar check was made out to The United Way. Kristin slammed another statement down and pointed her finger a dozen times at the dollar amount. It was a check made out to an orphanage for thirty thousand dollars. Kristin said she had researched where it was located. "It's in goddamn Peru!" she yelled as her eyes bulged out of her head.

Carol could see many more checks made out in lesser amounts. The donations added up to around a hundred and twenty-five thousand dollars. Kristin continued to laugh like a crazy woman. "I took these out of a locked drawer in the study. I picked the lock with a bobby pin, made copies, and put the originals back. I was pretty proud of myself," she said, making believe she was patting herself on the back.

Kristin handed Carol the papers. There were three adoption applications already filled out but apparently not sent yet. One was located in the states down in Miami, another in Peru, and yet another in Sudan. There was also an acknowledgment letter from an adoption agency in Detroit. "Yup, that's a good one. Apparently we're on the waiting list. I'm quite content with the family headcount we have. What are we, one of those jet-setting celebrity couples that picks up kids from every country they visit like they're vacation trinkets? The other night one of those Save the Children commercials came on TV. Kevin was sitting on the den floor playing with Keith. I changed the channel before he could memorize the toll-free number!" Kristin shrieked.

No, Kristin wasn't maniacal, but she certainly was propelling herself in that direction, Carol thought. They sat there looking at each other, taking turns to peer at the papers strewn across the table, and then shaking their heads in disbelief.

Carol broke the strained silence and finally said, "I'm not making light of the situation. It's quite serious, and if Kevin maintains this charitable-giving pace at the current rate, you guys will shortly join the ranks of the ninety-nine percent. I sincerely hope that's not his goal, to bankrupt the family. He might as well drop a wheelbarrow full of all the cash you have left from the roof of the Renaissance Building. When you started talking, I thought the worst—that Kevin had done something deliberately malevolent. His hidden antics here aren't completely condemnable. You can't crucify him for doing good deeds. You have to inform him that you're aware and somehow make him stop, or at least significantly tone it down. Forget about how you invaded his privacy. It was justified. I don't have an answer for the adoption thing. I just wonder when the heck he was going to clue you in."

Kristin got up, and they hugged each other. She was relieved that Carol appeared to be so supportive. She promised to be a better friend and invited Carol over for Easter dinner. She would no longer need Kevin's blessing. Carol told her to get her house in order first, and they'd see about Easter.

Kristin reached for her car keys and walked to the front door looking momentarily relieved. She grabbed the doorknob, sighed, and said with a smile, "Please don't be a stranger. I know I won't." She opened the door halfway, turned around, and added, "I was sorry to hear about your Uncle Sam. I hope he's going to be okay. Poor guy—first the hip replacement and now the heart valve operation coming up. Tell Edna he's in my prayers."

Carol looked at her at a loss for words, and Kristin knew right away that something was amiss. "I'm sorry. I thought you knew. I figured Edna already had told you. It's been two months since the hip surgery."

Carol informed her that she was right. Edna should have told her. She'd been in Edna's company more than a dozen times in the last two months, maybe more. She'd had ample opportunity to mention it. Carol concluded that Edna couldn't possibly have known.

Kristin went on with the story. "He came down here alone for his hip pre-op tests. Kevin went to Henry Ford with him. It's his left hip, so he could drive okay. The tests revealed an abnormality in his heart. He stayed over at our house that night, and the next morning Kevin took him for more tests on his heart. They determined he needed a valve replacement, but they said his condition could be temporarily controlled with medication. So they went ahead with the hip operation. I'm not sure when the valve operation is scheduled, but it's coming up soon. See, this is what I'm talking about. Kevin assumed you and I would never talk to each other, so I wouldn't be in position to tell you—unless he thought Uncle Sam had told Edna. I never thought about that. Kevin and your uncle chat on the phone all the time. I think it's very endearing. Why wouldn't he tell his own daughter? Maybe he didn't want to worry her, with him living so far away. Can you see lately how my mind has been working? I really don't like it. Everything seems so convoluted. There are more angles to consider than in a geometry class." She hurried down the steps, off to her tennis lesson.

Carol wished her goodbye and sent her off with a wave. Kristin had opened a door Carol hadn't envisioned. How would she sort things out with Edna? How strange that Kristin had left seemingly with a huge burden off her chest. Now Carol was the one with a burden, she thought, as she leaned against the door fretting over what to do.

Chapter 13

It was the morning of Holy Saturday. Another beautiful day was in the making. Carol was outside in her bathrobe filling the birdfeeder. She had been very diligent in fulfilling her personal promise to keep it filled. Her life wasn't exactly bustling, and chores, no matter how mundane, helped stretch out the day. Another week had gone by with no surprises, which was to her liking. She actually had gotten a lot accomplished around the house. She had changed a lot of the light bulbs and had cleaned the oven, which had been long overdue, and also had cleaned the windows.

Carol never had realized how many different kinds of light bulbs were in all the fixtures in the house. She needed vanity, sconce, three-way, indoor and outdoor flood, indoor and outdoor spot, halogen, and soft-white bulbs, all in different specified wattage levels. Her shopping cart at the hardware store was almost completely full of them. It was a rather stressful trip. After twenty minutes of indecision, she had to elicit assistance from a clerk. He asked her if she was moving into a new house, and when she had said no, his next question was why she needed to buy every light bulb on her list. Did they all need changing at the same time? She really didn't have an answer for that. This kind of home improvement, fixer-up store always intimidated her, and that question was proof again as to why. The fact that she always attracted the elderly clerk with the droopy suspenders, instead of the hunk with the tool belt around his tight jeans, made the shopping experience seem even more degrading. The smell that permeated the store added to her dour mood—a blend of rubber, plastic, lumber, fertilizer, and plumber and carpenter body odor. She'd take the scent of potpourri, candles, and perfume over that any day. The only positive aspect was that she had gotten all the right bulbs and didn't have to go through the drudgery of going back and making a return.

Carol hadn't seen Edna in a couple of weeks. She was stopping by later in the day, and they were going to the cemetery and then going out. Edna had gone away with Nick the weekend before to a cottage on a lake he had rented in Chelsea. The cottage was for sale, and Nick was interested in purchasing it. She was curious how they had gotten along. Edna always had an interesting story along that front. Carol thought Nick was a nice guy. He was well groomed and good looking. She thought Edna was overly critical of him at times, but she always spun things from a humorous perspective, which never made him seem that bad of a catch.

Carol and Edna had spoken a few times over the phone lately, but Edna's father was never mentioned. Carol hoped that Sam had called Edna and filled her in so she could be extricated from the delicate task of doing so herself. Now she had to put the pieces together quickly, as time was no longer on her side. She knew Edna would speak with her father over Easter, and the clock was almost striking midnight.

Carol had spoken to Chris earlier in the week and told him about her meeting with Kristin. He had asked what he could do to help, but Carol explained that the ball was in Kristin's court and that they should wait for her to give her an update on the situation. Chris had told Carol to call Edna right away, as she would just be passing along information that Edna had a right to know. *Easy for him to say half a country away*, Carol thought.

Chris was concerned about the safety of the estate money. Carol had thought about that but didn't feel right harboring such thoughts. Kevin was their brother, she told him, and they had to stand by him. Chris convinced her it was something to think about. He told her to separate the fact that Kevin was their brother from the situation at hand. They'd already had reservations about him before these new issues had come to light. If he was that out of control, he might be tempted to dip into their inheritance. He likened it to drug addicts who know that stealing from their family is wrong but can't stop. Carol wouldn't hear of it. Kevin wasn't some stiff skipping out on his bar tab. He never would shirk his financial responsibility at the expense of family. He had done an exemplary job already. That quelled Chris's negative thinking a bit, and he gave Carol a wary half-apology.

* * *

Edna and Carol stopped by the florist to get some lilies on their way to the cemetery. There still was a great selection of healthy-looking flowers, which was why they had decided to come on Saturday instead of Easter Sunday. St. Hedwig's was always less congested the day before a holiday. Heavy traffic on such restful hallowed grounds tends to denigrate the feeling of peace and tranquility. People double-park and box other cars in. There's two way traffic in a lane built for one car, which causes cars to drive on the lawn, and people always appear to be lost in a maze and agitated, as if the graves they're looking for moved to other spots just to piss them off.

The gravesites of Carol's parents and Edna's mom were only a section apart, so they could park the car and walk to both pretty easily, or so they thought. Both were wearing high heels, and they kept sinking into the grass and getting stuck. They had to take turns leaning against each other to free themselves, which wasn't easy, considering each of them had three plants corralled in their arms. Carol was wearing white open-toed shoes, which were now grass stained, and she feared her rose-colored freshly painted pedicure from the day before was also ruined. Edna had on dark green pumps. She looked down at Carol's now two-tone shoes, pointed to her own stain-free shoes, and joked she had planned it that way. Carol knew better. Edna always had that kind of stupid luck.

They got to Carol's parents' resting places first, placed the flowers down, and stood silently praying. Carol slightly trembled. She had gone to the gravesites last weekend by herself and was very despondent. It had been the first time since her mother's funeral, and her memory from that was too fresh. She could still envision what her mother was wearing, her shade of lipstick, and how her hair looked. There was a clump of fresh dirt carved out of the beautiful manicured lawn. Now grass was starting to grow, and soon her mom wouldn't stick out like a sore thumb, as she never had craved any undue attention. Edna held on to her tightly. Carol wasn't quite sure if it was to prevent her from falling out of her own sunken shoes, or to support Carol in her time of need. She didn't even realize she had tears rolling down her cheeks; the week before she had been wailing on her knees. She hoped this was possibly an evolutionary stage in the whole healing process. Carol nodded to Edna that she was ready to leave, and off they trudged to Aunt Helen's grave, which was closer to the side of the road, so they didn't have to ruin more of the lawn.

Carol noticed how beautiful the grave was. A lovely wooden flowerbed surrounded the grave and had an intricate design and an assortment of flowers. The bed was permanently imbedded in the ground. Edna smiled over the grave and gave out a sigh of satisfaction. It definitely was the most appealing in the area. Other graves had big fancy stones, but Aunt Helen's was so tastefully original. Still, this probably had cost a pretty penny. Carol hadn't been to the grave in two years, as the year before her mother was still recuperating from her health issues, and they didn't go like they usually did.

This was only the second time she and Edna had come to the cemetery together, and she saw the difference between them right away. Edna was more accepting of her mother's death now, although she would never get over the cause of it, while Carol still had to sift through more layers of raw emotions to get to that stage.

Edna retrieved a rag and a bottle of water from her trunk so Carol could clean her feet and shoes. Carol took off her shoes, and the grass stains came off rather easily. She scrubbed her feet hard and poured more water on them while they hung out the door, making sure not to chip her toenail polish. She gave Edna a wink, put her shoes back on, closed the door, and off they went. Carol felt relieved when they drove out of the cemetery, as she could wash away the stains from her feet, but not much else.

Edna had to make a return at a discount clothing store, and Carol went in with her. More time in the store meant less in a bar. They both went their separate ways. Edna was returning a blouse that had a small tear in the side she hadn't seen when trying it on. She found another one the same size, but with a slightly different print, as she couldn't find same one she had purchased. She liked the style, picked it up, and went up to the counter. Carol was already in line at another register buying a sports bra and watched in delight the encounter Edna was having with the teenage girl at the register. The girl scrutinized the top, taking note of the rip, and inspected it further to see if it was one of those "use it and lose it" kind of returns. She gave

Edna a suspicious leer and begrudgingly made the exchange. Edna let out a huff and walked away. Carol met up with her at the exit.

"Did you see that? The tags were still attached to it. What? I wore it out with those on it? Like I really want to advertise the fact that I paid nine dollars for that," Edna gruffly snapped.

Carol couldn't stop laughing and added, "I don't know which scene today was more precious, you getting the hairy eyeball from a malcontent teen, or the two of us creating divots across St. Hedwig's lawn."

The two decided to head to Detroit and go to a popular bar on the outskirts of Greektown. The Tigers were playing at home against the Red Sox, so downtown would be hopping. Both were wearing tight jeans and showing a little cleavage and attracted stares when they walked into the bar. Edna whispered into Carol's ear, "I don't know about you, but I think when they stop gazing is when we should be worried."

Carol laughed and ordered them two beers. It was elbow to elbow in the bar, and they settled into a spot by the men's room. Edna commented, "Boys all got to go at some point. This is prime scoping real estate."

Carol knew she was all talk. She asked Edna how her weekend with Nick was.

"It was fantastic. We had a great time. It was seventy degrees out, and the lake was so calm. The place wasn't what you might call a cottage. It was more like a four-bedroom lake house. The design and decor was like something out of a magazine, and the house was perfectly situated on the shore. I could see going there for a weekend escape. Ann Arbor is so close too. We snuggled by the fire pit Friday night and barbecued steaks. Nick made a reservation at a super restaurant in downtown Chelsea on Saturday, which was only seven miles away and really quaint. We got along surprisingly well too."

Carol was happy to hear that. Her belief all along was that Edna liked Nick a lot more than she let on. He wasn't as anal as Edna portrayed him to be. Carol pictured a psychological profile of Nick and compared it with Uncle Sam, as he was the only other constant male figure Edna had in her life. Her uncle was unpredictable, impetuous, undependable, irresponsible, forgetful, and not the best of providers. Not to mention, he had been a heavy drinker. Nick was highly intelligent and educated, well mannered, caring, self-assured, responsible, neat, stable, and prideful and made a decent living. A lake house isn't cheap, after all. He was the polar opposite of Edna's dad. Sam was more of an extrovert but less so when he was sober. Nick was no shrinking violet and had a Midwestern dry wit about him. Compared to her father, Edna eventually would see that he was like a panacea, Carol thought. She believed Edna already knew that, and why she tried to fight it was beyond her. Nick was the one who wanted to get closer, and when Edna would resist at times, he was clever enough to give her space, knowing that each time they reconnected she would be drawn deeper to him. Sooner or later, Edna would succumb to her feelings. Nick was a keeper. The lake house wasn't hurting his chances either, Carol thought with a chuckle.

Edna and Carol again talked about taking a vacation together and decided mid-June would be an ideal time. Airfares to the islands and Florida were much cheaper then, and the lodging rates were heavily discounted.

"Who cares if it's ninety-five degrees out with a hundred-percent humidity, with fanged mosquitoes the size of bats?" Carol joked.

A man behind them was laughing, and they weren't sure whether it was directed toward them. He turned around and playfully said, "Yes, I've been laughing at you girls for a while. You're quite entertaining, if I may say. Forgive me for eavesdropping."

Carol turned around and couldn't believe what she was looking at. The man was about six foot two with perfectly chiseled facial features, a lean athletic build, and salt-and-pepper curly hair. He was wearing a blue Red Sox cap. "Hi, I'm Tom. These are my two nephews, Brad and George. Brad is graduating from Boston College next month, and this is his present from me. We came in for the weekend from Boston for the baseball games. They're my sister's sons. George is just here for eye candy," he joked.

Carol thought that Tom certainly didn't need help in that department, as she gawked at his smoldering smile. "I'm Carol, and this is my cousin and best friend, Edna. Pleased to meet you. Congrats, to you Brad. What's your major?" she politely asked.

Brad shyly responded, "Economics. I figured it was the best choice. I could have a lot of options for work." Tom looked proudly at his nephew and said, "You girls should consider Maine for your vacation. I don't want to sound like I'm with the chamber of commerce, but I'm in the process of opening up a small inn in Kennebunkport. I may be in over my head a bit. It's slated to open the weekend before Memorial Day. I was a stockbroker in Boston for twenty-one years and decided to change my lifestyle. The business lost its soul, and I wanted out before I lost mine."

Carol could relate to that. "My brother lives in Ogunquit. He keeps asking me to come out and visit," she said. Tom shook his head, and Carol thought, *Please don't say "small world." It's so very cliché. Challenge my bland existence with a better comeback than that.*

Tom cheerfully said, "Ogunquit has the best beach around for sunbathing, as well as going for a long walk or a jog. The restaurants just aren't good—they're superb, ranging from eloquent, to farm to table, to lobster in the rough. It's just a half-hour car ride up the highway. You should drop by the inn. We have a bar, or I should say we will when it comes in. I'm having one custom made, and I'm keeping my fingers crossed it'll be ready on time." Tom's answer totally captivated Carol, and she immediately went into fantasy mode, imagining the two of them walking barefoot, arm and arm, toes in the water, stopping every other step to kiss.

She slightly shook her head to snap herself out of her romantic daydream, looked at the TV, and pointed to show Tom that the game was already in the bottom of the first inning. He didn't seem to mind and went on about how much they were enjoying their trip. They had tickets for the entire series, and he relished the atmosphere in bars steeped in tradition, such as the one they were in. He loved the old dark wood, meeting new and interesting people, and the fact that his nephews were now old enough to legally drink and they could now better share life experiences together.

Interesting people, she thought. *Guess that rules out piano teachers!* Carol was grateful that Edna had let her have Tom to herself, as she was making small talk with the boys.

She was curious what was underneath that baseball cap. How disappointing if it turned out to be a big red bald spot. It was hot in the bar, and she could see Tom's temples slightly beading up with sweat. Carol intentionally pressed her cold beer bottle against her forehead, hoping it would cause a reflex reaction and he'd lift his cap and show her the goods—like when someone yawns, others tend to as well. No such luck with that strategy. She attempted to entice him again and tactfully asked, "I was thinking of getting a Sox cap myself. I like the colors. What size is yours?"

Tom scratched his chin and said, "It's a large, or if you're in Europe, size seven-and-a-half." Carol was bummed. What man would know his exact hat size, unless he bought a lot of them to cover up his baldness? The search for the perfect man must go on, she guessed. Still, there was something quite engaging about him that she couldn't quite put her finger on.

She stared right into his baby blues, and as their eyes locked, she said in her best sexy voice, "If I ever get out to Maine, I'd love to stop by your inn, and I wish you well. It may be sooner than you think."

Tom gave her a semi hug and countered, "I'd look forward to that. I really would. Unfortunately I don't have any cards back from the printer yet with the inn's address and contact information, but here's my business card from my old firm. It has my cell number, and I'll jot down my email address." He took off his cap and ran his fingers through his curly locks. His hair was so thick and full.

Carol's knees buckled, and she felt the blood rush into her rosy cheeks, her ears feeling like they were on fire. That artful maneuver sealed the deal. She lovingly patted Tom on the shoulder, her eyes still staring at his hair and showing sweet approval.

"Come on, boys. Let's get out of here while we still have our wits about us. Off to the game now before they give our seats away," Tom joked before he said goodbye to Carol and Edna. He whispered into Carol's ear, "Call me even if you don't make it back east. It's less than a two-hour flight for me to come out. Heck, I'd fly halfway around the world for you. Trust me—I'm never this forward, but I am a strong believer in fate." They both smiled, and Carol kiddingly gave him a slight push toward the door.

"You made a face when I suggested we stand in this spot," Edna said. "Take it back now. That dude was handsome. Did you see all that hair—I mean, mane! He was smitten with you. I tried to distract his nephews as long as I could for you. I think I did a good enough job. Long enough, it appears, judging from your face. Let's do a shot and a beer to celebrate. He's gone. The coast is clear. You don't have to act like a lady any longer!" Edna shouted as she did a little dance.

Edna went to the bar to order, and Carol followed her, as there was an opening on top to put their purses on. "I just can't believe it," Carol said. "How a chance meeting can hold the key to possibly changing your life. I felt there was chemistry. He can't be married. What kind of an uncle would come on to someone at a bar in front of his nephews, his sister's kids, if that's actually the case? I couldn't take my eyes off him. We've only been here less than an hour, and I spent half of it talking to him. I wish I had that time back again. Maybe I would have said some things differently. I was so flustered and neglected to ask him what the name of his inn was. That's so self-centered!"

Edna laughed and said, "I was listening to you guys. I had my antenna up. You played it perfectly. Trust me. The only red flag he had up was the one between his legs."

Carol knew she really didn't need to do a shot. "Calm down, my cousin. Tomorrow is a big day. I'm most likely going to the eleven-thirty Easter service and want to try to get a quick run in beforehand, then my churchgoing ways will be put on hold until the holidays. I've had enough religion for a while," Carol adamantly said.

Carol always had thought Easter was a strange holiday. It was never on the same date, and every year she'd have to check the calendar to see where it fell. She knew it had something to do with an ancient calendar, in conjunction with some formula, but it was the twenty-first century. Why the crazy disparity? One year it falls in late April, another year late March. They should be able to figure out a better system. Why not celebrate it every year the last Sunday in March? Perhaps she'd have a chat with Father O'Malley tomorrow, and they could start a petition. *Fat chance of that*, she thought with a chuckle.

She was going over to Kevin's tomorrow. He had invited her during the week, his voice showing no sign of marital strife or tension. He had been in a great mood and told her the menu was baked ham, mashed sweet potatoes, string beans, and zucchini. Carol was going to order a pie to bring with her, but she made a couple of them Friday night, one apple and one blueberry. She was bored and hadn't cooked dessert in some time. She needed the practice, too. The pies could warm up in Kevin's oven before being served. Kristin never had followed up on their discussion, so Carol assumed she wasn't going to confront Kevin until Easter passed. *Good move*, Carol thought. *Let the kids have their fun.* A few extra days wouldn't change things much.

Carol's thoughts turned to Edna's plans for Easter. If she were planning to visit Uncle Sam, she'd already be there by now. It was a long drive for a day trip, and the roads up there were so dark at night. "You never told me what you're doing tomorrow. Obviously you're not going up north," Carol said. It wasn't like Edna not to tell her. If she were going to her cousins' on her father's side, she would have mentioned it. Carol could tell by the lag in Edna's response that she planned to spend Easter with Nick. She knew her behavioral attitude concerning Nick. Everything was so cavalier and matter of fact. God forbid she ever showed any emotion about Nick.

Edna sipped her beer and said, "Actually, I spoke with my father last night to wish him a happy Easter and said I wasn't going to make it. He invited me up the day of the funeral. You know how he can be. It's always an open invite with him. He knows it's a long haul and usually understands, but I detected a hint of deeper disappointment than usual in him. There was nothing specific. It was just a vibe. I told him I'd come up for Memorial Day weekend. I really felt bad when I hung up. I should have pressured him more when I asked if everything was okay. He usually jokes that he's stronger than the Energizer Bunny. Instead he laughingly likened himself to an old broken-down racehorse and said they should take him out back and shoot him. He asked how you were doing and told me to bring you that weekend, just so you know."

Carol didn't know what to say. She felt as if she were in an abyss. How could she find her way out? Not telling Edna about her dad's recent medical woes right away had been a mistake. Uncle Sam may have been trying the best he could to reach out to his daughter. He never was good about being serious and probably struggled to find the right words. His health was failing him, and Edna needed to know. Edna would have been there if she knew. Carol was more fixated on hurting Edna's feelings. Why would Uncle Sam seek out Kevin and not his own daughter? She would be devastated if she knew.

Carol thought the odds were against her getting any vindication the next day. She couldn't be forthright and bring up the topic of Uncle Sam, as that would tip Kevin off that she and Kristin had discussed the subject and could lead him to suspect they may have touched upon a variety of other issues. The only resolution would be if Kevin himself brought it up. Perhaps Kevin had assumed Uncle Sam already had informed Edna. After Carol faked being shocked by the news, she could then let him know that Edna couldn't be aware of the situation, because she would have confided in her, and then Kevin could express his opinion regarding what to do. Carol could then take the opportunity to tell Kevin that he should call Uncle Sam and be forceful with him that he should inform Edna. *It's the proper thing to do*, Carol thought. She had to put the idea in Kevin's head that Edna had to hear the news from her dad directly and not secondhand from either of them. This scenario would be the only chance Carol had at getting a reprieve. *Please, let it play out this way*, Carol thought.

"Are you just going to leave me hanging?" Carol asked Edna, as she had never answered the question about how she was spending Easter.

Edna played dumb for a moment then told her she was going to Nick's mother's house in Howell. She had met her at a birthday party a few months ago, so they already had broken the ice. *Funny*, Carol thought, *it must have slipped Edna's mind. She never told me about attending a family birthday party.* She hadn't even told her just now who the party was for, which made Carol pause to wonder how many other Nick-related family events she had kept from her. *Oh, sweet cousin*, Carol thought, *when are you going to throw in the towel and tell the world you love the guy?*

Edna patted Carol's pocketbook on the bar and chided her to get out Tom's business card. Carol blushed, pulled it out, and placed it on the bar beside Edna's hand. "Let's take a gander here. Thomas Quinn, managing director. He must be a very important person, a VIP!" she teased, pretending to stuff the card down her shirt. "There's an old song called 'The Mighty Quinn.' He certainly looked mighty fine!"

"Give it back, smart ass," Carol demanded. "I don't know why I got so excited anyway. He probably has too much baggage. His wallet was pretty thick, most likely from the pictures of all his kids stuffed in there."

Edna wouldn't hear such negative speculation. She enthusiastically said, "You have to accentuate the positive, my doubting cousin. I know you've been through a lot lately. A part of me senses your mother up in heaven has aligned the stars for you. I know it sounds mushy, but that's what I want to truly believe. She's looking down on you, and you should hold on to that belief too. Maine, here we come. It's our destiny!"

Chapter 19

Attending Easter Sunday Mass turned out to be a grueling experience for Carol. She was mad at herself for not going on her planned run. It wasn't from a hangover; she and Edna had eaten so much in Greektown the night before, and she hadn't fully digested it yet. The thought of all that feta cheese still swishing around inside her was nauseating. Plus she felt as if she were breathing hummus out of her nostrils. She purposely sat in the last pew in case she needed air. To add to her woes, a late-arriving worshipper heavily stepped on both of her feet as he attempted to balance himself while inching past her along the pew. After Carol received Holy Communion, she looked straight ahead as she passed the last pew, kept walking straight out of the church, and never looked back.

On the drive to Kevin's house, she put the air conditioner on full blast, with all the car windows down. It was a cool, seasonable April day, and Carol foolishly hoped it would help eliminate the pervasive stench of hummus that she feared had soaked into her clothes. She was wearing jeans and a maroon sweater and wanted to dress sensibly, as the ceilings in Kevin's house were so high and the rooms so large that it always felt cold when she visited.

It was a little past one o'clock when she pulled into Kevin's circular driveway. The fresh mulch, neatly raked along the perimeter of the front lawn, was a welcome smell. Kristin's black

Range Rover was parked outside the four-car garage. Carol could see the kids excitedly waving to her through the large picture window; little Kate, with a stuffed big-eared bunny in her arm, was running toward the door. The door was ajar, and Carol slowly pushed it open so it wouldn't strike the kids. They planted wet kisses on her, almost knocking her to the hardwood floor when she kneeled down, while each hand balanced a plastic-wrapped pie. Kristin heard the commotion from the kitchen and walked in with an inviting smile, still dressed in her church garb and wiping her hands clean with a dishtowel so she could rescue Carol from the kids. She welcomed Carol with a careful, warm hug and led her into the kitchen so she could put the pies down.

Kevin, dressed in a sport coat and tie, came in with a digital camera in his hand and gave Carol a quick hug, along with a peck on the cheek. "I'm afraid the little ones are on a sugar high. We tried to hold them off the candy as long as we could, but we let them enjoy some treats on the ride home from church," he said, pointing to a chocolate smudge on Kate's light-pink Easter dress. Carol pointed to her jeans and added, "I'm dressed in my best Easter outfit too."

"Okay. Let's get the pictures out of the way, and then we'll get these clothes off you kids," Kevin said as they all watched Kristin magically make the smudge disappear from Kate's dress with a stain-remover stick.

They all went into the living room by the picture window and took various combinations of photographs. The kids became a little rambunctious, and Kristin sensed Carol was getting impatient too. She called a prompt halt to the photo session, which was done more so for her family to see the kids in their Easter outfits than anything else, and led the kids upstairs to help change them. Kevin still had a smile on his face, and Carol informed him that he could stop smiling now, unless he was so happy to see her that he couldn't stop. His smile turned into a brief chuckle, and Carol actually noticed in the window's light that he had grown more than a few gray hairs, as obviously he had a lot on his mind. He offered Carol wine or a beer. She passed on alcohol until dinnertime and opted for water instead. Kevin opened a can of beer and handed Carol the water. "Would you like me to show you what I've been working on?" he asked. "Kristin thinks I'm crazy, but I find it soothing."

Carol instantly wondered whether Kristin had spoken to him about his secretive escapades. She wanted to say, "You mean, you find giving all your money away and accumulating children like Daddy Warbucks soothing?" Her tongue started to roll, but "Sure" was all that came out.

Kevin walked her out to the backyard and down a red-bricked path that led to a freshly planted garden about fifty square feet in size. "We're going to have zucchini, green beans, eggplant, radishes, and basil. When it gets a little warmer, I'm going to plant tomatoes. I already put in fertilizer. It'll be a lot of upkeep, but the kids will gain a little responsibility—that is, if they take an interest—and our reward will be fresh vegetables," he proudly said, as he tiptoed in the dirt.

Carol nodded in approval. "It's huge. You could feed a whole army," she stated. *Possibly an orphanage or two*, she also thought.

Kristin poked her head out the back door and told Kevin he should have changed his clothes before he walked in the garden. "Wipe your feet good, and go up and change," she gently said, knowing at least she had control over maintaining a clean house.

They strolled back into the house, and Carol went into the kitchen while Kevin obediently wiped his feet on the welcome mat and went upstairs to change.

The kids were watching TV in the den. Kristin peered around to make sure Kevin was upstairs and whispered to Carol, "Now it appears he wants to feed the world too. I'm still trying to get the nerve to talk to him. He came straight home from work this past Thursday. First time in months. It could be because of Easter break, though." Kristin's eyes turned to an unopened bottle of Merlot on the counter. "It's time for me. These days that time seems to be getting earlier and earlier," she said with a short giggle. She skillfully opened the bottle in a matter of seconds, plying the corkscrew with a sommelier's expertise, and noticed Carol's astonished eyes. She cracked, "Been getting in a lot of practice." She poured Carol and herself a healthy glass each, and they joined the kids in the den.

Kevin came downstairs and joined them in the den. He was truly in his element. Kate sat on his lap, still clinging to her stuffed bunny, and Keith was on all fours, pushing a tiny metal racecar along the hardwood floor, purring engine sounds out of his tiny mouth. Kevin asked where Edna was spending the holiday, and when Carol told him she was going to Nick's mother's house, he remarked how nice it was that she wasn't alone and then commented on how the relationship must be getting serious. "She's turning forty soon and not getting any younger. A lawyer isn't such a bad catch, if I must say so myself," he said with a chuckle.

Kristin chimed in, "Edna looks fantastic. She deserves to be happy at any age. Don't forget, mister—you'll be turning forty before her. By the way, I'm sure her blood pressure wasn't a hundred and sixty over ninety-five at her last checkup."

Carol put her hand over her mouth. Her mother had just died of a stroke, and their father had died of a heart attack; both had had high blood pressure. Carol's blood pressure was generally quite low, and she was thankful for that, given the family history. Her mother's blood pressure was always stable, within the normal parameters, until she started chemo treatments. Then she developed hypertension and required medication. Carol had monitored her mother's blood pressure daily, taking it three times a day. She also had kept a chart, administered all of her mother's medications, and kept track of the various doctor appointments. Her mother was strong willed and self-sufficient right to the end. Carol never needed any visiting care to help her, even when her mother was immobile from her broken ankle. She would help bathe and sometimes dress her, but those services were generally performed sporadically, far from routinely, depending on her mother's condition that day.

"Kevin, that's not a good thing," Carol said. "Did your doctor outline a plan to get that under control? Our family history isn't favorable. Often hypertension is stress related. You have a lot of responsibilities. What good is living here in Camelot if you become incapacitated by a stroke or something? Kristin has her hands full already. See to it please that you get that taken care of."

Kristin waved her finger at Kevin in an "I told you so" fashion and gave Carol a high-five. Kevin broke the temporary silence. "I know you're right. I have to go back to the doctor's next month. I've been trying to change my diet a bit, but please allow me to devour that salty ham we're serving today without any guilt," he joked, as he watched Carol and Kristin's disapproving expressions dictate that it was no laughing matter.

Keith asked why his Uncle Chris wasn't there. Carol explained that he lived in Maine and was eating with his friends. "You're lucky," Keith said. "You have two brothers. I don't have any to play catch with. I want a baby brother!"

Carol and Kristin looked at each other in shock. Carol wondered whether Kevin had coached him to say that or whether it was an innocent remark. Surely, Kevin's blood pressure was through the roof because of all of his extracurricular activities, but using his son to sway opinion was beyond contempt. Kevin just sat there, as if he were waiting for someone else to respond. Carol envisioned the doorbell ringing, and someone from an adoption agency shepherding two little boys into the house with their suitcases. She glanced out the window, saw no one outside, and felt relieved.

"You can always play with Mommy, Daddy, and your sister any time you want," Kristin lovingly said.

Kevin went into the kitchen, ogled the ham, and delivered it to the center of the dining room table, smacking his lips in anticipation. "It's almost three. Why don't we finally eat? How about it, kids? Who's going to say grace?" he cheerfully asked.

Carol helped Kristin with the sweet potatoes, zucchini, and string beans, and Kate brought in the rolls. Keith sat at the table next to his father, kicking his feet in excitement. He had volunteered to say grace and was instructing everyone where to sit. Carol was honored that Keith wanted her by his side and gave him a sweet tap on his knee to stop him from kicking his feet. He obliged, clasped his hands, lowered his head, and slowly said, "Thanks, God, for this food, all my candy, and for dessert. Pray for Mommy, Daddy, my sister, and Auntie Carol, too. Amen."

They all said "Amen" and lightly clapped. Kevin proudly patted Keith's head. Carol noticed how festive the table looked. The white tablecloth was embroidered with a snowflake design, more so fitted for Christmas than Easter. She gave Kristin a pass on that. The tall red water glasses glistened in the sunlight. They were elegant and looked more like chalices. The wineglasses were goblet sized. The silverware was wrapped inside a fancily tied red-cloth napkin, and the centerpiece was a round glass sculpture with shiny colored-glass marbles in the middle and four thin glass branches extending toward the ceiling, each with a lit white candle on the end. The china looked to be hand painted with an intricate floral design and was gold plated around the edges. Carol complimented Kristin on the table setting, and she responded that they hadn't hosted a formal dinner in a few years, ever since they had joined the country club. Kristin saw Kevin was staring down, scooping string beans on to Keith's plate, and rolled her eyes at Carol.

Carol stared into the gas-lit fireplace in the living room, entranced by the jiggling flames, and thought of Uncle Sam. Her window of opportunity was growing short, and she wanted to touch upon the subject before dessert. Almost everyone had been done chewing for a while, except Kevin, who kept going for one slice of ham after another, as if today were his last day on Earth. Protecting Edna was Carol's highest priority, even if that meant putting Kristin in a compromising position. Edna always diligently had Carol's back, and she'd do the same for her, as if they had an immutable covenant that would never flounder under the tests of time. Edna had even called her in the morning and encouraged her to grasp life and seek out Tom but joked that she should wait until the hummus completely left her system. Carol's allegiance was to Edna, and she would unabashedly have to render Kristin as collateral damage to complete her mission.

"Have you talked to Uncle Sam lately? How has he been?" Carol asked, staring intently at Kevin. She could sense Kristin's eyes looking at her in sheer horror.

Kevin stoically sat there, stalling for time, as he rubbed his mouth and chin repeatedly with his napkin. The silence was broken by the strangest of parties. "Uncle Sam is really sick!" bellowed little Kate. Everyone's eyes looked at her and then darted to one another. This was a totally unexpected scenario from what Carol had played out in her head. Little Kate was a messenger from God. Perhaps Edna had been right. Carol's mother was up in heaven warmly shining down on her and had enrolled Kate as her angel of mercy. She had to capitalize on this gift quickly.

"Sick? Is it just a bad cold kind of sick or something else?" Carol asked, as her head twisted in Kevin and Kristin's direction.

Kevin gave Carol a puzzled look and asked, "Edna hasn't been keeping you up? I don't understand."

Carol couldn't tell whether he was being sincere or playing along so as not to incriminate himself. At this point her main concern was that Edna find out, preferably from her father. Carol shook her head, leaned toward Kevin, and folded her hands together. He told her the exact story Kristin had told her, pausing to gauge Carol's reaction and to see whether she might interject with a question. He kept repeating that the prognosis was good if there weren't any setbacks from the surgery, which was slated to occur in four days. It was time for Carol to put on an Oscar-worthy performance.

"Why doesn't Edna know? She's his daughter. It doesn't matter. I don't care about the reason. You have to call him now and demand that he lets her know. Immediately! You have a great deal of influence over Uncle Sam, and you have to use it now, Kevin. It's the right thing to do. Put yourself in her place. How would you feel? Finding out that your father had not one but two major surgeries without your knowledge goes against any principle this family has ever known," Carol frantically exclaimed. She looked toward Kristin, who was undoubtedly impressed by Carol's acting ability and relieved she wasn't revealed as the source.

Kristin didn't have to be persuaded and followed Carol's vociferous lead, "Honey, Carol is right. I'd be terribly hurt and upset if one of my parents kept me in the dark, especially about something so serious. It's not like this is idle gossip we're discussing here. Please say something to Uncle Sam. Don't put Carol, or yourself for that matter, into the painful position of telling Edna."

Kevin respectfully listened. Both Carol and Kristin were overwhelmingly convincing, and he couldn't logically offer any excuse to defend Uncle Sam. To do so would only make him look bad. He was skilled in a courtroom, but this judge and jury wasn't going to cut him any slack, and he had no choice but to acquiesce to their demands. He nodded, grabbed the cordless phone, and dialed Uncle Sam's number. Carol could hear Uncle Sam's booming voice answer the phone, and Kevin walked into the den to speak privately with him.

Kristin smiled, walked over to Carol, and topped off her goblet of wine in a passive show of victory. Carol picked up her glass, raised it to her in appreciation, and took a well-deserved gulp. She was well on her way to absolution, and when Kristin had reinforced her stance and followed it up with her own opinion, it instantly had become two versus one, and Kevin's odds were greatly diminished. Her sister-in-law had become her advocate, just when Carol was about to give her up. The irony of it all gave Carol goose bumps. Kristin walked over to Kate, who had sat there quietly, as if by divine design, during the whole discussion; gave her a big kiss on the top of her head; and told her, "You are our little angel." Carol couldn't help notice how luminous her niece's smile was.

Kevin was in the den talking with Uncle Sam for quite some time. Carol wondered whether he was complicit in some kind of plot with Uncle Sam. He had appeared unsure of what to say until Kate had spilled the beans. If so, the situation could be merely as benevolent as Uncle Sam not wanting Edna to worry and a case of Kevin wrongfully abiding by his wishes. It felt peculiar to depict her brother as being that blind, and it didn't seem logical for that to be the case. He could innocently have been under the impression that his uncle would have surely told his own daughter about his medical plight. Either way, Carol wouldn't fully exonerate him until she had a chance to examine the facts more fully.

Kevin came back into the room with the good news that Sam was going to call Edna later that night to disclose everything that had been going on. Sam had been reluctant to do so, but Kevin convinced him otherwise. Kevin didn't go into specifics, but Carol was pleased with the outcome for the most part. The only lingering doubt she had centered on why the conversation took over half an hour if Uncle Sam's only motive was to simply protect Edna from worrying. Why would that take so long?

Carol gave Kevin a hug as Kristin brought out the pies, which had been warming in the oven. Keith ran behind her with a can of whipped cream, and Kate followed with a tub of chocolate ice cream. Everyone in the parade was all smiles. Kristin gave Kate a slice of apple pie, and she shoved it in front of her stuffed bunny, which was seated in the chair next to her. They all laughed loudly at the sweet gesture. Even though Carol's anxiety wasn't completely relieved, she couldn't have been more content about how the day's events had unfolded. What had appeared to be an unsolvable conundrum had evolved into a satisfyingly fortuitous resolution.

Chapter 15

It had been three hours since Carol had awoken, and she was concerned that Edna hadn't called yet. Surely Uncle Sam had called his daughter by now. The night before, Kevin had given the impression that the phone call would be imminent. Maybe Uncle Sam had a change of heart, or perhaps Edna was tied up at the office and had missed his call.

Carol was getting anxious and decided to go for a run to relieve her stress. She put on her running outfit and ran down the stairs to the front door. As her hand touched the doorknob, she froze, as the possibility of missing Edna's call while she was out overcame her. She decided to forge ahead with her run, as she desperately needed to wash away the food-and-drink sins she'd committed over the weekend.

Just as she opened the door, the phone rang. She dashed to the kitchen, saw it was Edna on the line, gave a deep sigh, and picked it up. Edna was quite upset. She told Carol her father had called a few minutes before with the news that he was to be operated on this Thursday. He said he didn't want to spoil her Easter and wanted to wait until it was over to inform her. Carol feigned surprise but didn't want to overact, in the event that Edna may surprise her with a question, which she hadn't yet rehearsed in her head. She asked Edna what she could do to help, and Edna informed her that her father was driving down to Dearborn alone and would stay at her house Wednesday night.

His operation was scheduled for seven the next morning, and Edna asked her if she could keep her company at the hospital until the doctors informed her how the surgery had gone. "You didn't have to ask. Of course I will," Carol responded.

Edna profusely thanked her and apologized because she had to rush off the phone. "You're always there for me. I'll fill you in on more details later. I forgot I had a meeting," Edna added, and then the line fell silent.

Carol stood there holding the receiver and hadn't realized that both her arm and neck were tangled in the long cord. She felt like she was tied up in a lasso at a rodeo. Her mother always preferred the kitchen phone, and Carol hardly ever used it, but it had been much closer to her than the upstairs cordless phone when Edna had called. While extricating herself from the dastardly cord, Carol wondered why Edna hadn't mentioned Uncle Sam's prior hip-replacement operation, along with Kevin's role pertaining to it. Perhaps Sam had omitted it on purpose, or Edna was so flustered she had forgotten to fill in the blanks. It was an integral part of the story, sequentially connecting all the dots. An ominous cloud would be hanging over things if that portion was left untold. Carol vowed never to use that phone again, unless it was to strangle herself, and went out for her run.

It was around dinnertime when Edna called back. She sounded more upbeat, as she had scoured the Web for hours regarding heart valve replacement surgery and was confident that her father would pull through just fine. She joked that the depth of her knowledge about the procedure was now so extreme that she could perform it herself, chewing gum, with her eyes shut, while standing on one leg, in heels. Carol was relieved to hear the positive attitude, and Edna's laugh, but knew it was her worrisome cousin's way to mask her true feelings. Still, Carol didn't mind hearing the façade. After all, they say laughter is the best medicine, and besides, Edna was the queen of the masquerade.

"It'll be all right. We have to be thankful they found out that he needed a new valve before it was too late. You never told me how they found out," Carol coyly asked, as she wanted to know how Uncle Sam had spun the story to Edna.

Edna paused for a moment and offered, "Huh...you know, I never asked. I was in such a state of shock that I forgot. He'll be here in less than two days, and I was more concerned with his current state of health and how he was going to get here. He was strangely insistent on sleeping at a nearby motel instead of the house. Why wouldn't he want to sleep in familiar surroundings? It took all of my powers to convince him to stay with me. I had to pick up another line a few times, and I was so nervous that every time I picked the phone back up I lost my train of thought. I'll ask him about that for sure. I assume it was at a checkup near where he lives, and he felt the level of care was superior at Henry Ford. Years ago he had his gallbladder taken out there, and he couldn't say enough good things about the doctors and nurses. Hey! Contact that Tom guy! It'll give us something to talk about Thursday. I gotta go. Nick's buzzing me on my cell. I'll see you Thursday."

Carol could understand Edna forgetting to ask. However, why wouldn't Sam tell his daughter that information? Carol would have to be in limbo for a couple of more days.

* * *

It was around a six forty-five p.m. Carol sat in bed with her knees bent, her laptop and phone by her side, clutching Tom's business card, trying to decide whether to call or email him. She already had firmly decided to take some course of action, rather than let the opportunity slip by. There she was, in the same bedroom all these years—the comforting spot where her heart had skipped beats as a teenager. She reminisced about all the crushes she'd had, the euphoria of lying in bed and smilingly staring up at the ceiling after her first kiss ever with Bobby Cheever, as well as the heartbreak scene of her lying facedown, sobbing into her pillow, when her boyfriend of three weeks, Steve Roscoe, had broken up with her, as her mother rubbed her back and gently consoled her.

A phone call to Tom would appear very forward, so she decided to email him. She rationalized that it would be forward enough if she eventually traveled to Maine to see him.

She sent him a cordial note to say that it was nice to meet him, asked him how the rest of his vacation was, and wished him well on his new venture. She really didn't stress over the exact wording, as it was strictly a reaching-out overture, so she kept it short and sweet. Her most hopeful result was a timely response; anything to keep the lines of communication open would suffice, and any romantic implication would be a big bonus.

Carol pressed the "send" button then clicked on the TV. Despite having two hundred channels in her cable package, she found nothing of interest and finally settled on a *CSI: Miami* rerun. She always found comedic value in that show because the plots were so farfetched and the acting was so atrocious.

Suddenly her incoming email alert pinged, and she peered at her laptop in earnest. It was from Tom. It had only been seven minutes since she had sent the email, and her heart raced as she opened it. It read, "Where are you and what are you wearing?" Carol gushed and put her hand over her mouth. She knew it had been too good to be true and closed her laptop in disappointment. Her blood boiled—how could she have misjudged him so badly? How could she be so infatuated by such a slime ball? She got up to leave the bedroom, as she didn't want to ruin any memories she had there. Certainly, email dirty talk wasn't on her agenda. Her email pinged again, and she debated whether to open it up. Her curiosity won out, and she angrily opened it up. It read, "So very sorry. I hit the wrong button by accident. My phone icons are so tiny, and I don't have my reading glasses with me. We decided to extend our time here for two more days. If you haven't eaten yet, will you please come join us? That's why I asked what you were wearing and if you're close by. Call me!"

Carol laughed at herself for having been so presumptuous. She had run through a gamut of emotions in a few moments. She reached for the phone and called Tom. He answered on the first ring and furthered explained, "Hi. Heaven knows what you must have extrapolated from that first message. I'm sitting in our dark hotel bar, and I'm terrible enough typing with this phone—never mind without my glasses. We decided to visit Ann Arbor tomorrow, and I was able to get tickets to the Wings game tomorrow night. The weather looks awesome! We may even go fishing for a few hours, too. We have a rental car and can meet you for dinner, if you're up to it on such short notice. I didn't want you to have to get all dressed up if you were already settled in for the night. Of course, the boys are old enough that they may even appreciate a night away from their boring uncle. I can just meet you by myself."

Carol laughed and blurted out, "I started to write you off. Your excuse seems plausible enough, though. It appears your smartphone made you look dumb. For a moment I didn't know what to think. I suppose we can meet somewhere. What do you feel like?"

Tom excitedly responded, "It doesn't matter. I have a GPS in my rental. Somewhere comfy that has charm and tradition and is far from pretentious."

Carol had just the place in mind. "How about Mueller's Grill in Dearborn? It fits the description, and it's right on Michigan Avenue, so you won't have to make a lot of confusing turns. Unfortunately I've been the victim of a rogue GPS before. Those suckers aren't a hundred-percent accurate, you know. I'll email you the address, in a large font," she teased. "Wow, it sounds like you're the only person in there. Does eight thirty sound good?"

Tom laughed and said, "It's just me and the bartender. I haven't even ordered yet. I was obsessively staring at my phone when he passed by, hoping you'd call. The boys wanted to check out some sports bar. I had to make a few time-consuming phone calls regarding the inn, so I passed. I'm going to call my nephews now and let them know they're on their own. I'm looking forward to seeing you."

Carol was elated by the impromptu meeting with Tom. She had been getting ready to make a boring grilled chicken salad to eat alone in her kitchen. Now she was about to go out on a date with a guy she had met two days ago. Her mundane routine wasn't just broken; it was shattered. She caught her breath and wondered whether this was really a date. An old-fashioned date is made days in advance, for a Saturday night, when a man comes to your house, rings your doorbell, gives you flowers, opens the passenger-side door for you, and takes you to a fancy restaurant, where he made a reservation at a perfectly situated table. This was a last-minute meeting, on a Monday, at a burger joint, in a booth, she told herself.

Carol went into closet overdrive, as she whipped three pairs of jeans, half a dozen tops, and three belts onto the bed. She ran into the bathroom and turned on the shower then spun back into the closet, grabbed a black skirt, looked at it, and decided to put it back. She was like a whirling dervish as she jumped into the shower. Tonight would be special, with no generic hair-and-bath products; she'd use her expensive Clinique collection. She laughingly concluded that this was a date after all.

She decided on a pair of designer jeans she had irrationally splurged on, five margaritas deep, while vacationing with Edna in Playa del Carmen; a black short-sleeve V-neck top; a silver belt with rhinestones; and black pumps. The only jewelry she wore was a thin silver bracelet on her right wrist and small silver hoop earrings. No need to break into the trinket arsenal yet, as they were only going to a bare-bones place. Her hair was down and parted to the side. The other day it had been styled more in a "bangs look." Tonight she would tantalize him with an alluring, intermittent, hand-swept hair flip. Carol paused to look at every mirror in the house on her way out, grabbed her keys and her black shoulder bag, and skipped down the steps.

* * *

She walked into the bar but saw no sign of Tom. She seated herself in a booth near the back and checked her lipstick, as if things had changed since the ten-minute ride over or when she had just checked it in the parking lot.

"Are you getting prettied up just for little old me?" a voice out of nowhere slyly asked. Carol looked up to see Tom, sans cap, his curly locks begging to be petted. He was wearing a short-sleeve gray golf shirt, jeans, and black loafers.

Carol smiled and playfully replied, "I guess I'm busted. The answer is yes. A girl has to look pretty, you know."

Tom sat down and complimented her looks and her choice of where to meet. He went on about how easy the place had been for him to find and how the decor was very authentic and full of character.

While his eyes danced around in amazement, Carol responded, "Face it, Tom. It doesn't matter how many fancy adjectives you use, it's obvious that you're drawn to dive bars. What is it? The cheap prices, the easy women, or both?"

They both looked at each other for a second. Apparently, Tom was trying to figure out how serious she was. Carol was anxiously awaiting his response, as she had purposely tried to startle him. Their eyes met, and both started to grin, and when that turned into laughter, Tom placed his hand on hers for a fleeting moment, and frankly admitted, "I believe, for the first time in forty-five years, I've met my match, You scare me in a good way, Carol, if you want to take solace in that."

Carol explained to him the place had a legendary reputation for grilling the best burgers in Detroit, and people came from miles around to eat them. They both ordered plain hamburgers and a round of beers. The chatter flowed easily; it had been a long time since Carol had felt so at ease with a man. She learned the most important fact right from the start—that Tom was never married and had no children. Everything said after that was music to her ears. He had grown up in Malden, Massachusetts, a blue-collar working-class city, situated about seven miles north of downtown Boston; attended public school until high school; then went to Malden Catholic High and then Boston College, where he had majored in economics. Even though he had lived on campus, he wanted to be near his close-knit family, so he chose to remain in Boston instead of moving to another state. He had an older sister, Beth, and a brother, John, as well as a younger brother, Chris. All were married with kids and still in their first marriages. Tom had been engaged once when he was in his twenties; it didn't work out, but it was an amicable split. His last relationship ended two years ago and wasn't so clean. He and his girlfriend had been together seven years off and on, had lived together for the last nine months of their relationship, and at the end had argued over personal belongings as well as some unsettled financial issues. He heard she had moved to California with her new boyfriend and hadn't seen her since. He was the one to break it off, as his instincts told him it wasn't meant to be.

Carol reciprocated with highlights of her life story, and Tom listened to every sequence with keen interest, his blue eyes appearing so deeply caring. He deliberately didn't interrupt her. He crafted his questions with such sincerity; most of them, respectfully, were about her mother. Every mannerism and action he displayed exceeded Carol's expectations. He was also intrigued that she was a piano teacher and told her it took a special gift of patience to teach, which was bestowed upon her by God.

Carol didn't want the night to end. Her heart raced at every word Tom uttered. He could have sneezed all over her, and she would have bathed in it, she grossly thought. He didn't appear self-centered and just referenced his professional accomplishments a couple of times, more for Carol's benefit, so she could better follow the story, than his own. Carol thought that was a great quality and told him so outright.

The bartender walked over to them and wisecracked, "I hate to interrupt the Mutual Admiration Society meeting, but I'm calling last call a little early tonight. Everyone must have overindulged this weekend. I have to clean up for a half-hour or so. Please feel free to stay." He grabbed the empties and walked back with two fresh ones, without even waiting for a response from them. Carol suspected he was a romantic who knew something was in the grease-filled air.

Tom raised his bottle to Carol. "This guy must be psychic," he joked.

They continued talking for some time, and the conversation turned to the prospect of Carol coming to Maine. Tom appeared a little flustered as he timidly asked if she was coming out, as if he were afraid to hear the answer.

Carol thought it was cute and responded, "Hey, big boy, I promise I'll work on it. Is that a pout I detect? Your lower lip is kind of curling up there." She teasingly poked at his lip with her finger, and he slowly grabbed her hand away, caressing her palm with his fingers. "Is this officially the first time we've held hands?" she said. "We may need to throw the red challenge flag, like in the NFL, and have a referee look through that peep-show machine to determine if it is."

The bartender walked up to the booth to clear off their plates, smiled as he noticed there wasn't one crumb left, and said his two cents' worth. "I officially rule no. All fingers have to be entangled for five seconds or more. That was a two-second touchy feely. You folks must love my impeccable timing."

All three gave out a hearty laugh. Tom cracked, "You see, the character in these places I love to frequent, which you describe as dive bars, is ingrained in the people who work here also, not just in the wood design. They make these bars so special."

Tom got up to pay the bill with his credit card. The bartender pointed to the cash-only sign, and Tom fumbled through his wallet, only finding a five-dollar bill. Carol had forgotten to inform him of that earlier. She had known for years that they didn't take credit cards but was so caught up in the moment that it had slipped her mind. She slowly pranced up to the bar, slapped fifty bucks on it, and teased, "You get the next one." She headed toward the exit, purposely over-shaking her behind, while her hands reached up to the ceiling.

Tom followed, saying he hadn't been embarrassed like that in a long time and wanted to repay her. Carol silently wished it were in trade, with a kiss. She impulsively rushed toward him and pressed her lips hard against his. They kissed for a few seconds and glanced around to see if the bartender was looking. They both embraced and instinctively guessed right which way to turn their heads so their noses wouldn't collide. Tom smiled, and his hands softly touched her cheeks as the two passionately kissed in the dark, desolate parking lot, beautifully serenaded by a concerto of semi-truck airbrakes and a smattering of blaring car horns from busy Michigan Avenue. Carol didn't mind one bit. To her, they were in Maui, surrounded by lush greenery, exotic birds cawing, and feeling the refreshing spray from a nearby waterfall as the beaming sun poured over their naked bodies. Still embracing, they broke their lengthy kiss for a moment.

Tom looked toward the entrance of the bar and boastfully said, "There isn't any need for the red flag on that. We had it covered!"

They walked to her car and kissed again. Tom opened the door for her and made sure she was seated safely before closing it. Carol awkwardly rolled down the window, and Tom was amused by the effort she displayed turning the handle so quickly. "I haven't seen one of those in a while. Remind me to stay away from your left hand," he snapped, as he went into a mock boxing stance.

Carol began to realize that it might be a while before she saw Tom again. She could tell by his puppy-dog eyes that he was thinking the same thing.

"What's next? How do we figure this out?" he calmly asked.

Carol rubbed his arm. She didn't want to seem too sad. She forced out a crooked smile and said, "I really believe we may have something here. Obviously we have no choice but to take things slowly. If there's a will, there's a way. My mother always told me that. Let's work on it one day at a time, and we'll connect sooner than later. My schedule almost grinds to a halt a week or so after Memorial Day. I know your plate is full. The inn will consume your time. There's a ray of sunshine—it'll make the time pass faster until we see each other again. I promise to keep in touch any way I can."

Tom smiled, and nodded his head, keeping it more down than up. "I promise too," he reassuringly said, as he touched the top of her hand. He turned around and slowly walked away, turning back to make sure Carol's car started. Carol watched as he got into his rental car and drove onto Michigan Avenue, and she pulled out behind him.

"Not again!" Carol screamed out loud, as she followed Tom down the road in the middle lane. She floored the engine and switched to the right lane. Tom was slowly driving ahead, completely unaware of the madwoman beeping her horn behind him. Carol caught up to him at the next stoplight, and Tom rolled down his window. He smiled when he realized it was Carol struggling to lower her window. She popped her head out the car window. "What's the name? What's the name of the inn? You never told me," she frantically yelled.

Tom leaned in and yelled back, "The Nautical Inn!"

They shared one last smile as the light turned green and they went their separate ways.

Chapter 16

Carol wondered what Tom was doing as she drove to Henry Ford Hospital to meet Edna. She had decided to wait until this morning to fill her cousin in on the other night with Tom. It was past nine, and her uncle was already in surgery. She found Edna sitting in the waiting room texting away. Her phone pinged, and she saw it was a text from Edna.

"Should I bother to open this, or do you want to tell me?" she asked Edna.

Edna laughed and said, "I was texting you to pick up some coffee on the way. We can head down to the cafeteria now if you like."

Carol thought it was a great idea, as the cafeteria was a better spot to chat, certainly more upbeat. The waiting room was very quiet, and too many people were milling around, all looking worried and morose.

They got their coffee and found a table in the corner. Edna was very nervous as she told Carol about the night before. Uncle Sam had appeared so distant, like she no longer knew her own father. His gait was measurably slow, as if he were unsure of his balance. He claimed it was due to his arthritis getting worse. He acted as if the house were haunted and wanted to sleep on the hard pull-out couch downstairs instead of the comfortable bed in her parents' old room. "Wouldn't that aggravate his condition even more?" Edna asked Carol. He barely had touched his food and had passed on dessert. She attributed his actions to his dwelling on the surgery.

Even scarier, in the middle of the night, she had heard him sobbing. She went down to check on him and found him lying on the couch, talking out loud. She couldn't understand what he was saying, as his sobbing was so loud. She noticed he was rocking a picture of her mother in his arms, and she quietly went back upstairs, because she didn't want him to see her, as she had started to cry.

"He probably misses her very much, and being in the house again brought back all the memories he has of them being together. I think it's sweet that he still has those emotions for your mother. Don't forget, we have to consider that he's pushing eighty, and he's not exactly getting a tooth taken out today," Carol consolingly said.

Edna took comfort in that, sipped her coffee, and added, "You're probably right. It was just unsettling to see. Even today, before they wheeled him into the operating room, he said something odd. They already had him under sedation, so I don't know if that affected his thinking. He told me he was sorry and that he loved me. I asked him, 'Sorry for what?' He looked like he wanted to tell me something but decided against it and waved his hand as if to eliminate what he was about to say from his mind."

Carol smiled and said, "There comes a time when we become the parent and they the child. Perhaps that threshold was just crossed. It's a role reversal of massive proportions. Sometimes it happens overnight, which tests your will even more, and you have to be more caring and understanding than you thought you'd ever have to be in your life."

Edna looked at Carol and laughed. "So now you're Confucius, and I'm Grasshopper? The doctor said the operation should take four hours minimum, possibly five. He'll have to be in here for about a week and then come back for follow-ups periodically. We have another three hours to kill at least. Nick's not coming until early this evening. Did you make contact with you know who?"

"What do you mean by 'contact'? Would you mean lip-locking in Mueller's parking lot this past Monday night? Would you consider that contact?" Carol asked, raising her eyebrows and smirking nonstop.

Edna leaned back, bent the back of the plastic chair, pushed her lips together, and scratched her nose. "Are you pulling my chain? How could that happen? I thought he was back east," she excitedly said, as she lightly punched Carol in the arm. "Yeah, and then you snapped out of your dream, all sweaty, with drool on your pillow. You have to wake up early in the morning to fool me."

Carol sat there, still smirking, and exclaimed, "I completely swear on the Bible. It's one-hundred-percent true! I figured this was the best time to tell you." She filled Edna in on the whole story from the beginning. Edna sat there laughing, watching her cousin's face all aglow, as she spared no detail. Edna was so happy for her and looked out the window, with her eyes as big as saucers. Carol knew what that gesture meant. Maybe there was something to Edna's theory that her mother was mystically watching over her.

"I'm telling you—I'm right about that. Aunt Mary, keep doing what you're doing for my sweet cousin please," Edna pleaded.

Carol changed the subject and asked Edna about the wonderful flowerbed on her mother's grave. She was just getting ready to ask her at the bar the other day, right before they had bumped into Tom. Edna responded that she didn't know who was responsible for it. Two years ago she had gone to visit the grave, and there was this beautiful creation, brightening up the whole area in striking splendor. She assumed her father had it done, but when she asked, he was evasive and never implicitly took credit for it, so she dropped the subject. She concluded it had to be him. Who else could it be?

Carol and Edna went back to the waiting room. It was past noon, and less crowded, as people had left for lunch. Edna knew Carol didn't have much time left and hoped they'd hear some news shortly. They found two seats together, and Edna was curious how Carol and Tom had left things.

"One day at a time. After all, it was just one date," Carol rationally responded.

It was Edna's turn now to offer advice, solicited or not. "You have to make the best of it. I mean, managing your time and balancing your emotions. At this point you're just *interested* in Tom. You're not head over heels in love. Although, I must deduce, that things are off to a positive start. Let love naturally nurture at its own crazy pace. The current separation in distance will better allow that to occur...for now," she said.

Carol smiled, and they carefully butted heads, leaving them leaning against each other.

* * *

Edna lifted her head as a man wearing surgical scrubs walked toward her. She quickly stood up, and the doctor gave her a big smile. "He came through fine. There were no complications. We have him in the recovery room now. He should be in there at least two hours, and then he'll be moved to the cardiac intensive care unit. It'll be at least dinnertime before he's all settled. I suggest, if you haven't eaten, to go out and enjoy the beautiful day and then come back," he suggested with a smile.

Edna and Carol hugged each other after hearing the great news. "I wish we could go out to celebrate together, but I have a piano lesson to prepare for shortly," Carol regretfully said. "I'll check back with you tonight. You and Nick should go somewhere nice later." They hugged once more, and Carol walked away thinking, *Any time you leave Henry Ford or any hospital with a smile, that's reason enough to celebrate.*

* * *

A week had passed, and Uncle Sam was convalescing at Edna's house until his first follow-up visit, which was in a few days. Carol had visited him a couple of times in the hospital and was amazed at his progress. Due to the faulty valve, his heart had been working overtime, and Edna said he had appeared gaunt and lackluster before the operation. The day before he was released, his color was excellent, and he even danced with one of the nurses. Apparently, Nick and Uncle Sam had gotten along fine, and he even invited Nick to go fishing over Memorial Day Weekend.

Carol could hear the satisfaction in Edna's voice. It was important for her to have a tighter bond with her father. She was always disappointed that he had moved out shortly after he went through the twelve steps at AA into a studio apartment in Allen

Park. She couldn't understand why he would forgo living in a house he already owned to pay someone else rent. He had paid the mortgage balance off right before he left so Edna would always have a roof over her head. It was very noble, but it didn't soften the hard feelings she harbored.

She had watched in silence as her mother helped carry his drunken body into bed and made excuses for him when he was late for a job or when he didn't show up at all, or when he embarrassed someone with an off-color remark. It would make her upset to see her mother continue to accept his misgivings, and she didn't understand the concept of how someone could love another so deeply that they looked the other way. Carol thought how nice it would be if all the emotions her cousin had festering inside for years went away and she could wipe the slate clean.

The doorbell rang, and the UPS guy was on the stoop holding a package. Carol opened the door and signed for the delivery. She saw the return address was from Kennebunkport, and her pulse raced. She opened the box right away, and inside she found a smart-looking, violet, collared shirt with a "Nautical Inn" insignia. There was a note inside from Tom that read, "Hope you like this sample. I also have jackets, aprons, T-shirts, key chains, and beer and coffee mugs, all in assorted colors, but you have to come out here to collect them." She smiled, wiped away a few tears, and immediately tried on the shirt. It was a medium and fit pretty well—a little snug in the chest but far from tight.

She texted Tom a picture of herself wearing it; she was all smiles. They had kept in touch daily, and her fondness for him had grown a notch with every call, text, and email. The week before, Edna was firm in her belief that it was too early to label it love, but Carol wasn't so sure. All she knew was that a sublime feeling endlessly bubbled inside her—a warm scintillating whirlpool of passion, lust, and desire that pervaded every brainwave and heartbeat. Every sense was on high alert.

Tom had a salutary effect on her, which was so evident. Her wrinkles seemed to vanish, her legs flowed faster when she ran, and her psyche was very optimistic. She had transcended the boundary of love and wanted to bravely forge ahead. She peacefully surrendered to her feelings, without any trepidation or fear of being overly quixotic. Edna seemingly could remotely control her feelings with the click of a button. Edna's cautionary plea for Carol to take things slowly, however, was swept aside by a tidal wave of loving emotion.

Carol couldn't keep it inside her any longer. It was now the first Saturday of May, Kentucky Derby Day, and as she watched the pre-race party on TV, she felt inspired by all the women wearing those uncomfortable-looking hats, sipping their mint juleps, and thoroughly enjoying themselves while standing in a crowd of more than a hundred thousand inebriated horseracing fans. She decided to join the party and made herself a vodka and grapefruit. Then she phoned Chris to make plans for visiting him. He was glad to hear her voice and excited that she and Edna were coming out. He insisted they stay at his house the entire time. That gave Carol the opening she needed to mention Tom, as she had waited to tell her brother about him until she felt comfortable in her feelings.

Chris was still at the deli and poured himself a glass of red wine in a paper cup to hide the fact that he was drinking on the job. He didn't want his sister to drink alone, or so he claimed. He was a fool for romance and relished her story, etching every detail into his memory. Chris had no idea a new inn was opening in Kennebunkport and teased Carol that he and Arthur should book a room there before her visit to check it out—and to scope out Tom.

"Don't you dare!" she ordered, knowing it would never happen anyway.

During the conversation, Chris assured her that they had such a large circle of friends that Edna would never feel like a third wheel; she'd be constantly entertained. He referred to them as a barhopping, roving gang of straights, gays, transsexuals, blacks, whites, psychotics, and narcissists. Carol heartily laughed at Chris's depiction, as she contrasted that wild scene in her head with the stuffy Kentucky socialites partying on her TV screen. She heard voices ordering food in the background, and left her brother to his customers, promising to follow up with her exact travel arrangements.

Chapter 17

It was Mother's Day, the first one without Carol's mother alive, and she was feeling very melancholic. She went over to the Keurig coffee machine, poured water into it, placed a K-Cup in the designated spot, and waited for it to brew. She had recently bought the machine figuring she rarely had company, and making a pot for just herself was a waste, as she had no one to share it with. As she stared at the coffee dripping into her solitary mug, a feeling of loneliness washed over her. She wished anyone would be there to keep her company. The mailman, the neighbor next door she didn't even know, one of her student's parents—she wouldn't discriminate, as long as she heard another voice. She sipped her coffee, satisfied with the result but not with the quiet, when the phone rang. It was Edna. She was on her way to pick her up to go to the cemetery together, and she wanted Carol to have a cup of coffee ready for her upon her arrival. At least she was getting her money's worth out of the coffee machine, she thought.

When they arrived at the cemetery, it was packed. This time they were both sensibly dressed in sneakers and jeans. It had rained heavily the evening before, and the cemetery grounds were muddy. They did the same routine as before, going to Carol's mother's grave first, as it was closer to the entrance. They each placed a tulip plant on the grave and prayed. Carol was less emotional this time. She missed her mother just as strongly, but all the horrid images, such as her mother being found dead on the parking lot pavement, were not as implanted in her memory, and the grave itself, now fully covered with grass, appeared more blended in with the scenery, which further assisted in camouflaging her recollections.

Edna held her arm as they both turned to walk toward Helen's grave. While approaching it, they saw Kevin standing by it in the distance, all alone. He was uncontrollably sobbing. They stopped in their tracks and looked at each other. He appeared much more distraught than when his own mother recently passed. Carol found her brother's current state of despair rather odd, and she could distinguish from Edna's expression that she felt the same way. She didn't want to startle or embarrass her brother and waited to see if Edna wanted to move forward. Edna grabbed her, and they ducked behind a skinny tree.

"This is stupid, I know," Edna whispered. "He could easily see us here, but I don't know what to do. Should we run to the car and come back later? I'm kind of freaked out, to be honest. My mother has been dead for almost twenty years. I don't even cry nearly that deeply over her anymore. He's crying like she just passed yesterday, and he's making me look bad. What do you think?"

Carol paused a moment to think. "Yes, it's a bit creepy, I must admit. We can discuss this later. It sounds like things are quieting down. Let's talk loudly from here to announce ourselves. It'll give him a moment to regain his composure. For God's sake, let's get away from this tree."

The women stepped forward chattering loudly, and they saw Kevin wipe the tears away from his eyes. Edna yelled out his name, and he turned around to greet them with a smile. It seemed like it took forever to reach him, and they all gave one another an awkward hug.

Kevin was impeccably attired in a dark-gray suit with a red, patterned tie. His lapel and sleeves were wet from tears. He tried in earnest to recover quickly from his sobs after being taken so off guard. "The flowerbed's awesome. We should do this for Mom's grave," Kevin emphatically said, in an attempt to distract their attention from him.

Carol nodded and asked him where Kristin and the kids were. Kevin informed her that they were at home. He and the kids had made breakfast in bed for Kristin and had baked a Bundt cake for dessert later, after they had an early dinner at the country club.

Carol's mind drifted to poor Kristin. She despised the country-club scene and now had to be subjected to it on Mother's Day. It was her own fault, though. If she voiced her opinions more strongly, on a variety of issues, she wouldn't find herself in these predicaments. There didn't appear to be much in the way of compromise in her brother's marriage, from his side, and Kristin had to assert herself more. How peculiar—usually a sister would defend her brother along such lines, but Carol actually felt sorry for Kristin, and she didn't feel the least bit disloyal, especially after Kevin's recent behavior. To make matters worse, he apparently didn't have a clue that there was any discord in his marriage, with his wife obviously choosing to be silent rather than confront him. *The longer Kristin maintains this passive posture, the less likely it'll be that Kevin will resolve his issues before things get to a level of disrepair*, she thought.

Edna and Kevin were discussing their fortieth birthdays, which were coming up later in the summer. Carol suggested a dual celebration, at her house, as they were born weeks apart. It would be more of a family scene than a wild party. Kevin was a little hesitant at first but was still a little woozy after his crying episode and didn't object. "We're not talking Vegas or shots of tequila. We'll have a couple of nicely decorated cakes, and the kids will love it," Carol slyly said, fully knowing that using the kids as leverage was always a game changer.

Kevin looked at his watch and mentioned that he had an arrangement of flowers wilting in his trunk, intended for their mother's grave. He asked Edna briefly about her father and was happy to hear that he was back in Marquette doing fine. They said their goodbyes, and the women watched him drive away. They were in such a state of shock that the tulips were still in their arms. They placed them on the grave, said a prayer, and stood in silence for a few minutes.

"Something is amiss with Kevin. He gets my vote for the most sharply dressed today, though. Why the duds? It's as if they were part of a ritual. Did I mention how creepy he seemed?" Edna observed.

Carol couldn't argue with her and felt the timing was right to fill her in on some of the other things going on with respect to her brother. Perhaps another viewpoint would add some clarity to the situation. She and Kristin were too close to the situation, and Edna would be more objective. "Let's go somewhere to talk," Carol said. "Forgive me for not confiding in you much sooner, but I was hoping things would get resolved favorably and quickly, so I wouldn't have to talk behind my brother's back. However, today's behavior sent me an alert signal, and I believe that talking about things might actually help him, as well as myself."

They drove to a coffee shop, and Carol told her about the whole ordeal, starting from when Kevin had run out of her house after going over the estate, to Kristin's revelations. Carol omitted the sidebar about Uncle Sam's hip operation. A father neglecting to inform his only child about something so severe, and turning instead to his nephew, wasn't right, and Carol still was of the mindset that sheltering her cousin from that was wrong but a necessity for the time being. Edna and her dad recently seemed to be on their way to tightening their relationship, and Carol didn't want to get in the way of that.

Edna always had looked up to Kevin. He had been instrumental in giving her financial advice and helping her resolve numerous household issues. For example, when Edna had new gutters installed, the work was done in a shoddy manner, and they leaked badly. She was unable to get the company that did the work to come back and do the job correctly, as guaranteed, and asked Kevin for assistance. He called the company right away and threatened them with legal recourse, and they fixed the issue the next day.

Edna considered Kevin to be a brother to her. She felt beholden to him for having saved her father's life and felt close to Kevin due to a special bond they shared. Years ago, when both of their mothers were having issues conceiving, they had driven to a legendary church on the outskirts of Quebec City renowned for its miraculous baby-making powers. Their parents had to climb a hundred steps up the bell tower on their knees, stopping at every step to say a prayer. It was a painfully grueling ritual. The Canadian pilgrimage was the last resort their parents had. This was long before the era of artificial means. In those days, kid-starved couples mostly relied on old wives' tales, such as changing sexual positions or embarking upon unappealing diets of liver and the like. Within a month, Helen and Mary became pregnant, and Kevin and Edna were born healthy within a few weeks of each other. The story became part of family lore, often repeated at parties and on holidays. Kevin and Edna were the miracle babies, and Mary and Helen grew more faithful to the church because of that.

Edna's view of Kristin's role in this was much more negative than Carol's or Chris's, which hardly surprised Carol. Edna had been exposed firsthand to her mother's submissive behavior while growing up, and she was very petulant regarding Kristin's similar pacifism. However, she did faintly praise Kristin for coming forward but stressed she had done so to seek assistance. It was the initial step, but Kristin should see to it that the job was finished. Edna suggested a family intervention, which could only be effective with Kristin on board. A united front would be much stronger. Otherwise, Kevin would know his wife was the weakest link and exploit that. Kevin had to see that his wife had taken the leadership reigns to help him not betray him—a stigma that's tough to erase but certainly doable with the visible backing of others.

Carol thought it was a great idea. They both agreed that Kristin had had ample time to take action and confront her husband. Somehow she had managed to suppress her original feelings, against all instinct and common sense, making herself an impediment to fixing the situation. Carol had to convince Kristin to get back on the course she had started but seemingly abandoned. She had morphed into being part of the problem, not the solution. Edna volunteered to be part of the intervention if necessary but stressed that the immediate family was most affected and that the intervention should probably be limited to Kristin, Carol, and Chris, from Skype or speaker phone if he couldn't physically attend.

Carol was very impressed by what Edna had to say. Her opinion was derived from both a personal and professional standpoint. At work, the lawyers handled many divorce and family law cases, and Edna was highly exposed to many unsettling situations, including drug and alcohol issues and physical, psychological, and sexual abuse. Her experience in this area, of course, was mostly relegated to depositions and interviews, but she knew how the cases were handled, along with the strategies implemented to resolve the issues, both inside and outside of the court system. Carol had completely forgotten this component that Edna brought to the table and took greater comfort in her decision to take Edna over the wall, so to speak.

Carol needed a little blind luck. Kristin was guilty of being a bona fide enabler, and if Carol didn't act swiftly, she would share that guilt. Edna had profoundly enlightened her to that fact, and Carol lovingly told her, "Once again, you've come through for me, as you've done countless times. I never tell you enough how much I love and appreciate you."

Edna cut her off and said, "Don't squander the opportunity. Hit Kristin head on tomorrow. It's your only recourse, and let me know what she says. Stop with the lovey-dovey crap. You'd do same for me. Now let me get home to my exciting laundry-filled night. I'd drive, but just to add to my miraculous deeds, I think I'll walk on water with you piggybacked on me."

Edna dropped Carol off, and as she unlocked her front door, her phone rang. It was Tom. She really needed to hear his voice tonight. "Hi," she gleefully said. "It's been a long day, and your voice is just what I need to hear! Tell me something good!"

Tom told her he'd had a wonderful day visiting his mother and seeing the family but was stuffed from nibbling all day and couldn't wait to go for a run the next morning. He was driving up the Maine Turnpike and said he needed to hear Carol's voice before settling into his empty inn.

Carol could relate to what he was feeling. It's not easy spending time with friends or family and then coming home to an empty house. She was glad it was her voice he had sought out and wondered whether there would ever be a time when they'd be happily going home with each other.

Tom went on to say, "I was wondering if you'd object if I came for a visit for this weekend. I got a lot done at the inn last week. The bulk of the furniture arrived, and I hired some key staff. The painters are almost done, and there's an unexpected lull. The bar will be ready next week. We could actually open now, way before target, but the grand-opening date already has been printed in the local newspapers, pamphlets, periodicals, and on the website. I even had kids put fliers on car windshields around Fenway Park during a game, and as far north as downtown Portland. Next weekend there will be quarter-page ads in the Quebec, Boston, New York, Providence, and Hartford newspapers that will run once a week until mid-July."

The boundless excitement in Tom's voice had become contagious as Carol emphatically responded, "That's so great! You sound like you've covered a lot of ground in a short time. You told me you were in over your head. From my perspective, that's not the case. You've devoted a great deal of time, energy, and sweat to the inn. I suppose I can squeeze you in this weekend, but I insist you stay at my house—unless your goal is to continue to properly court me. You could stay at a hotel if you want, but there's only my older brother left alive for you to ask my hand in marriage. I'd like to be a fly on the wall for that!"

Tom let out a chuckle and quickly said, "The anticipation of seeing you will get me through the next few days. I'll be like a prisoner scratching a notch in the wall for every day until he's freed. My thought is to fly in late afternoon on Friday, just in time for happy hour and leave mid-morning on Monday."

Carol responded, "Whatever works best. I'll be here anxiously awaiting your arrival." She further teased, "Try to not drive off the road. Friday will be here before you know it. I feel like a warden, giving you an early release for good behavior."

They both heartily laughed as they hung up. Carol sat on her couch, thinking of the delightful surprise she had just received, and kissed her phone. A frozen smile was planted on her face. Her sneakers tapped the floor, as if they were drumming the countdown until she had Tom in her arms once again.

Chapter 18

It was the Monday morning after Mother's Day. Carol looked at her watch; Kristin was expected to arrive shortly. Edna had given Carol more clarity on the situation than she could have hoped for, and she had to be firm and concise with Kristin. She had texted Kristin the night before but offered little insight as to why she wanted to meet with her. All Kristin knew was it was about Kevin. Carol had to convince Kristin in person to do an intervention. She reasoned that talking over the phone would reduce her powers of persuasion, and luring Kristin to the house was the best way to succeed. She couldn't prevent her sister-in-law from hanging up the phone, but she could try to stop her from leaving if the conversation wasn't productive.

Kristin walked in the front door and called out Carol's name. She located her in the kitchen, a box of muffins in hand, and they gave each other a warm hug. They both had on sneakers and jeans. Kristin said she was still taking tennis lessons, but she was such a novice that she couldn't play with anyone in their circles, because they had played for years and were much more advanced. It had been Kevin's idea that she take lessons so she could fit in more. His heart meant well, but after watching the other girls play, Kristin felt even more isolated, so the lessons were having the opposite effect. Carol thought, *Yet another example of Kevin's pull over her*. After hearing that, she was more determined than ever.

"Did Kevin tell you we ran into him at the cemetery yesterday?" Carol asked. She knew right away that Kristin was unaware and waited for her to respond.

"He told me he was going, and I grabbed my bag to come with him, but he said he wanted to be alone. All week I had assumed we'd go together. Please, don't be mad that I wasn't there. I planned on stopping by on my way home today," Kristin said, her voice shrouded in shame. "I figured that since this was the first Mother's Day since she passed, Kevin wanted to be alone, and I told him I understood."

Carol held Kristin's hand. "You're missing my point," she said. "He never informed you that he saw us. Edna and I saw him at Edna's mother's grave, not my mother's. We found him sobbing uncontrollably at his aunt's grave—an aunt who has been dead a long time. He hadn't even been to his own mother's grave yet. You'd think that would have been his first choice. You had to be there. We watched Kevin for five minutes. It was quite an animated display of sorrow. I'd never known my brother to be so close with my aunt. Uncle Sam—that's a much different story. It was very unsettling to see, and maybe you should be glad you didn't witness it. I'm trying to come to grips with what I saw. Has he ever mentioned my aunt and expanded on the depth of their relationship?" Carol pointedly asked.

"Hardly ever. Years ago, when I had just met your family and Kevin and I were still dating, I asked him about her death. When he told me the horrific way that she had died, I was so saddened and appalled. Poor Edna. It's a terrible topic to bring up, and every time I see her I want to mention it but can't. All I can think is that it may be possible that your mother's recent passing helped release some latent emotions Kevin didn't know he had concerning his aunt. He also could have been crying over both of them at the same time. You don't have to be officially standing over someone's grave to mourn," she offered, in steadfast defense of her husband. "My best friend growing up, Belinda, passed away two years ago from breast cancer. The other week I dropped Kate off at her best friend's house for a sleepover. It reminded me of all the fun times Belinda and I had shared, and I cried the entire way home. I didn't have to be standing over her grave to feel sad."

Carol could relate, as she had found herself many times weeping at home, triggered by a particular moment shared with her mother. Such flashbacks could occur at any place or time, so what Kristin had said could be correct. Nevertheless, Carol was fixated on the fact that Kristin wasn't even in the house for ten minutes and already had made two excuses for Kevin, the first concerning her tennis lessons, the second about yesterday's behavior at the cemetery.

"So the fact he didn't tell you he saw us doesn't bother you? And the fact that he was so shocked to see us there and couldn't wait to leave doesn't bother you either?" she asked, quizzing Kristin like a trial lawyer bullying a witness. *Edna would be proud*, Carol thought.

Kristin's body language showed her discomfort. Her hands were clenched, her elbows leaning against the table. Carol tried to make her feel at ease. "I'm sorry. I didn't ask you to stop by for this—to make you feel uncomfortable or to argue, I mean. We should focus on helping Kevin and ultimately saving your marriage. My interpretation of his actions yesterday may be debatable, but you weren't there. It's my suspicion, from everything you've told me, that Kevin was crying for help yesterday. He looked too despondent to just be mourning. Who his tears were ultimately intended for, we don't know, but what's important to note is that we are alive, with four compassionate ears, along with four welcoming arms between us, and instead he cries to the dead, not us."

"You're right," Kristin said, as she sat back and unfolded her hands. "I kept hoping that whatever had bothered him had passed. I was happy to see his Thursday-night routine had stopped, and the way he responded on Easter when he called Uncle Sam gave me additional hope that he had reclaimed his sanity and that everything once again would be normal in our household. Now I'm not so sure."

Carol incisively stated, "Which is the reason I think an intervention may be best. You, Chris, and I, united in our resolve, would be the most tactful way to go about it. I know that means unveiling yourself as the instigator, but we'll ensure that he perceives you as a savior not a traitor. We have to instill in him the fact that we love him and want to help him, but we can't until he tells us what's going on."

Kristin's hands locked again, as she flagrantly shook her head. "I can't allow it. It would render our marriage useless. I don't think he'd ever trust me again. I hear about all these divorce cases filed on the grounds of irreconcilable differences, and I'd rather take the chance to wait for him to confide in me," she sternly said.

Carol tried to reason with her another way and asked, "What if it's too late by the time he decides to tell you what's going on? You could lose everything by then—that great house, his high-paying job, and your sanity as well as his. All you would have left in the end, maybe, would be a sham of a marriage. The only positive would be that you'd be free of that country club. Can you honestly say without reservation that your marriage is on solid footing?"

Kristin couldn't believe how relentless Carol was. Her face showed she knew Carol was right, but she hadn't expected such a Draconian method of her seeking the truth. The psychological punishment would be too much for her to bear, even if the crime was based on good intentions—that is, if there was any crime committed at all, which was they had yet to confirm.

"This is asking a lot from me," Kristin said. "I have the most to lose. Can you let me monitor things a little longer? I haven't had any new information to tell you in almost a month, or else I absolutely would have. I'm glad you care so deeply about Kevin. Cut me a little slack here. My intent to confide in you had more to do with my sanity. Originally I wrongfully assumed Kevin was cheating on me, and I feel bad about it. I admit I sought out advice, but I just wanted to understand your brother more, not to immediately force any resolution or learn something I may not want to hear."

Carol knew Kristin was trying to placate her with stall tactics and never would follow through with a planned intervention. She tried not to show her disappointment, but Kristin could detect it in her eyes.

"I don't blame you for being disappointed or even angry," Kristin said. "I've already experienced those emotions regarding myself, but I'm not at a crucial breaking point yet. Call me weak, naïve, or irresponsible, but let me cling a little longer to the belief that the man I married, had two great children with, and love may have a secret agenda for the good of mankind and that if he divulged it now it may jeopardize his plans. I'm just not inclined to relinquish that dream at this time, as foolish as it may sound."

The women hugged each other. Carol didn't want her to leave on bad terms, and she knew Kristin felt the same way. "I was considering having a small family celebration for Kevin and Edna's fortieth birthdays. I didn't know if you were making any plans along those lines also. What do you think? I can take them out for dinner instead if you have plans," Carol pleasantly said.

Kristin laughed. "I tried a few different ways to organize a celebration, suggesting a romantic trip up north, a house party, or dinner at a restaurant in a private room. I even offered to throw Kevin a party at that dreaded mausoleum of a country club. He passed on everything and made it clear he'd be furious about any surprise or formal party. He was so adamant that I dropped the subject."

Carol informed Kristin that she had resorted to using the kids as bait and that Kevin had agreed to a small family gathering. She joked that she didn't feel proud stooping to that level, but sometimes the ends justify the means. It was her way of urging Kristin to reconsider things one last time. Kristin nodded in full understanding and walked out the front door. She shuffled down the steps and turned to see whether Carol was looking at her. She was. Kristin smiled, as if to show her everything would be all right, and they both waved goodbye.

Carol stood dejectedly on the stoop, her arms folded, her mind cluttered with "what if" scenarios, her ego dented, as she acknowledged her failure. She usually accepted defeat with grace but not now. She watched Kristin's car move out of view then slapped the side of the house. It had been as if they were in a boxing ring, and Kristin wouldn't fight back, yet Kristin had still managed to win. It was a prevailing strategy of peaceful resistance, as if designed by Gandhi himself. Carol could understand Kristin's pious faithfulness to Kevin to a certain degree, but he was keeping a secret from her that involved great sums of money and that could potentially affect their quality of life and harm the entire family. To Carol, the consequences greatly outweighed the repercussions, and Kristin's servile decision lacked both courage and pragmatism.

Carol called Edna's cell phone, expecting it to go straight to voicemail and was startled when she answered. "Kristin just left. Can you talk now?" she asked in a deep whisper.

Edna laughed and responded, "You know, it's a tad annoying—in a cute way, though—when you whisper knowing that the person you're talking about is miles away."

Carol mockingly laughed and said, "You do the same thing yourself, if you hadn't noticed." She went on to inform Edna about the conversation with Kristin, stopping and starting over again to ensure every sentence was in chronological order so there would be little confusion. She was waiting for Edna to interrupt and harshly criticize her, because it was easy to decipher the eventual outcome of the story, but Edna was courteous enough to let her go on until the bitter end.

Edna paused for a moment, expressed her dismay, and joked, "You can only lead a horse to water. I've always hated that cliché, but that girl is in serious denial. You know what this is? It's a pitiful combination of Tammy Faye Baker and Hillary Clinton, with Tammy Wynette singing 'Stand by Your Man' in the background for special effect. You tried everything you could to reason with her, so don't be despondent. Give it some time. I know it's hard. You still have another option to consider, which will take an iron stomach to attempt. It's called tough love, but sometimes you have to overstep the boundary. You could tell Kristin the intervention is still on, whether or not if she's involved. She would be exposed and left all alone to defend herself from Kevin's wrath. Here's another cliché to think about, 'She who hesitates is lost,' which could sway her to your side. I'm not sure Kevin has done anything illegal or immoral. He's been an admirable, levelheaded person all his life, and there's probably a logical explanation for his actions, filled with good intentions. Kristin stirred up a hornet's nest, and now she's fearful of getting stung by the truth."

Carol shuddered at the thought of the last option. It was like using a nuclear bomb. She had failed miserably at diplomacy, but such a preemptive strike might polarize her from Kevin's family for life, and she would never want that. She could threaten Kristin with that harsh option, with the intent of never carrying it out, but she feared Kristin would see through that and call her bluff.

"Thanks," Carol said, "but I don't want to feel like President Obama with my finger on the button. Oh, one more small thing to tell you. Tom is flying in early Friday night around five and staying until Monday morning. He'll be staying at the house. I don't know whether to buy a seductive negligee or keep it simple."

Edna yelled over the phone, "One last thing? You should have led with *that*! I always opt for the good news first. That's so great! Hmm...I'd go with the negligee. Wear your silver crucifix necklace with it. He might be into that 'dirty Catholic girl' look. You could also wear your old blue-plaid Catholic high school uniform, with the navy-blue knee socks, in your 'do me' pumps while sucking on a lollipop. I'm sure you can still fit into it, and you'll save money that way. Be careful that Tom doesn't place a hidden camera around. You don't want to go viral in that outfit."

Carol eliminated Edna's last bedroom wardrobe selection right away. "That's a little over the top. Maybe it's best to just wing it. I don't want the stress of deciding what to wear to carry over into the bedroom. It's been a while, you know," she sensibly said. "There are no concrete plans. I think I'll cook something nice on Sunday night, though. I'll see what his thoughts are, and maybe we can all get together for a bit. He may want to work on 'us' first."

Chapter 19

It was five o'clock on Friday, and Carol pulled into the airport to pick up Tom. She had moved her last lesson to the next day at ten and was free afterward, as her other Saturday lesson was canceled. She decided on curbside parking, even if it meant she had to circle the airport a few times. It was always a painstaking experience to meet someone at the baggage claim area, with everyone jostling for positions up front, the distracting conversations, the tearful embraces, and the awkward silences as people's attentions zeroed in on finding their bags. Carol preferred a one-on-one scenario. Her thoughts turned to Edna. She was so important in her life and even had been instrumental in her meeting Tom. Edna had picked the bar and the spot where they'd stood that fateful day, and she was Carol's good luck charm. Edna always had a way about her that lifted Carol's spirits, even in dire circumstances, and she succeeded again in doing so during the past week, when Carol had called her to inform her of Kristin's decision. It had been a repetitive theme throughout her life. In fact, earlier in the day, Carol had found her old school uniform and tried it on. Edna was right again; it still fit and even may have been a little big in some spots. She had more baby fat in high school and was much leaner now from her workout regimen. That added to her natural high that day, but there was still no way Tom would ever see her in that outfit.

She checked on her phone, and Tom's flight already had landed. There were security guards in sight to shoo her away, and just as she turned to look for Tom, there he was tapping on her rear window for her to unlock the door. He climbed in, and they gave each other a quick kiss, and he quickly said, "I traveled light and didn't check a bag. I could neatly squeeze all my stuff in my carry-on. Thanks for picking me up. I'm so thrilled to see you again. I'm almost out of breath!"

Carol laughed and playfully said, "I know this airport. You're out of breath most likely because your arrival gate was a mile away. It had nothing to do with me. I'll give you an A for effort, my little teacher's pet."

She was glad her choice to do curbside parking was the proper one. Otherwise she would have paid a hefty price to park in the garage for nothing. The one thing they hadn't discussed was whether Tom was going to check his bag. *This is another good omen*, she thought. Carol drove out of the airport and toward Dearborn. She quickly glanced back at Tom's duffel bag and said. "I guess you were serious after all. That bag looks a little tiny to contain any Nautical Inn goodies."

Tom shrugged, laughed heartily, and said, "I meant every word. It's so beautiful there, and you must visit. You have to pay the toll before you get on the ride. I have a bonanza of stuff for you that I've put aside."

Carol looked at him and said, "Hmm, bad choice of words, mister, seeing as I picked you up and will be squiring you around all weekend. Perhaps I should start running the meter now." They both shared a long laugh.

It was apparent to Carol that Tom appreciated her wry sense of humor, and vice versa, and it was a big reason why they seemed so instantly compatible. She wouldn't yet declare that fact to be a cornerstone of their relationship, because the physical attraction was too strong and overbearing. She could reflect on Tom's many personal qualities and give them their proper grades in the future, when her other senses were in better standing. Right now, as she looked at him, assuaged by his inviting smile and alluring scent, the tingling sensations stirring within her body were all she could comprehend. She wanted him with great fervor, and the thought that he had come all this way just to see her magnified that feeling a hundredfold.

Tom suggested, "Why don't we hit the ground running? I must admit, I'm astonished Michigan still has a legitimate happy hour. Back home, all the drinking establishments can legally do is discount meals and appetizers. Here, you can do that and discount booze! I don't want you to think I'm some a raging penny-pinching alcoholic, as I agree with the law. It just happens to be a nostalgic part of my life that I fondly miss."

Carol always had been a big fan of happy hour herself, being on a teacher's salary and in her current dead-end, low-paying job. "There's a bunch of places in Dearborn, all within walking distance of each other. We'll make it an adventure and try a few," she said, smiling in anticipation of a wonderful weekend.

It was decided the Barrister Bar would be their first stop, which was a happening place with a nice after-work crowd of mixed ages. They grabbed a beer at the bar, walked to the back, and went outside, where there was another bar and an abundance of tables. Their eyes simultaneously spotted a lone unoccupied table. Carol grabbed Tom's hand, and they made a mad dash for it, plopping themselves onto the chairs, while laughing at their good fortune. It was a typical spring evening, and they both had light jackets with them. Tom mentioned the outdoor seating season was so short that he always tried to take advantage of any great weather, and Carol wholeheartedly agreed.

They talked about the inn and how quickly everything had come together. There was one issue that Tom was uneasy about, and that was his head chef. He had hired a highly skilled local chef, Maurizio, who had worked at numerous places but not for very long, as he had a mercurial personality. He did have strong references, though, and was the best candidate for the job. However, Tom added, there had been a short list of candidates, as the inn was a startup. It was getting close to the grand opening, so he had felt pressured to make the hire.

The inn had ten rooms, Tom said, as well as a large dining room that could seat more than forty people. The dining room would be open for dinner only, Wednesday through Sunday, as well as for lunch on Saturday, with a limited pub-style menu, and for Sunday brunch. The bar would open at four p.m. on Wednesday through Friday and at noon on the weekends. On holiday weekends, the bar would be open on Mondays at noon but serve the pub menu only. There was a small partition with a long railing separating the bar and the dining room. Along the railing on the bar side were a half-dozen or so high tabletops with comfortably padded barstools. The bar itself was L-shaped and would seat a dozen people, with plenty of room to stand. There were six tables in the bar, one of which was large enough to seat eight. The inn's menu would be more suited for fine dining, leaning heavily toward seafood. Tom's goal was to serve at least two creative entree specials daily. He wanted everything to be upscale and felt that if people were paying a rate of more than three hundred dollars per night in season, they deserved to be treated right.

Mesmerized by Tom's vision for the place, Carol listened to every detail. He was so very noble, she thought. He wanted to treat people as he would want to be treated, and she loved that quality in a person.

"I'm sorry. Am I boring you with all this?" Tom asked, as he placed his hand on top of hers, which instantly gave her the tingles.

Carol firmly responded, "No, please don't stop. I want to hear it all. I think it's fascinating, and I'll save my questions for later. Tom, I feel so attuned to your whole philosophy. Please continue talking, and keep holding my hand too, if you don't mind."

Tom giggled as his smile lit up the twilight sky, and he continued to describe the inn. The entire house had been gutted. His list of new additions went on and on. Installed in the house were new wiring, plumbing, a new roof, insulation, state-of-the-art soundproofing, a new heating-and-cooling system, heated tile bathroom floors, and reinforced hardwood flooring. Every room had a forty-two-inch flat-screen TV, Egyptian three-hundred-thread-count sheets, a wet bar, an iPod dock, a Bose stereo alarm clock, a separate shower and tub, upscale toiletries, a desk, and a sitting area with a couch, coffee table, chair, and a large closet with a safe. The rooms even contained bidets so the French-Canadian and European clientele would feel at home. There was also free Wi-Fi throughout. Tom strived to create an upscale traditional inn with modern flair and amenities. He lamented that there wasn't suitable room for a small gym and that he couldn't get the planning done in time to build one.

It was obvious to Carol that there had been a great deal of expense involved, but as she studied Tom's tone and body language, he didn't appear to be worried about money at all. His entrepreneurial spirit was so evident, and he was very confident and showed little fear of failure. He seemed more concerned with having his vision come to fruition than anything else. She was curious as to what drove Tom to take on such an endeavor and politely asked, "What made you want to shift gears so suddenly in life?"

Tom responded, "People ask me all the time. As you know, I worked in the brokerage business for a long time. The bad times get all the headlines, but the good times truly outweighed them. The first twenty years were financially great. I made some successful investments in limited partnerships, stocks, and real estate that greatly exceeded my salary and bonus some years. There was a lot of luck involved, and I managed to get out of things at the right time.

"The game changed, for the worse, within the last five years, not just on an income level, but my morale also plummeted. I was an equity trader, and the trading community was like a brotherhood. Our overtime wasn't dictated by a time clock. It was a nice steak, bottles of wine, and a fine cigar with coworkers and clients. We were like knights in shining armor sitting around the round table at all the bars in the financial district. We had access to all the sporting events and concerts. Due to the recent scandals, that all came to a halt. The clients migrated to executing their orders by computer themselves, because that way was faster and much cheaper, and when they did give you an order, they mandated that it be done by computer also. The human element eroded on a daily basis, and there was no turning back. I used to be on the phone all day long, chatting with clients and executing orders. Nowadays, the main mode of client contact is done via IM, email, and other electronic sources, all monitored by compliance departments, making it more difficult to foster new relationships and maintain old ones, as small talk and personal conversation occur less and less frequently.

"It became drudgery coming into the office, and I wasn't having fun any longer, plain and simple. There were shocking turnovers in senior management. Many old allies were unceremoniously shown to the door, replaced by a much younger set, with unattainable mandates to carry out and lacking in managerial experience. A cutthroat culture was instilled and encouraged. I found myself drifting toward the middle of the pack, and it would only be a matter of time before the younger puppies devoured me. I didn't want to take that dreaded walk of shame down to the elevator bank, carrying a career's worth of sentimental belongings in a cardboard box after being fired. It was better to do things on my own volition and reinvent myself with an open mind and positive attitude, rather than attempt to resurrect a suffocating career that was depressing me. When I pressed the 'down' elevator button for the last time, all I felt was jubilation and liberation. I had an ear-to-ear grin that lasted all the way out of the building!"

The wind picked up a little just as Tom finished speaking. They both looked up at the darkened sky and acknowledged the increasing breeze. Tom breathed deeply, taking the freshness of the air into his lungs. Carol noticed the symbolic display just put forth. "The wind whisks away the staleness of the air and invigorates the senses with life-changing pulsations, offering a rebirth of hope for the future," she poetically stated, holding her beer bottle in the air.

Tom stared at her in wonder and asked, "I'm serious—did you just make that up or is it a quote from some famous author? Were you trying to indirectly say I'm an old windbag because I talk too much? Please, humor me."

Carol laughed, with her hand over her mouth, and said, "I did just make that up. I think you were impressed and won't tell me the truth. Here's to new beginnings. Now tell me why you chose to open an inn."

A moment passed as Tom collected his thoughts, and he told her he had stayed at the inn many times when someone else had owned it. He liked the location, but over the years it had become rundown. It wasn't from sheer neglect. A loving elderly couple from Manhattan had owned it for quite some time, and the husband had passed away. The wife attempted to run it on her own and was doing fine for a few years, until she got sick and was unable to maintain the property. The couple's children had no interest in running it, and when she passed they put it up for sale. Tom had driven by it last fall, saw it was for sale, and immediately wanted to restore it. There were some back-tax issues that held up things, but it gave him time to consider whether he really wanted to go forward, and so far, so good. He had the chance to meet interesting people and form new friendships, and he wanted to slow things down in his life.

It was getting late, and they hadn't eaten yet. Carol suggested they grab a pizza to go and head back to her place, and Tom was all for it. They walked across the street holding hands, ordered a pie, and grabbed a beer while they were waiting.

As they pulled up to her house, Tom was surprised by how close Carol lived to the pizza place. "You could cook a two-minute egg and would have a minute still left," he cracked.

They walked into the house, and Carol carried the pizza into the kitchen. Tom placed his bag on the hallway floor and noticed the piano in the parlor. Carol found him standing over it, gently running his fingers along the keys. He turned to her, and they passionately kissed.

Always the gentleman, Tom briefly separated from her, looked into her eyes, and said, "I lay awake last night dreaming of this moment. Your eyes are so bright even in this dim lighting."

Carol interrupted him by putting her hand over his mouth and led him upstairs to the bedroom. She had planned ahead and had strategically placed a few candles on the bureau. She lit the candles as Tom kissed the back of her neck. Then she turned around, lifting her shirt over her head. Tom followed suit, and they became entangled as they kicked off their shoes and wiggled out of their pants while lying on the bed. The candlelight danced around the room as they created a rhythm of their own. Their mellifluous moans flowed through the air as they rolled back and forth in each other's arms. Carol caressed Tom's sweaty muscles as she slowly squirmed up and down in trembling delight. Tom gazed into her eyes as he knelt on top of her, slowly thrusting, until he let out a roar of satisfaction and carefully rolled over, making sure their glistening legs were still intertwined.

All that could be heard for minutes was their beating hearts, as they tightly held each other. Still panting somewhat, Carol laughed and said, "I just realized something. I've been sleeping in this room for thirty-seven years, and this is the first time I've made love in here. In fact it's the first time ever in this house. You must be either scared or flattered by that, hopefully the latter."

Tom softly brushed his foot down her leg and responded, "That makes two of us. I made out a few times in the bedroom I shared with my brother, when he wasn't around bugging me. However, I grew up in a small Irish Catholic household. Between the crucifixes and the pictures of Jesus and the Pope hanging on the thin walls, it was a little intimidating, to say the least. My parents, especially my mother, always reminded us that giving in to temptation leads to eternal damnation. I never truly believed that, but just in case, why risk fate?"

Their eyes both locked on the crucifix on the wall next to the bureau, and as they watched it shimmer in the flickering candlelight, Tom said in a deep mock-scary voice, "Even now it seems to be admonishing us, as if it's shaking a 'no, no, no' at us—kind of creepy."

Carol kiddingly punched him and voiced her opinion. "I prefer to think Jesus is nodding his head, giving us his blessing and approval." She sweetly kissed his ear and ran her hand through his curly locks. "I believe you called out to God a couple of times moments ago. You can't be too much of a scaredy cat. Hey, your belly is gurgling. It's a tad past midnight. Let's go downstairs and have our gourmet dinner, even though it feels more like dessert now. You're not off the hook yet from your last visit. You still owe me a decent meal tomorrow. On Sunday I'd like to cook us something special."

* * *

Tom woke up the next morning to find the bed empty beside him. The clock read nine a.m., and he was embarrassed that he had slept in that long. Carol, running a brush through her wet hair, emerged from the bathroom in her robe. She saw his eyes wide open, ogling her, and bent over and kissed him on the cheek. It had been a long time since a man had looked at her like that, and she was enjoying every second of it.

"How did you sleep?" she asked. He shook his head and responded, "I never sleep this late. I'm actually groggy from oversleeping. I had one of those dreams that you don't want to end, I guess."

He got up and gave her a hug. Carol imagined how great it would be to start off every day with a smile and an embrace from Tom. She was living her dream. "I neglected to tell you that I have a piano lesson in an hour. I have one of those single-cup coffee gizmos, and there's bagels on the counter. Just relax, and do whatever pleases you. Let me know if you need help with the coffee," she said.

Tom told her he was familiar with Keurig coffee makers. He had forgotten to mention the previous night that he'd placed one in every room at the inn.

"Do you also have a butler come to the room and brew coffee for the guests while he draws them a bath? God forbid they have to pour the water in the machine themselves," Carol teased.

Tom couldn't let her have the last laugh, even though he adored the way she teased him. "Well, now that you brought it up, the inn has the commercial version where the machine is connected to the plumbing, so the guests don't have to pour their own water into it. I figured it was a nice touch, and it makes it much harder for them to run off with the machine in their bags," he said in a matter-of-fact tone.

Carol snapped her towel at him, and he ran out of the room so she could get dressed in privacy.

The music from the parlor was awful as Tom sat in the den, catching some scores on ESPN. Every now and then, he'd peek over to watch Carol. He was amazed at her patience and how gently she grabbed the little boy's hand to show him which keys to hit, over and over. Her smiles of encouragement were so genuine, and she gave him a tiny hug when he got it right. Tom wanted to sign up for a lesson just for the hug factor. If his reward was a hug from her every time he played something right, he thought, he would be a concert pianist. The piano sounded so sweet when Carol played. The short snippets from her dancing fingers were certainly worth the wait, Tom thought as he looked on, marveling at their fluidity. He watched as Carol gave the boy one final hug and led her beaming student out the door, making sure he safely got into his parents' car.

She turned to Tom and said, "I hope that wasn't too bad for you. He's a beginner, and he's trying hard."

Tom joked, “It wasn’t the music that bothered me. More so it was that the boy received thirty hugs, and I only got one today so far.”

Carol snapped back, “Jealous of a little boy? Don’t forget, his parents paid fifty bucks for those hugs. Yours don’t cost a cent. Don’t worry. I’m sure you’ll pass his total by the day’s end if you’re a good boy.”

Chapter 20

The weather wasn't cooperating, as it was showery and overcast. To Carol, the day wasn't the least bit dreary. They sat on the couch in the den, unconsciously trading love taps, looking at each other agog, stopping to kiss every few minutes. Having recently visited, Tom already had taken in most of the tourist sites in the area, and Carol wondered what they could do for entertainment. Dearborn really wasn't an easily walk-able city where you could stroll aimlessly and discover things on your own.

Tom appeared content watching a baseball game, and Carol tried to focus on the game with him. A batter had just popped a ball in the air, and Carol yelled out, "Infield fly rule. Batter is automatically out, and the runner may advance at his own risk!"

Impressed with her knowledge of the game, Tom turned to her, gave her a high-five, and said, "The men around here must be nuts to let you slip through. If I had the time, I'd write each of them a sincere thank-you note."

Carol smirked and gave him a soft elbow to his side. It was great that he had a strong interest in sports, especially baseball. She loved to attend games, and she actually went to enjoy the action not just to people-watch.

As if Tom knew what she were thinking, he said, "In Red Sox Nation, we have female fans they call 'pink hats' for obvious reasons. A lot of the male fans ridicule them because they think they cheer for the cutest players and don't know much about the game's nuances. On talk radio, some callers say they actually boycott Fenway Park because there are too many pink hats. I'd never do that. Those guys need to get a life."

The game was slow moving, and Tom asked if they needed to make reservations to wherever they were going to eat later. He also added that he wouldn't object to seeing Edna again and inquired whether she or anyone else wanted to join them later for dinner. Carol was delighted to hear that. Tom was aware how important Edna was to her, and that fact that he wanted to be in her company spoke volumes about his character. She texted Edna and got a reply back that Nick had made reservations at an Italian restaurant at nine p.m. for two but that they could easily switch the reservation to four people.

"Do you feel like Italian tonight?" she asked Tom. "This restaurant rivals any in Boston, I promise. They make their own pasta." Tom was all for it and looked at his watch as Carol texted Edna back.

They both were excited at the prospect of seeing Edna on such short notice. Carol had only met Nick a few times, but she felt confident that he and Tom would hit it off. Tom was so good natured that he could get along with anyone and make them feel at ease, she reckoned. They went upstairs to get ready, as Carol instinctively knew Tom would want to sample another bar before they ventured over to the restaurant.

It was seven p.m., and a little misty out, when they walked into Howley's. Carol was certain Tom would savor the atmosphere here. It was a serious drinking establishment. Almost everyone ordered a sidecar with their beer here. Carol ordered two beers with a Jack chaser.

"We're one and done here. This place is a throwback. We can go to Bennies next door afterward. The restaurant is a block away. They have a decent bar and a nice wine selection," she told him.

Tom smiled at Carol and said, "I couldn't be happier. It feels so good having all my decisions made for me. Last week I stressed for an hour while picking out silverware for the inn. I really could have used you for that."

Howley's was tightly packed. Tom introduced himself to an old grizzled local sitting nearby and chatted with him about the Tigers. Carol stood by quietly and smiled every time Tom glanced at her, as he tried to ensure that she was included in the conversation. The local yelled down to a patron standing at the other end of the bar that Tom was from Boston, and in a matter of moments, Carol and Tom were standing within a circle of people, shaking hands. Soon the group was listening to Tom tell a story about how he had met Al Kaline, an all-time Tiger great, when he was a little boy.

Carol admired the magnetic personality Tom possessed, and it didn't matter to her that he was just captivating a few weathered locals. She was confident he could converse perfectly with people from all walks of society. He was a natural to own that inn, she concluded, as she pictured herself standing alongside him, greeting excited vacationers checking in, showing them their rooms with great anticipation, and sharing stories with them at the bar. It was only a pipe dream, of course, she thought, but the comment Tom had just made about wishing she were there to help pick the silverware had ignited it.

Her mind drift got sidetracked by a local as he grazed her arm with a fresh beer, and she looked at Tom while accepting it. He nodded to her, and she could tell it wasn't to give her permission, but to let her know it was the last one, as they were just being gracious to their hosts.

They chatted a little longer, and Tom set up the circle standing around them with more drinks, while apologizing that, as much as he was enjoying their company, they had to rush off to meet people for dinner. After a series of backslaps, handshakes, and hugs, they wandered into the quiet of the misty night.

"I'm sorry. Things kind of snowballed in there," Tom said with a chuckle. "They kept calling one guy 'the mayor,' but I'd like to believe Dearborn's mayor wouldn't wear a lumberjack outfit on a Saturday evening and would have more than five teeth in his mouth."

Carol let out a silly laugh and loudly added, "When you said we had to split for dinner, one of them pointed to that disgusting jar of deviled eggs behind the bar to lamely convince us to stay longer. Oh, yup, give us the whole jar, buddy, and set up the whole place! Let's take another lap in the pool, fellas—or should I say, cesspool! Don't get me wrong. They were very nice people, and I like that bar, but the night would have gone down the crapper if we had stayed, hence the cesspool comment. All we've eaten today has been a bagel and a leftover slice of pizza each. A deviled egg would have been the frosting on the cake!"

As they stood in front of the next bar, Tom peeked at his watch. His face was red from laughing so hard, and they looked at each other cackling again, for no apparent reason other than they both couldn't believe how hard they were laughing.

"Let's go to the restaurant. We still have an hour, but I'd like to enjoy the bar, and I get the impression we should jump off the tour bus while we're ahead," Tom said, failing miserably at trying to stop laughing.

The bar at Camogli's was crowded, and Tom commented on how elegant the place looked. "This is one of those places that looks plain from the outside, but once you step inside, it has that certain 'wow' factor," Tom said.

Carol cracked, "Kinda like when you first walk into my house!" She reached for Tom's hand and led him to where Nick and Edna were seated at the bar. Tom already had spotted Edna and greeted her with a hug and a kiss. He introduced himself to Nick, and the bartender came by for their drink order. Tom saw that Edna and Nick's martini glasses were almost empty and looked at Carol, and she nodded. He ordered four of whatever they were having.

Carol was thinking how much she and Tom seemed to click, when Edna asked where they had come from. Edna and Nick smiled and heartily laughed, as Carol told the story.

"We used to go to Howley's when we were much younger, in our early twenties. I hope Carol made that clear to you," Edna joked. "Nick and I have been here since seven and snagged these seats right away," she added.

Nick suddenly offered Carol his seat, followed by an apology. She declined and stated, "That's very sweet, but I don't want to get too comfy drinking martinis. I might not be able to walk to the table for dinner."

The reservation was running a little late, but they didn't mind, as the conversation flowed, and it gave them time to have another drink. They eventually were seated at a corner table. Tom graciously mentioned he felt as if he were in an Italian seaside village. He admired the ocean-themed decor and complimented Edna and Nick on their restaurant choice. They ordered various pasta dishes and split an antipasto for the table. Tom asked if everyone wanted red wine and then ordered two bottles of Chianti.

Carol noticed how at ease Nick was, as he was being very talkative and smiling a lot. He and Edna had been spending more time together lately, and Carol was silently congratulating him in her thoughts, as it appeared his patient ways finally had shown Edna the light. Edna was even displaying a little public affection, as she playfully bumped shoulders with Nick and patted his arm, which was a bit out of character for her.

"I have a question for you guys, seeing that we have people with finance and legal backgrounds at our table," Carol said. "It seems there's been a lot of news over the last few years about a number of embezzlers and Ponzi schemers. How do these people get away with it for so long? How do people get so snookered by them? What safeguards are in place to make it harder for them to succeed?" Carol looked at Edna to make sure she understood what she was getting at—namely Kevin.

Nick and Tom glanced at each other, and Tom gave him the floor with a polite wave. "Most of the time these scams start with the simplest of intentions, but things get out of control. I'm not showing empathy for these crooks, even though I'm a criminal attorney. These devious people seem to have a flaw, almost genetically, which makes them think they're much smarter than others. And what better way to prove it than to take someone's—or a company's—most prized possession, their own cash, away from them, without them knowing it? Almost all embezzlers, when caught, declare their intention was always to replace the money at some point. I find it plausible but not likely, in most cases, as they've already bought houses and boats, gambled, and went on extravagant trips with the money. Embezzlers are much more secretive and know how their workplaces operate very well, so they can better cover their tracks and remain undetected for long periods of time. In many cases they're trusted mid-level employees who have continuous access to the books, or disgruntled partners. I find the Ponzi schemers much more fascinating, as it takes more creativity and, quite frankly, balls. I'll leave that to Tom to explain."

The waiter stopped by and refilled their water glasses, and they all passed on another martini. Tom expanded on what Nick had to say. "Nick is right on. The Ponzi guys are usually already legitimately quite successful, with a high standing in the community. It's like a switch gets turned on all of a sudden, and it won't shut off. They get introduced to new targets from fancy country-club connections or hedge-fund consultants with high net-worth clients. Unlike most embezzlers, these are high-profile people who contribute to many charities with their own money, as well as with the funds they've stolen. Making these lavish donations relieves the guilt a little, but it also gets them on the boards of even more charities, as well as corporations, so the scope of their network widens and their number of unsuspecting victims increases. It's self-perpetuating."

Edna chimed in, "It's like a merry-go-round. The money keeps going around and around. They pay one victim as they collect from the others, but sooner or later the music stops, and when more than a few large investors demand their money at the same time, the scheme gets exposed, because they can't get access to the money quickly enough to pay them."

"The scale of the deception is staggering," Carol said. "They look a lot of people in the eyes while they're stealing and depleting their hard-earned money."

Nick interjected, "Usually at first they know their victims reasonably well. I mean, they have to start somewhere, but as their network and reputation increase, more people—like registered advisors who get massive fees—are unwittingly doing their dirty work by raising more money for them. Consequently they never meet the majority of the people they're bilking."

The entrees arrived, and the table grew quiet. Tom took a sample of his shrimp over homemade linguini and commented, "The pasta is cooked perfectly al dente, just the way I like it, and the fra diavolo sauce is delicious. I hope you girls aren't thinking of embezzling, or something else of that ilk. At least wait until dessert before you start."

Edna noticed her cousin in deep thought, as Carol basically had ignored Tom's last words, and assumed it had to do with Kevin. "A lot of people I know have a lot of mistrust in the stock market, especially when they see headlines about highly educated, smart people and celebrities getting fleeced almost daily," Edna explained, as her eyes met Carol's.

Nick and Tom nodded, as both where too busy twirling their pasta to respond.

A chorus of satisfying groans overtook the table. "There's no way I can eat a morsel of dessert," Edna declared, as the rest of the group nodded in agreement.

The waiter cleared the table, and Edna and Carol excused themselves to go to the ladies' room. Upon entering, Carol looked underneath a few stalls and whispered, "I have Tom here, and all I can think about is Kevin. He could be in over his head and headed for big trouble. He fits the psychological profile, as he's smarter than most people. I have to shake off this feeling. I hope Tom didn't find me uninterested back there. I didn't mean to tune him out."

Edna whispered back, "I think the boys had food on their brains. There's no other way to describe Tom other than charmingly pleasant. You two look great together!"

Carol snickered as she looked in the mirror and applied some lip-gloss. "I see you and Nick are looking very blissful this evening yourselves. For a second there, I thought the waiter might have had to pry you two apart with a crowbar when the antipasto arrived."

The girls were still giggling as they walked back to the table. Tom paid the tab, over Nick's objections, and said, "You can get it the next time we get together, and I sincerely hope that's soon."

Carol enjoyed hearing that, as it was more than a hint that Tom thought of them as a couple. Edna picked up on it too and gave Carol a silly wink. Nick offered to buy a nightcap at the bar, but the women declined, and the four of them walked out into the misty night.

* * *

The house appeared so inviting as Tom and Carol entered. They kicked off their wet shoes in the hallway and kissed each other at the bottom of the stairwell. Carol led them up the stairs, removed the crucifix from her bedroom wall, and carefully placed it in her top bureau drawer. She cracked, "We don't want Mr. Boston College to get spooked again."

Tom laughed briefly as he went into the bathroom to prepare for bed. Carol quickly opened her dresser drawer to find an old teddy but decided Tom deserved something new and not one she had worn for someone else. He came back in, and she shuffled into the bathroom. She came back to find Tom had lit the candles and was lying in bed, smiling at her wistfully, underneath the covers on his back with his hands folded behind his head. She slowly walked over to the bed and enticingly disrobed so Tom could see her naked body. He cupped his hands over her breasts as she ripped the sheets off him to find him fully aroused. They both let out a pleasurable groan as Carol climbed on top of him, and they made love so deeply that their bodies trembled for what seemed like hours.

Unlike the night before, when hunger pangs shortly followed their first lovemaking session, they both lay down, caressing each other, sweetly sharing stories throughout the candlelit night. Carol's ears tingled with joy at Tom's every syllable, and when his last sentence turned into a slight mumble, followed by a brief snore, she gently kissed him goodnight on the cheek. Her eyes became heavy as she introspectively examined the status of their relationship and happily concluded that this was not a whimsical, whirlwind romance but one manifested with incredible compatibility and long-lasting staying power. The boyishly handsome man softly purring beside her, as if he were singing a comforting lullaby, was indeed "her" Tom.

Chapter 21

It was Sunday morning, the last full day of Tom's scintillating, impromptu visit. Carol tried not to dwell on that sad fact and vowed to make the dwindling time that remained as pleasant as possible. She rolled over to catch a glimpse of her Prince Charming and found herself smiling at an empty bed. She picked her bathrobe up from the floor and walked to the top of the stairs. She yelled Tom's name out but received no response, and a slight sense of panic gripped her as she held onto the railing to hold up her sleepy legs. Her temporary feeling of abandonment quickly subsided, as she smelled coffee and heard the back door close. She repeated Tom's name, while shuffling down the stairs, her left knee cracking loudly. "Tom, is that you stirring about down there?"

There he was, dressed in workout attire, holding a bag of birdseed, greeting her with an infectious smile and those inviting blue eyes. "I was sipping my coffee out back and noticed the birds flying up to the feeder, only to be denied their breakfast. I found the birdseed by the door. I hope you don't mind. They're putting on quite a show now," he said, hoping for a sign of approval from Carol.

She peeked out the window and saw a cardinal helping itself and warmly responded, "See the cardinal? It visits all the time. I can't tell you for sure that it's always the same one, but my mom insisted it was. She loved sitting out there watching the feeding frenzy. I made a personal promise to keep the feeder full, but I'm ashamed that I've fallen short on that lately. Thanks for picking up the slack. I owe you."

Once again a mystical feeling overcame Carol. It was as if her mother had sent a signal from heaven for Tom to refill the feeder. Edna would have insisted that to be the case if she were present. Carol wished she could share her happiness with her mother. Perhaps, in some way, her mother knew how her life had changed. *Please, mother, keep writing the script, and don't ever let this magical story come to an end*, Carol thought, as Tom patted her back while they were entertained by the vibrantly beautiful cardinal feasting in the sun-filled yard.

The moment passed as the content cardinal flew away, and Tom asked Carol whether she felt up to going for a run. She jumped at the offer and sprung up the stairs to change, her legs now fully underneath her. They decided on a scenic municipal path a short drive away. It was about two-and-a-half miles long and interspersed with a few wooden bridges immersed in a bucolic array of shady woods, dandelion-covered rolling meadows, babbling brooks, and an industrial park with a perfectly manicured lawn.

They ran at a leisurely pace, with Carol leading the way, pointing out the flora and fauna like a personal tour guide. After reaching the path's end, they turned around, ran another ten minutes, and began to walk briskly.

Tom was invigorated by the fresh air, as well as the natural beauty of the path. "This sure beats running around the block. You wouldn't even know we were in the middle of the city," he boasted, as if they had engineered the path themselves.

The whole experience was uplifting for Carol also. It was the first time they'd done anything athletic together, and she was impressed by Tom's high level of fitness for a man in his mid forties. On the ride home, she added another mental checkmark in the plus column for the two of them.

Carol and Tom lazily shared the afternoon doing a crossword, falling one word shy of completing it; swapping sections of the Sunday paper; watching golf; and munching on assorted cheeses and crackers. Carol was enamored by how magnificent the state of soulful seclusion was going, which had been her goal for the day all along. There was little chance of sharing Tom with any audience today, and she judged that he hadn't devised an escape plan, as he sat on the couch barefoot, slowly running his fingers through her hair as her head rested on his thigh.

The afternoon began to drift into early evening as the shadows on the front shades crept larger and larger. It was nature's alarm clock signaling Carol to open a bottle of wine and to prepare dinner. She got up from Tom's lap, gave him a loving kiss, and asked him if he wanted a beverage.

"Surprise me!" he excitedly responded. She came back holding a can of Bud in her left hand and a glass of Merlot in her right, saying she couldn't make up her mind regarding what to serve. Tom politely grabbed both and smiled, sarcastically thanking Carol for the overly generous offer.

"Okay, enjoy the drinks and also all that laughing by yourself. The kitchen is off limits. No peeking!" she playfully ordered.

Carol had a relatively easy menu planned, as she didn't want to spend a lot of time away from Tom. From beginning to end, they were having mushrooms stuffed with sautéed pancetta and bread crumbs; a warm spinach salad with goat cheese, walnuts, and dried cranberries; center-cut, double-thick pork chops drizzled with a Dijon mustard sauce; microwavable sweet potato fries; and store-bought apple pie for dessert. She had gotten all the necessities on Friday morning, before picking up Tom, and was determined to have everything ready within an hour.

The TV was turned on to some fashion show, when Carol returned to the den to briefly check on Tom and to pour him some more wine. He commented on how unhealthy looking the models appeared as they pranced down the runway. "There's nothing to grab on to, and look at those unsightly ribs," he observed. Carol felt relieved that he was watching the show as if he were gawking at a grisly murder scene, and she took pleasure in seeing his disgust as he flicked back to ESPN.

It would be awkward for the two of them to eat at the large dining room table, Carol thought. She fancied the kitchen more of a comfortable setting. It's where she had eaten the most throughout the years, and she also could dim the lights to create an illusion of intimacy. She set the table, along with the oven timer for the pork chops, and joined Tom in the den.

He looked at her, then toward the kitchen, and proclaimed, "It smells so good. I'm so honored to be with you and appreciative of every moment we've shared during this visit. I want you to know, from the bottom of my heart, how I truly feel. I feel wired to you in every dimension. It's as if we were perfectly molded and cast together, through a master blueprint, designed from the man above."

As their eyes locked, Carol realized she had never witnessed Tom be so sincere and heard his voice so animated, with unwavering conviction. She was rejuvenated by his candidness and felt compelled to reciprocate. "Tom, I know what you mean. I'm smitten in every way, shape, and form," she said, as she fought off the erupting urge to say the "l" word by squeezing his hand.

Tom smiled and said, "The horse has left the barn."

Carol grinned and responded, "The genie has left the bottle also, I suppose."

The timer went off, and Carol lightly slapped Tom in the behind and said, "It's the pork chops' turn to leave the oven. Let's meander into the kitchen, or would you prefer eating in your stable, my starving stallion?"

The kitchen wasn't the ideal "table for two with a view" spot, but it was all they needed. Looking at a serene lake, a yacht-filled harbor, or a snow-covered mountain would be no match for Tom's effervescent smile and would even be distracting, Carol reasoned. For the next two hours, they dined in their small oasis, softly chatting about family, current events, history, travel, favorite foods, movies, and celebrities. The cornucopia of interesting topics stretched on and on at times. Tom mentioned that he felt as if they were seated in a corner table at a Parisian bistro, and their waiter instinctively had left them alone to pass the night away.

Tom had no idea that Carol was so adroit in the kitchen. The pork chops were juicy and moist, and the entire meal was exquisite. The endless list of dishes she had cooked with her mother, however, were quite extraordinary in imagination, and Tom was envious he hadn't been a recipient of all that fine cooking.

"I like to experiment with foods that test boundaries," Tom said, "but you won't find me devouring monkey brains and chocolate-covered leeches, like that guy on the Travel Channel. You claim this was one of your 'simple' meals, but it was better than restaurant quality! My compliments to the chef."

Carol giggled and responded, "I was looking for leeches at the supermarket. Fortunately they were out."

After the meal, they partially cleaned up then went upstairs to get ready for bed. Tom came out of the bathroom and started to rearrange his duffel bag. Carol half-kidded, “Rats, I forgot to hide that bag.” It was either tears or a vain attempt at humor, she decided.

Tom nodded, sadly looked at her, and without uttering a word, dejectedly climbed into bed next to her. They silently embraced each other with their thoughts focused on the future and when they would see each other again. There would be no carnal delights this evening. Instead it was a poignant time to exhibit amiable affection, patient soul searching, and gracious acceptance of the gift they shared, as they calmly drifted into a sound slumber. Their relationship had just evolved to the next level, without generating a drop of sweat, a moan, or a word.

* * *

The next morning, when Carol awoke, her mind was cluttered with a mishmash of foggy dreams that had no apparent relevance to one another. Sometimes she would lie in bed for a while and attempt to make sense of her dreams, but it was usually a futile exercise. Today, for sure, the jigsaw puzzle wouldn’t be completed, as the most important piece was flying away in less than two hours, leaving a gaping hole in her heart.

The ride to the airport was better than Carol imagined it would be, thanks to Tom. He was very talkative and upbeat about how they could make things work. Some of the scenarios he threw out were unrealistic, such as his flying out every other weekend when he had an inn to manage, but Carol wasn’t in the frame of mind to rule out any suggestion. The most overriding and endearing theme she heard was that Tom wanted to be with her. Whether he was grasping at straws or being delusionary was of secondary importance. It was the bottom line that mattered most.

Carol pulled up to the terminal, and they passionately kissed in the car. She leapt out of the car, almost forgetting to shift it into park, and ran around to Tom, who stood on the curb, and hugged him hard. He stumbled for a bit, and they both laughed while clumsily clenching each other. Their hands slowly separated as Tom walked toward the automatic doors. Carol couldn't bear to watch much more and quickly got in the car and slowly drove away, checking a few times to see if Tom was running after her. She was stopped at a red light by the airport's exit when her phone beeped. It was a text from Tom in upper case, "I MISS U ALREADY." Carol texted back, "I HEAR U. MISS U 2" and sped off to prepare for her first lesson of the day.

Chapter 22

Carol got an excited phone call from Tom when he landed. He informed her that the bar at the inn was in place and almost fully assembled. She knew the inn already had three reservations for Wednesday evening and was almost booked for the upcoming Memorial Day weekend, so that was a relief to hear. Tom desperately wanted to open the inn with the place fully intact, and now that would occur on schedule. Carol was elated by the news and wished him good luck once again.

It was back to the everyday routine for Carol. She longed to have something different to do, but for now it was daytime piano lessons sprinkled with evenings out with Edna, which were becoming less frequent, as Nick seemed to take up more of her time. Carol was very happy for Edna and desired the same for herself—the sooner the better. Edna and Nick were trekking up to see Sam and Patty this weekend, so Carol really didn't have much to do. She was more concerned with the weather in Maine than anything else, for the sake of both Tom and her brother. The forecast looked perfect, and her visit there couldn't come fast enough. Edna was still in the process of determining the exact dates she could take off work, as her firm had a hectic trial schedule before the summer slowdown began. Carol would head to Maine with or without her cousin, but she preferred it if Edna came along.

* * *

It was Memorial Day, and Edna called from the road on her way back from her visit up north. The reception was terrible, and all Carol could gather was that she wanted to drop by the next day after work. Carol wondered whether there was anything important from her trip she wanted to divulge or if it was just to catch up. Things had been pleasantly quiet on the home front. There had been nothing blackish lately from Kristin regarding Kevin. Chris seemed better than okay when Carol had spoken with him last. All she wanted to hear was fluff; she didn't want to be used as a sounding board for any serious issues. Her karma had been good since meeting Tom, and she didn't want any disruptions to break it. Her outlook on life always had accentuated the positive, but never was it more buoyant than now.

* * *

The kitchen was agonizingly hot as Carol scrubbed the oven with a wire brush. She wore thick, long, yellow gloves; her hair was full of grit and grease; and her body was covered in sweat. It was Tuesday, and she had been on a cleaning mission for the last three days.

Edna startled her as she walked into the kitchen. "I rang the bell, but you probably couldn't hear it with your head stuck in the oven. The rest of your weekend with Dreamy Eyes wasn't that bad, I hope," she kidded.

Carol cackled, out of breath, "I got so into it and lost track of time. The back is the hardest part. I polished the floors yesterday. They say cleanliness is next to godliness."

Edna gave her a shove out of the kitchen and said, "Good. Now that you put it that way, go clean yourself up. It's a lovely evening, and we're going out for a spell."

Carol obediently marched up the stairs and hopped into the shower. Edna seemed to be in a great mood, and Carol dismissed the notion of any troubling news coming. She quickly showered; toweled herself off; blow-dried her hair, leaving it slightly wet; and slid into her jeans. She pulled a black T-shirt over her head as she hopped down the stairs. "How's that for time? Less than twenty minutes," she declared. Edna clapped as Carol picked up her black sandals next to the front door, walked barefoot to Edna's car, and tossed them on to the floor.

Carol's phone rang as Edna drove. It was Tom. She showed Edna that it was his name on the display, and Edna waved for her to pick it up. He was calling to say hello before meeting some friends for dinner. His voice sounded so good to hear, and Carol chatted with him or a while but finally begged off when Edna pulled into the parking lot across from the bar.

They grabbed a table outside, and Edna ordered two dirty martinis. Carol's intuition detected that something was up. A few minutes passed, and Edna was being unusually fidgety. "Do you have the day off tomorrow, or is there a new Tuesday martini special here?" Carol asked, fully knowing Edna was up to something.

The waitress placed the martinis on the table, and Edna waited for her to walk away. Her face was beat red, and her eyes were beaming. "I have something to ask you." She paused for a moment. "Would you please be my maid of honor?" she nearly shrieked.

Carol's eyes filled with tears as Edna lifted her left hand from underneath the table to reveal a sparkling diamond in a white-gold setting. "Oh, my God! It's beautiful!" she told Edna. "You rushed me into the shower, and then Tom called. I can't believe I didn't see it!" Carol shouted.

Edna told her how sweet Nick had been as he had asked permission from her father while they were fishing Saturday afternoon. He had gotten on his knee to pop the question by the fire pit Sunday evening. They were all alone, and it was so romantic, under the star-lit sky. Edna had no idea it was coming but instantly responded in the affirmative. "I didn't hesitate one second to say yes. The word flew out of my mouth. I was surprised by that more than anything, and I never second-guessed my decision. A person can do a lot of thinking during that torturous eight-hour drive back home. It can play tricks on your mind!" she happily said.

Edna wasn't sure of the timing, she said, but they were aiming for a small September wedding, and Italy was the leading contender for the honeymoon. She added, "More than ever, I want you and me to go to Maine and whoop it up. I have a lot of vacation time coming. I should know—I helped create the vacation policy, and I oversee the entire schedule, partners included. I promise I'll find a way to make sure it happens, even if I have to resort to a little chicanery."

Carol was ecstatic to hear that, but it was Edna's night, and the protocol was for her to be supportive. An engagement is a prelude to marriage and a commitment of colossal proportions. She had been right the entire time concerning Edna's relationship with Nick, as she knew her cousin so well. Edna admitted to herself, and eventually to Carol, how amenable she was to the idea of marrying Nick. In reality she had fallen in love with him in her heart months ago. It just took a while for it to escalate to her brain. Edna was in love and was no longer apprehensive about it. She was radiant, fearless, and ready to profess her love to the world. "I feel ashamed that I put the guy through hell, but I love him so much!" she blissfully crowed. Her eyes looked toward the sky, and her head slightly bobbed, as if the word "love" still reverberated inside her head.

"Nick is a great guy," Carol said, "with many qualities most men don't possess. He's the whole package." They clanged glasses, and Carol had to shake out one barb. She flippantly said, "Some people could see that within a couple of minutes of meeting him. For others, I guess, it takes more than a year." Edna broke out in laughter, patted her heart, and ordered another round.

* * *

The next afternoon, Edna called with the dates best suited for her to take time off. She had maneuvered things around to create a large window for them and could take a week off anytime between the last two weeks of June and the first week of July. Carol jumped on the opportunity and instantly called Tom at the inn. Happy to hear the news, he fumbled through his calendar to check the inn's availability and told her they could stay only Tuesday through Thursday during June, as weekends and the week of the Fourth of July were all booked.

"Check with the airlines and get back to me," he told Carol. "My heart is going to jump out of my chest. This morning I went for a nice run along Kennebunk Beach and was thinking the whole time how you would have liked it."

Carol expressed her dismay that she hadn't been there and told him she'd call right back. The online reservations were a breeze to make. They would leave on a Saturday morning in mid-June and come back the following Saturday afternoon.

Carol planned on staying with Chris the first three nights and then at the Nautical Inn for the next three. They still had to figure out where to stay the last night, but she wasn't worried. Within ten minutes, she had called both Tom and Chris to inform them, saving Edna for last.

When she did call her, Edna immediately said before she could get a word out, "Let me see. Everything is all set. You didn't waste a moment of time."

Carol laughed and told her the only hitch was the last night, but they would make an adventure out of it. Edna agreed and hurried off the phone to get back to work.

It was early evening, and Carol called Uncle Sam to congratulate him and see how he was doing. He picked up the phone and seemed very happy about Edna's engagement. "I understand you played a major role," she said.

Her uncle chuckled. "I don't know about that. We were out in the middle of the lake fishing, and Nick asked me for her hand in marriage right out of the blue. That's very old school. I was tickled. He seems like a nice, levelheaded guy. I told him I had no objections at all. He looked a little timid at first, like he was afraid I'd throw him in the lake. It would have been a lot more memorable, though, if we had caught a single fish."

Carol asked how he was feeling. He told her, "So far so good" and mentioned that he had another follow-up appointment at Henry Ford on Friday, July sixth.

A light bulb went off inside Carol's head. "The timing couldn't be better. I'm having a small fortieth birthday celebration for Edna and Kevin. That weekend would be perfect, since they were born seventeen days apart. It wouldn't be complete unless you were there...and Patty too, of course. Where are my manners? I'm going to double-check with Kristin now and get back to you. I already know Edna's free." Uncle Sam said he was all for it, and Carol felt better than ever about having called him. How great for Edna's dad to be there!

A burst of energy shot through Carol's veins. She had accomplished so much in a short span, and her fingers moved so uncoordinatedly that she had to redial Kevin's home phone number three times before getting it right. Kristin picked up and sounded glad to hear from her. Carol told her about Edna's engagement, and the two of them carried on for about ten minutes, mostly about wedding-related topics. Kristin assured her they were free for her party. "Anything to get a weekend day away from that country club," she kidded.

Carol was tempted to tell Kristin about Tom before they hung up but ultimately decided not to bother, as the verdict was still out regarding how tight they actually were. Until she had credible evidence that Kristin was ready for a more reciprocal relationship and not acting only in her self-interest, she would keep her in the dark. She wanted a deeper bond with her, but at this point, Kristin was on "need to know" footing, and for certain she didn't need to know about Tom.

Chapter 23

The small jet's tires screeched as they made contact with the landing strip. "Welcome to Portland, Maine. The local time is two p.m. Please stay seated until the plane comes to a complete stop," the flight attendant cheerfully said.

Carol elbowed Edna in anticipation as the plane taxied to the gate. "The current temperature is sixty-seven degrees, with partly sunny skies," the attendant added.

Carol clapped in excitement. She was the only one on the full flight to do so. "Amateur," Edna whispered while playfully hiding her face.

Chris was anxiously waiting for them at the baggage claim area. The bags came out quickly, and they hopped into Arthur's black Infiniti, which Chris had left running curbside. "Advantages of a small airport," Chris explained. "The drive to Ogunquit will be about thirty-five minutes. It's much quicker on the turnpike. The scenic route takes twice the time, and I have to go back to the deli for a couple of hours after I get you girls settled in," he said.

About halfway into the ride, they passed the Kennebunkport exit. Chris pointed it out, and Edna laughed from the backseat. "Carol was panting like a dog in heat on the plane. She actually applauded when the plane landed. I was surprised she didn't start barking," she kidded.

The car turned off the turnpike, and as they headed farther east, Carol smelled the ocean. The salt air was something a Midwesterner could never take for granted. The first sniff of it instantly put Carol in vacation mode. Edna rolled down the window, stuck her head out, and sucked the air into her lungs.

Chris sensed the girls might be a little too pumped. "Okay sisters," he said. "Here are the ground rules. Ogunquit is a tiny village. Everyone knows one another. Arthur likes to think he's a pillar of the community. Myself, I know better and have little aspiration to achieve that lofty status. Please, no drunk-and-disorderly actions, and if you have to vomit, do so either in the ladies' room or back at the house, preferably in the toilet," he cracked.

The girls laughed. Edna still had her head hanging out the window, pretending she was throwing up, as Carol barked loudly in the passenger seat.

They drove through downtown Ogunquit. The car turned onto a hilly street just outside of town and pulled into a short gravel driveway fifty yards up the hill that led to a white, wooden, shingled, two-storied house with lavender shutters. In the front and on the sides of the house was a short white picket fence. A white wooden lattice trellis, surrounded by stunning rose bushes, led to the brick front steps. Carol noticed a small porch with four white wicker chairs and a coffee table made out of lobster traps.

As they walked up the front steps, Carol and Edna commented on how beautiful the exterior of the house was. Chris carried their bags and opened the door for them. The interior was immaculate and modernly designed, with a funky open floor plan.

"Arthur gets credit for ninety-nine percent of this," Chris said. "He gutted the house and redesigned it himself. I might have done a few things differently at the beginning, but everything in here feels like home to me now. I wouldn't change a thing."

He gave them a hurried tour of the house, starting in the kitchen. It had stainless-steel appliances with a commercial six-burner oven, a huge overhead steel fan, and a bright blue-tiled backsplash. The floor had deep-blue Spanish tile. The cupboards were made of maple, and the black soapstone counters, as well as the island with two blue padded seats, created a chic look. The kitchen sink was also stainless steel and was very deep to better clean large pots and pans.

"I could take a bubble bath in this sink. This is a serious kitchen," Carol commented.

Next they went into the master bedroom. It had bamboo flooring with an inviting king platform bed situated between two windows. The walls were sponge-painted in light gray, and the black bureau with matching armoire were antiques made in a factory in Maine during the early 1900s, Chris explained. The master bathroom had been completely redone in solid black. There was no tub, just a glass shower, which was about six by four feet, with a black marble bench, as well as two spray jets on each side and a rainwater spout in the middle.

"I see there's no TV in the passion pit," Edna joked.

Carrying a suitcase in each hand, Chris led them up the blue-carpeted stairs. The hallway had bamboo flooring. There was one bedroom with a queen bed; the room was sponge painted in lavender. The second bedroom was slightly bigger with two double beds and the walls painted a dark gray. The bathroom had an old-fashioned white soaking tub. There was a gray fiberglass shower stall, with a glass door, about the size of a phone booth. The floor had tiny alternating black and light gray tiles, and the sink and toilet were white. Carol threw her bag atop the bed in the queen room, and Edna left her bag in the other bedroom.

They all met back in the kitchen, and Chris gave them a set of keys, told them to help themselves to anything, and scampered down the hill, back to the deli. "I don't need to shower or change. I already did before picking you up. I'll be ready to hit the ground running in a little over two hours. Just take a right at the bottom of the hill, and you'll find me," he yelled out from the street.

Carol and Edna broke out in laughter. "Nice of him to inform the neighbors that he already bathed," Carol noted.

The girls didn't know what to do with themselves at first. Carol grabbed two bottled waters from the fridge and handed one to Edna, and they both sat on the porch for a short spell, taking in the salt air. Carol texted Tom and said they had arrived, and he texted back, saying he had made arrangements so he could come down the following night to have dinner, which Edna had suggested when they had originally discussed their agenda. This way, Tom could meet Chris as soon as possible, something she knew was important to Carol, as well as Chris.

They agreed to freshen up first and then do some exploring. Carol came down first, adorned in a long, flowing, blue sundress and comfortable black walking sandals. She walked into the dining room, which they had bypassed during the mini tour, and was struck by the size of the table. It was made of dark wood with a few chips here and there, which gave it character. Around the communal-like table were ten wooden chairs, and there was a matching hutch, with dozens of plates stacked on it. It was apparent that Arthur and Chris entertained quite a bit. How nice, Carol thought, for her brother to have so many friends. She took comfort in knowing he was far from alone and knew their beloved mother did as well.

Edna joined Carol in the dining room, dressed in light-beige shorts, a white short-sleeve shirt, and brown canvas boat shoes. She took one quick look around and wisecracked, "They have to be running a soup kitchen out of here."

They moseyed into the den where a monstrous fifty-inch flat-screen TV greeted them, taking up an entire wall. There was a black leather recliner in the corner by the windows begging to be sat on, and a deep-backed gray fabric couch and matching ottoman placed opposite the TV for optimum viewing. A sleek ergonomic chair filled out the rest of the room. The black lacquered coffee table looked to be an antique. On one wall stood a minimalist print of brightly colored stick-figure bicyclists. The other walls had contemporary sea-themed watercolor paintings that appeared strikingly similar and were signed by the same artist, most likely a local. Carol picked up a Detroit Tigers coaster from the coffee table. "Very little fairy dust sprinkled throughout this house. It's almost too macho for my taste," she joked.

Edna picked up a framed picture of Arthur and Chris standing side by side. "I assume this is Arthur. Your brother depicted him as being chubby, which certainly isn't the case here. So it's either an old photo, or it's very recent and he's lost a great deal of weight," she commented.

The women walked slowly down the hill to the main street, which was bustling with an after-beach scene of people carrying lounge chairs, coolers, and towel-stuffed beach bags. The smell of coconut suntan lotion filled the air. They both saw a shirtless, heavy-set, badly sunburned middle-aged man covered in sand, walking sideways, undoubtedly drunk, forcing people to scoot out of his way. "That guy is going to be one hurting puppy when the booze wears off," Edna cracked. "That is, if he doesn't get hit by a car first."

They strolled past the quaint pubs, trinket shops, clothing boutiques and decided to visit them at a later time. Finally they came upon the deli. It was much bigger than Carol had imagined. Chris was at the register when they entered and greeted them with a big smile. "You timed your arrival perfectly. I'm out of here at six. Arthur will stay until closing at seven and then meet us wherever we are. Feel free to walk around for a few minutes while I finish up," he said.

The deli counter was enormous and filled with various meats, cold cuts, cheeses, salads, olives, pickles, and prepared dishes. One aisle was devoted to various olive oils from Italy, Greece, and Spain; another was full of assorted pastas; and another was stocked with desserts imported from Europe as well as plastic-wrapped cookies and delicacies from local bakers. The deli also sold beer, wine, and nonalcoholic beverages, as well as nuts, chips, breakfast bars, magazines, and newspapers. It clearly wasn't targeted just for the beach scene. The homemade sausages, along with the specialty-cut meats—such as pork chops, ribs, steaks, veal cutlets, and ground pork, turkey, and beef—also gave it the feel of a local butcher shop. It truly was a year-round operation, and Carol felt more confident than ever that the place would thrive.

Arthur came out from the back, dressed in his kitchen whites, wearing a blood-stained apron, and sweating profusely. Chris immediately introduced him to Carol and Edna. He playfully punched Chris in the ribs then rubbed his hands clean with a towel and enthusiastically shook their hands. "I told you I didn't want them to see me like this. For heaven's sake, you only get one chance to make a good first impression, and I'm afraid I've blown it. Hello, girls. I'm so pleased to meet you. Oh, my, will you look at the blue eyes on these luscious ladies? Rain check on the hugs all around, please. Sorry again for my appearance. I clean up well," he blurted.

Edna laughed. Arthur was definitely quite the character, and she commented, "The store is awesome. The food looks delicious. You look even thinner than in the picture of you and Chris in the den."

Arthur flashed a smile and placed his arm around Chris, who immediately brushed it away from his clean shirt. "I joined a gym down the street when Chris went to Michigan for the funeral," he boasted. "I wanted to surprise him. Again, I'm so sorry for your loss. From what I hear, Mary was a great lady and one heck of a cook. Anyway, I work out five days a week, lifting weights and using the treadmill. Now that the weather's better, Chris and I walk and run on the beach early in the morning, and I go to the gym for a little lifting. I've cut back on a few things and have lost twenty-two pounds since March. We all should go for a nice walk tomorrow morning."

"What's your ultimate goal?" Carol asked.

Arthur patted his belly and joked, "The only goal on my mind right now is to show you girls a great time once I get out of these filthy duds. The word is out that you're in town. Wait until you see our circle of friends. We're not in Mayberry, sisters. Get ready for a lot of f-bombs from these quirky clowns. The quicker I clean up out back, the faster I can boogie home to get ready. See you real soon. Don't get too much of a head start on me."

They walked out of the store with Chris leading them to a street that led to the beach. They crossed a small bridge, with a tidal pool beneath it that led to a small sandbar where people were lounging about in beach chairs. Adjacent to a small inn was a tiny porch that had been converted into a tiki bar with about a dozen carousers whooping it up. A couple of excited men called out Chris's name as they approached, and the trio joined the festive scene. The girls were mortified, as the throng of men instantly stepped over one another, introducing themselves and hugging and kissing Carol and Edna as if they were long-lost friends.

Carol was taken aback by the friendliness of the welcome committee and felt like a celebrity. She was the sister of their friend, and the outgoing show of support was for Chris's benefit not hers, which made her extremely proud to be his older sister.

Edna's face was red from embarrassment, and she softly giggled in Chris's ear, "I'm afraid of what they'd do to us if we set up the bar."

Chris remarked, "The boys aren't even laying it on thick. They genuinely love people. It's that accepting attitude that makes this town much more than a tourist destination. There's a legitimate sense of equality here, where gays and lesbians can openly express their freedom and prosper without any repercussions. The social barriers to entry here were broken years ago. You'll see plenty of intermingling between straights and gays."

Edna joked, "I feel like a goddess. I've never had so many men throw themselves at me like that. I'm assuming this gaggle of geese must be all gay. Such is my luck."

They had a few beers while enjoying the sunset and chit-chatting with the locals as the sky became a mixture of burnt orange and silver. Some of the guys had left to get out of their beach attire and shower, imploring Chris to meet up with them later. Those who stayed behind were treated to last call on the house, as well as three boxes of complimentary pizza. The owner explained there was a mix-up with the order and that it should have been delivered more than an hour earlier and insisted he wanted to see it all gone The girls deftly took advantage, eating two slices each, since the last time they'd had anything to eat was a burger during their short layover in Albany. Chris explained the place only opened for a few hours a day until a little past sunset. "Don't worry, girls. The sidewalks aren't getting rolled up around here," he joked.

Off they went to another bar situated on a corner, about a five-minute walk from the previous spot, called the Front Deck. They went upstairs, where there was a piano bar with a musician playing and singing popular tunes to mostly gay patrons, some singing along with him. Around the piano was seating for a half-dozen crooners, who loudly belted out the lyrics to Neil Diamond's "Sweet Caroline." Chris led them to a table where Arthur was seated and talking to a few people.

"Here are my Michigan mamas," Arthur said. "I'd like you to meet our friend Luigi, his wife Valerie, and her cousin visiting from New York, Francesca. Place your tooshes down, and make yourselves comfortable."

Edna and Carol introduced themselves, and Carol added, "You must be the Luigi who's responsible for the wonderful artwork in Arthur and Chris's den. You're very talented. I recognized the name from the signature."

Luigi nodded and thanked her profusely, expressing his gratitude by shaking her hand once more, as his wife proudly beamed while massaging his shoulder. Arthur rubbed his other shoulder and added, "I love this big lunk. There's nothing he can't do—sculptures, paintings, clothing design. He can reupholster any kind of furniture and even makes handbags and custom jewelry. Other than that he's boring as hell." The entire table laughed as Arthur ordered another round.

Carol continued to focus on Arthur. He was really in his glory, stopping in mid-conversation to sing along for a few words, with his arm around Chris, who was constantly smiling. He seemed larger than life, as people in the room periodically stopped by the table to say hello and hug him. He was wearing a light-blue, long-sleeve dress-shirt open at the top, revealing a thick braided gold chain and fuzzy chest hair. He had on an expensive-looking watch as well as a sapphire-and-gold pinkie ring on his left hand. He was tan, which made his shiny teeth appear very white. His eyes were dark brown, and his hair was jet black; it was thinning a bit on top but still had tight curls on the front and sides. He wasn't strictly matinee handsome. More so he had distinguished features that made him appear more mature for his age. He was far from shy and a bit crass—not in a belittling manner but in an overly descriptive way, to further punctuate his stories. Carol could understand why Chris was drawn to him.

The mood at the table couldn't have been merrier. Carol had been in a few predominantly gay bars when she had visited Chris in New York, and having a gay sibling gave her a heads-up regarding what to expect. She had been a bit fretful that Edna might feel uneasy, but those fears were expeditiously abolished, as she witnessed her cousin frolicking between two dancing guys on her way back from the ladies' room. Edna waved her hands, encouraging Carol to join them. Carol got up, danced along for a few songs until her thirst caught up to her, then headed back to the table, leaving Edna gyrating in the middle of six guys. She was slowly pushing her hair up sexily with her hands to cool off, acting like a junior in college.

Edna finally came over to the table and downed her vodka drink in one swoop. She had been dancing for so long that the ice had melted, causing her to gag for a bit, while yelling into Carol's ear, "I don't know what it is! I feel so powerful around all these men!"

Carol shook her head in disbelief, and responded, "Right. Listen, Superwoman, you might as well have kryptonite between your legs. You don't have the right anatomy to compete in here with over half this crowd, which renders you powerless."

Edna laughed and explained, "That's the fun of it. When there's no sex factor involved, you don't have any misguided preconceptions, and you feel unencumbered."

Arthur overheard their conversation, laughed heartily, and jokingly offered some unsolicited advice while looking at the men dancing. "Be careful. You don't want to get in the crossfire of a sword fight out there. You might get accidently poked by a misguided cucumber, if you know what I mean." The entire table roared as Arthur ordered another round, gave Edna a warm embrace, and sweetly kissed her on the forehead.

More people stopped by the table, and Arthur hopped to the surrounding tables, asking if he could take a chair here and there so the new arrivals could sit down. Carol watched as he pushed the incoming chairs to the table. It was as if everyone was his personal guest and he couldn't relax until he knew they were comfortable. He was a take-charge kind of guy, with a magnetic persona, which made people want to be in his presence, Carol concluded.

The night was getting long in the tooth. Carol yawned and noticed that the crowd around the piano bar had thinned out. She judged the piano player as being very good, given how he could stop on a dime, tell a funny joke, and continue playing where he had left off with perfect timing. He was more entertainer than pure piano player at present, but Carol decided, by examining how his fingers moved with little effort, that he could play at a more advanced level.

Both Edna and Chris noticed her looking toward the piano. "Are you tempted to join him?" Edna quietly asked, so no one could hear and embarrass her cousin into going up there.

Carol hadn't given it any thought. She was on hiatus and felt no emotional attachment to playing the piano. All she pined for was to tickle Tom, not the ivories. "The piano and I are on a trial separation. Besides, I want to let my nails grow for a change," she kidded.

Chris gave her a wink. He knew what she was going through, and he secretly yearned for her to fall in love with Tom and move to Maine. There was little reason for her to stay in Dearborn. Their mom had passed, and Edna was to be married soon, starting a new life of her own. Carol needed a fresh commitment, a sense of duty, a cause, anything to escape the dreary confinement of her current situation. He reasoned that personal growth does indeed leave a few regrettable and hurtful emotional scars along the way, but they're a necessity. They enable one to insightfully navigate life's convoluted journey, and their marks shouldn't be feared, perceived as a detriment, or used as an excuse. If his sister's budding relationship with Tom wasn't the right impetus, so be it; she would need to seek out something else, wherever it took her.

Chris knew he was being somewhat selfish, wanting his sister to be so close to him, but he couldn't let go of the possibility that their lives could be on a parallel trajectory—i.e., both of them moving to Maine to be with the ones they loved. He was a romantic fool and always felt love should be impulsive. He couldn't wait to meet Tom the next day.

"It's getting late, Arthur. Drink up. Let's go. You'll thank me tomorrow. Think about how much better it will be walking along the beach with the girls in the morning. It's well past midnight," Chris sensibly said.

Arthur paid the tab, tuning out everyone who was trying to donate to the cause. He made sure to hug every person at the table, as well as a few more, and tossed a twenty-dollar bill into the piano tip jar to acknowledge the entertainer on the way out. They walked down the steps into the breezy night singing the theme song to *The Love Boat* on the short trip home.

"We're at our port of call," Edna announced as they entered the house.

Chapter 24

The morning sunlight never had felt so welcoming to Carol. Her senses were keen and her thoughts clear. Her body felt fine, as she had wisely avoided the dreaded first night of vacation pitfall of overindulging; instead she had increased her water intake as the night went on and switched to beer for the last few rounds. She wanted to feel healthy and refreshed for Tom. It was a little too early for him to see her at her worst. She couldn't wait to start the day walking on the beach and didn't care whether it was anxiety, energy, or ants in her pants generating her mobile thoughts.

Not so much for Edna. "Go away!" she whined to Chris, as he tapped on her door to awaken her. Carol floated out of bed, put on her sports bra, and quickly got into her workout clothes. She slowly opened Edna's door. "I'm coming, just feeling a bit shaky this morning. They put too many drinks in front of me. I didn't want them to go to waste," Edna calmly stated, trying to make sense of her malaise.

Carol watched as she tried to step into her shorts and kept putting both legs into the same opening. "How sad. I can't watch this. It's a walk, not a three-legged race. I'll see you downstairs, unless you need help hopping down," she joked.

The boys were in the kitchen anxiously waiting to get rolling. It was already six thirty a.m., and the deli opened at eight. Carol complimented them both on how good they looked, especially considering the night before. "You could say we're seasoned pros at this," Arthur said. "At least you girls can get a little shut-eye on the beach. No matter—we'll be ready for this evening. We close at six on Sundays, so we can drink early and often." Everyone laughed as Edna trudged down the steps. "You looked like you were on *Dancing with the Stars* last night," Arthur cracked.

Edna slumped against the kitchen counter and responded in a weak, monotone voice, "I feel like I should be on *Celebrity Rehab* this morning."

A short while later, they all walked down the hill, across the street, and over the bridge, passing the tiki bar from the night before. Edna puckered her lips, gave the place a nasty look, and grumbled, "First scene of the crime."

The end of the street led to the beach. It was extraordinarily long and wide, at least a hundred yards to the ocean. To the left, all Carol could see on the horizon was miles of sand. "It's about two-and-a-half miles to the end. That would mean five miles total," Chris offered, looking in Edna's direction with a mischievous smile.

They walked along the shoreline, where the sand was hard packed. Seagulls, terns, and sandpipers swirled around them in uncountable multitudes. Their chants were somewhat muted by the seemingly angry roar of the smashing waves. Many joggers and walkers were sprinkled about. Some were with dogs, defiantly ignoring the signs that read, No Dogs Allowed on Beach. Carol pointed to two brave souls waist deep in the ocean, getting tossed about, screaming at each other in a familiar non-English tongue. "French Canadians," Arthur observed. "They jump in this frigid water as if they were in Miami."

The pace was ferocious, far from a leisurely stroll, with Edna taking the lead, berating the crew and bragging about her recuperative powers. Chris replied, in an attempt to set her straight, "Ha, you neglect to mention the power four Advils possess. Another thing—the glare from the monster bling on your finger is blinding us."

They continued their walk, pointing in awe at the funky beach homes dotted along the way. A large rock seawall obstructed their path, and Chris signaled for them to turn around. Arthur jogged up to the much deeper dry sand farthest from the shoreline, and they all followed. The conversation slowed immensely on the walk back. The footing was challenging, and there was a brisk headwind. Edna began to lag behind, much to the delight of the guys up front leading the charge, who had received the brunt of her earlier braggadocio.

Carol turned around, urging her on, "Less than a quarter-mile to go. I can see the spot up ahead where we started." Edna gave a crooked smile, ran up to Carol, then zoomed past the startled guys. Everyone ran after her until they all made it back to the beach-access ramp.

"You're my vixen queen!" Arthur puffed out when he finally caught up to her.

All four were invigorated by the scenery and the boot-camp-style walk. "It's a great way to start the day. I could get used to this," Carol chimed in, as she noticed the line forming at a breakfast spot along the way. The aroma of coffee, fresh muffins, and bacon rapidly invaded the group's flared nostrils.

"My suggestion, girls, would be to stop by the deli, and we'll make you breakfast sandwiches," Arthur said. "All the sit-down breakfast joints will be too crowded. It could be lunchtime by the time you get seated. I left you a shoulder cooler in the kitchen. The beach chairs are in the side yard. You can fill up the cooler with whatever you want. It's going to be a near perfect beach day. You don't know how badly we both wish we could join you."

Back at the house, Edna and Carol showered quickly, put on their bathing suits, and slathered up with SPF 50 tanning lotion. They both wore one-pieces. Carol's was bright red; Edna's was black-and-white polka dot.

"You look like a lifeguard," Edna said.

Carol quickly retorted, "You look like a Dalmatian."

They grabbed the chairs and flip-flopped down to the deli. It was crowded with people waiting in line for sandwiches. Chris and Arthur had a high-school student on summer break helping them. It was her first day, but she didn't seem frazzled by the anxious customers as she rung them up and counted out the change with patience and poise. Chris glanced toward her, then to Carol and Edna, and they all made eye contact with one another.

"Hi, I'm Glema," she said in a Scandinavian accent, revealing a mouthful of braces as she smiled. Her long blonde hair flowed over her sparkling blue eyes as she bent over to hand them a plastic goodie bag each. "There's egg and cheese on a toasted English muffin, along with a turkey, cheese, and avocado sandwich in each bag. Chris wants you to help yourself to the ice, drinks, and snacks."

Edna and Carol quietly thanked her, trying to not act conspicuous as they walked past the customers standing in line. They grabbed ice, diet cola, bottled water, and pretzels, and filled the soft cooler outside on the sidewalk with red faces, as they weren't used to such preferential treatment.

The two cousins marched along with an army of beach enthusiasts, all happily heading for a fun-filled day by the water. Once their toes touched the golden sand, the incoming crowd broke out of formation, scurrying about for a prime spot. Carol directed Edna to a barren area near a rock formation. They situated their chairs facing the ocean and sat down, taking in the gorgeous landscape. Edna let out a sigh of relief as she ravenously bit into her sandwich and guzzled down some water, looking instantly replenished. Carol slowly ate, licking her lips and savoring each nibble, as she checked out the burgeoning beach scene, quite satisfied with their semi-reclusive sunbathing spot. It was just far enough away from a small congregation of harried parents chasing after screaming infants, and a gaggle of giggling teens with a loud boom box. It wasn't exactly a chamber of silence, but it wasn't in the middle of the commotion.

It didn't take long for both women to ease into a sound sleep, facilitated by the heavenly breeze, soothing sun, and the billowing waves. Carol dreamt in anticipation of the upcoming evening, seeing Tom, and introducing him to her brother. Her body felt as if it were softly floating into the sky, bobbing along the white puffy clouds. It was a sensation of unabashed freedom she hadn't experienced in her entire life—void of responsibility, guilt, or worry. She was on a boundless adventure without a care where it had begun or a snippet of curiosity about where it ended; she was living only for the illustrious moment.

A familiar tone entered her buoyant dream, totally disrupting it. Carol slowly came down from the clouds, still half-asleep, and rumbled through the beach bag for her phone. All thumbs, she picked up the vibrating handset and dropped it in her lap but recovered fast enough to answer without seeing who was calling, hoping to hear Tom's heaven-sent voice. It wasn't meant to be. It was Kevin.

"Hi. Just checking in to see how the trip's going. How's Chris? What do you think of Arthur? How's the weather?" he asked in machine-gun fire.

Carol thought it peculiar for Kevin to sound so inquisitive. Maybe she was still asleep, but one glance at Edna's shiny engagement ring, along with her own belly-button reservoir of sweat, answered that question. "Everything's been great so far. Chris seems happy. Arthur is a wisecracking movie character right out of central casting. They both work hard. Today, on a Sunday, ten hours," she explained. "Edna and I are at the beach. She's beside me in a coma. Too much alcohol for her last night."

Kevin laughed and then asked, "How's their house? Are you staying there the whole week?"

Carol didn't know how to respond at first. Kevin didn't know about Tom and probably wouldn't understand their "dalliance," or whatever it was. She hesitated then decided to tell him the truth. "Actually, Edna and I are heading up to Kennebunkport on Tuesday morning and staying for a few days at an inn owned by a new guy I'm seeing. I met him a couple of months ago in Detroit, and we've been hitting it off ever since. He's driving down for dinner this evening to meet Chris. He already knows Edna. I was with her when we first met," she rambled.

"I guess I deserve being left in the dark. I haven't been a good brother. It's bothered me for a long time, years in fact, and I just don't know how I can make it up to everyone," Kevin ruefully said.

Carol felt a searing pain in her temples from the shock of her brother's sobering words. "Kevin, you're scaring me. Why the drama all of a sudden? Everyone? Who is everyone?" she asked, nervously digging her feet into the sand, waiting for a response. She thought she heard a faint sniffle on the line. "Kevin, are you there? What's going on with you?" Her troubled voice awakened Edna, and Carol stood up, walking in circles around their cozy encampment.

"I didn't mean to worry you. Things are fine. I've made decisions in my life I've never been happy with. That's all. The more I try to rectify things, the harder it gets," Kevin said in exasperation.

Carol stopped orbiting and said, "I forgive you for whatever grievous mistakes you've made. Just talk to me! Are things okay with you and Kristin? Is it work? Do you have a student loan twenty years past due? Did you run a red light? Did you get caught cheating at golf? What could be so bad? You could talk to me more often and make a concerted effort to take an interest in my life. That's all I've ever wanted from older brother all these years. Start communicating with me, your closest blood relative, right this instant!"

Edna rose from her chair with her mouth agape, moving her arms about, pleading for a clue as to with whom Carol was talking. Carol waved her off, and she held the phone tightly with both hands trying to concentrate on Kevin's response, turning her back to Edna.

"Have a great rest of your vacation," Kevin said. "I'm happy for you. I hope everything works out with this new guy. It's time for you to start caring about yourself instead of others. Your life hasn't been easy these last few years." There was silence on the line. Carol stood there fruitlessly calling out his name, clinging to the hope that Kevin was just pausing for a moment, until it became apparent that he had hung up.

Tears rolled down Carol's face. Her emotions had just run the gamut. In one swift moment, she had gone from defying gravity up the stairway to heaven in restful bliss to crashing into the ground, eyes wide open, without a parachute.

Edna saw the look on her face. "It's Kevin, isn't it?" she asked.

Carol nodded and said, "Yes, I'm worried. I told him about Tom, expecting him to counter with a few cautionary words, as a protective big brother should, but he unexpectedly expressed remorse that he hadn't been a very nice brother to me. Then he said he wanted to make things up to 'everyone,' which can mean a whole bunch of unsuspecting people. He wasn't specific about anything when I pressed him. It's much more complicated than a simple mea culpa. I can feel it. He wants to divulge a secret, but he can't channel himself to do so. I've never known my brother to sound so vulnerable. Something was already stirring inside him when he called. He just inadvertently fired a flare in the sky. Some search-and-rescue crew we are. I guess we know where to find him, but the real issue is that we need the special code to unlock whatever is festering inside him, and I'm not sure how to find it."

The area around them had become more populated while they had snoozed. The new neighbors to their immediate left were a spry elderly couple. Edna and Carol grinned as they watched the husband carefully peel a banana. He inspected it, gave his approval, and took a tiny bite before lovingly handing it to his appreciative wife to enjoy. In front of them, tainting the pristine ocean-view, a sand-covered, twenty-something couple dry-humped on a flimsy motel towel.

Edna shook her head. "When will the director of this skin flick yell 'Cut'?" she asked in disgust. "Back to Kevin. It doesn't sound to me a covert operation is necessary. We won't have to resort to pouring truth serum in his drink or using hypnosis. He's already torturing himself, which saves us from that task at least. He'll be spilling his guts soon enough. Let's try to enjoy this awesome day. Look, it's lunchtime now. Come on, cousin. Sit down and read one of your scandal sheets, and you'll feel better seeing how bizarre other peoples' lives are."

Chapter 25

The padded chair on the front porch was a welcome relief from the beach chair Carol had sat on for five hours earlier in the day. She took a sip of her lemonade in the cooling shade, rubbing the sand off between her toes, which the shower hadn't washed away. She was dressed in jeans, a black blouse that smartly sprouted out at the bottom and showed off her taut behind, and black sandals. A circling hornet buzzed close by, left, then reappeared. It was more curious than threatening and exited for good within a minute. Carol hoped Tom didn't find her as boring as the insect did.

Arthur and Chris walked up the steps. "That Glema seems on the ball," Carol told them.

Arthur laughed. "Yes, she's a friend's younger cousin from Norway. She goes to UNH, speaks better English than I do, and will be a big help. Not my type of course, but I saw more than a few boys noticing her."

Carol laughed as Arthur scooted into the house, motioning for Chris to stay out on the porch. She told him about what had transpired earlier in the day with Kevin. He reached the same conclusion. "The guy called out for help. He's not lost in the car asking for directions. He's in his own personal purgatory and must expiate his sins before he can move on. In the meantime, we sit helplessly in limbo, hoping the stain from his sins doesn't fall upon us," he said in preacher-like prose, then quickly switched gears. "Hey! I'm excited to meet Tom. Let me get ready."

Edna stepped onto the porch, a glass of white wine in hand and wearing tight jeans, a sleeveless pumpkin-colored top revealing her tanned shoulders, and navy high heels. Her hair was up in a bun. Carol couldn't help notice how striking her cousin looked, as the shadow eclipsing the porch gave her a brushed radiance. Tom texted Carol, saying he would be leaving the inn shortly and would meet them at the restaurant. She tried to call Kevin to clear her conscience but got his voicemail and hung up without leaving a message. She always delved into humor when in crisis mode and wondered whether Kevin had been put off by her rash comedic attempt earlier, as she tried in vain to extract the truth out of him.

Convincing herself it was time to look ahead, she checked on the boys and was surprised to find them both ready, pushing each other away from the hallway mirror while primping their hair. Both were dressed in jeans. Arthur had on a pale-yellow, long-sleeve dress shirt. Chris wore a short-sleeve black V-neck and was flexing his biceps.

"Summer guns. Got to have them, my sister," he joked. "You look great. You've got a little color in those cheeks for lover boy."

* * *

They walked into Antone's and informed the bubbly young hostess that she could find them at the bar when their reservation was ready. It was like stepping into someone's den. Carol noticed a tiny bar against the far wall that sat eight people, and also three couches, each placed alongside a wall. The setting was more for people waiting to dine than for a nightly destination. The smell of garlic-infused mussels saturated the air. Carol and Edna sat on one of the couches. Chris sat next to them, and Arthur sat atop the arm, balancing himself on Chris's shoulder. Before they could order a drink, Tom peeked in. Carol spotted him and hoisted herself up to usher him into the room. He was casually dressed in khaki shorts, a thin-striped light-blue golf shirt, and brown loafers. His outfit screamed summer. Arthur warned the group in jest, "Oh, my. This one will get eaten alive in this town. Don't let him out of your sight, even if you have to follow him into the bathroom." Fortunately, Tom was too occupied embracing Carol to overhear him.

After a round of introductions, the hostess informed them that their table was ready, and they left the bar for the dining area, which consisted of three rooms different in size and decor, all dusted in intimacy by candles, dark lighting, and warm, enticing smiles. Carol envisioned the room as it may have looked years ago, a piano in the corner by the large window, a maroon rug, a crystal chandelier, intricate crown molding, and perhaps a mahogany table on which to serve silver plates of finger sandwiches and scones to go along with afternoon tea. "It feels a smidge as if we're sitting in what once was the parlor," she observed.

Arthur nodded, and offered, "We chose this place because of the layout. With all the walls, the background noise gets muffled so we won't have to yell at one another. Is there such a word as 'smidge,' by the way? Is it imported from Michigan? The food here is very creative, especially the pasta dishes."

Carol took offense, playfully responding, "You're questioning my grasp of the English vernacular? You're one to talk. I believe you used the word 'poppycock' last night. I was surprised I didn't hear 'balderdash' also. Those words were burned at the stake years ago back in England."

They all laughed at Carol's tenacity. The waiter came by and took their drink order, starting with the women and ending with Arthur. "I'll have a vodka and soda water, and could I please have a 'smidge' of cranberry juice with that?" he asked, checking to see whether the waiter knew what he meant. The group all laughed at him as the waiter left the table without inquiring what a smidge was. "And another thing, 'poppycock,' I'm sure, has a whole different meaning in this town," he said in a defensive tone.

Tom was his usual jovial self, trading stories with Arthur about politics, favorite restaurants in the area, and the economy. Both were so charismatic that Carol could sense people at the surrounding tables straining to gather tidbits of the constantly flowing conversation. Chris loved it when Arthur took center stage and held court, but Carol could tell he was more engrossed by Tom. His words were so thought out, never confrontational, with his captivating blue eyes scanning the table, appealing for others to join in. His delivery was polite and polished yet still full of wit. If Tom were at an audition, he would nail the part. Chris stared deeply into his sister's eyes. Edna caught his eyes traversing the table until they settled onto hers, and he camouflaged a quick, reassuring smile. Tom already had won him over.

At the end of the meal, Arthur scanned the collection of empty plates and polled each of them individually about their dishes. He was an ardent foodie, always searching for a flawless combination of flavors, and he listened with unbounded enthusiasm, filing away their descriptions while smacking his lips, rolling his eyes, and wiping his chin with his napkin, as if he had sampled each meal himself.

Tom clearly respected Arthur's passion. "I love to eat a nice, relaxing meal. This has been so pleasurable, as well as educational for me. I'm such a novice and never took into account the finances involved in running a restaurant. I can't thank you guys enough for the insight you provided me," he said.

There were just a few stragglers left in the restaurant. Arthur asked for the bill, and the waiter informed him that Tom already had paid it when he had returned from the restroom.

"At the least let me get us a nightcap. You're more than welcome to stay over, my new friend," Arthur said in appreciation.

Tom sighed and said, "One drink. I wish it could be more, but I have an early breakfast with the local chamber of commerce and want to make a good impression."

They all moved to the bar. The bartender was in the process of placing the garnish tray in the cooler. Carol noticed a rag and spray cleaner on top of the bar. "I'm still open," he cheerfully said. Arthur ordered five lemon drops as they all sat down at the bar.

Chris brought up a funny story about the previous Halloween. "The area got hit with a blizzard the night before that dumped over a foot of snow on the ground. It started at nightfall on a Saturday, which added an eerie dimension to the well-renowned Ogunquit holiday festivities. There were dozens of marauding men in costume, slipping and sliding in the middle of the street, wearing dresses and high heels, unable to get up due to the icy conditions. Anyone trying to assist them ended up in a prone position. Arthur and I had a window seat at the bar around the corner. We already had done the costume scene at a house party the night before, and after hearing the weather forecast, we decided not to dress up. If you must know, I was Daisy Duke, and Arthur went as Pamela Anderson, so you can imagine how skimpy our outfits were. Anyway, we watched the high jinks from our warm, cozy perch, and then the bar lost electricity. They passed out candles, and even though the cash registers weren't working, they kept the bar open, making change with the use of flashlights from a cigar box full of money. It was surreal. Most other places would have closed shop, but there's such a sense of community here that the bar decided that creating an everlasting memory was a higher priority than losing a little money from the few scofflaws who ran out on their tab. I can't speak for Arthur, but it was the first time it felt like home to me here."

Smiling profusely at the fond memory, Arthur gave Chris a tight embrace. Tom cleared his throat and added, "I have an interesting fact to share. In beautiful Carmel, California, it's against the law to wear high heels without a permit. I was at the nineteenth hole at a golf outing out there, and I vaguely remember someone telling me that."

Arthur joked, "Really? Fess up, Tinkerbell. Are you sure if we venture into your closet we won't find a pair of stilettos? Be careful, Carol. We may have a secret cross-dresser in our midst. Maybe you should wear your pumps to liven up your breakfast tomorrow with those old stodgy stuffed clams."

The group erupted into laughter, Tom being the most vocal, wiping a tear out of the corner of his eye. Carol rubbed his back. *He's such a good sport*, she thought.

Knowing Tom could take a joke, Chris added, "We don't go up to Kennebunkport. We could get tarred and feathered and run out of town by those God-fearing conservative zealots. I hear there's a cerebrally challenged former head of the free world who summers up there and had his favorite electric chair shipped in from Texas and makes his grandkids sit on it, all strapped in, for a little punitive quiet time. I wouldn't want to play musical chairs in that house."

Tom couldn't stop laughing. "I assure you there are only skeletons in my closet and no women's shoes. You guys are most welcome at my inn. I can't be held responsible for whatever happens once you stray from the property, though. Maybe I should get an electric fence," he joked. "I really don't want to go, but I should leave while the going is good. I hope to see all of you soon. Edna, I look forward to seeing you very soon."

He reached into his pocket, got his keys, and gave the gang goodbye hugs. Carol measured that his hug with Chris was a few seconds longer, which filled her heart with joy. She tightly took hold of his hand and walked with him out to his car. It was a plain SUV that was far from new. Tom explained that he used it for practical purposes, almost sounding embarrassed. Carol thought it was cute, but she was never one to judge others by what they owned and never raised that way. After seeing her humble house, riding in her clunker, and meeting her brother, Tom had to know that.

They passionately kissed, holding each other tightly, each one not wanting to let go. "I'll see you the day after tomorrow. I can't wait to see the inn. I purposely didn't open up the website so I'd be surprised. It was tough to do. After all, it's so much a part of you," Carol said, aware she might have sounded a bit corny.

Tom responded, "When I hear your voice, all I want to do is be with you. Sometimes it feels better to email, because it's less personal, and talking to you over the phone makes me want to crawl through the line so badly."

They both smiled. "Okay. It's a toss-up," Carol whispered, as Tom slid into the SUV and drove away.

Carol went back into Antone's to find Arthur paying the drink tab. "Tom's a great guy," Chris told her. "Well rounded in every sense. Edna's so right. You two look great together."

Arthur turned around. "I found him to be absolutely delightful. Next time he comes here, I'm going to cook him a meal he'll never forget."

On the walk back to the house, Carol felt relieved the night had gone so well. She wondered why she had been so nervous in the first place. Everyone said their "good nights" upon entering the house. The boys weren't on vacation, and Edna, who had been unusually quiet during dinner, was still feeling the effects from the night before. Carol wasn't particularly sleepy and looked out the window. She noticed how bright the stars were in the clear sky. In Dearborn, they were dulled by the city skyline and had a far-away twinkle, making life appear so dim. Here the stars appeared vibrant and ethereal, filling her with optimism about what the next day might bring. She'd had similar feelings while on vacation in the past but always knew the reality of going home within days would extinguish them. This trip had a sense of permanence. It felt more like an opening chapter to a novel. Only this time it wasn't fiction, or about somebody else's life.

Chapter 26

Carol heard a slight tap on the bedroom door.

"Are you awake?" Edna whispered.

Carol was reading a DIY magazine and told her to come in. "Do you know how easy it is to install a garbage disposal yourself?" Carol asked.

Edna sat next to her and rolled her eyes. "Grinding one's hand into hamburger meat doesn't sound appealing. It may be a wee bit difficult to play the piano without any fingers," she joked. "Although I saw the way you glared at that piano the other night. You looked as if you wanted to set fire to it. I thought it was just the piano at your house you had anger issues with. Apparently no piano is safe."

The front door slammed shut, followed by the sound of footsteps, confirming that the boys were off for another long day at the deli. Carol felt a little guilty and wished they had the liberty of playing hooky for the day. "I just remembered a strange dream I had yesterday at the beach," she told Edna. "I was playing the piano while floating on a cloud. Faceless people were sitting on countless clouds in the distance. All the clouds rolled closer to me, forming one large peaceful audience. I was playing 'Born Free,' and for the first time in years, my heart and fingers were in tune. The only way the assemblage could express their appreciation was to rub the clouds together to produce a thunderous applause. A driving rain immediately followed the clapping thunder."

"I could see smiles on every person floating on the horizon," Carol continued. "When I looked below, I saw people scurrying to escape the downpour with frowns across their faces. The people in the sky were in a glorious mood while the people below were miserable. Then I heard music, and on the cloud next to mine sat our mothers smiling at me, their features so angelic, literally the only faces in the crowd. The music grew disturbingly louder and louder until it startled me out of my dream. It was my phone ringing, and Kevin was on the line. I just remembered the dream now. I know it means something, but I can't interpret it," she said in frustration.

Edna got up and pretended she was floating around the room. "Who knows? Dreams never make sense. Here's what I think it means. As much as you try, it's impossible to please everyone. One team always has to lose. You didn't come across any dark clouds up there. No rainbow either. What kind of dream is that?" she kidded, content with her wishy-washy analysis.

Edna was back to her wisecracking self, which bode well for the rest of the trip, but Carol was a little disappointed. Edna was always the one who looked to heaven to gain any sense of why things happened on Earth. Her indifferent dismissal of the dream came as somewhat of a surprise. Carol rationalized it may have been that Edna's body had rebounded from a good night's sleep, and her mind was racing too much for her to slow it down and concentrate. Her biggest concern was to make sure her cousin never felt out of place during the trip. She feared Edna may have felt like a fifth wheel at dinner, but perhaps it was purely a case of cobwebs having overtaken her mind. Melting under the sun for five hours surely didn't help either, even if she did sleep for a couple of hours.

"I have so much energy today," Edna said. "Let's hit the beach for a couple of hours, then walk around, do some shopping, and have a lobster roll and a few drinks."

Carol put her hands up. "Slow down, and catch your breath. Conserve a little of that giddy-up. I'll do whatever you want," she said as she got up to change into her bathing suit. "I'll meet you on the front porch in fifteen minutes. Do some yoga or something in the meantime. I swear I can hear your thoughts ricocheting in your head."

There was a slight fog cover overhead as the women stepped outside, which was predicted to burn off well before noon. The sun occasionally made a cameo appearance and teasingly warmed their toes, but they weren't in the mood to play peek-a-boo and lollygagged their way into town. They had resisted the temptation to go shopping for a couple of days and didn't need much of an excuse to do so. They lazily zigzagged throughout the area, buying cheap lobster-claw key chains and other items of that silly nature, challenging each other in jest as to which of them could purchase the dumbest piece of junk.

It was almost noon, and they stopped by the deli to get some refreshments. The place was nowhere near as busy as the day before. Chris explained it was usually slower during the week—today was Monday—but stressed that the cloud cover wasn't helping, and the weather usually dictated how busy they'd be. "We pay attention to the weather forecast more than a postal worker does," he said. "Over time we've gotten a feel for how much inventory we should have. Being at the mercy of Mother Nature is never a comforting thought."

He recommended a walk down to the tip of Perkin's Cove where they could find a few restaurants perched on the water to grab lunch and enjoy the view. Glema nodded in agreement and innocently said, "Do you have your IDs? My uncle got carded at a place there, and he's forty."

Edna snarled, "Wow, he's almost ancient. I hope he got an elderly discount. Maybe we can too!"

Glema gave her a nervous smile and headed back to the register. Chris shot Edna an amazed look and scolded her. "Nice! She doesn't know you're turning forty in a couple of weeks. You took it the wrong way. I believe she was attempting to convey that you look young."

Carol let out a quick burst of laughter, stopping instantly when Chris gave her an icy glance while giving Edna an urging elbow. Edna reluctantly walked over to the register, her head down and eyes facing the floor. "I'm sorry, Glema. I overreacted. I know you were trying to pay us a compliment. Is that right?" she meekly asked.

A whole mouth of tinsel responded, "Yes. I'm sorry you took it the wrong way. You both look very young for your age."

The women scurried out of the deli. "I still say she meant the opposite," Edna said. The kid didn't know when to quit when she was ahead. 'You both look very young for your age.' What nerve! You know what I want for my birthday? I want a nice big pimple on my face so I can feel young again!"

Carol laughed heartily, stomping her foot on the ground once they were out of sight. They strolled down to the cove, stopping on a whim to do some serious shopping and add to their junk collection.

It was the kind of carefree time Carol greatly desired with her cousin. Getting lost in the day was what vacation was all about and she concluded the deli had been aptly named. They finally went into a restaurant situated on the tip of the cove and luckily found a window seat where they could watch the waves pound against the rocky shoreline, leaving behind a bubbly white froth. They opened their bags, laughing at all the stuff they had bought, until Carol added up her receipts. "Oh, my. I spent over fifty bucks on stuff I'll never use!" she proclaimed, holding her hand over her face, knowing all the while that every time she opened her junk drawer at home, she'd cherish each item, because it would remind her of the time she'd spent with Edna. She hoped Edna felt the same way too, as she watched her examine her own trinkets.

They gabbed over a cup of chowder and a lobster roll each, and slowly sipped a few Bloody Marys with a colossal shrimp placed on top. Even their server was entertaining. She was a middle-aged character with a husky voice and an axe for a tongue. Edna hit it off with her from the start. *Surprise, surprise*, Carol thought, listening to them yak about how disrespectful kids were these days. The time flew by.

Finally the waitress informed them that the evening shift was coming on and asked if they could settle the bill before she left. Right to the end, she had them in stitches. "I don't know why I'm in such a hurry to get out of here. It's not like I have to freshen up before a big night out. There aren't enough eligible bachelors around here who appreciate a seasoned woman of the world like me with four bratty kids, three cats, two dogs, and a dropped bladder," she wisecracked.

* * *

It was almost six o'clock. Carol and Edna sat on the front porch reading magazines from the boys' extensive collection, no doubt unsold leftovers from the deli. They looked up to see Chris and Arthur walking up the hill looking exhausted. Carol suggested to Edna that it may be more prudent to stay in so they could all relax; they both were still full from the long lunch.

Edna agreed. "Hi, guys. You look so beat. We don't need to be shown the sights tonight. Believe me—we covered enough ground today," she told them as they walked up the steps. Arthur held onto the railing and looked toward Chris, who looked up to the sky. "Thank you God," Chris said in appreciation. "We were just discussing the options, and the best we came up with was getting some pizza and having a few glasses of wine. We haven't spent any time with just you two, and you both are off to greener pastures tomorrow. I can't wait to drive you to Kennebunkport and get a tour of the inn."

That night they all sat on the front porch, protected from a passing light shower, dining alfresco and sharing stories about romance and adventure. Edna lit up talking about Nick, their honeymoon plans, and how he strangely seemed to bring her closer to her father. During the conversation, Carol felt as if she were at the low end on the happiness meter. She was making assessable progress, however, and understood wholesale life changes don't happen overnight.

Her brother appeared regal, sitting on the wicker couch in silhouette, his right leg crossed, his foot grazing Arthur's knee, sounding so optimistic about the prospects of their life together while declaring his love for Arthur. A sense of clarity shot through Carol as she silently sat and compared her brothers. All these years, she believed it was Kevin who'd had it all: a trophy wife, beautiful children, an enriching career, and an expensive home. Now Kevin appeared to be a fragile wreck, unsatisfied, sullen, and twisting in the wind looking for direction. It was Chris who had been the stronger brother the entire time, facing adversity at such a young age, dusting off every time he had fallen down, and springing right back up. Her mother had comprehended the illimitable power of his inner strength years ago. Things had come easier for Kevin. He was almost forty and had yet to fall down. Carol wondered whether her older brother ever could fully recuperate from his afflictions. She loved them the same, but she always had been twice as worried about Chris. No more. In terms of worry, the pendulum had swung to Kevin's side by a huge factor.

Chapter 27

It was about four p.m. on a sunny day as Chris turned into Kennebunkport's Lower Village, joining a crawling procession of cars, scooters, and horse-drawn carriages. Carol and Edna excitedly rolled down the windows, taking in the buzz, and getting a whiff of fried clams, boat fuel, and, as they went over the Dock Square Bridge, the stench of low tide. The town center was tightly packed on both sides with numerous stores, restaurants, and bars overlooking the river. They veered onto Ocean Avenue and slowly passed art galleries, inns, and bed and breakfasts.

Carol's heart fluttered as she saw the sign for the Nautical Inn. Chris turned left and drove up the long paved driveway, stopping halfway so they could study the view. The three of them sat in complete amazement. It was more majestic than Carol had imagined and surpassed Tom's unassuming description. Even if she had peeked on the website, the pictures wouldn't have done it justice, she reasoned while scratching her goose bumps.

"This place is postcard perfect," Chris stated, as he watched a middle-aged male guest donning a Yankees cap relax in an Adirondack chair reading a book, looking back at them, and probably guessing whether the idling car would ever move forward.

"I feel like we just hit the jackpot," Edna chirped.

Chris parked the car near the designated check-in sign, and they walked up the steps to the sprawling porch. They entered through the door to the reception desk, where Tom stood chatting with a couple.

"I'm glad you guys are here!" he called across the room. "Allow me to introduce you to two dear friends of mine, Jim and Gina McDonough, who are staying here this week. This is Chris, Edna, and Carol."

They all shook hands and Gina declared, "Carol, I've heard so many nice things about you. Usually sports and the stock market are all Tom talks about, but you've been dominating the headlines since we got here. I hope to see you girls later."

Carol was thrilled with the warm greeting and gave Tom a hug. He grabbed a room key, put his arms around Chris and Edna, and steered them into the lounge, looking back for Carol to follow. She moved along, not knowing where to look first, overwhelmed by the plush interior and the view of a Great Blue Heron standing still in the marsh outside the floor-to-ceiling windows, as if it were posing for a photograph. She could smell the leather on the new bar seats and the varnish on the wood molding. Tom gave them all drinks to sip while he showed them around. They passed through the dining room. The tables were all set with thick white cloths, detailed silverware, and tall wineglasses.

Tom led them through the swinging doors into the large kitchen. It was stainless-steel appliance galore. Chris was smitten with the two large walk-in freezers. He dragged his fingers along the oven as he complimented Tom. "These are all top-of-the-line brands," he said, undoubtedly calculating the cost in his head. They dodged a worker stirring a vat of lobster bisque, and Tom motioned for them to watch their step as they hopped over a crate of tomatoes on the way out.

"I'll show you to your room now, and I'll bring your luggage up in a jiffy," he said, as he pressed the elevator button. "You ladies have a corner room on the second floor. I figured it would be quieter, as it's the farthest from the elevator. You have a great view of the marsh and the side lawn," he explained.

The room was exceptionally elegant, yet practical, with more than enough room for luggage. It had all the bells and whistles that Tom had described to Carol during his visit to Dearborn. She saw a pair of queen platform beds with retractable lights on the wall for night reading. From the bath products to the linens, Tom had overlooked no details.

Carol looked proudly at his beaming smile. "You did a really great job," she said warmly. "I love the design. The soft music playing is a nice touch also."

The group left the room and took the stairs down to the lobby. "Where do you live?" Chris asked, as the group followed Tom out the rear door to another large porch that faced the marsh. In between stood a manicured lawn that curled to the left and led to a newly restored carriage house situated in front of a large barn. The impressive house was a diminutive replica of the grandiose inn.

"Over there," Tom humbly said, pointing to the carriage house while waving for them to follow him. Carol was surprised. Tom had told her he lived at the inn, but she assumed it was in one of the rooms. "I had it completely rebuilt with every intention of renting it out, but once I saw the finished product, I selfishly wanted it for myself," he explained, as they curiously walked inside. "This house is more than a thousand square feet larger than our biggest guest room in the main house. I figured it's more suitable to entertain in here."

The house had an open floor plan. There was a large main room with exposed wooden beams that had a stone fireplace that took up almost the entire far wall. "This room is bigger than my entire first floor," Carol said in amazement.

The kitchen was small with four barstools around a granite counter. There were two bedrooms. One small one was fitted with a queen bed that was situated next to a bathroom with a stand-alone shower. The master bedroom had a king-size platform bed. The master bath had double sinks with granite counter tops. It was equipped with a good-size tiled shower with a glass door and a rainwater shower spout.

"I absolutely love it. Your taste is impeccable. I can't blame you for wanting this. Being confined to a room isn't your style. This is a more of a home," Chris acknowledged.

Tom graciously thanked him and turned to the women. "This is where you'll stay on your last night. I told you I had it covered and not to worry," he said. Edna gave him a hug and teased, "Thanks. Carol and I can take the master bedroom."

The tour ended back in the lounge, where the group settled into the comfy chairs at the bar. Carol noticed that Tom had even placed hooks underneath the bar for patrons to hang pocketbooks or shopping bags. "I can feel myself dangerously melting into this seat," Chris stated, as he regretfully passed on another drink. "I have to get back. It's the first time Glema has been left alone at the counter. I'll try and get up here before you girls leave. Tom, let me help you with their bags."

Carol and Edna giggled as they looked around the lounge. "A girl can get used to this," Edna said in a teasing tone. "Can't you picture yourself living in that dreamy love nest?"

Carol didn't respond. In fact she already had envisioned herself reading by the glow of the fireplace, sipping a hot chocolate with a throw blanket over her, as Tom affectionately massaged her feet. Edna allowed her cousin to have a short moment to herself, knowing the boys were due back any moment. "I know you're in love with him," she finally said.

Carol was stunned and just sat there. She had had accepted that notion weeks ago but was fearful of confiding her true feelings to Edna, particularly since she had advised her to take it slowly.

"It's okay, Carol. I have no doubt he feels the same way. Falling in love is the easy part. Figuring out the rest is, too. He's not going to move to Michigan. Your decision is simple."

A couple of men dressed in dark suits walked into the lounge. Carol watched as they took off their sunglasses and scoped out the place. She whispered quickly into Edna's bent ear, "I am in love with him. It'll take a lot for me to move, though. There's the issue of the house where I've lived my whole life, and Kevin and the kids, and you, of course. Most important, he hasn't asked me to come out to live here. I'm certainly not going to invite myself."

The conversation abruptly ended when Tom and Chris returned. The men in suits, who had never taken a seat, were looking out toward the marsh. One of them seemed to be measuring the width of the rear door with his hands. Tom walked over to them, and they quietly conversed for a few minutes. They stiffly stood at attention while Tom spoke calmly, leaning against the partition, which separated the dining room from the lounge. They eventually left after Tom gave them his business card. Tom returned to the group.

"IRS troubles already?" Edna snapped.

Tom let out a laugh. "It appears our former president, the older one, has heard some good reviews about the restaurant and may stop by in the near future. Those were Secret Service agents on an advanced scouting mission," he said.

Carol gave him a slight tap on the arm and said with a pinch of sarcasm, "Those guys looked like a lot of fun. You shouldn't let any riff-raff come in here, ex-head of the free world or not."

The group all snickered as Chris said goodbye. "That's my cue to leave before they run me out of town," he joked.

Carol and Edna returned to their room to freshen up. Carol splashed some water on her face and leaned against the sink as she looked into the mirror. Her thoughts turned to Edna's earlier comments. She could merrily dream all she wanted about her future with Tom, but all she had known was a lifetime mired in mediocrity. She didn't know what he saw in her at all. Except for a few excursions here and there, she was far from a worldly adventurer, choosing to live at home all these years. Financially, she was barely above the poverty level put forth by the government guidelines. It was great she had some financial footing, courtesy of her thoughtful parents, but it wasn't enough for the long term, and it was currently tied up for the time being. She was thirty-seven-years old and for years had struggled with the fact that she never had married. Tom must have wondered what was wrong with her. She feared he might decide to exhaust every resource to unfold a flaw or any unflattering characteristic before committing to a relationship that didn't involve a half-a-continent commute. Edna's words of encouragement did alleviate some of her anxiety. As usual, her cousin wouldn't allow her to grow despondent, and she loved her for that, but Carol had to push aside any thoughts about her future with Tom and enjoy the moment. She was his temporary guest for now. She had never been skilled at making demands or being aggressively persistent, and she wasn't about to use Tom as target practice.

He didn't deserve to have any distractions thrust upon him right now. He had a business in its infancy to run and could only juggle so many balls at once.

The women went downstairs to the lounge and were delighted to see it was crowded—not packed but lively enough for a Tuesday evening. They bellied up to the bar and noticed Gina McDonough was motioning for them to sit next to her. "Hi, girls. The boys are going over some paperwork at Tom's bungalow. Jim has handled all of Tom's insurance needs for more than twenty years. They've been friends since kindergarten and may be a while," she explained.

They learned that Gina had worked as a paralegal for years before motherhood called. She and Jim lived in a suburb south of Boston with their seven-year-old twin boys and their two-year-old black Lab. Edna hit it off Gina her right away, discussing the tribulations of working at a law firm. Gina was in prime vacation form, ordering drink after drink, not worried one bit about what was taking the guys so long. Carol liked her effervescent personality. She was petite, with dark-brunette hair cut extremely short, which showed off her wide bubbly brown eyes. Her skin was flawless, although a little pasty for the summertime. She certainly didn't seem as frazzled as Kristin, who also was raising two young children.

The men finally showed up with Tom's arm on Jim's shoulder. Carol couldn't get over how comfortable in his skin Tom always appeared to be. She watched as he cheerfully bopped around the lounge and introduced himself to the patrons like a bright bumblebee hopping from flower to flower. Every now and then, he glanced in Carol's direction and flashed a smile, causing her cheeks to tingle. There would be no lovemaking until the last night, she decided. No sneaking off in the middle of the night to the carriage house. She didn't want to make Edna feel uncomfortable, even if her cousin urged her to do so. Her desires would have to take a respite for a few days.

Right now her only craving was to get something to eat. Matching vodka drinks with Gina was beginning to take its toll, and Carol marveled at her new friend's liquor tolerance. Carol noticed Tom coming toward them with some menus. Carol began to think he could read her mind, but that notion was proven not to be the case, as he informed them the kitchen was closing shortly. Jim and Gina apparently already had eaten an early dinner, which explained why Gina didn't seem to be as wobbly as Carol. Tom wasn't very hungry; he said he'd had a late lunch. Edna and Carol both ordered a grilled chicken sandwich. Tom got the lobster bisque.

Armed with a bevy of brochures, Tom gave them some sightseeing tips and restaurant recommendations for their stay. "Let me see... You're a bellhop, official greeter, and the concierge all in one," Edna observed.

Tom's brows pressed against his eyes, as he ducked his head between them and whispered, "Hopefully I won't have to add chef to my duties. Ours is a real head case, and I'm not a fan of how he berates the kitchen help. He's a great cook, and we've only had one complaint about the food, but I'm a firm believer in treating everyone with respect. The kitchen is my Achilles' heel. I can fry an egg or grill a burger, but that's about it. I'm more suited to the lounge, if you hadn't noticed. I lie awake in worry about this."

Carol gave him a concerned look. "You'll find a solution if he doesn't work out. I have complete faith that you'll overcome this," she said, while patting his hand.

The food arrived, and things got quiet for a while. Carol noticed the bar had filtered out a bit. "I'm encouraged by the bar traffic. A lot of first-timers who came in off the street were in here tonight. I hope they become return customers," Tom said, knocking on the bar for good luck.

The eleven o'clock news was on the TV. Carol hadn't realized it had gotten so late and let out a big yawn. The McDonoughs, Edna, and Tom all yawned along with her. It was a foregone conclusion as the weary group headed for bed. Tom sweetly gave Carol a kiss on the cheek, wished everyone a good night's sleep, and departed through the rear door.

Edna gave Carol a funny look as they headed for the elevator alone. "I think it's cute. I feel like a sorority mom. I'll gladly look the other way if you want to break curfew," she teased.

They snuggled into their beds. Edna squirmed around while softly dishing out a chorus of oohs and ahs, and went on about how comfortable the mattress was and how soft the sheets were, lauding Tom as the ultimate host. "I may never get out of this bed," she purred.

Carol's phone beeped. She grabbed it from the nightstand. It was a text from Tom that said, "I understand. You are a class act. It's what I love about you. See you tomorrow." She sat up and stared at the word "love," and after a few moments decided it was just a descriptive word in a sentence and dismissed it as an official declaration. Her Tom certainly wouldn't do that in a text. She wrote back, "Sometimes the right thing to do can feel so wrong. See you tomorrow." Carol put the phone back on the nightstand and curled up in bed.

Edna watched as the phone's glow slowly faded. "I still think it's cute," she mouthed, her tongue struggling to fling out the last word.

Chapter 28

The next two days were blessed with great weather. Carol and Edna shopped up and down Kennebunkport's quaint village, occasionally stopping for a drink by the river or to nibble on some sweet fried clams from a famous stand, always finding their way back to the inn right on time for the complimentary wine-and-cheese hour on the rear porch. Carol had just begun to get a feel for how Tom spent his day. Mornings were the most hectic for him, as he checked guests out, accepted deliveries, and inspected the rooms and grounds. The four p.m. wine-and-cheese hour was his first opportunity to mingle with guests. He was a great schmoozer, sharing stories, offering advice, and answering questions, always with a sincere smile. Carol loved to hear the superlative feedback he received from his pleased guests. The girls got little face time with him at the gathering, but they didn't really mind. The delicious assortment of cheeses got most of their attention, Carol especially. She'd wait for Tom's back to turn toward the cheese tray, and then she'd stack her plate with cheese and crackers, slinking out of view to munch in secrecy, as Edna laughed loudly.

The daily late-afternoon gathering had sputtered out, and Tom began to move the wine bottles inside. Carol and Edna grabbed a few bottles each to help. When they entered the lounge, Tom was standing outside of the kitchen door, as the head chef, Maurizio, verbally accosted him. They watched in horror as he pointed his finger in Tom's face, complaining that food was missing from the morning's delivery, and swearing loudly. Thankfully no guests were lingering around. Tom's face grew red as he swore back and demanded that the chef retreat into the kitchen.

Carol's heart went out to Tom. She rushed to his side as Maurizio forcefully slapped open the kitchen door, causing it to whip the side wall. Tom and Carol watched through the small round hole as he slammed a pan onto the stove, still swearing away. It was a good ten seconds before the door stopped violently swinging.

"I'm sorry you had to see this. Now you know I wasn't exaggerating," Tom said.

His face was redder than Carol had ever seen it as he inspected the wall for damage. It was the first time she had seen him display anger. She found herself much angrier at Maurizio than Tom appeared to be and fully understood why he had to control himself. Still, she abhorred seeing him in such a compromising position. This incident hadn't been with the kitchen help; it was with the proprietor of the inn.

"Apparently Maurizio doesn't discriminate between the kitchen crew and his boss—you know, the guy who pays him," Carol fumed, as she menacingly leaned toward the kitchen door.

Edna sensed Tom needed time to calm down and assess what had happened. She was also fearful her cousin's stirred emotions might cause her to cross a boundary with Tom. He already was reeling in embarrassment and may have not welcomed Carol's meddling. "Let's put away the rest of the stuff, Carol," she suggested.

The two walked out to the rear porch. Carol stomped her foot and exclaimed, "All my life I've walked away from conflict, and just now I wanted to knock that guy's head off. Tom shouldn't have to endure that kind of insolent abuse. It makes me so mad. The poor guy is stuck between a rock and a hard place."

This was the first time Edna had seen her cousin exhibit such voracious loyalty to someone outside of the family. "Listen," she said. "It's very admirable sticking up for your man's honor, but you can't morph into some princess warrior like that. Give Tom some space to sort things out."

Carol took in a few deep breaths, taking Edna's advice to heart, and poured them another glass of red wine. They sat on the back porch for an hour or so mesmerized by the tide creeping in, sipping their wine while discussing where to eat dinner, and agreed it was best to avoid the inn for a night. "That loose cannon of a cook might poison everyone. Besides, there isn't any wine left out here. Technically we did put it away, just for the record," Edna quipped, patting her belly in laughter.

Carol and Edna walked into town, and Carol eventually texted Tom to tell him where they were. Within minutes he showed up all smiles, suggesting they move along to another bar across the street that offered sunset entertainment. The three of them walked down a pathway that passed a boatyard, and an incoming whale-watching excursion inched up to the pier. A crewman jumped out and tied the boat to a post as he reminded an overanxious passenger to stay aboard until it was fully secured.

Tom turned to the girls and whispered, "It's four hours long. Not my cup of tea. You've seen one whale, you've seen them all. I'd much rather fish. Don't tell anyone, but when I see older guests, I recommend the whale-watching tour to them. There's not much else for them to do around here except eat fried clams and gulp down ice cream. Pardon me for being such a hypocrite."

The women gave him a smile. "I believe I saw a whale-watching brochure in our room," Edna responded. "Don't forget to give us the AARP discount."

The bar was the perfect venue. They sat on the deck listening to a solo guitar player strumming 1960s folk songs. In between, he told tongue-in-cheek stories about life in Maine, which the tourists in attendance found very entertaining. Tom had completely brushed off the incident with Maurizio at the inn. Carol observed him intently while he clapped along to the music. It was the first time she had seen him deal with adversity, and she concluded he wasn't putting on a façade. Edna also had noticed how adaptable he was, sitting there so blithely, facing the small stage, rollicking in laughter, and intermittently checking to see whether she and Carol were having a good time. She made eye contact with Carol and shrugged in disbelief, prompting Carol's eyes to widen. Both were relieved the night wouldn't require a handholding session, as Tom appeared far from glum.

They dined on boiled lobsters with French fries and corn on the cob with all three passing on the bibs. "Might as well let everyone know you're a tourist. It's okay to get a little messy," Tom declared in amusement, knowing Edna and Carol were novices, as he watched Edna figure out how to tie her bib. He laughed when the women instantly folded theirs back up and decided not to wear them.

Carol realized this was the first time she had ever eaten lobster while seated outside by the water. It felt so rustic and soothing as she cracked a claw. The reward for getting a little wet was a delicious piece of tender meat. It became almost a game to her, scavenging through the lobster to find every morsel of meat, delicately separating the meat from the shell with surgeon-like precision, dipping it in warm butter, and swirling her prize in her mouth, before devouring it with a victorious swallow.

"I'm proud of both of you. A buzzard would pass over your plates," Tom said in delight.

They walked back to the inn for a nightcap, pleasantly finding the bar almost full to capacity. Tom disappeared for a moment and returned with two cases of beer. Carol watched as he ripped open a case and stocked the cooler in less than a minute. It was hard to imagine him sitting at a desk surrounded by computer screens all those years. Maurizio came out from the kitchen, a white towel draped over his left shoulder, his head dripping in sweat, as he carried a large empty glass. He went behind the bar, filled his glass with ice, and squirted soda into it. He turned to Tom, smiled, gave him a pat on the back, and walked toward the kitchen, stopping to cordially shake hands with a table of patrons in the dining room who were showing appreciation for their meal. "What's up with that?" Edna softly asked Carol.

The night quickly went by. Tom swept the floor for a bit while Carol and Edna sat on the front porch finishing their beers. He poked his head out and asked them if they wanted to go along with him for an early-morning walk along Kennebunk Beach the next day. Edna politely declined, and Carol jumped at the chance to finally get some alone time with Tom. After all, it was the last day of their vacation, and she had deprived herself long enough. Abstinence on their parts was a noble experiment, but the test of wills was nearly over, and she sensed they both couldn't hold out much longer.

Tom tiredly walked over and sweetly kissed Edna on the cheek just as Nick called to say good night. "He has the best timing," she kidded, as she picked up the phone and walked into the lobby. Through the open window, Carol and Tom overheard Edna telling Nick what a great time they were having. It had been a couple of days since they had spoken with each other, as Nick had been occupied with a long murder trial. Tom grabbed

Carol's hand and gently lifted her out of the Adirondack chair. They both watched as Edna paced around the inn incessantly talking, sparing little detail about the last couple of days.

"Poor Nick. He's involved in a big local murder trial that probably been all over the news. Something tells me he won't get a chance to mention it for a while," Carol observed.

Tom let out a chuckle, and they valiantly kissed each other, looking toward Edna again in deep satisfaction that their sacrifice had paid off.

Chapter 29

The smell of muffins and pastries lingered in the hallway as Carol eagerly bounced down the stairs to fetch a cup of coffee before going on her walk with Tom. A few guests sat in a circle, discussing the upcoming day's events by the raging fireplace. It was overcast and a little chilly, and the warmth from the fire on the back of Carol's legs felt so good as she stood by the coffee urn. Tom was buzzing around, dispatching himself into the kitchen to retrieve some butter before welcoming her with a smile. He was wearing a navy-blue Nautical Inn pullover and had one folded in his arm as he implored Carol to try it on. She excitedly obeyed. More than content with the fit, she flipped her ponytail a few times, posed for a moment, and gestured to him in gratitude with a blown kiss. It was barely eight in the morning, and she already had received a present. *What a way to start the day!* she thought.

Carol and Tom walked through the quiet village, only seeing an occasional jogger or someone walking a dog. The day tour buses wouldn't arrive until a few hours. A lobster boat chugged along the river in the light morning murkiness. Tom explained that the boat was coming in from its catch, and the crew would be having a few beers shortly. He laughed as Carol imagined herself drinking so early, crinkling her nose in repulsion and sticking out her tongue. "I wish I could have taken a picture of that face," he joked.

They walked past an old monastery and eventually came upon the inlet to the beach. A few kayakers slowly paddled past them, their bright-yellow colors taking the place of the sun and adding some brightness to the gloom. They came upon the white-capped ocean, which looked both angry and majestic.

"I love the ocean and the sky on mornings like this. I choose to interpret the dreariness as nature hitting the reset button," Tom philosophized.

Carol could understand what he meant, but her mood was far from dismal. She jumped over the seawall and ran toward the water. A flock of terns hopped out of the way, granting a path for her. The whipping wind made her stop to secure her sunglasses on her nose. Tom caught up and cradled her in his arms, kissing her along the back of her neck. Suddenly everything seemed so calm and serene; she never had felt so secure in her life.

They walked arm in arm in the sand until the terrain in front of them turned into jagged rocks that cut into the ocean. Then they walked onto the sidewalk and headed back to the inn. The fog had begun to lift, and more people were out and about. To those folks, it was all about the promise of a new day. Carol's mind reverted to dwelling on her long-term future with Tom. She did all she could to put aside those thoughts as the enchanted inn came into sight, making her feel as if they were about to enter Camelot together as king and queen.

When Carol arrived, Edna was packing her suitcase for the big journey across the lawn to the carriage house. She informed Carol that her phone had been buzzing, and Carol was happy to see a text from Chris saying to expect Arthur and himself around seven for dinner. Edna was elated to hear that both of them were driving up. "The two of them are so entertaining," she said. "It's like you never know what's looming behind the curtains inside their minds. They even keep an old whippersnapper like me on her toes."

After Carol took a shower and got dressed, they rode down the elevator with their luggage. Tom met them at the front desk and carried their bags to his bungalow, making sure to give Carol a set of keys. She told him that Chris and Arthur were stopping by for dinner, and he promised to reserve a table by the rear windows for them all so they could enjoy the view of the marsh. It was past eleven a.m., and Carol and Edna decided to do one more go-around at shopping and seize their last opportunity to eat a Maine lobster roll. Tom apologized that he couldn't join them, as he was expecting a full house for the weekend and wanted to be hands on. He gave each of them a designer Nautical Inn umbrella, which made Edna double over in laughter. "Another word out of you, and I'll rescind the rest of your going-away present," Tom snickered.

After an hour, Carol and Edna quickly lost interest in shopping. It was the only iffy-weather day for the whole trip, a bit breezy and cool, and it appeared the clouds were thickening. They came upon an eatery that also sold wholesale seafood and gave it their stamp of approval. As they walked in, they were overwhelmed by the abundant selection of fresh seafood from the Atlantic in the iced-glass showcase. This was something they seldom saw back in Michigan. They ordered their lobster rolls at the counter, deciding to also get a cup of seafood chowder each to warm their bones, and sat down at a plastic table and chairs.

A burly man donning a leather apron with a face to match and sporting a scruffy beard delivered their food on trays. He looked like he may have lived at sea for years. The bountiful amount of lobster was a treat. It was the first time they'd both had lobster meat tucked into a round roll and also with just butter brushed on top, without any mayo. The chowder had scallops, shrimp, clams, and whitefish in it, without any potatoes. "This place is a hidden gem. It's the best lunch, bar none, that we've had on this trip!" Edna exclaimed.

Stuffed, they drooped in their bending chairs, yawning up a storm. Carol could tell the long week had caught up to them. Edna was glassy eyed and looked ready for a nap. "Why don't we take advantage of the fireplace at Tom's and read some magazines, watch a little TV, and chill?" Carol suggested.

Edna gave her a high-five, and they headed back. It was comforting for both of them to know they were still in sync on the last day of their vacation.

Tom's carriage house was like an oasis. They watched back-to-back reruns of *Friends* and dozed off for a couple of hours. Carol awoke first and was stunned to see it was past five o'clock. She thought about flinging a throw pillow to awaken Edna, but decided to let her sleep a little longer. The mixture of salt air with the serenity of the house had proven to be the right formula for sheer relaxation, as neither one of them usually napped much, unless there were extraordinary circumstances. Carol felt very at home. She looked around and couldn't find one fault with any piece of furniture or decoration. It was as if she had picked everything out herself. There was one naked corner that screamed for a bar, a pool table, or some other boyish delight, though she couldn't see Tom playing foosball. He was much too sophisticated for that. At least she hoped that to be the case

She looked out the window. The tide was coming in, which meant more wildlife would appear, going with the flow of nature. Tom even had a pair of binoculars placed next to the window to better experience the incoming spectacle. Carol wondered how many different lives—human, fish, and animal—were affected by the tide.

The door opened, and Tom walked in with a bottle of red and a cheese plate. "You don't have to sneak around tonight," he cracked.

Carol put her hand over her mouth. "How did you ever see me?" she asked in shock.

Tom laughed, waited for a brief moment, and explained. "I didn't. Another guest mentioned a woman was hogging all the cheese, and you matched the description."

Carol got up, purposely grabbed four slices, and stuffed them into her mouth. "Did she say I was eating like this?" she mumbled, as Tom pinched a big cheese crumb from the side of her mouth and placed it in his own mouth. Carol's heart raced. The moment had shifted from one of initial embarrassment, to one of humor, then to strangely romantic. They silently stared into each other's eyes. Over the last few days, their emotions had been reaching a crescendo. The downtime was almost over. Tonight would surpass the buildup, Carol knew.

"You two are sickening," Edna remarked, rising from her slumber. "What's next? Slurping shots of tequila out of each other's belly buttons? I'm going to get ready."

Tom laughed, pretending he was about to slug Edna, and left for the lounge.

Carol and Edna freshened up, changed their tops, and put on jeans. They left the house for a couple of steps and immediately returned to fetch jackets. They had been spoiled for hours by the warm fire and had forgotten it was a little nippy outside. They entered the lively inn through the rear porch door. The sharp contrast from the house to the inn ruffled Carol's senses a bit. The dining room was full, and the bar was crowded. Even the lobby was brimming with guests positioned by the fireplace.

Chris and Arthur already had arrived. It had been a slow day at the deli, they explained, and they had taken turns showering before closing time so they could drive up right away and surprise them. "I'm so glad to see you guys again," Carol exclaimed. Chris hugged her hard and for a long time, hoping it would be a regular occurrence in the near future.

Arthur declared that Tom had given him a tour of the grounds, but he didn't get a chance to see any of the rooms because they were all taken.

"Did you guys walk through the kitchen?" Carol asked.

Arthur responded, "Just a few feet in so we wouldn't disturb anyone. I know how temperamental chefs can be when someone invades their kitchen—kind of like a mama bear protecting her young. It's fabulous, though."

Perhaps Maurizio was a harmlessly rude diva after all, Carol thought.

Their table was ready, and they all followed Tom to the best vantage point in the entire inn. "We've been treated like royalty this whole trip, boys. Thanks to all of you," Edna chimed.

Carol graciously smiled, thinking how Nick always had treated Edna like a queen, and he would continue to do so upon her return. Carol, on the other hand, was going home to her empty life, fending for herself like a serf, under house arrest by her piano. That ugly box of chords and keys owned her, and in truth, the piano was the real lady of the castle. This week had been nothing more than a furlough, and she had to figure out how to do a jailbreak. If there truly was a God, he would have let her out early for good behavior.

A waiter handed Carol a menu, rustling her out of her morose stupor. Tom reached for her hand and squeezed it for a moment. It was like shock therapy. Every time he touched her, she felt a jolt of positive vibes. She gave him a squeeze back, and all her woes were forgotten.

Once again the meal was delicious, and the time was delightful. Everyone at the table had ordered a seafood dish and commented on how moist and tasteful their choice was. Maurizio and the crew had done an outstanding job. It was the kind of creative cooking that Tom had in mind in the beginning for the inn. Edna, Chris, and Arthur's halibut steak special was masterfully presented with colorful vegetables atop lobster risotto. Thankfully, Tom had been able to sit through the entire meal without any interruptions and seemed utterly relaxed as he listened to Arthur's riveting stories about life in Greenwich Village, when the gay lifestyle wasn't taken too kindly by the mainstream media or people in general. Tom was spellbound by Arthur's historical perspective, which was heavily laced with comedy concerning his own experiences. Carol got the feeling Tom could listen to Arthur for hours.

Their waiter arrived from the kitchen with a round chocolate cake, guarding the flames with a small dish, and placed it on front of Edna. She looked at Carol in surprise. "I had nothing to do with it," Carol offered.

Edna's eyes turned to the men in appreciation. "You didn't really think we forgot that your birthday is next week?" Chris said.

Edna looked down at the cake. Her face appeared a little flushed as she held a knife, deciding which spot to ceremoniously cut. "You would have been in big trouble if the number forty was written on this sucker," she quipped, as she carefully cut pieces for everyone to enjoy, licking her fudgy fingers in the process.

The bill arrived, and Arthur and Chris insisted on paying it. Tom objected, but Arthur reminded him it was his turn and promised they'd come up and spend a night during the slow season. He apologized that they had to leave so soon because they had to get up early the next day.

"No apology needed. We're so tickled you boys came up and weren't sick of us. We all have to get up early tomorrow. Our flight is at eight," Carol said.

They all walked out to Arthur's car, wishing Chris and Arthur a safe trip home and thanking them for generously picking up the tab. Carol and Edna were too stuffed to continue the evening at the bar. They sat on the front porch in the dim of the night, chatting with people coming out for a smoke and welcoming guests returning from dinner elsewhere. It was past ten, and Kennebunkport only had a few eateries and bars that stayed open later than that.

Carol informed Tom that they were heading back to the carriage house, and he pledged he'd be right along in a few minutes. More than ready for bed, Edna shuffled into her room. Carol had a spring in her step as she plopped into Tom's comfy bed. She squeezed out of her jeans, twisted out of her underwear, and got up to brush her teeth. She stared at her breasts in the mirror, declaring them still firm and sexy for a woman her age, and put on a Nautical Inn T-shirt Tom had left in a gift bag, as promised. She sat in bed and fidgeted with the sheets, waiting for her man to take her, hoping Edna wisely had chosen to wear earplugs for the night.

The door opened, and Carol heard Tom walk quietly into the bedroom. She scooted down to the foot of the bed and jumped into his unsuspecting arms. "I love you. I love you with all of my heart," she fearlessly stated. "I've been waiting to say those words for a long time."

Tom kissed her gently on the side of her ear three times. "Each beauty mark deserves its own kiss. They remind me of the three ballerina stars up in the sky. Every time I glance to the heavens and I see that trio of twinkling galactic spheres in a row, I think of you. What I'm trying to say is that I love you too," he proclaimed.

Chapter 30

The kitchen looked like a cafeteria as Carol examined the delicacies on the counter. She had made stuffed eggplant, a broccoli-and-cheese frittata, penne with meatballs, a spiral ham, and a Greek salad. For dessert she had baked oatmeal-raisin cookies and two apple pies. The only item she didn't make was the birthday cake, which she had ordered from the local bakery. She took a picture from her phone and sent it to Tom so he could see what he was missing.

It had been two weeks since she had seen him, and she couldn't stop thinking about the sleepless romantic night they had shared; she cherished every touch, every word, and every second. The memory was so strong that she could still smell his body even while she stood surrounded by the piping-hot food.

Carol was happy that everyone could make it to the party, Uncle Sam and Patty especially, since their journey was so long. Edna came into the kitchen with Nick to help Carol take the trays of food into the dining room. "Kate looks so heavenly in that blue dress, like a little lady. Your mother's eyes always sparkled when she looked at her," Edna fondly remembered. Kristin joined them, and the four of them carried the food out of the sweatbox of a kitchen.

Uncle Sam was in great spirits. The day before, he had gotten clearance from his doctor to resume limited physical activity. He still did a lot of volunteer handyman jobs, mostly for widows, but had been unable to do so for a while. Patty joked that she could finally get a little peace and quiet around the house.

Kevin offered Carol a beer, and she placed it against the side of her face to cool off before opening it. He reminded her that it had been a while since she had attended a Tigers game and said he had tickets for her anytime she wanted to go. He asked about the trip to Maine, and Carol filled him in as best she could. Edna filled in the blanks on what she had omitted, embellishing a little. Oddly enough, Kevin didn't prod Carol for any facts about Tom, especially since he had gotten so upset about being left in the dark about him. Tom's name came up about a dozen times during the conversation, but Kevin stood there silently. Carol wondered whether he was listening at all.

Evidently, Kristin had picked up on it. "Who's Tom?" she innocently asked.

Carol leered at her brother. Why he hadn't told his wife about the new love in her life was beyond her. Obviously he still had a long way to go in polishing up on his brotherly skills, which he had pledged to do a few weeks earlier.

As usual, Edna came to the rescue, elbowing Carol so she'd stop giving Kevin the hairy eyeball. "Tom is the new guy Carol is seeing. He owns a dreamy inn in Kennebunkport on an estuary. We randomly met him downtown a few months ago when he was out here for the weekend with his nephews. Chris and Arthur met him a couple of times, and so did Nick, when Tom came out here again. Everyone, including myself, has given him the thumbs-up," Edna explained, leaving out the part that Carol was madly in love with him.

Now it was Kristin's turn to look at Kevin with scorn. "You knew about this?" she sternly asked.

Kevin put his head down for a moment. "I only found out when I called to see how the vacation was going. I swear I didn't know how serious it was. That's why I never told you," he sheepishly explained.

Satisfied with his answer, Kristin looked at Carol in despair. "Your older brother was left out in the lurch?" she asked with a confused expression.

Carol didn't know what to say as Kristin waited for an explanation, standing with her arms folded, tapping her foot as if she were counting the seconds for a satisfactory answer. Carol was being blamed for her brother's shortcomings, and Kristin's uneasiness was bordering on anger. Even Edna was at a loss for words as the four of them stood in silence.

Kate suddenly ran up from the basement, followed by Keith. She tugged on Kristin's arm, still not breaking her stare at Carol. "Mommy, Mommy!" she yelled, tugging harder each time. "Daddy's got a girlfriend in the basement! Come see! Come see! Hurry!" She grabbed Kristin's hand and led her down the basement steps.

Carol was relieved and went to grab another beer. Edna followed, leaving Kevin standing in the hallway by himself. "Little Kate's an angel of mercy," Edna whispered. "That scene was about to get ugly. Your brother is clueless. For his sake, I hope there's not a blowup doll down there, or the kids didn't find a smutty magazine."

Kristin entered the den with a smile on her face. "Angela Sheridan loves Kevin! How sweet puppy love is!" she declared, directing her comments for everyone to hear. She walked up to Kevin and rubbed his shoulder. "Did she break your heart?" she kiddingly asked.

Carol had never known Angela to have gone down to their basement. She only had been in the house a handful of times, mostly to fetch Jack for dinner or to sell cookies. She asked Kate to show her what the fuss was about. The two of them went downstairs, and Kate pointed to a wooden beam in the unfinished part of the basement. She explained that she was standing on a box while playing hide-and-seek with her brother when she saw her father's name carved in the beam. Carol turned and looked at the beam. Just reading Angela's name beside her brother's gave her the creeps. He was more than four years older than her. There was no way he had ever seen the etching, or else he would have carved over it. This wasn't as innocent as Kristin wrote it off to be. Kevin would have to answer to Carol also for this, knowing how she felt about Angela, even after all these years.

Carol came up from the basement with her hand over her mouth as she walked toward Edna. She whispered, "It's worse than everyone thinks, I fear. No good had to have happened down there with that girl."

Edna smirked and put her hand over her mouth. "You may be overreacting. They were kids," she said.

Just as the words came out of her mouth, Kevin blurted, with tears in his eyes, "I'm sorry. I'm so sorry!" he sobbed, looking in Edna's direction. "Everyone, please stay. I'll be back shortly. Please. I can explain everything."

Kristin had no idea why he was acting this way. She ran after him, pleading, "Honey, it's not a big deal. Come back to the party! I think it's cute!"

Uncle Sam sat on the couch in silence, hands clenched, his head down, almost in prayer.

Looking confused, Nick walked over to Edna and Carol. "Is there anything I can do?" he asked out of concern. "Should I go after him?"

It was nice of Nick to offer. He barely knew her brother, but Carol knew Kevin had something to unleash from his conscience. She respectfully thanked Nick and told him to stay put. Kristin walked over, trying to keep her composure so the kids wouldn't get upset. Kate had begun to whimper after seeing her father so upset and thought it was her fault.

"Who's this Angela and why is my husband acting this way?" Kristin demanded, looking at both Carol and Edna.

"She's the sister of Kevin's best friend growing up. I honestly don't know why he's so upset. I never even knew Angela was down there," Carol responded. "I'm just as curious as you are."

Kristin rubbed Kate's arm. "It's okay. This has turned into one of those mystery 'whodunit' parties grownups sometimes have. We'll get to have ice cream and blow out the candles after we solve the case," she calmly said, as her astonished eyes drifted toward the basement door then to Carol's flustered face. "You uncovered a very important clue, Kate. Nice job."

Carol made the kids a plate of food and told everyone to help themselves. Nick, relieved he was more of a spectator to the show, had no issue with his appetite, as he made himself a ham sandwich and sat in the den across from Uncle Sam, who was nervously hunched over in deep thought. Patty got up to get some food and asked Uncle Sam if she could make him a plate. He didn't respond.

Edna, showing concern, walked over and repeated Patty's question, placing her hand on her father's arm to get his attention. He grabbed her hand, looked her in the eye, and told her that he always had loved her.

"I love you too, Dad. It's nice to see the two men in my life sitting together like this. I'm sure everything is going to be okay with Kevin. You never answered Patty. Do you want some food?" she asked. He weakly squeezed her hand and shook his head no.

Carol and Patty stood next to the dining room table. Patty thanked Edna for her help as they all observed Uncle Sam sitting there, ignoring Nick's comments about the Tigers game.

"I have no idea what's eating him. He was in a great mood, but he just turned into a zombie," Patty offered.

Edna observed her father once more. She had seen that look of dread on defendants' faces during court proceedings numerous times right before the jury would issue its verdict. She whispered to Carol, "I think your brother may have consulted with my father about things. He's acting like he knows something. I mean, how bad can it be? You know how old folks sometimes tend to worry too much about things."

It had been close to an hour since Kevin had left. Kristin sat with the kids on the den floor, playing a game on her iPad, badly pretending she didn't have a worry in the world as she kept glancing toward the front door. Edna sat next to Nick watching the game. Her eyes darted from her father to Patty, who rolled her eyes back in confusion.

Carol looked at the wasted food in despair. What was supposed to be a fun family celebration had evolved into a somber occasion. She tried to remember the last time Angela may have been in the house but grew agitated as she came up empty. Why did her brother deliberately look at Edna on his way out the door? Perhaps Edna was right, and her father knew what the fuss was about. If so, her instincts told her the unfolding drama hadn't been relegated to one incident. It was intertwined with a much larger story. Possibly a grim secret ironically had been unveiled by the bright, inquisitive eyes of an innocent child hiding in the corner of a dark basement.

The sound of a car door closing caused Carol to breathe a sigh of relief. Kristin sprung up from the floor and ran to the window. "It's him!" she exclaimed and ran back to the kids with a reassuring smile. A second car door was heard, and they all looked at one another in bafflement. Kevin slowly walked into the house, and emerging out of the shadow behind him was Angela Sheridan. Carol unsuccessfully attempted to contain herself and let out a gasp. Angela was wearing a nurse's uniform and stood in silence.

The kids ran toward their father, and he gave them a long hug. "Guys, why don't you play in the backyard for a little bit?' he calmly asked.

Kristin got up and grabbed a plastic football from the floor. "Come on, kids, just for a bit," she softly requested.

Feeling secure the kids were out of hearing range, Kevin introduced Angela to everyone. Angela's smile became short-lived when Kristin impatiently asked, "So what is this about, Kevin? Are you having an affair, or is she just here for show and tell?"

Kevin positioned himself and Angela in the hallway so they could be better heard. "Let me start by saying that's not presently the case. However, we did have a thing back when I was in school before I met you," he responded, his words failing to ease Kristin's concerns, as she knew there was another facet to the story. "The only one who ever knew was Uncle Sam. I confided in him and asked for his advice. You see, Angela was the sister of my friend Jack, and I didn't want him to know about us, thinking it would ruin our friendship. Angela was four years younger than me, almost five, and at sixteen she was still considered a minor," he explained.

Kristin brazenly interrupted, "Okay, so this 'thing' ended many years ago, I assume. Are there any children between you two? Why did you feel the need to parade her in here?"

Angela gently pushed Kevin's arm and softly responded, "There's nothing going on. We were briefly infatuated with each other for a few summer months, but there's more to the story. I'm here on my own free will and feel it's my duty to be here."

Everyone turned to Kevin, desperate to hear the rest of the story, as he sadly shuffled his feet and spoke. "It was eighteen years ago on a debilitating hot summer day. Uncle Sam and I had toiled for hours under the unforgiving sun, fixing a fence around the corner from here. Sam had consumed a few beers to quench his thirst, nothing more than usual. When we finished, the plan was to drop off some tools from his Jimmy truck and restock it with supplies for our next job, which was in East Dearborn. I was to drive the truck back home and pick him up for work the next day.

"Angela was walking down the street and decided to come along for the ride. Uncle Sam drove while I sat in the passenger seat. Angela sat in the back. It was stifling hot. The truck's air conditioner wasn't working, and it was like sitting in an oven. The truck turned the corner by Uncle Sam's house. I was talking to Angela with my head turned toward her. I saw a blurred figure bounce off the side of the truck and then careen against a parked car. Uncle Sam had passed out, and the truck was still moving down the street in a straight line. How he didn't veer into a parked car, I don't know. I turned around and saw a body lying in the street. We were a good fifty feet away and still moving. I grabbed the wheel and quickly put my foot on top of Uncle Sam's to stop the truck. Then I put the car in park and yanked him as hard as I could over my body, switching seats with him. I panicked and drove away, riding around in circles, not knowing what to do. Angela and I were uncontrollably crying. Sam finally woke up, and I dropped him off at the house, making sure to drive there from another direction. He didn't know what had happened."

Edna let out a shriek, "What are you saying, Kevin? Are you telling me my own father ran over my mother?" she frantically asked. "Nick, Nick, tell me I'm hearing this wrong. Is he saying they drove away and left my mother in the street like a dog? It is my mother you're talking about, isn't it?"

Kevin stood there dejectedly and explained, "We didn't know who it was until after I got home. I know that's not a good reason."

Uncle Sam got up and approached Edna. "Don't blame your cousin. He was only trying to help me. I'm so sorry, Edna. It's been eating me up all these years. Words can't describe the sorrow I feel," he emphatically said. Edna turned away from him, and he retreated to the couch as Patty held her heavy heart.

"How can you be sure who was driving? Maybe it was Kevin who was actually driving and made you think you were," Edna suspiciously asked.

Her father scoffed at the idea. "He didn't tell me until a year later, after you mentioned your concerns to your Aunt Mary about my drinking. Kevin was responsible for me quitting drinking and straightening out my life," he said in staunch defense of his nephew.

Edna cried out to her father, "All these years, sitting across from me at the holiday table, laughing and eating, having a jolly time, harboring this secret, knowing you denied me of my mother... For heaven's sake, she was going to the store that day because you neglected to do so the night before when she asked you to pick up bread and milk! Your irresponsible behavior put her in front of that big truck of yours in the first place! I can never forgive you. No wonder you couldn't stay in the house any longer and moved as far away as you could. You were afraid Mom was going to haunt you."

Kevin responded, "My whole life I've been trying to right this wrong. I'm so sorry, Edna. I've been going crazy inside from massive guilt. I vowed, along with your father and Angela, to become a better person and devoted myself to helping others to the highest reaches. I wanted so badly to have some good come out of this tragedy to the point of being overly obsessive. I can't begin to tell you how much money I've donated to charity. Even my bosses at work have been questioning my sanity lately because of my extreme civic mindedness. It's like I want to do everything possible to please your mother to attain her forgiveness but never can do enough. When my mother passed away, the guilt got worse and things began to spiral out of control. I felt like she now knew everything, and I had to get absolution from both of them."

"Angela turned her life around," Kevin continued. "She went from being a rebellious teen to a caring nurse and volunteers her spare time at hospices in the area. We promised each other that we would live better lives and will continue to do so in honor of your mother, Edna. Please, we need every ounce of your forgiveness, all of us," he begged.

Kristin walked toward her husband and gave him a firm hug. His secret was finally out, and there was now a somewhat rational explanation to his odd behavior that had been weighing mightily on their marriage.

Edna, however, wasn't offering any leniency. "You expect me to buy into this whole Robin Hood thing? As far as I'm concerned, it's a conspiracy, a damnable cover-up, and you orchestrated it, Kevin. This is criminal, and all of you share responsibility. Nick, the authorities may be interested in hearing this. Funny, they had designated my mother's death a cold case all these years. They were right—there's nothing colder than driving away as my mother's lifeless body lay in the street. I don't care how hot it was that day."

Nick sat quietly and wisely let Edna vent, looking to Carol for guidance as he rubbed Edna's back. It pained Carol to see her family so distraught. She even sympathized with Angela, who, even though had been complicit, was by far the least responsible, and a victim of being in the wrong place at the wrong time.

Carol tried to console Edna and pointedly said, "It was a tragic accident. There isn't any doubt how contrite they all have been. Kevin admitted he panicked and had no knowledge who was lying on the ground at the scene. I know you're upset, and rightfully so, but considering the idea of putting them in jail sounds more than harsh."

Edna stared at her cousin in disbelief. It was an implied rule that they would always look out for each other. To her, Carol's words amounted to a treasonable offense, and she was stunned as well as hurt. "Come on, Nick. We're out of here. It appears the perpetrators actually have been the victims. Nice party, Carol. I guess it was sort of a twisted surprise party after all," Edna crisply said, as she grabbed her purse and headed toward the door.

Nick silently followed in fear that any words he spoke might get misinterpreted. Minutes earlier, he had erroneously believed he was immune from the situation. Now he was as tormented as everyone else and had the tough task ahead of getting Edna through this shocking ordeal.

Hoping to stop Edna from leaving, Carol rushed to the door and urged her cousin to stay. Feeling besieged by her own family, Edna wildly swung her pocketbook at her in tears, as she ran out of the house in hysterics. Nick understood that Carol wasn't taking any sides and that Edna was too emotionally stung to think rationally. He gave Carol a comforting nod and followed Edna.

"Please take care of my cousin. She's going to need you more than ever," Carol rattled, still envisioning the agonizing look on

Edna's face when she realized it was her beloved mother that Kevin was describing. All this time, Carol and Edna had thought it was Kristin who would suffer the most from Kevin's ostensible indiscretions. It must have been unbearable for Edna to decipher Kevin's ominous words.

Angela bid goodbye to everyone and made her way out of the front door. Carol followed after her. "Please tell me one thing, Angela. You are responsible for the flowerbed on my aunt's grave, aren't you?" she asked.

Angela stood at the bottom of the stoop and smiled slightly. "Yes, I couldn't get myself to visit the grave until a few years ago and decided it was the right thing to do. I went there right at dawn before my shift started and spruced it up from time to time. Even though Kevin and I have stayed in touch throughout the years, I never told him. It's a shame that this tragedy ultimately tore our brothers apart. To this day, Jack is dumfounded by how their friendship dissolved, but I could never tell him the truth. Kevin just felt too uncomfortable around him. He blamed himself for getting me involved and couldn't face Jack. We never thought this secret would last this long. I feel for Edna," she regretfully said.

Carol watched her get into her car and drive away. She looked at Angela's old house across the street, thinking how petty it had been of her to despise the girl. Carol's mother had been right about Angela the whole time. She was crying out for help, and in the end, she had admirably conquered all of her problems without the benefit of anyone else. Everyone inside the house had a support system. Kevin had Kristin; Uncle Sam had Patty; Edna had Nick; poor Angela only had herself. Jack had reasoned that his sister's changed behavior was the beneficial result of an epiphany. Strangely the bizarre circumstances surrounding Aunt Helen's horrible death had been the cause.

Chapter 31

It had been a few days since the infamous party. Carol had decided to let things settle for a bit. She surveyed the situation from every perspective. Right after the accident, Kevin had seconds to react and had chosen to flee the scene to protect his uncle. Angela, so very young, frightened, and impressionable, had gone along with the scheme. Uncle Sam had passed out from alcohol and possibly heatstroke and didn't know what he had done until a year later.

Carol tried to put herself in their shoes. Aunt Helen was gone. Did her uncle deserve to go to jail? Kevin and Angela didn't want their secret out either. She was underage at the time and Kevin's best friend's sister. It was immature of her brother to be with her, especially considering all of the options he had on campus—educated sorority girls and the like. The thought of them having a tryst in the basement right underneath her nose bothered her. Kevin had taken a monumental risk and was fortunate not to have gotten caught. Ultimately the plot unraveled because Kevin could no longer live with his conscience. Carol asked herself whether Edna was better off knowing or not knowing. Edna always had yearned for closure...but this? Some mysteries are better left unsolved, she thought.

Kristin had gotten her long-sought answers and terribly more. She initially appeared relieved that her husband wasn't an adulterer, embezzler, or con artist but then was troubled by the thought that Edna might notify the police. Her sympathetically hugging Kevin was imaginable, but it had unintentionally antagonized Edna. Over time, Kristin had to reconcile herself with the fact that the man she had slept beside for more than a decade had kept a secret of such magnitude for eighteen years.

It finally had been time for the secret to come out. Kevin, Angela, and Uncle Sam all had appeared as if a huge burden had been lifted from their shoulders. Angela didn't have to be there, but she never would have felt cleansed if she hadn't. Uncle Sam didn't want to take the secret to his grave either. He knew Kevin was about to implicate him and didn't try to stop him; he even corroborated Kevin's story. It was only natural for Kevin to break the seal of their promise, since he had initiated it.

Chris was heartbroken when Carol had called him after the party. It was the just about the worst news he had ever heard, and he feared Edna might never recover. In fact he wished his brother had been a white-collar criminal instead. Covering up a deadly accident in one's own family for so many years was an unfathomable stretch. It must have been nearly impossible for Kevin to be around his relatives. It made perfect sense now why Kevin had spent most holidays with his wife's family; why his personality abruptly had changed his senior year in college; why he had grown distant with him and Carol; and why he jumped at every chance to help Edna. Chris was compassionate toward all involved but mostly felt for his brother. It wasn't about loyalty; Kevin wasn't responsible for the accident. The person behind the wheel had been responsible but hadn't even witnessed what he had done. Kevin had to relive that horrid memory the rest of his life—something someone else did. To Chris, that was more of a crime than Kevin fleeing the scene.

Carol was thankful Tom hadn't been able to attend the party. What a way for him to meet the rest of the family! At first she decided not to tell him about what had transpired, but after observing firsthand how harboring a secret for such a long time can be so destructive, she thought better of it. Tom didn't condone what Kevin had done, though he did admit it had taken a lot of courage for him to stop Uncle Sam's vehicle before it crashed into something else, access the situation, and swiftly administer a moral judgment call that would change the rest of his life and the lives of others. He believed it took even more courage for Kevin to come forward and didn't see it as Kevin reneging on his promise to Uncle Sam and Angela. All three more than adhered to their promises for years; it would have been only a matter of time before Angela and Uncle Sam succumbed to the pressure. Kevin's issues had compounded to the point of no return, and breaking the silence was the first step in what would be a long healing process.

Carol was relieved that Tom stayed on the line and offered encouragement. He could have headed for the hills and written her off as a bad investment. Instead he consoled her and offered advice. He said he didn't believe her relationship with Edna was unsalvageable and urged her not to get discouraged if Edna didn't take her phone calls. He said Carol should go see her and talk to her directly.

It was still early enough in the evening for Carol to drive to Edna's house. Since Edna wasn't fielding Carol's phone calls, she would have to go unannounced. She collected her thoughts on a pad of paper because she feared Edna would only allot her a limited time—that is, if she opened the door at all. Carol's phone rang, and it was Tom again. She hoped he might have a few more pearls of wisdom for her and rushed to answer it.

She could tell from his voice that he was upset. "What is it, Tom? Something's wrong. I can feel it. I want to help you. Please tell me," she said, afraid to hear, since she had spoken with him a few hours earlier and he had seemed fine.

"I'm in a bit of a pickle," Tom solemnly said. "My worst fear about the inn has come to fruition. It's Maurizio. I had to let him go and he didn't take it well. I almost had to call the police. A few guests overheard and got scared as he stormed out screaming while hurling a chair at me. When you were here, he confided in me that he was manic-depressive. His doctor tinkered with his medication and said he would be fine. I always believe in giving people a chance. Over the last week, however, he was unbearably rude. I couldn't depend on the guy. Late this afternoon, a friendly conversation turned into a loud, threatening argument for no apparent reason. It was like he was daring me to fire him. If I didn't act, no one in the place would ever respect me."

Carol's heart went out to Tom. It was smack in the middle of tourist season—the first one ever for the inn—and now the kitchen was in chaos. "All the good chefs are already employed for the season," Tom said. "I can't try to hire anyone else's chef—it would tarnish my reputation in the community. The crew in the kitchen is very capable but more so for prepping or flipping hamburgers. There's nothing like the cache of having a distinguished chef to attract customers. Without a creative chef, we're just another pub...barely. I want you to know I love you very much," Tom added. "For weeks I've been trying to figure out a way to ask you to come out here and be with me so we can be together and give this relationship a shot. I know it's selfish, but you're a fantastic cook. Would you consider coming to help out?" he feverishly asked.

Carol was stunned. She had been waiting for him to ask her to live with him; in fact she constantly had dreamed about it ever since she had gotten back home. They'd never discussed it, however, and were still in a "taking it one day at a time" mode. They had left off with Tom mentioning a tentative weekend visit to Michigan in October. It didn't matter to her that he needed her. There was a reason Maurizio hadn't worked out. Maybe this was God's way of getting her and Tom together sooner. All she knew was that she loved him and he needed her. It was a call to duty, just as taking care of her mother had been. To her, love was defined by loyalty, trust, and helping those close to you get through the toughest of times.

Jumping at the chance, Carol exclaimed, "I'll be there as fast as possible. I'm a good cook, not an accomplished chef, but I'll try my hardest, and we'll take it one day at a time, as we always say. I just need to talk to Edna. She already thinks I've been disloyal. Now I have to convince her that I'm not abandoning her on top of everything else. That's not going to be an easy task. I also have to check in with my brother. There's the matter of the house and all."

Carol's heart was pounding after her conversation with Tom. She sadly looked around the house. It had been the only place she had ever lived, but now she would have to leave it unattended. Kevin would have to check on things for a bit. Her brother had been so distraught by Edna's reaction that he had decided to take the week off work and hole himself up in his mansion. Edna's response had been worse than he ever had visualized. Forgiving one person was hard enough, but his cousin now had to consider three people. There was no way she could pardon one or two of them and not the other. It had to be a package deal and also tough for her to swallow, especially given the bitter taste she already had in her mouth. Carol had to help Edna sift through the situation, and now the process would have to be accelerated, as she was unexpectedly leaving Michigan very soon. She prayed that Edna would be understanding and didn't want to leave on bad terms with her.

Chapter 32

The lights were on in Edna's house as Carol pulled up to the curb. She sat in the car shaking. This would be the last time she would see her cousin for a while, and she would miss her terribly. She kept telling herself to be overly patient. She was there to broker the peace among the family and not to blatantly come to anyone's defense.

Nick answered the door, looking glad to see Carol. She walked into the hallway. Edna was sitting in the den in her sweats looking disheveled with a box of Kleenex beside her. She showed little emotion upon seeing Carol, not really even acknowledging her presence, as she stared at a picture of her mother. It was an awkward moment—no shared smiles, no hug, and no words. Carol asked permission to sit down. Edna just waved her hand, almost cringing when Carol leaned toward her.

"I'm worried about you, and I've been thinking about you," Carol said. "I know this wasn't the closure you wanted all these years. I can't imagine what you're going through. It's a terrible thing to digest. We're all dismayed by this. I understand your being upset with the world. I just want to help. I'm here for you, Edna. Please...what can I do?"

Edna grabbed a tissue and wiped a tear from her eye. Nick, who had left them alone, reappeared to offer Carol a drink of water, but upon seeing Edna in tears, he went outside and sat on the stoop. Edna's eyes followed him as if she longed for him to stay in the den. It was obvious Carol wasn't entirely welcome, and Carol was beginning to feel uncomfortable.

"Edna, you have to find it in your heart to forgive your father. He needs your support. He never wanted this to happen. Your mother never would want you to punish him. He's been through enough. He's so frail, and he's had had to live with what he's done every day for many years. Imagine what that must be like—waking up every day knowing what he did."

Edna sat there crumpling her tissue in her hand and finally said, "She always protected him, made excuses for him, and lied for him. What good did it do? That was the thanks she got! Who protected her? I don't care if it was an accident!"

Carol was relieved that Edna finally had spoken. "What bothers you more, the accident itself or the fact that we all were misled all this time?" Carol gently asked. "What would you have done differently if you had known the day it had happened? Would you have wanted your father to go to jail back then?"

Edna tapped her foot against the coffee table. Carol could tell where the crux of the problem lay. It was natural to want revenge but tough to seek it out against your own flesh and blood.

"I feel like a fool," Edna said. "All these years they kept this from me with that insane promise they made to one another. I remember that day so vividly. It was unbearably hot. No one was outside. Everyone was hunkered inside with their air conditioner blasting. So not one soul could hear or see what had happened. Your brother and Angela never took it upon themselves to be Good Samaritans. They were probably her only chance. God knows how long it was before she was found. She had no pocketbook with her, no ID. All she had was a twenty-dollar bill. The police canvassed the neighborhood for three hours looking for where she lived before they tapped on our door and drove us to the morgue. All that time I was wondering where she had gone while my father snored on the couch. I feel as if I'm reliving her death all over again, but now I can fill in all the blanks. She deserves another funeral. The first one was a farce, especially with my father going up to the altar to receive Communion. He even had a chance to come clean a year after it happened and take responsibility for what he'd done. But no, he decided to be the dastardly coward he is."

"Did you ever think he wanted to protect you?" Carol asked. "Just like Kevin wanted to protect his uncle? He looked up to your father. I'm not agreeing with his decision by any means, but please don't crucify them. You saw what they were going through, with your dad clutching a picture of your mom and crying himself to sleep, and Kevin's extreme behavior almost bankrupting his family. If any of this got out, Kevin's firm would part ways with him. He'd lose everything. No firm would hire him, and he might even get disbarred. Look at all the good he has accomplished—all three of them for that matter."

"Do you really want to be that vindictive and take that away?" Carol continued. "Would the world be better off? Would that really make you feel better, knowing your dad and my brother's family were suffering? Would your mother want you to inflict so much pain? That's a lot of petulance inside of a person. You have to repress those feelings. Do you really want to go through life trying to rectify a wrong like Kevin, Angela, and your dad have been doing? It would be a willful, premeditated action, knowing the consequences would ruin lives if you publicized this. Kevin had no time to think; he didn't have that liberty. He wasn't trying to ruin anyone's life. He was trying to protect everyone in that truck, especially your father, as well as yourself. I hope you can come to the same conclusion. We were all blindsided by this. All of us." Carol took a sip of water, as her mouth was dry from her lengthy sermon.

It was obvious Edna was working her way through a wretched inner conflict. The power to issue a verdict eighteen years past due, and the ramifications of it, clearly made her uneasy. Carol had said everything she could on the issue. Edna needed to get past her anger before she could forgive, and she still hadn't cooled off much from the day of the party.

Carol decided to switch gears. "I have something else to tell you. Tom asked me a few hours ago to stay with him at the inn. He fired the chef and needs my help. I don't know how long I'll be gone. Once he called, all I wanted to do was come here. I don't want you to think I'm deserting you. The timing is awful. For the first time in my life, I'm really stepping out of my comfort zone. It hasn't been much of a life to begin with, though, except for my times with you. I didn't want to leave without telling you in person. I'm scared, but if I have your blessing, it would make things easier," she said, hoping Edna finally would smile and embrace her.

Carol waited a moment. There would be no celebratory hug or screaming with happiness as when Edna had gotten engaged and Carol had tried to hide how hurt she was. Edna merely sighed and said, "I'm really happy for you. How convenient... everything neatly wrapped up with a nice big pretty bow. Don't worry. I'll be fine."

Carol found the acerbity in Edna's voice bothersome. It was as if her cousin were a coiled rattlesnake hissing at her. Carol decided she didn't want to get stung by Edna's venom and tearfully said goodbye. Edna didn't even get up to politely escort her out. She just quietly let her walk away, knowing she might not see her for a long time. Carol walked past Nick, who was sitting on the stoop. She knew he had been eavesdropping, as the windows were open.

"You take care, Nick," Carol said. "I'm sorry about all this family strife. Edna's mad at the world right now. For some reason I'm being lumped in with the others. I don't know where things stand between Edna and me. All I've ever wanted was for her to be happy. By the way it wasn't the best way to treat one's maid of honor," she gruffly said, as she walked to her car in tears.

The emotions Carol felt ranged somewhere between pity and sorrow. She had expected Edna to cop an attitude in the beginning but never figured she would be so sharp tongued and bitter during the whole visit. Carol knew Nick was a sensible guy. She convinced herself that he ultimately would guide Edna in the right direction. She wasn't sure whether a criminal complaint filed regarding an accident that occurred eighteen years ago was something that still could be prosecuted. Nick had most likely already advised Edna on that. Carol was counting on him; he currently had the most influence on her. Airing stained family laundry would only serve the media and little else. In a few days, the story would be yesterday's news and forgotten, but Edna would have to wake up to the same headlines every day the rest of her life, just as her father, Kevin, and Angela had. Hopefully, Nick could instill some sense in her. From the start, Carol had estimated that Nick was right for Edna. Now her hopes for a quick resolution were vested with him of all people, a criminal lawyer. It was ambiguous as to where that fit into the equation, which heightened Carol's powerless state of mind.

She decided to call Kevin. She had only spoken to him once since the day of the party. He had called out of concern for Edna and was depending on her forgiveness so he could get on with his life. He believed he needed forgiveness from the family en masse so he could have a better chance of attaining it in front of the eyes of God, Aunt Helen, and his parents, reasoning that he had no shot in heaven if he wasn't forgiven in this life first. Carol offered her unconditional forgiveness without hesitation. Kevin was her brother, and she admired his guile and sense of duty to his uncle. She didn't believe Kevin should burn in hell. He had suffered enough. In her mind, the punishment already had exceeded the crime.

Carol told him about her visit with Edna and asked him to be patient because the healing process probably would take a long time, then she switched gears. "I have exciting news," she said. "Tom has asked me to come to Maine and be with him. I love him and told him I would. He needs my help in the kitchen at the inn, and I didn't want to let him down. Besides, I was afraid if I declined his invitation our relationship never would be the same. I've never done anything this impulsive before, but I can't deny myself a more enriched life any longer. I need to take a chance. There's more to life than that damn piano. I feel like it's been weighing on my back, and it's only a matter of time before it crushes me. Every note seems so sour—it feels like I'm punching the keys with my knuckles. I don't know anything about cooking ten different entrees at once, but I'm up for a challenge," she enthusiastically rambled.

"I think it's fantastic," Kevin told her. "I'm not in the best position to give a blessing, but you know what I mean. I'd really like to meet Tom. Do you think Kristin and I can visit for a few days in the fall? We really need to get away. I have to make amends for a lot of things. Kristin and I are actually going to set up a charitable foundation together. She'll be materially involved in all the decisions, and she's really excited," he proudly said. "Don't worry about the house. I'll check on it and make sure the lawn is mowed."

Carol couldn't ask for a weightier endorsement from her big brother. It didn't matter to her that he was short on words. The tone of his voice was astoundingly genial, reminding her of years past when he had been a wide-eyed freshmen optimistically leaving to attend college. Edna would be impressed by his upbeat attitude, if not for the surrounding circumstances. "Don't forget to fill the birdfeeder," Carol playfully ordered. "Mom will be watching."

Satisfied somewhat by her brother's comments, she dialed Tom before she could get cold feet. It would be better to just pack her bags and leave town before she had a chance to think things through. She was worried about keeping her family together and also leaving the house. If Tom had called another month or so from now, it would be easier, she thought, but things could very much continue to be in a state of flux, and her life had been in a holding pattern long enough. Playing it safe had become much too painful. It was time to extract herself from atop the picket fence, take a leap of faith, and hop over it. Carol wanted to be part of the action and not observe it from afar like some lonely voyeur. Oddly enough, even during this current family fiasco, she basically had been a non-participant for years, suddenly forced into a clean-up role after the fact. Who knew hosting a simple family party could bring so much unwanted skin to the game? She knew she wasn't escaping from the past. All that mattered to her was the future.

"Hi, Tom. It's me. I can be out there on the first flight possible. I can't wait," she cheerfully told him.

Chapter 33

Tom picked Carol up at the airport the next day. She was emotionally drained. She'd had a three-hour layover in Albany and was still laboring over the mess she had left behind in Michigan. All it took was one look at Tom's bright smile and curly locks, however, and she was infused with energy and bubbling with joy. She consulted with him about some new menu ideas, and he seemed very receptive. The last thing she wanted was to inundate him with her family issues.

"This isn't a business trip, Carol. Tell me the latest, if you'd like. Maybe there's some way I can help," Tom offered.

Carol smiled, as there really wasn't anything new to add. He was such a good listener that she already had told him the far-reaching story a few times, giving him numerous updates and details she unintentionally had omitted along the way. She couldn't blame him for wanting to hear more. It was good drama after all, but she wished it would be someone else's. "Nothing new. I'm still persona non grata with Edna," she ruefully said.

The ride was rather enjoyable. Tom had picked her up in his vintage bright-orange 1965 Pontiac GEO convertible, and the wind felt great as they whipped down the highway merrily waving at passing cars that honked in appreciation. Carol didn't even know Tom was a classic car buff; she had thought he only loved classic bars. She yelled, "How many other cars do you own?"

Tom laughed and yelled back, "I have a leased BMW in Boston. Hey, they're beeping their horns at the babe in the passenger seat, not the car."

Carol's heart raced as they entered the driveway to the inn and turned left toward the old barn across from the carriage house. The roof was missing some shingles, and the frame slightly tilted to the left. It was in dire need of a serious makeover. Tom explained that he was using it as a garage until he figured out if he wanted to convert it into a spa and gym.

"So you've have been hiding this car in here all along? Holding out on me already, I see. What else have you been keeping from me?" she joked, with her fingers crossed, as her heart couldn't take another jolt of bad news. All she wanted was good surprises for a long time.

Tom didn't say a word as he smiled and led them to the door of the carriage house while carrying her bags.

The house was nice and airy as they walked in. Tom had left the windows open so the refreshing sea breeze could filter inside. "Aren't you going to lug me across the threshold?" Carol snapped.

Tom laughed as he stood next to a dark object adjacent to the fireplace in the spacious living area. Carol followed slowly behind and watched as he sidestepped out of the way to reveal a huge mahogany piano.

Tom smiled widely. "It's a beauty, as close to the one at your house as I could find. I bought it at an estate auction a few weeks ago. The delivery guys had a tough time getting it in. I neglected to measure it to see if it would fit through the door. Fortunately it made it by less than an inch," he happily said, eager to see Carol's reaction. "I wanted it in here so it would always remind me of you."

Carol put her hands over her mouth, but in horror, not joy. Tears rolled down her flushed cheeks. Tom's frozen smile quickly melted as he surmised something was wrong. "Don't you like it?" he meekly asked.

Carol didn't know how to respond. She was concerned that Tom wouldn't understand, but she wanted to be honest with him. "I don't want you to think I'm ungrateful. It's a wonderful gesture on your part. I don't expect you to understand, but the piano has become a symbol of negativity to me, like a ball and chain. I was tethered to it for years. When I left the house to come here, I slammed the keyboard lid shut in defiance, like I was getting in the last word and that was my exclamation point. I actually looked out the back window to make sure it wasn't chasing after me and breathed a sigh of relief as the house disappeared out of sight. I know it sounds nuts, but it looks so similar to the piano back home, minus the kinks and scratches, of course. It's like it beat me here and got in the last laugh," she said, at her wit's end.

Trying to mask his disappointment, Tom nodded as if he fully empathized with Carol. He knew she was going through a period of adjustment, and the emotional baggage from the goings-on back home might have been heavier than she had led on. "I can get rid of it without a problem. It's just that when I saw you teaching that little boy at your house you looked so naturally happy. I couldn't take my eyes off the two of you," he said softly in his defense.

Carol gave him a hug, her tears soaking his shirtsleeve. "No, maybe I'm being a little flighty now. Let's keep it. Perhaps I'll feel differently in time. It's very handsome, just like you," she said in an attempt to quell Tom's hurt feelings. "Hey, it's getting late in the afternoon. I have to acclimate myself in the kitchen before the dinner rush," she said, changing the subject.

"Are you sure you want to jump right into the frying pan? We have a fair amount of food in stock for what's on the menu. We can get through another night without any specials unless you want me to grab something quick from the fishmonger before he closes," he said.

Carol had the menu memorized and decided a couple of specials would help. "Okay. I need you to get some sole and some bay scallops. Make sure they're the small scallops," she quickly said. "Get enough for about fifteen entrees. I'm going to change and head for the kitchen now."

Impressed by her sudden shift in mood and hard-charging attitude, Tom headed out the door, reminding himself that Carol had been in Maine barely an hour, and he had to temper his expectations somewhat and go about things at her pace. He smiled as he fastened his seatbelt, thinking it probably wasn't going to be a smooth ride for a while.

Carol introduced herself to the kitchen staff of two—Mitchell, a clean-cut twenty-something who just had began studying at a culinary institute in Portland, and Eduardo, a Columbian immigrant still in his teens, whose family lived in nearby Sacco. They had been splitting duties for the last two days, Mitchell spearheading the entrees and Eduardo helping with the appetizers and side dishes as well as the prep work. They both informed her with laughter that the boss had washed the dishes for the last two nights. Ordinarily that was Eduardo's responsibility. Carol explained her situation to them, and both pledged to help in any way they could.

Tom came back with the food Carol had requested . He was glad to see the young men already had warmed up to the new chef. "I understand the boys relegated you to dishwashing status," she teased.

Tom laughed and said, "They did a fine job. We had one little rush last night, but they worked so well together getting everything out. I would have been in the way, holding up the works."

Carol inspected the produce in the walk-in fridge and wrote the first special on the blackboard—baked filet of sole stuffed with bay scallops, baby carrots, roasted potatoes, and wilted spinach. The second special she wrote down was bourbon-infused filet mignon, two baked stuffed colossal shrimp, fingerling potatoes, and sweet corn salsa.

She looked over her penmanship, fixed a few smudges with a spit-wetted finger, and proudly went into the dining room, introducing herself to the three-person wait staff. Then she went over the specials with all of them, making sure the bartender also knew. Everyone seemed genuinely nice and professional. She couldn't have asked for a better reception and felt like a guest more than a coworker. She wondered whether she was being treated so well because the word was out that she was the boss man's girlfriend. Carol knew she would earn their respect over time, hopefully, but she had too much to do to be paranoid about such things.

The first few dinner orders were a snap. Timing the meals to come out relatively close to one another was her biggest concern. So far, so good. She was glad the specials were going out the door, especially the surf and turf, because there was a disproportionate amount of filet mignon in the fridge. She had correctly figured that including it in a special might help sell more of it.

The commercial ovens were a bit intimidating at first, but Carol was amazed by how quickly she could cook with them. She laughed to herself, thinking that her mother would have fed the entire Dearborn police force if they'd had this kitchen at home. The line to get into the funeral home at her wake would have been around the corner, with hundreds of cops all dressed in uniform. Tom interrupted her vision, as he walked up to her with a frown and a perplexed expression.

"What's wrong? Did someone complain about the food?" Carol quickly asked, thinking the worst. Tom waltzed her into the walk-in fridge and kissed her on the lips. "I've always wanted to do it in thirty degrees next to a bucket of mussels while on top of a crate of lettuce," her freezing lips chattered. "How seductively romantic you are. Maybe you should slip into your dishwashing apron."

Tom put his hand over her mouth and whispered, "Shush. Two Secret Service Agents are standing in the dining room next to the kitchen door. The ex-president and his wife are sitting at the table against the far wall with another couple. They're here for dinner. That's right. You're about to cook dinner for a former US president, the senior one!" he exclaimed.

Carol slowly stepped out of the fridge and peeked through the kitchen door. At the same time, a bald man with piercing eyes dressed in a dark suit gazed into the kitchen, startling Carol. She let out a whimper and scurried back in front of the stove. "It's my first night, Tom! What am I supposed to do?" she said as she felt her blood rush to her cheeks. "Do those guys have to taste the food first? I don't know how these things go!"

Tom tried to calm her down. "Just do what you've been doing. I don't know if they'll come in here and observe. Right now they're guarding the kitchen door. There are two more outside. It's all very exciting, Carol. There's nothing to be scared about," he said, patting her on the back. "I'm going back into the lounge to scope things out."

The head waitress, Ruth, walked into the kitchen. "That's my order that just hit the system. It's for you know who," she whispered, with a fearful look in her eye.

Carol was glad to see the president and his guests had ordered both specials, two of each. She quickly went to work on them. Suddenly the skillet seemed very heavy, and she had to use both hands to steady it. She took a deep breath and noticed the boys in the kitchen walking toward her.

"I'm so glad you're here tonight. I don't know if I could do it," Mitchell offered. "It's going to be okay."

Eduardo didn't say a word. He just smiled and did the sign of the cross. Carol knew they meant well, but no one could be as reassuring as Tom. This was a monumental night, and she didn't want to let him down. After all, that's why she was standing in the cavernous kitchen in the first place, but she hadn't expected to get tested like this on her first night.

The orders were ready, and Carol buzzed Ruth to come and deliver them. Ruth rushed into the kitchen and placed the hot dishes carefully on the tray, gave Carol a wink, took a deep breath, and walked out confidently with the orders resting on her shoulder. Carol watched the door swing a few times, hoping she wouldn't hear the sound of dishes crashing. The silence couldn't have sounded better, and she focused her attention on the next order that buzzed on the computer screen. Her nerves steadied. She was confident the meal had come out well. She couldn't wait to tell Chris, and Edna of course, if she would ever listen to her again.

About a half-hour had passed, and Tom came back into the kitchen. Carol was grateful he hadn't stood over her back while she was cooking the president's meal. Tom smiled, rubbing his hands excitedly, and said, "The president requested that you stop by his table."

Carol's heart pounded as she looked at a chicken breast sautéing on the stove. "Don't worry. I have it," Mitchell chirped. "You can't keep him waiting."

Tom grabbed her by the hand and led her out of the kitchen. All eyes in the room turned to them as they approached the president's table. Carol noticed it already had been cleared, so she couldn't determine how much of their meals they'd eaten. Tom introduced her to the president as the new head chef. Carol slowly extended her hand and watched in awe as the president stood and leaned in to shake her hand. He also introduced his wife and the couple they were with. "I just want to say my filet special was so tender and delicious. The ladies kept commenting on how sweet and slightly tangy their stuffed sole was. We'll definitely be back. You're the new chef? When did you start?" he inquired as he sat back down.

Carol blushed for a moment and knelt on the floor, thinking it would be rude and awkward to talk down to him. "Actually, tonight is my first night. Thank you so much for the compliment. I have a great crew working with me. Tom has devoted an immeasurable amount of time and energy into this place to ensure everyone has a memorable experience. He deserves all the credit," she nobly said.

The president's wife clapped her hands in praise. "I don't think this is a case of beginner's luck. You're very talented, Carol. I may have to ask Tom's permission to borrow you for a catered gathering we're hosting, if that's okay," she said, looking at Tom, who nodded.

Carol gave out a resounding yes and extended her hand to the table again, asking whether there was anything else she could do for them. "Just keep doing what you're doing!" the president exclaimed. Carol smiled and headed back to the kitchen.

Eduardo and Mitchell greeted her right away at the door. They had been gawking through the round kitchen window. "It was like you were bowing to a king," Eduardo joked as he got down on one knee. "Maybe we should be bowing to you. Hail to the queen!"

Carol thought, *If only Mom were alive to see what just happened.* Her mother deserved all the credit. All those years of cooking together had paid off. It was as if her mom had prepared her for this all along. Carol had been at the inn less than a day, and she already felt like royalty. She pulled Eduardo up from the floor. "Okay, buster, this anointed queen still has another hour of slaving in the kitchen to do," she kidded.

Chapter 34

A week had gone by. Carol sat on the front porch assessing her life in the afternoon shade, sipping an iced tea, occasionally smiling at guests as they went about their business. In the short span she had been in mystical Kennebunkport, she had cooked for a former US president, made friends with the various staff at the inn, met interesting acquaintances from all places and walks of life, and woken up every morning to the man of her dreams. Not to mention, she was twenty minutes up the road from Chris. There was something about mingling with the guests, however, that she found odd, and it bothered her a bit. She could converse with them, get to know them, be entertained by them, but at the end of the day, she received the most pleasure knowing she wasn't beset with their problems. When they checked in and out of the inn, they were also entering and leaving her life. She wasn't used to being so hands off and uncommitted. There was nothing for her to get saddled with, no stress, remorse, worry, or guilt. It was kind of like watching *Ellen* or *Letterman*, or any of those talk shows. A celebrity guest would get introduced; chat about his or her latest CD, movie, or baby for ten minutes; and wave goodbye. Then the next guest would stop by to do the same puffy routine. It was light entertainment, and her life right now clamored for a heavy dose of that fluffy babble.

Carol had been running on pure adrenalin and had little time to reflect on the burning issues back home. Today felt different. Life seemed to slow down a bit. Tom had been very patient and supportive, which made the transition much easier for her. As reliable as he was, however, he couldn't replace Edna's role in her life. She could humorously pick apart an insane situation and restore sanity to it, even if it applied to her—understandably, except for this one gut-wrenching time. Carol feared the current circumstances might be too insurmountable for Edna to overcome. There was a huge void in her life, one that Tom couldn't fill, and Carol tried to mask it from him, hoping he wouldn't catch on. She wanted him to think things were perfect. Between them, they certainly were, at least in her mind.

Carol grabbed her phone and debated the idea of calling her cousin. It wasn't a case of being homesick. She just felt lost and lonely without sharing her life with her. Edna would have gotten a hoot out of hearing about her first day on the job. The only person she had talked to about it was Chris, who wouldn't believe her until Tom sent him a picture of her shaking hands with the president. Her hands began to sweat, and she almost dropped the phone.

She found Edna on her contact list and hit the button. A taxi slowly turned into the driveway, and Carol quickly hung up without knowing if the call had connected. She wanted to be fully attentive to the needs of any newly arriving guests, as she didn't know whether Tom was currently commandeering the front desk or had gotten called away. It would be the guests' first impression of the inn, and Carol knew how important the check-in process was in all of the travel reviews. The inn was so new that one negative write-up could dissuade a lot of potential guests from staying there. She got up and leaned against the railing as the cab came to a stop.

Her phone began to ring, and she saw it was Edna calling. In her mind, Edna superseded everything else, and now she would have to explain why she had hung up after one ring, assuming that's what had just transpired, as the chances were slim that Edna was calling out of the blue. She prayed Tom was at the desk and nervously answered her phone.

"I'll forgive you for hanging up on me only if your butt comes down the steps and helps me with my bags," Edna yapped.

Carol let out a shriek and ran down the steps as Edna stepped out of the cab. They jumped up and down, hugging each other and creating such a scene that Tom came out on the porch clapping his hands. Earlier Carol had thought it was strange that he kept poking his head out to check on her. "You knew, didn't you?" she asked him.

Edna walked up the stairs and hugged Tom. "Leave him alone," she proclaimed. "I called him. You see, I'm still a bit peeved that he picked up the bill the last time we were here. I told him not to say a word about my coming unless he really wanted to get on my bad side."

Carol was stunned when she spotted Nick standing by the trunk of the cab, getting the luggage out. "Oh, I'm sorry, Nick. I had no idea you came too!" she screamed as she ran into his inviting arms. "Thank you. I know you had a lot to do with this," she whispered in his ear.

Nick shrugged. "I can't take all the credit. Tom had a lot to do with it, too. He knew you weren't the same person since you arrived. We both wanted the girls we fell in love with to return to their old selves," he softly said.

Edna walked up to Carol in tears. "I'm so sorry about everything. I visited with Kevin yesterday, and we had a long heart to heart. I realized he was under intense duress at the scene of the accident, and he's been devastated by that decision ever since. It was a lot for him to bear and really took a toll on him," she firmly said, with no hint of indecision in her voice, as she rubbed Nick's back.

Tom grabbed a bag from Nick and led them into the carriage house, sensing the scene was much too animated for them to be standing on the front porch of the inn. They all sat down in the great room, relaxing for a bit. Carol was delighted to hear that Edna and Nick planned to stay through the weekend. Tom asked Nick if he could give him a tour of the inn to give the women some privacy, but they wouldn't hear of it.

"We're all in this together now, like it or not," Edna stated, motioning for Nick and Tom to sit down.

"Except for the few guests who may have overheard us when we arrived," Carol added, as she ran her fingers through Tom's hair and snorting out a wet laugh.

Edna and Carol held hands like two long-lost souls. Edna trembled and cried out, "It was your dream, Carol. The dream you had on the beach about the clouds that I pooh-poohed. I mistakenly disregarded it as rubbish, but I know now that it was a message from our mothers. All along I've been saying that your mother was guiding you from above, without considering she may have had an accomplice. My mother was trying to tell us to forgive Kevin. It's so clear now, and I made fun of it. The same thing goes for my father. He and I couldn't fully connect until I knew the truth. My mother knew his hidden guilt had been sabotaging our relationship for years. He ostracized himself from my life, and his sickness finally brought us together. He tried to tell me, albeit in a heavily medicated state, when they were wheeling him into the operating room. He wanted badly for me to know in case something went wrong. He didn't want to take his secret to the grave."

Carol comforted Edna and added, "I know. You and I have been thinking such mystical thoughts for a while. Edna and I believe you were heaven sent, Tom. We had just come from the cemetery when we bumped into you."

Tom chuckled and said, "No, I'm really an alien from another planet. I set my flying saucer on course for the Motor City by mistake. I wanted to go to Battle Creek to visit Tony the Tiger from the cereal commercial, which I watched from afar via satellite when I was younger. Instead my navigation system took me to see the Detroit Tigers." They all laughed at Tom's silliness.

"You sound like you're from another planet at times with that thick Boston accent of yours," Edna cracked.

"I suspect our niece Kate has been their emissary. My mother always called her a little angel. It was by no means a coincidence that she found Angela's scribbling in the basement," Carol emphatically stated. "There's been a cryptic chain of events ever since our mothers were reunited."

Nick had been quiet for a while. Carol got up and offered everyone a beer. "The timing is perfect for a toast. We have something else to share. Go on, Edna," Nick urged.

Edna smiled and guzzled her beer, wiping some drizzle on her chin with her arm. "I'm pregnant," she said, as everyone stared at the half-empty beer bottle in her hand.

Carol looked at Nick and saw he was a little agitated. "No! Stop fooling around! You're going to give your cousin a heart attack. Those words are making my chest tight. Be serious!" Nick ordered.

Carol gave Edna a whack on the arm. She appreciated Edna's humor much more than the guys did, craving it for days, and she let out a belly laugh that seemed to release the last of her morose worries.

"Well, with Kevin's help, I'm setting up a charitable arm at work. We're going to take on pro bono cases as much as fiscally possible, and we're going to raise money for select causes. I'm going to be the administrator for it all. The partners were so receptive and approved it right away. It's something they'd wanted to pursue, but no one had been prepared to take the bull by the horns. I didn't have to shame them into it one iota. I was prepared to do so, believe me—you know me. I feel so good inside already!" she proclaimed, as her smile brightened up the room.

Carol gave her and Nick a high-five and looked at Tom. She still felt terrible about ignoring the piano and went over to hug him. She slowly placed her hand on his, one seductive finger at a time, forming a tight grasp, and led him to the neglected mahogany piece of art, sitting him down next to her on the padded bench.

"Oh, my God. I didn't even notice that there. That spot is perfect for it. I love the wood!" Edna exhorted as she raised her beer in celebration. "Nice touch, Tom! Here's to you, my mother, and Aunt Mary,"

For the first time in ages, Carol's heart called out for the piano. She longingly looked at the keys, feeling lucid and inspired. They no longer seemed dismally black and white. Her being had ceased to live in a bleak monochrome state. The present and the future were now a kaleidoscope of uplifting color swirling about.

At long last, harmony resonated within her. Joyful notes danced inside her spinning head, magically flowing unconstrained down her arms into her awaiting fingers. She smiled at the gang and played "Happy Days Are Here Again" as an amusing warm-up then eased into a rendition of "Let It Be" by the Beatles, going from memory, without the benefit of sheet music. She turned to Edna, who nodded her head in reverence. Carol began to sing the words, "When I find myself in times of trouble, Mother Mary comes to me… Speaking words of wisdom… Let it be... Let it be." It was a fitting spontaneous tribute to her mother. The notes sounded sweetly superb and full of everlasting promise as the music drifted throughout the room ceremoniously in step with her new lease on life.

Carol stopped for a moment, turned to the group, and triumphantly declared with a satisfied smile, "I think I'm going to give lessons for free from now on!" She kissed Tom on the cheek as she giggled at the strange phenomenon taking place. In a roundabout way, the piano was tickling her, and she didn't want the music to ever stop.

Paul Mazzarella has lived in Greater Boston for all 54 years of his life. He currently resides in Lynnfield, Massachusetts with his loving wife of twenty years, Susie, and their mischievous two-year old Vizsla, Dante. Paul had a lengthy 30-year career as an equity sales-trader for investment banking firms and no longer wanted his life defined by cold impersonal numbers. He decided to pursue his lifelong dream of writing fiction and has treasured his newfound creative freedom. Paul is an avid sports fan and fitness enthusiast. A warm-hearted friendly person, he loves to travel and engage in spirited conversation with interesting people from all reaches of the globe, preferably in a lively tavern. Paul is looking forward to having a steady dialogue with his readers.

www.ingramcontent.com/pod-product-compliance
Lightning Source LLC
Chambersburg PA
CBHW071524260626
47170CB00002B/490